POISONED IN LIGHT

Poisoned in Light

BEN ALDERSON

OFTOMES PUBLISHING
UNITED KINGDOM

Cover Art by Gwenn Danae
Cover design by Eight Little Pages
Interior book design by Red Umbrella Graphic Designs

CONTENTS

CHRISTINE, MY WEE FRIEND WITH AN
OPPOSITE OF A WEE HEART.

CHAPTER
ONE

DEATH HAD A smell.

It reminded me of the early autumn days on Fa's farm when the apple trees dropped their fruits. A vile stench would infect the air as the plush red skin of apples turned black, and its once fresh juices spoiled. It was both sweet and sickly. Even the unignorable taste would stick to the back of my tongue, and no matter how many times I coughed, it would never clear. Water couldn't wash it away. Only time would rid it. And time was not a luxury I had anymore.

Even pressing a cloth over my nose and mouth was a wasted effort.

I walked through the streets of Lilioira, Gordex ahead of me, Marthil by my side, as a silent prisoner. The streets were lined with Gordex's army of animated dead. Shadowbeings. Hollow lifeless shells of decomposing bodies used as soldiers by the Druid. But they were not to blame for the strong scent that filled the city.

I blamed the overpowering aroma on Gordex's newer recruits; civilians of Lilioira who had been killed since Gordex's took over. It took a few days for their organs to decompose within their animated bodies. The black smoke that controlled them seemed to feed off the rotting. But still they stood tall, life like, even though their eyes were glazed over and empty.

I'd learned not to get too close. Not if I wanted to keep my food down. It was vital I didn't waste my energy source when it had been rare that Gordex provided me with food over the past weeks. I had to play along, act calm. It was how I'd survived this far, and I was not about to give up.

It'd been over three weeks since my companions got away. Three very long, tempestuous weeks. With every blink, I saw the back of Nyah's head disappear into the dark tunnels in the prison cells. And Hadrian. He'd gotten out with Gallion; there was no telling if he was alive or not. All my worry and anxiety for my friends was what made eating hard. The dull ache within me had become one of my only constants.

Marthil kicked the back of my leg and urged me forward. I shook my head and carried on, burying my thoughts until I was in the safety of my own room.

We'd made it to the main street of the city. It acted as a vein for the entirety of Lilioira, a place that connected each part of the city with small side alleys and walkways. The very same that Hadrian, Emaline and I had been paraded through before Hadrian lost himself to the Heart Magick. It was the first time I'd been out in days. Since I'd fought back during the first outing with Gordex he kept me locked within my room like a well caged animal. I still had the bruises he and Marthil gifted me even days later.

Instead I'd watched from my balcony as Gordex and Marthil took daily walks around Lilioira, making their presences known amongst the survivors. I thought today would be no different until Marthil came knocking for me and demanded I followed.

"Eyes up and smile," Marthil demanded next to me.

I raised my stare from my boots and examined the street before me. Besides the rows of shadowbeings, the streets were empty of *true* life. The surviving civilians in the city never left their homes anymore. Behind shuttered windows, they looked out through the slats with hate. At me, at the Druid. They thought I was to blame. That *I* had a hand in this.

I suppose it didn't help that I was the one pulling the chain, the long silver tether that connected my wrist to *their* Queen.

Queen Kathine stumbled behind us, an obsidian collar wrapped tightly around her delicate throat. Now and then, she would falter and fall. But for her safety as much as mine, I would tug on the chain to keep her moving. I'd learned my lesson as to what happened when I tried to help her stand. She had angry welts across her shoulders and back as proof. They'd healed since Gordex had gifted them to Kathine, but it was obvious no one had helped clean them out since my outburst. *If I had just acted calm, she would never have been punished.* Gordex never hurt me as punishment, not since the first time. It was always Queen Kathine after that. So, as she stumbled again, I pulled gently and silently urged her to keep up.

This had been our routine for Gordex since he conquered the city. After the first two weeks, time seemed to just bleed together in the city of light. It was more aptly referred to as the city of death by Gordex. *My city of death*, he would laugh, hands rubbing together greedily.

It started with a morning feast accompanied by Gordex and Marthil, where they would bask in their destruction. A feast that I would usually sit and watch. Food was never brought out to me when I was with them both. Only scraps would be left in my room at the end of the day. What would follow their morning feast was the parade through the city of Lilioira. A reminder to those civilians who hid in their houses that the Druid had won, using Queen Kathine as a means of getting his message across.

Then Marthil would leave for the gates. Gordex would retreat into the libraries, and I would hide myself in my room, hoping, *wishing*, to hear something from my friends. But with each day that passed, that hope dwindled down to a dim glow.

I did wonder what Gordex was looking for. Something to combat the looming threats from the shores of Thessolina and Morgatis, perhaps? There was tension brewing beyond the city. I could tell in the constant pinch of Gordex's brows when we spoke of what his scouts saw during breakfast. He always kept his words brief around me, but there was an unspoken look between Marthil and him when I would leave the room. A look that suggested there was more story to tell.

"Out my way!" Marthil hissed. I'd stood on the back of her foot and almost tripped to the floor over my own weak, clumsy legs.

I cocked my gaze away from Marthil's intense glare and took steps back, mumbling my apology.

Our parade had come to a stop. Strange, it never happened around this part of the city. We were standing beside the remains of the water fountain. It'd been destroyed during Marthil's free reign of destruction during the first days. When the city was her playground. The stone woman no longer had a head. Instead, it lay at her cracked feet in two pieces, each eye looking in a different direction than the other.

"Well, this *is* a surprise. Pray tell, what brings you out of your watch holes today?" Gordex's voice was steady, unlike my hands that shook fiercely at the thick tension in the air. *My* air.

There was some commotion ahead. No more than muffled words that lacked confidence as they were tossed towards Gordex. I peered over Marthil's shoulder to get a better look and spotted a small group of civilians standing in the Druid's way. I counted five.

"It is-is time you leave," a younger Elven boy called, stumbling over his words. He stood at the front of the group, hands held behind his back. His chest was pushed forward, his chin held high. For such a youngling there was nothing but bravery in his stance, but his tone seemed to lack it.

"Very brave you are to stand forward and command me within my own city," Gordex said, taking steps towards the line of five. Two shadowbeings went to follow him, but he raised a hand, and they stopped. "Each day I have walked this city, and each time you stay in the shadows of your homes. May I inquire why it is today you have decided to greet me at last?"

"Don't answer him," a blonde elven girl called from the group. Her face was dusted with black smudges, her clothes dirtied and ripped from her bodice to skirt. "Just do it."

"Yes, just do it and see where it gets you." Marthil's shoulders raised and neck leaned forward. Nothing but aggression was evident in her stance.

Gordex peered to his second, back now faced to the group. "Now, now, dear girl, let us show our friends kindness."

"Enough, demon. This ends today," one of the five said, a tall woman with ivory skin and midnight hair. She, like the other four, looked tired, dirty and thin. The long while she'd survived within locked houses with minimal food and supplies was clear across every inch of her frame and expression.

"Ends?" Gordex laughed. "I am afraid it has only just begun."

His calm reply scared me more than knowing what was coming next. No one had dared go against him. They knew what would happen. He would kill them, resurrect them for his army of death. I wanted to shout. To tell them to back down and return to their locked homes. But the burning hate in the groups' tired eyes told me she'd *never* back down. This truly was the end. But not for the Druid, no, for them.

"We have sat back and watched you display your creatures through our city. You take *our* Queen, cause her pain and suffering. You steal our family, our friends for your twisted, demonic rituals. So yes, *Druid*, this is the end. For our Queen, we will not backdown." The elder woman of the group gathered spit in her mouth and hacked a gob at Gordex's feet.

Gordex knelt slowly and put his thumb and

forefinger into the mucus by his feet. Standing, he rubbed it between his digits as if it was nothing more than ointment. "The admiration you hold for your Queen is beautiful. Truly. My only displeasure is that you do not hold it for me." Gordex looked truly disappointed.

"I have something for you." The young boy revealed why he had his hands behind his back by pulling them forward and pointing a rusted sword towards the Druid. Not even the day light flashed across the red and brown coated steel. It only shook ever so slightly in his small hands.

"This is no place for toys," Gordex said quietly, raising both hands beside him to show he was not threatened. "All actions have consequences, young boy, are you prepared to find out what it will be for pointing that *play-thing* at me?"

"No one will stop fighting until you are dead, Druid. Kill us and more will follow." The rest of her group pulled weapons from concealed places. Dull axes with chipped handles and short swords. Each made from the famous Alorian metals. These, unlike the first sword, were not rusted and old. The cobbled streets danced with reflected light. One even flashed briefly across my face, causing me to shy away.

"I have no doubt. I invite them to join you. It will only benefit me in the end. And you know I am right. I can see it in your eyes. If you want to join my army, all you have to do is ask."

"Keep looking in these eyes," the blonde girl called out again. "I want them to be the last thing you see as I snatch the life out of you."

"No!" Queen Kathine screamed, her voice hoarse. She tugged back on the chain and tried to stand, but her attempt to be heard over the groups battle cry was wasted. Her knees slammed back into the ground, the sound of bone against stone echoing off the tall buildings around us.

Before I could turn to help her, all five of the rebels swarmed Gordex, flashing blades towards him in a rush of shouts and curses.

The world seemed to slow. I watched with bated breath as Gordex dipped in and out of the blade's paths, his hands clasped behind his back. He moved like billowing wind, twisting and turning away from the incoming attacks. Not a single advance got close to him to draw blood.

A chorus of grunts from the group only intensified as they swung messily at him.

The sharp tug of the chain made me turn away from the battle.

"Zacriah," Queen Kathine mouthed, "do something."

I tried to ignore her, but her wish was embedded

into me. Even before she pleaded me to act out, my fists were clenched and my magick lurked in the corners of my very being. It was no anger I felt but more intense panic.

"You are the only one," she whispered, tugging the chain again.

My palms grew sweaty, and my magick begged to fight.

A scream cut through my consciousness, and I watched one of the five tottered to the ground, his own blade protruding through his stomach. He was so young, clear from his perfect face and soft eyes. I'd not seen how it had happened, for Gordex's hands were empty and still behind him as he dodged the attacks.

My vision blurred, and my body faltered—a sign of Gordex calling upon my power.

A burst of wind echoed in the distance as Gordex raised a hand and called for it. When he used my magick, it caused me great discomfort. Like a splinter in a hand, it was a long, dull ache. One I could ignore but never forget.

With a giant push towards the ground, Gordex barely missed the swing for his head. But it didn't matter. The wind collided with the ground and spread out all around him. The four still captured in the battle flew from their feet and scattered in the distance as the force of the wind backfired.

As if Gordex used my wind to spread his shout farther than natural, his voice boomed over the city.

"Take this as a lesson. You will fight me, and you *will* lose. This does not need to happen. I will welcome you all with open arms. Join me, and you will no longer need to hide within rooms that my army could enter with a simple command. I have spared you all long enough."

The four scrambled from the ground, trying to get away as the winds sang throughout the city. Their hair and ripped clothing bustled around them beneath the force of the unnatural winds. It was so strong I was certain they could be taken adrift at any moment. But the shadowbeings moved forward and ceased them from going anywhere, dead arms wrapped roughly around the remaining four.

"I have shown you all patience, but I see that you do not appreciate my kindness. Too long have I waited for your cooperation and acceptance." There was a long pause. Gordex scanned his eyes over the four trapped by the shadowbeings, then to the many who watched behind the safety of their homes. "You have until tomorrow to join me in life. If not, you will in death. My soldiers will go through your homes one by one. Either go with them peacefully, or they shall take you. These are the repercussions that you have forced me to make."

Besides the wind Gordex controlled, there was no sound. The four that had fought Gordex could not make a noise with the pointed spears pressed at their throats.

"Heed my warning, for you shall not have the luxury of another."

Gordex flicked his hand, and a collective gasp broke the silence. The shadowbeings thrust forwards, pinning the spear heads through the necks of the four rebels. Their eyes rolled back into their heads, flashing only white. Gold blood bloomed across their necks, spilling down their chests and onto the floor around them. It created one united puddle, which caught the suns light and blinked fiercely.

Queen Kathine screamed with pain, slamming her cut hands to the floor over and over. Her wailing turned my blood to ice. It stabbed right through me, making all the hairs on my arms and neck stand on end. It was a sound that would haunt me for the rest of my days.

You could have stopped him.

"I introduce my new recruits," Gordex called out.

Slowly, he raised both his hands, and black shadow seeped like hungry clouds towards the five bodies. One by one, the shadow disappeared into their open mouths and filled them entirely until not a sliver of shadow was left out.

"Stand." I shivered under Gordex's command.

It seemed the entire city watched from hidden shadows as the five bodies stood from the ground, spears and blade still stabbed into them. Their bodies clicked aloud as the shadow made them stand, controlling them like a new born fawn with no grasp on the use of its legs.

"Monster," Queen Kathine spat. I was not sure if it was aimed at Gordex or me. "Goddess knows you are a monster."

I could have stopped this.

It was all so wrong. They were nothing more than kids. Brave enough to face an enemy, but naive not to see he would destroy them.

I should have stopped this.

Burning heat crawled up my legs, numbing my body and mind. Anger.

My own taunting message spun in my mind in a violent vortex of hate. I didn't register as my hand slacked and dropped Queen Kathine's chain. My mind was occupied on the magick I released and the wind I connected to. My power, it was tainted, vile and alien since Gordex claimed it. But before it was his, it was mine.

Gordex snapped his head towards me, but it was too late for him. Even Marthil didn't have time to reach out and stop me.

With a breath, I thrust my air forward until it met shadow.

My move had been made.

I siphoned my magick into the five bodies that stood before us. Silver strands of visible power forced their way into the newly created shadowbeings, and it followed my one command. I annihilated all shadow within them, just like I'd done at the temple in Thalas. It was exhilarating, latching onto my power for the first time in days. It was stronger, hungry and fresh. Heart Magick. It sang in my blood like purple light, urging for more of my mind. It was a physical representation of fury. Overwhelming and wild.

The five bodies dropped back to the ground, dead. This time, for good. I was too late to prevent their deaths, but I could at least make sure they were free of Gordex's ungodly grasp.

A flash of light lit my mind, and I faltered. A cold bite nipped into the left of my stomach, and my knees collided with the ground. I released my magick, now focused on the warm in my side. My vision doubled, but I didn't need it to see what had happened. I could feel the dagger that was lodged to the hilt in my skin. It tickled my insides, draining my magick as I bled down myself.

"It would seem you have not learned anything, Zacriah," Gordex said, his voice dripping with humor. I peered up, looking away from the blooming patch of red at my side. His yellowed smile was the last thing I saw before darkness swallowed me entirely.

CHAPTER
TWO

I CAME AROUND to the soft brush of a finger across my forehead. Round and round, it danced in circles, sending pleasurable shivers down my arms and legs. I nuzzled close into Hadrian. The haze was still thick in my mind, enough for me to forget. But it took seconds for the clouds to pass and reality to return.

I bolted up, gasping for breath. A spasm of discomfort pinched in my side, so I slammed my hand above it. I was topless, a patch of white cloth had been placed above the origin of my pain.

"I have been waiting for you to wake for a while now," a deep voice uttered beside me. I had been too focused on the memory of being stabbed to check my surroundings. I scolded myself instantly for my lack of awareness.

"Petrer?" I croaked, vision blurry as I took a moment to get used to the light.

He was perched on the edge of my bed, his hands half hovering in the air. The tickling, it was not Hadrian.

It had been Petrer. My stomach turned, jolting violently. He'd touched me with his vile, murderous hands.

"The one any only," Petrer replied, a grin overtaking his entire face.

I mumbled over my words, shaking my head and rubbing the sleep from my eyes. Surely this was an apparition, an illusion of kinds caused by the stabbing. I'd not seen him since the fight on the ship when he dragged his knife across Browlin's neck.

"Stop jolting about unless opening your wound is what you want to happen," Petrer said, reaching across the bed and grasping the tops of my arms. "I'm not happy about it, but the lack of willing healers meant I had to stitch you up myself. Goddess knows I didn't inherit my mother's ability to knit."

"Get off me!" I muttered, yanking my arms from his grasp.

Red crawled up his neck. "Zac, stop."

His hands clasped on with more vigor, and he hissed as he attempted to pull me back again. Having his hands on me repulsed me to the edge of madness. I didn't care if the stitches ripped; I wanted him away from me.

"Get off!" The clapping sound of my hand connecting with his face was blissful.

His head snapped backwards. As he turned to look at me, he had his own hand pressed protectively to his cheek. I peeped the red mark I had left him.

"Touch me again and it will be much worse for you." My warning boiled in the space between us.

"Now, Zac." He dropped his hand to show the river of red leaking from the corner of his mouth. With one great swipe of his tongue he dragged the blood and smeared it across his lips. "Is there much need for such disdain towards me? All I have done is help you, but I see our time apart has not helped you distinguish my kindness from the warped view you have of me."

"Leave now. Get out." My voice cracked. Was it fear from him being close or the lack of my own energy that scared me? I couldn't fight him off, not with this stabbing pain in my side.

"Not until I check on your wound," Petrer said, his smile melting from his face. "Unless you would prefer the Druid to do it himself?"

I paused. I would rather they both not check.

"I'll do it myself."

"No, Zac. No, you won't. Lie back down and keep your hands to yourself," he commanded.

I flinched as he reached out. Laying myself down before he could reach out and make me do it, I bit down on the insides of my cheeks to still the repulsion that flooded me.

"I'm *truly* happy to see you again, Zac. We left on such bad terms, and I've been sick with worry since. This seems to be the universe's way of giving me a chance to make it up to you again. To get back to those old days between us."

I winced as he pulled back the bandage to reveal my wound. I got a quick look at the raised mark, enough to see that it was free from infection. It was red, but no more than any other minor mark would be.

"I've found it to be terribly lonely without you. Your company always got me through those boring days back home in Horith, and it has been lacking since *he* took you away from me."

I tried my best to block out his words. I didn't believe them, nor did I want to hear them.

"You want to harm me, don't you?" He gently placed the bandage back down and withdrew himself from me. "Your eyes burn with your desire to cause me pain."

"Do you blame me?" I said, unsure where my question came from.

Petrer was deranged and a murderer. As I looked upon the boy I once knew, I could see his expression when he dragged the dagger across Browlin's neck.

He shrugged and stood, his frame towering above me.

"Then why don't you do it?" he asked. "Why not finish me off right here, right now? Nothing is stopping you, and between me and you, I quite fancy a little tussle. Just like the old days." He winked, his dark eyes reflecting with malic and hunger. "Well?"

I pushed myself up to sitting, trying not to show the discomfort my side caused me. "Not now."

"Of course not." He laughed. "That wouldn't be your style, would it?"

"You don't know the slightest thing about me, Petrer." I spat his name, allowing my hate for him clear with each letter.

"Maybe I don't." He took a breath, running his eyes up and down every inch of me. "Your wound is healing nicely, I think in a couple of days you will be right as rain. Until then, you must rest and let your body heal naturally. Marthil is growing something that may help speed future healing along, but I'm certain you will not be acting out again. Isn't that right?"

I didn't reply. Never again would I make promises to comply. I twisted in my seat, causing my wound to burn like liquid fire.

"You know as well as I that Gordex would never have hurt you if you didn't go against him. And so publicly. That didn't help your cause. Why didn't you learn from the first time?"

The first time Gordex had caused me pain was no more than a few slaps across my face and his fingers around my throat. This was different. I'd grown used to him not punishing me that I was blind-sided when he stabbed me.

"And I suppose you would have stopped him if you

were there? Save me?"

"Who knows what would have happened, Zac. Stop acting like the hero. You might end up with a few less scars."

Hero? I'd acted like no hero. I'd stood back and hid in my room as the rightful Queen was taken through her city with a chain like a prized animal. I was a bystander, which, in a matter of ways, was worse than that of a person who committed the crime and horrors.

The many days had given me more time to think than I cared for. All I wanted was to go home, not to save the world, not to have this power anymore. I wanted home. The smells of the hearth mingled with Mam's baking. The farm. The dusty books Fa brought home for me. And my friends. I wanted them back.

Hadrian. I wanted him more than anything else.

"Why *are* you here?" I tipped my head to the side, squinting my gaze at Petrer. His complexion glowed in the morning light that shone from the open balcony. "Why now? After a week of me being kept here you decide to show up when I'm hurt. It would seem that it is you who is acting as the great *Hero* now."

Petrer rocked back on his feet, sticking his hands in the pockets of his trousers. I caught the hilt of a dagger strapped to his waist. Only briefly but it was there. Of course, he came with protection of his own. The last time we were in a similar situation I was captive on a ship after he forced a band of gold around my wrist. He didn't look much different from then either. His short, coal-colored hair was still in perfect curls. He'd eaten in the past weeks, that was clear. Even trained by the looks of his bulging arms. Not a single sign of suffering visible on the boy before me.

"I am no hero. I just picked the right side, simple as that. And to answer your question, the other loyal shifters and myself have only just arrived in this city. Otherwise, you would've seen my face sooner."

Only just arrived? What was keeping them from Lilioira for so long?

"And I was the first thing you had to see?"

"No question about it. You might not believe it, but I have worried about you. Stuck with that prince, nothing good would come for you. I'm glad, beyond words, that you are here. Back with me where I can do my job and keep you from harms reach."

A deranged laugh burst past my lips. "The day I believe those words is the day I no longer can hear. Go, Petrer, before I make you." I injected as much threat in my voice as I could muster.

Reaching for my magick pained me still. Knowing the Druid was linked like the tight binding of a chain always made it harder. But wind listened to my call and roared beyond the window of my room. Petrer regarded it for a moment and took a few steps towards the main door.

"I will not give up on you like you gave up on me, Zac. I will keep fighting for you until I prove you are mine."

"Don't you see? There is nothing to fight for. You lost me when you bedded someone else. Now get out."

A strange shadow passed behind Petrer's wide, dark eyes. A twisting snake of black that moved to make itself known. The Druid's power. Still it leaked within him.

Petrer reached a hand for mine which lay on the bed. As he moved, I yanked it from his reach and snarled. I thought he would give up. But with speed of a beast he lunged forward, encasing my hand in his vice grip.

"If kindness is not what you respond to, I will use other means. You have forced my hand, Zac. This *is* your fault."

I cried out as my fingers clicked beneath his force. Then as quickly as he held on, he let go. Hugging my hand to my chest, I looked up at Petrer through tears. Not of sadness, but of hate.

"What happened to you?" I croaked through a cry.

"What hasn't?" Petrer responded, turned and left me to my own thoughts.

The rest of that day and the two that followed, I hardly slept. And when I did, black feathers and eyes full of hate were all I could see. There was something about Petrer that made me feel more unsafe than I had with the

Druid alone. A strange twisted evil that I had hoped was the result of Gordex and his strange grasp on Petrer. But I was wrong. Petrer always had a seed of potential revulsion within him.

He just needed the Druid's power to water it and give it life to flourish.

Only King Dalior's chest moved. The rest of him was as still as stone. I'd spent hours staring at him, hoping to see a sign that he was finally waking and not lost to this eternal slumber. But it never happened. His chest would rise and fall, his mouth parting ever so slightly. But not once did his eyes open and the flush of life return to his paled skin.

He was not dead. No, this was different. Perhaps even worse.

Since Gordex had taken me to see King Dalior on the day Lilioira fell, I had visited him as often as I could. Every moment that was not occupied with feasts and hiding, I came here.

I hoped the King dreamed as he was laid within his glass coffin, sealed from the world beyond. That simple thought warmed my heart. I wondered often if he saw his son, Hadrian, during his peaceful slumber. Was he unaware of the turmoil the world beyond his coffin was in? There wasn't any point trying to open it, Gallion had warned me of that. He said if the glass broke, King

Dalior would die. So, instead, I would just watch from the side, taking in the figure of Hadrian's father.

The glass coffin was a strange contraption. It was made half from wood and the top from a clear glass that allowed me to look in without blind spots. Silken, plush cushions kept the sleeping King aloft, his head raised slightly compared to the rest of his tall frame.

Just as the Druid posed as him, King Dalior's long midnight hair shone. Although his eyes were closed, I could already imagine the gray eyes that I had seen back in Olderim. The very eyes that Gordex wore as part of his disguise. He was full and looked healthy. Asleep. Alive. Not dead as we first thought. I'd cried, wasted countless moments in pure disarray that Hadrian had no clue of his father's state. I couldn't tell him he was alive. It broke me inside, ripped my heart in two every time I laid eyes upon the sleeping king.

"The Goddess told Hadrian you were still alive," I said, opting to tell him this story today. "If only you could understand the hope it gave him. Hadrian would give everything to see you. He missed you dearly. Just as I miss him now."

It was the silent moments when I looked upon the King that I thought of Hadrian. He'd escaped with Gallion before the Druid's siege, but had they found a way back to Nyah? Was Hadrian awake and well? All questions I would ask when I could risk communicating with Nyah.

It wasn't that she hadn't tried. I'd lost count of the number of times her cold trickle ran down my mental wall. But with Gordex close, I wouldn't risk it. I worried he would find them if he sensed her trying to get through. He seemed to know she was doing it when he stepped through the dark portal into Lilioira.

Gordex kept me close for some reason. Was he waiting for me to communicate, so he could use his mysterious powers to locate them? I would rather be alone and know they were away from his reach. I only hoped they would find a way back soon though. I didn't know how long I could keep this up here.

A shuffling of feet sounded behind me. Turning on my heel, I expected to see Petrer, or Gordex. But it was Marthil who watched me from the shadowed doorway of the dark room. She leaned up against the stone archway, bright eyes standing out even in the dark.

"Thought I'd find you here." Marthil stepped forward into the cramped room.

I'd not shared many words with her in private, only passing snarls she gave me and burning looks. Never had she activity come looking for me.

"What do you want?"

"Many things."

She was dressed in a muddy brown tunic that was cinched in at her waist. Her boots were laced up to her knees which blended seamlessly into the black trousers she had opted to wear today. She looked like a vagrant, one who'd seen much in a short life.

I moved from King Dalior's glass coffin and towards the door. I was in no mood for conversations with my captors.

"Gordex told me to speak to you. You see, he's fed up waiting for you to heal now. I've been told to tell you that you're not allowed to miss supper tonight. A lot has happened whilst you've been sleeping, and Gordex wants to see you and update you on all the exciting events you've missed."

"I am tired. I need to rest." I kept my head down, trying to get out of the small room. "I've still not healed fully—"

"Here, I've something that might help." She thrust a hand out. In it was a strange vial. "It's for your wound. Taken me days to grow the right herb, so don't say you are not taking it because I'll make you. Should sort out that little cut of yours."

As she referred to my wound, the stitches in my side twanged. The pain and swelling had reduced tenfold over the past days, but it still caused me discomfort. The threads had grown loose, even beginning to fall out of my scabbed scar.

"I think I'll pass on that," I said, side eyeing the vial with distrust.

"Take it. Unless you like the thought of getting an infection. The longer that *cut* lingers the more of a chance you will catch some nasties inside it."

She referred to it as a cut, but we both knew it was much more than something so simple.

"And why do you care if I heal or not?" A dark feeling turned within me. It didn't belong to me, but I didn't have a moment to register how fast it came on.

"Because Gordex is in a terrible mood and has been since he was forced to put you down. Take a guess as to who is getting the brunt of that mood? Me. I don't care if you want to heal, but I do care that his attention is put back on you." Marthil thrust the vial again. "Don't make me force you to take it."

"And I should trust you with whatever is in this? What if you are just trying to kill me yourself?" I said, knuckles white as I held onto the vial.

"Trust me, when I kill you, it will be messier than poison." She took steps forward until the slip of light from the missing bricks in the ceiling illuminated her sharp face. This close I could see the few freckles that dusted the skin beneath her eyes. "I'd tell you what I am going to do. But then again, what would be the fun in that?"

I snatched the vial from her hand. "And I almost thought I found trust in someone." I held my ground. Gordex had Marthil's Heart Magick yet she still used it with ease. If she tried anything, regardless of the Druid's link, I would show her what mine could do.

"Take the herb. Heal so you can get back to normal, and Gordex can take his woes out on you. I miss it."

She turned and moved for the door. As her spindly hand reached for the doorframe I called out.

"What is it? The herb."

"Forbian. Grown personally for you. One drop in the morning and another at night, that is all you will need."

"I know about Forbian," I snapped.

"Then you will know that it stays in your system for a while. Don't take too much. You might get a taste for it." Marthil winked in jest and skipped from the room, leaving me with the vial and the sleeping king.

CHAPTER
Three

I POPPED THE cork of the vial the moment I stepped through the doorway to my room. Marthil had said to only take one drop, so I took two for extra measure. Maybe it was my own rebellion or just the throbbing of my wound that urged me to do it. But the moment the sweet liquid coated by throat, cooling its way down into my stomach, I felt the effects.

A rush of numbness spread across my body. I gave it a few seconds before touching the bandage. I expected to feel the same discomfort that had replied every other time I'd touched it. But this time, I felt nothing. I prodded again, hardly feeling the own touch of my finger against the numb skin.

"Strong stuff," I mumbled to myself, closing my eyes against the wild rush of my light head.

It was known that shifters did not succumb to the side effects of Forbian. To anyone else, it would put them to sleep as it worked on their ailments. But for me, being Dragori, I was untouched by the curse of drowsiness. It was the very same as when Gordex had spilled it into the food during the feast when I first arrived in Olderim. It seemed like someone else's history I peered into. So much had happened since that it was hard to remember that it was in fact I who went through it.

Opting to keep the herb close, I corked the vial and placed it in the pocket of my trousers.

The rest of the day passed without any interaction. I could hear the shadowbeing guards beyond my door, shuffling up and down the corridor. But that was it. Petrer didn't return, nor Marthil. When the sky darkened with welcoming night, I almost got into bed when the three loud raps startled by lapse in comfort.

I stopped moving, my gaze pinned to the door. Should I call out for them? Before I made my mind out a voice called for me.

"May I come in?" Gordex called serenely from the other side.

Even if I wanted to refuse, it would have been pointless. Gordex would do as he pleased. I knew that by now.

"Yes." I kept my reply short.

It was not common for Gordex to be alone when I saw him. Seeing his sole presence made me panic. I took deep breaths as the door opened and he stepped inside, turning his back on me to close it again.

"Petrer passed on the report that you finally awoke today," Gordex said, taking a few steps forward and stopping with his hands behind his back. He was dressed in all black. The robe had a slight sheen to it which, I saw as he got closer, had symbols stitched on in a different material. Gordex raised his open palm and a flame spluttered into existence. The orb of fire, Hadrian's fire, jumped from Gordex's hand and split midair in two directions. Each flew towards an unlit pillar candle at either side of the room, creating new light. "And I know Marthil's message reached you about the feast this eve. Yet you do not seem to be ready."

"What can I do for you?" I ignored his comments, only getting to the reason why he came to visit me. He'd never done this, only the first time I'd awakened after Marthil had stopped me from escaping alongside my friends.

"I have been meaning to come and check on you myself, but I have been awfully busy since your outburst. I apologize for my tardiness."

His kindness was fake and reeked of malice. "There is no need for your visit."

"Oh, there is a need. I thought I would come and collect you myself to ensure you do not miss the feast this evening. Eating will only help you regain some strength. Look at it as my own way of apologizing for stabbing you. Truly, I do not want to see you hurt,

Zacriah. You may not believe me, but I really do not."

I couldn't ignore how honest he seemed to be.

"If you don't want to see me hurt, why bury a knife in my side?" I asked, squinting in his direction. I wanted to test just how far this kind nature of his would go.

Gordex chuckled, hand over his pinched mouth. "Perhaps. Come now, let us walk and talk. I am beginning to enjoy your company."

"I'm not hungry," I said, holding my ground.

"Then you can watch me eat." Gordex waved a hand to dismiss my attempt at refusing his offer. "You are not missing another meal."

I had two choices. One, to go with him and sit through whatever meal he had planned. Or I refuse, but I could already imagine how that would go. So, I picked up my ego from the floor and followed him out of my room, still keeping some distance between us.

We moved through the ruined palace in silence, stopping only when we reached the door to the dining hall. I could have walked this route with my eyes closed. It was the same place my shadowbeing guards would flank me to every morning since Gordex took control of the city.

It had been a beautiful room, draped with curtains of ivory and ocean blues that had once covered the walls and spilled across the slabbed floor in waves of material. Those had been ripped down and tossed into the flames days ago. Now I could only see hoary stone walls. The large rug had been left untouched, as well as the large dining table made from some type of sturdy wood. At the head of the table was a grand window that looked upon the city below. I could imagine how stunning the views would have been. Queen Kathine and her small family could have watched their people from this vantage point. But that view was no longer a happy one. It was empty, broken and lifeless.

"Please, sit," Gordex said, pulling a chair back for me.

I slithered across to him, shoulders hunched. "Will no one else be joining us?"

"Not tonight. I felt that it was important we have uninterrupted time with each other. There is a rift between us that I would like to spend time mending."

The chair squeaked as Gordex pushed me towards the table. His strength was physically hidden beneath his large robe, but it was there none the less. My neck jolted by the sudden movement, hands grasped the table to still my violent shake.

"I don't see how that will change." My reply was ice cold.

"Much can change, Zacriah. You see, I need your cooperation, not your resistance. I have plans, and I am prepared to do anything to see them through. It hurts me to say this, but you *are* standing in my way. I do not know how many more times I have it in me to forgive you."

My brows creased. "I'll *never* help you."

"And why is that? Why the resistance always, Zacriah. You are stubborn; it does not suit you."

The doors opened behind me, and four elves strolled in. I didn't need to turn to know they were still alive, unmarked by Gordex's power. Their skin was flushed, dirty but full of life. I tried to get eye contact with one of them, but each kept their heads down as they laid out the trays of food between us.

"Zacriah?" Gordex said, resting a hand on my knee to get my attention.

Immediately I jolted back, chair squeaking and hand flying to push his away.

"I want to go back to my room," I said.

"Sit down."

"No—"

"Sit yourself down!" Gordex voice burned with heat. "I will not ask you again."

Shaking, I complied.

"You truly have forced my hand, Zacriah. I have tried kindness with you, but that clearly is not enough motivation. But I have other means to make you cooperate." He reached for a bowl of charred meat, allowing the juices to spill down his dirtied fingers. But not long before his tongue caught every last drop from spilling onto the table.

Just as Petrer had threatened in my room, Gordex too said the same thing.

I spared the food a glance but couldn't find it in me to eat. Gordex had no problem ripping into the meat with his teeth like an animal. But he never spoke with his mouth full. No matter how deranged he looked whilst he ate, he would pick up the table cloth and dab the corners of his mouth before he carried on.

"I have a question for you, Zacriah, and I know you will answer it. Tell me, do you think your family misses you? Do you think they would want to see you as soon as earthly possible?"

Shivers ran up my arms. I looked up through my lashes to Gordex, who smiled like a waiting cat. I was his mouse, and he had just made his move. I gripped onto the edge of my seat, wood threatening to snap beneath my vise grasp.

"You see, it would not be impossible for me to retrieve them. In fact, I cannot help but think it might be a fantastic idea. I am sure you would just die to see them safe and sound. Do you have anything to say to that?"

Tears pooled in my eyes as I looked upon this physical representation of evil.

"Oh, Zacriah." Gordex picked his napkin up and extended it over to me. "Do not cry. I thought this might make you happy here." His voice dipped with sincerity. Even his face melted slightly as he offered me his napkin.

"I will give you tonight to think about it. Come morning I will have a task for you. You can either comply and do as I ask. Or, you know what I will be forced to do."

"I hate you," I said, lips trembling. If I bit any harder into my lip I would have ripped it into shreds.

"Of course, you do." He smiled. "Now eat up, I am going to need you on top form in the morning. You have a busy day ahead."

The narrow pathway of stone and earth that once led to the gates of Lilioira no longer existed.

I'd not ventured this far from the city since I'd arrived, alive and together. Now I stood at the mouth of the walkway where we dismounted the horses and looked upon the rubble of rocks that blocked it. Marthil had done this. It had her magick written all over it.

When Gordex had asked her to stop anyone coming in or leaving, she must have taken it literally and brought down the mountain walls on either side of the walkway, blocking the stretch to the gates. This meant there were only two ways in and out. One was from the air, flying over the mountain face, but that was a treacherous journey. One griffins could do, but armies would not be able to follow. Slaughtering the griffins within the city was one of Gordex's first tasks. He'd gloated about it for an entire day after he spilled their blood across the stables in the south of the city.

That left only one other way out of the city. Cristilia. Her Morthi abilities could create a shadow portal as she had done to get the Druid into the city in the first place. But she'd been locked up beneath the palace and not seen for days. Gordex had expressed his concern with her using that power to escape. Now it was locked within the Staff of Light, stolen from the woman that once used it. She was powerless now.

Whatever tunnel Tiv had taken to get Illera, Nyah and Emaline from the city was now blocked and out of the equation. That too was down to Marthil. I often wondered where their path had taken them to, but the answer was not important to me. Not as important as knowing that they *did* get out and were not in Gordex's unrelenting web.

By the time Marthil had blocked it with rock and earth, it was never an answer I could get. Unless I simply asked Nyah. Again, I was not prepared to risk communication with her with the Druid close.

"Took you long enough to get here," Marthil hissed. "Didn't Gordex ask you to be here by first light?"

Last night, after he'd finished eating, he had told me what to do. *Go to Marthil or force my hand to retrieve your parents.* I didn't know how honest his threat was, and I wasn't ready to test it. Though, I wanted to see them beyond belief. The urge was stronger these days, so much so that it caused me physical pain in my chest.

"I would have been here sooner if you hadn't destroyed the path," I replied, sharp. After last night's meal, I'd gone to bed with a pounding head and anxious heart. It was an easy decision to make when I woke up. I would do as he asked. I would not allow my family to be used as pawns in this game.

I awoke to a note from Gordex telling me to meet Marthil at the city entrance in the mountains, but it said no more.

"Sounds like you have got some balls back. The Forbian is working then?" Marthil asked sarcastically. It had been. By the time I woke this morning, the wound had healed more than it had in the days before, and it was almost impossible to see any scarring. The herb had worked quickly. I'd taken another drop when I awoke, even though I didn't need it.

"What is it we have to do?"

"Scouts suggest we will be having some visitors this morning. And it is our job to make sure they get the warmest of welcomes when they try to get through."

Visitors? My heart almost stopped.

"Once they get in, they will have a shock seeing what I have done to the passageway," Marthil said. "And what I still have to do."

We both looked in towards the dust ridden, rock

covered passage way as the banging of something against the metal of the gate sounded in the far distance. Whatever was being hit against the gate was enormous. It made the ground vibrate beneath each hit.

"You decided to leave half the path open?"

Wind rushed around us this far up. I peered back down over the city and my stomach leaped.

"I have my reasoning." Marthil smiled, rubbing her hands together. "When they, whoever it is out there, takes down the gate and gets through. I'll bring the rest of the passageway down on top of them." A chilling horror spread over me. Her plans were premeditated. "I'm only sad that I'll not see their faces when they finally realize what waits for them."

I looked towards the hollow banging. A trap. What if it was Nyah, Illera and Emaline? Hadrian or Gallion? Possibilities flooded my mind, sparking a slither of hope. What if this was their attempt to break me free?

"I can't let you do that." I didn't look at Marthil when I told her.

"Can't you? Oh, I think you can, and you will," she replied.

"Marthil." Slowly, I faced her. "I'll not stand back and let you do this."

In that moment the threat on my parents disappeared from my consciousness. A strange, dark anger bubbled within me, starting in the pit of my stomach. I couldn't let Marthil kill anymore. I wouldn't. The thought that my friends, no, my family, might be beyond those gates about to walk into a trap was enough to let me sink my claws into the building anger and reign it for my own.

Wind twisted on the ground at my feet as I clenched my fists. It spun into small vortexes, enough for Marthil to look down briefly. Her smile faltered as she watched my power; the banging of the gates echoed my own pounding heart.

With a flick of her hand, the sand and dirt that was caught in my twisting wind stopped dead and was pulled from its grasp. It hovered beyond my air under Marthil's control.

"You *really* want to try this?" Marthil warned, fingers clenching into fists as the earth gathered around her hands. "I don't know how well wind will fair when stopping an avalanche of mountain. I think I'd bet on my magick above yours."

I readied my power. "Isn't the trick when winning a bet, you always choose the underdog?"

My sarcasm was wasted on Marthil, as she shrugged, a blank expression covering her face. "Who knows? No one ever told me…"

A loud screeching had me clapping my hands over my ears. It rang across my mind, blinding my senses. I could see out the corner of my eye Marthil also cowered, her mouth open in a shout of discomfort.

Whoever desired entrance beyond the gates succeeded in their wish. The gate was down. The pounding of footsteps echoed within the passage way. Marthil straightened up, face white with panic, and pressed both hands onto the rock face. I barely moved an inch to stop her when the ground began to shake, and dirt rained down above us.

CHAPTER
FOUR

SCREAMS OF TERROR spoiled the skies. It was a short burst of noise that ignited my own horror as I watched the rock tumble down from the sheer mountain face.

Then there was only silence. Bursts of dirt and dust rushed out of the passageway, coating Marthil and me and blinding our vision. I managed to cover my mouth with my hands, but my eyes were not so lucky. Grit scratched at them as more waves of it billowed out. My skin stung beneath the dirt's wrath.

I couldn't see Marthil in the cloud of her own destruction, but I could hear her coughing heavy yacks as she tried to rid the earth that invaded her lungs. I called for my air, which responded with its own rage. In moments, I cleared all dust and grime until my vision was clear once more.

"What have you done!" I shouted, heart pounding in my throat. I could feel the odd anger burning in me again. My palms pushed into Marthil's shoulder, and she stumbled steps back.

"I only completed the task that *our* master bestowed on us," she replied, physically shaken by her own power. My head snapped back and forth between Marthil and the rumble-covered pathway. Even now small rocks followed suit, rolling down the mountain to lay atop the bigger boulders and rocks that had fallen first.

"You don't need to listen to him," I screamed, moving for the passageway to look for any sign of life. The ground trembled again, an aftershock of the avalanche. No one could have survived that. No one.

"Monster," I muttered. "No better than him."

"Speak up and face me if you have something to say. And watch what insults you choose, some are more like compliments to me."

I turned slowly, the anger now a twisting hurricane begging for a release.

"You are mistaken," I said, preparing myself. "It was not you I called a monster. It was me."

Before I could lift my hands to stop her, Marthil lunged forwards. In a few swift steps, she had turned me around until my back was no longer facing the ruined passageway. Then she pushed. One hard knock to my ribs ripped me off my feet. Over the edge of the pathway and into the abyss I fell.

I clawed for dirt, rock, stone, anything to stop me from falling. But it failed. I was a prisoner to the air that screamed past my ears as I free fell over the lip of the mountain's pathway. I was frightened for only a moment. Although my body was numb from shock, my mind still whirled at a speed that gave me control.

For the first time in weeks, I shifted. My wings melted into existence, spreading wide. I caught the wind beneath my leathered limbs and jolted to a stop. Looking up, I gave them one command. *Fly.*

"You demon!"

I screamed as I raised above the lip of the pathway. But something heavy caught my stomach and knocked the words from my lungs. Winded, I lost control for a moment and rocked backwards midair. Marthil was standing, ready, with slabs of stone floating around her. Looking down, I could see it falling into the chasm below.

"I've waited for someone to train with. Using my powers against someone unmatched is pointless. But with you, I can flex my full potential. I think it's time I see just how much control you have." Marthil's narrowed her gaze, the corners of her mouth lifting ever so slightly. "Your move."

Slashing a hand through the air I sent a slash of condensed wind her way. Never had I seen it so physically before, strands of moon silver and faint purples, as if my power gave its own appearance in the air. Like Hadrian's blue fire. Heart Magick, it must be. I felt it feed off my anger as I forced more wind towards Marthil, my arms moving quickly to overwhelm her.

Marthil moved stones before her as protection, just as I gambled. My wind slammed against her rocky shields as a distraction. At the last possible moment, I willed the air to aim for her unguarded feet. In a turn of events, it crashed into her. The sound of her back hitting the harsh ground was beautiful. She spluttered on her breath, unable to catch another quickly enough.

I allowed more of my anger to seep into *my* air. Like a twig caught in the stream of a river Marthil was forced backwards, skidding along the ground until there was no more to move on. She was my fly, I was her spider, and my air was the web.

"Regardless of what the Druid says, you don't need to kill. That is your choice and your choice alone," I screamed, pushing more wind on top of her. *Crushing her would be easy. So very easy.*

Even if I wanted Marthil to respond, she couldn't. Not when she was buried beneath my pressure. It allowed no room for her to move, let alone open her mouth. I could see her face turning a hint of blue from her lack of breath.

A shuffling of feet made me turn to the narrow walkway. Shadowbeings ran forward, rusted swords raised to stop me. Gordex knew what was happening. Good. He knew all along. This felt like a test of sorts.

And if my instincts were right, I would make sure to succeed in it.

Relaxing my hold on Marthil, I allowed her to drop to the floor. Out the corner of my eye I saw her scratch at her throat as the color returned to her face. She was no longer my problem.

I knocked my hand to the left, sweeping my air towards the shadowbeings until they each were knocked like reeds in the wind. I didn't stop until each one fell from view, disappearing into the abyss that waited to devour them. A small part of me twanged with symphony. They'd once been people, elves with lives and loves before the Druid came and stole their choice to live.

But I knew the fall would not kill them. I'd learned that only severing the head would truly end a shadowbeing's imprisonment to Gordex. Or blessing the dead bodies with my air, forcing the power out of them.

A scattering of dirt scratched my face. Sent as a gift from Marthil, who still struggled on the floor. Her eyes wide in terror, his hands raised as she tried to call for her element. The ground groaned, but she failed to connect to it fully. Only specs of dirt rose to greet me.

"I should kill you myself. Avenge the many deaths you have caused. But you have spilled enough blood for the both of us. I'd hoped there was something left in you before Gordex poisoned your mind." The vial of

Forbian grew heavy in my pocket. The only act of misplaced kindness Marthil had shown me.

"Go on, do it. End me. Do you think he will let you?" Marthil asked, black blood covering her teeth and dribbling down her chin. Her voice was hoarse and appearance disheveled. "If he wanted the Dragori dead, he would have let me kill you days ago. But he didn't."

"I am not like you. I don't kill for gain," I shouted back. "Why should I give you the easier route out when you deserve to suffer for what you have done?"

Marthil looked up through her lashes, giving her face a demoness appearance. "Then who would become the monster?" She raised a dirtied finger and pointed at me.

"Didn't you listen to me, I'm already a monster."

I thrust forward my hand, reaching my winds into her throat. My presence forced her mouth open. I fumbled amongst veins of black blood to find the source of her life. One clot of air and she would suffer pain like no other—

A cold trickling slammed into me with such force, more than I'd felt before. Nyah.

She begged to get through.

Again, it hit me, this time so cold it was freezing. I yanked my air from Marthil, and she stayed on the ground. For good measure I flicked a single burst towards her, causing her head to snap backward. It collided with the wall, and her eyes rolled back into her skull.

Closing my own eyes, I brushed the cobwebs from my metal door and brought down the barrier that protected it. Nyah's awareness flooded into me.

I am sorry.

Nyah?

I could feel her regret as if it was my own.

You need to listen to me. I don't have much time.

Where are you? I sent my question to her, imagining she was beneath the rubble of the passageway.

I have failed. We had one shot to get you, and I failed. Nyah forced her words into my mind. Just hearing her again, no matter the clear panic in her voice, calmed me. I'd dreamed about this.

Tell me where you are. I will help you!

A dark laughter filled the air. It raised from the city far below. It should not have reached me from this height, yet it did. Only Gordex had powers so mysterious he could cause sounds to travel beyond their natural constraints.

He has me.

Her presence left mine in a blink of an instance. I tried calling out for her, but the door was no more, instead a stone wall stood in its place. She'd blocked me out.

I flew for the city. My wings pumped with vigor, power and panic. I didn't stop pushing the limits of my energy until I reached the palace. *Nyah was here.*

Gordex waited for me in the throne room. I touched down on the floor beyond the room and strolled towards the closed doors.

I shot wind forward, smashing the doors wide to signal my entrance. I'd under estimated my force, which ripped the doors from the walls and sent them twisting in opposite directions. They crashed towards Gordex, where he sat on his new throne.

He didn't flinch. With a brief lift of his fingers, shadows spilled forward and encased the doors before they could reach him. The shadows were in control now. They moved the doors to the side and lowered them slowly to the ground. That was all it took. With a wave of his hand they fell quietly beside him.

"Back so soon?" he said, peering down to his nails. "I did not expect your task to be over with so quickly."

"Where is she," I shouted, wings spread wide like a swan under threat. Their span was so great, it was twice the length of my arms on either side.

"May I ask who you are referring to?"

"Stop,"—my wind wailed around us— "playing these games. I know you have her."

"Ah, of course," he said, shaking his head as if he had forgotten so clumsily. "That nifty little connection you have with her would have given it away. And here I was hoping to surprise you." Gordex released a breath and tutted. "I really do not like that. I am going to have to think about what I can do to ensure you both stop using it. I suppose there is one thing I could do to put an end to it permanently."

"If you harm her…"

"I admire your anger, but these empty threats are getting quite boring."

"Gordex, please. Do not hurt her." I couldn't hide the begging tone embedded in my voice.

"And what is it you will do for me if I agree to your request? Yet again I give you freedom to show me loyalty, and then you leave your *sister* unconscious. Again, you have failed. Punishment is due for you, Zacriah."

I was speechless.

Disappointment dulled his dark gaze. "Nothing to say?" Gordex reached into the folds of his robe and pulled out a jar. It was glass, small and lidded. Even from across the room I could see something emerald speeding around inside it.

"Since we are all here, I have a few questions I want to ask your friend before dinner." Gordex said, "Marthil, may you do the honors?"

I snapped my head around. Marthil stood right behind me, her face screwed with hate and covered in her own element. I had not heard her come in, and now it was too late.

"My pleasure," she said.

Her fist connected with my stomach. My knees slammed into the floor as the wind was driven from me. I looked up as another came straight at me, head snapping back, chin screeching in agony. Marthil's fists were like pure stone. I raised my hands to try to stop her constant smacks.

"Sweet dreams." Marthil's cocked her head, studied me, then moved like lightning. Darkness overwhelmed me when one final punch hit true. No matter how much I desired to stay conscious, I couldn't.

CHAPTER
FIVE

I DIDN'T NEED to open my eyes to know my wrists and ankles where bound in stone. I recognized their rough bite as it rubbed against my skin. The bindings were cold. Stone cold. They left no room for me to flex my fingers, let alone twist my wrists to ease their tightness. I groaned, and awareness to reality crept back to me.

It took a moment for my eyes to open. Then another for them to adjust to the dark lighting of the room. My head throbbed, my face burned with pain. All I could think about was my dire thirst for water. I couldn't tell how much time had passed since Marthil had knocked me out, but I was no longer in my Dragori form. My exhausted body was enough proof of that.

"Welcome back," Gordex cooed from his throne, fingers tapping loudly on the arm rests made completely from bone. How he could touch it so freely sent my stomach twisting.

I narrowed my gaze. If it could kill, he would have

been littered with daggers of hate with just one look.

"Nyah," I croaked, throat as dry as the stone binding me. "Where is she?"

No longer could I see the jar in his hands. I searched frantically around his throne for any sign of it but came up without.

"All good things come to those who wait." He waved a hand at me as I sat in the scuffed chair. "I am sure you can understand why I have tied you up. Cannot have you acting out again when I have many questions. I thought it best you are not tempted to try to stop me. Marthil also deserved her repayment for the little tussle you had with her."

Gordex looked disappointed. From the pinch of his face to the disregard he had for me as he spoke.

"What have you done with her?" I asked again, crystal clear.

"Looking for this," Marthil said behind me, so close her breath caused the hairs on my head to dance. I'd not noticed her presence. Not until she lifted the jar over my shoulder and into my vantage point. "What a small creature. Her coloring is beautiful, although I am bias. Green *is* my favored color."

She gave it a great jolt and the moth within bounced on either side of the glass. The movement left dust across the glasses surface from Nyah's small wings. I jammed my tongue between my teeth and bit down to still my cry. Copper filled my mouth, overwhelming my sense of taste.

"Oops." Marthil giggled. "This reminds me of what I'd do when I was a youngling. But I'll keep it to myself. I would not want you to worry with my stories."

I turned away from Marthil as much as I could, unable to look at her in the face. Her smile unnerved me, but her dark stare was what truly frightened me. It was full of intent. Intent to cause pain. I couldn't urge her on when Nyah was held so dangerously in Marthil's careless grasp.

"Go on, my dear, tell him." Gordex pushed for her to carry on. "I for one would love to hear your story."

"I don't want to hear it." I tried to push as much strength into my reply but ended up sounding as anxious as I felt.

"Oh, Zacriah, do not be such a spoiled brat." Gordex waved a hand this time and Marthil continued.

"After my own people disowned me, pushed me from my home and forced me to live in exile beyond the protection of their wards, I had to find a new way to occupy myself. The Deserts of Doom were vast and empty. Beside the terrible sand serpents and small insects, I found no company. Being lonely can drive even the strongest of minds to insanity. I'd collect anything I could find: insects, small snakes, even smaller lizards, anything brave enough to venture my way. Then I would name them. One for each person I'd left behind. Then I would crush them. Smash them. Kill them. One by one and over and over..."

She didn't need to say any more. I knew where this story was going. Although it sickened me, I couldn't deny the small sadness I felt for her. Being pushed away from everyone she had loved just because of their deep routed fear, it was no wonder why she was so warped. It made Gordex's latch onto her like a leech. Made easier with her heart already full of hate. Just like Petrer.

"I always had an interest in creatures with wings. After I came into my own I'd wonder what would happen if they simple disappeared. I tested my wonders by plucking said wings from the insects I stored. Pretty little moths just like this one." Marthil lifted the jar up before her eyes so they crossed with the object being so close. "Reds and greens, ocean blues and the darkest blacks. I wanted to know if they grew back. Can you guess what my marveling resulted in?"

She moved the jar right in front of my face until my breath fogged across its smudged surface.

"They died," she whispered her answer just for me. Shivers ran down my spine and across my arms until all my visible hairs stood on end. "Dead, dead, dead."

"Don't hurt her," I said through bared teeth, spit hitting the glass jar before me. "I swear it, if you do—"

"Marthil will not harm the shifter," Gordex said,

plainly. There was a paused moment of silence before he broke. "That will be my pleasure, and mine alone."

Gordex stood from the throne and walked towards us. His hand extended for the jar.

"No," I begged, tears pooling and blurring my vision.

I knew it was wasted effort, but I yanked at the stone bindings and thrashed in my chair. "Please, no." Seeing him so close to her caused panic to burn through me hotter than any fire Hadrian could ever conjure.

"Ah, ah, ah, you stay still, my boy. I want you to watch." Gordex turned his back on me and walked for the throne, jar in hand. "You see, I have some questions for the shifter girl. And I am prepared to do anything to ensure I get them. Anything."

Lightning fast, Gordex raised the jar above his head. In the next moment the sound of glass against stone vibrated around the room.

I spluttered a gasp, trying to see Nyah amongst the shards that littered the floor. I screamed, a sound so deranged that it pulled on the animal inside of me. Spit linked my open mouth and splattered across my chin. "Leave her. LEAVE HER!"

"It pains me to hurt one of my creations, it really does." Gordex raised an open palm towards the broken jar. In response, black smoke leaked into the air, revealing Nyah in her elven form, spread across the floor. She wore Alorian armor, silvers and whites. Her hair tumbled around her head, fanned out across the floor and glass. She stirred but did not rise.

At the sight of her, my breath halted. Only did I inhale when I saw her finally move. Putting both hands atop of glass shards, she raised herself up and look directly at me. The whites of her eyes were blood red, her skin the color of fresh snow.

"Zacr—" Gordex kicked his foot into her jaw, stunting her words. A cry of pain broke past her cracked lips. Pain, her pain was so intense I could feel it in my own being.

"Marthil," Gordex called for her. "Would you please restrain our guest here."

"Happily, master," she replied, the ground rumbling with the twisting of her fingers.

The floor around Nyah's hands and feet raised like water. It snaked up, rising like a wave before it broke. It enveloped Nyah's limbs and solidified once again. She was trapped. From a glass prison to one made of stone.

"Nyah." Gordex pronounced every letter and sound of Nyah's name. It had a taste of possessiveness, the way he drew out the syllables in his deep husk. "Since you have so aptly returned to my city, I think it only right that we bypass formalities and move strictly onto the situation at hand. I must admit, I was disappointed that it was you who tried to deceive me. I would be lying if I said it was not Emaline I hoped would return. But, I suppose, you shall do just fine in the meantime."

Gordex walked around her where she was pinned to the floor. Her eyes rolled, following his every move. Her hair spilled around her head, which Gordex didn't bother walking around. She flinched as he stepped on it.

"I can't say I agree, *Druid*." Nyah spat blood, which landed on the base of his robe with ease. A grin broke out across her face, pleased with her aim.

"Do not be like that, my dear girl. Hostility is not needed when this dance for answers could play out very smoothly."

"You'll not get anything from me." Some color flushed back into Nyah's cheeks with each refusal she threw at him.

Her small acts of defiance, although brave, would only end in pain. I knew all too well.

Gordex released a breath. "Oh, I will." He raised his arm and opened his palm as if reaching for something within the air. On cue, the Staff of Light flew across the room from where it was placed, resting against his throne. I cringed under the sound of wood slapping into his open, waiting hand.

"Do you know what it feels like to be impaled by a crystal?" Gordex asked, studying the onyx stone at the end of the staff. His brows knotted with interest as he turned it around for us all to see.

"Do you?" Nyah sneered.

"No." He shrugged, turning his gaze back to Nyah. "That is why I asked. I have always wondered. If you do not answer me, we will find out, won't we?"

Nyah arched her back as far as she could. "Ask away. I am in no rush. I have nowhere else to be."

Gordex spun the Staff around, so the crystal pointed towards her. Then, slowly, he pressed it against her exposed ankle.

There was no reaction at first. Nyah's face lifted into a smile, but it soon melted away as her mouth open in a hushed scream. The noise soon followed, exploding from her mouth as the hissing of the crystal against skin melded with it.

"STOP!" I shouted. Marthil clapped her hands down on my shoulders to stop my struggle.

Gordex ignored me. "My first question is one merely of interest. The distraction at the gates, was it your idea?"

Nyah's lips pinched white as she kept them closed. "If it was my idea, it would've worked."

"Good." He held the crystal on her skin. "I would have been disappointed in you if it was truly your plan that failed. You seem, stronger, smarter than that."

"Would you look at that." Nyah had gained some control on the lingering pain. "You seem to know me pretty well."

Gordex's smile faltered at Nyah's sarcasm.

"My next question you will answer without encouragement. Emaline, where is she?"

Everyone waited for Nyah to answer. Even the air stilled, worried it might muffle her reply. But one never followed.

Nyah pinched her lips together, cheeks swelling with a scream, but not a sound came out of her.

"Hmm." Gordex sagged his shoulders, disappointment marked across his gaunt face. "I truly hoped it would not come to this. But I see your stubbornness is as strong as your stupidity."

Nyah's mouth opened, spit linking her top lip to her bottom as she cried out in agony. Her scream of pain shocked me. I saw the smoke lacing up into the air around the crystal. Then the sound hit me, a light hissing as it burned away at the skin of her ankle.

"But you are also strong in more ways than one. It truly is a shame to hurt you. My *shifters* were supposed to be obedient creatures, but I have clearly missed a link in the chain with you." His lips pulled into a snarl and he pressed the crystal in more. "Now tell me. This pain only stops when you do."

Nyah's screamed, and my stomach lurched. Yet I refused to look away. Then, to my surprise as well as Gordex's, she stopped her cries. Pain still creased her face, pinching at the corners of her eyes and turning down her mouth, but she did not cry out again.

"Answer me, girl. Tell me of the final Dragori and her location."

"So, you can bring your demons back?" she spat, half in a cry and half in a shout. "I'd rather die than ever be a piece to this plan."

"My brethren deserve a chance to return. I will stop at nothing to make it happen. That includes not getting the answers I desire from you."

"Then kill me."

She shook her head sharply, biting down on her lips until a rivulet of red leaked out the side of her mouth. Veins in Gordex's forehead stood out as he pressed down harder with the staff. The stronger the force he gave her the louder the hissing of her skin burning became.

Nyah kept quiet. Her eyes, full of determination, were pinned to the Druid. But she didn't speak, nor cry out.

"Now she is quiet," Gordex said, lifting the staff finally.

I wanted to break free, to run to Nyah and hold her close. Her eyes fluttered into her head, as if she battled to keep consciousness.

"How will you get answers from her if she is not conscious?" I shouted at Gordex, hoping he would cease her pain at least.

He turned on me. "You are right, Zacriah, we cannot have her passing out. Not yet anyway. I will just have to alter my methods."

My muscles clenched as Gordex stepped for me, anger burning the whites of his eyes black.

Marthil clenched down harder as I tried to resist. I could see my own confused reflection in his large eyes as he got closer.

"If Nyah can resist the pain and stay quiet, then I will see if she can resist seeing you in the same pain."

"Zac," Nyah panted, eyes staining down her chin to see me. A single tear leaked out the corner of her emerald stare and dribbled down into her lips.

"I can taste the answer now." Gordex smiled, shrugging his shoulder as he placed the crystal onto my forearm. "So close. Nyah, I shall ask you again. Tell me where I can find the final Dragori." Gordex looked over his shoulder at her as he spoke.

Her lips trembled as she held my gaze. I shook my head at her. *Don't tell him*, I thought. *Don't do it!*

"Nothing to say? Then you leave me no choice, girl." Gordex shrugged, looking at the space on my forearm which the crystal hovered over. He truly looked shaken by his next action, as if he really didn't want to hurt me. Then he pushed the crystal forward until it touched my skin.

At first, I felt nothing. Then it was cold, freezing

cold, as if I had placed my hand in a mound of fresh snow and held it till my skin turned blue. I sucked in a breath, shocked by the sudden addition of flaring heat.

My scream brewed in the deep pit of my belly. It rumbled through my body, exploding out of my mouth as the pain intensified. I arched my back, trying to pull free, trying to get away, but Marthil clamped down harder.

"Nyah," Gordex sang over my screams, "I can keep this up for as long as you need."

It was getting harder to hear him above the throbbing in my mind. I could feel myself slipping into an oblivion, a peaceful place where no pain existed. Peace, that was what was waiting in the darkness in the corners of my consciousness. If only I could grasp it.

Nyah was speaking, but I could not make out her words. Not with the welcoming sleep seeping into my body. I could only hear the sweet tones of her voice.

The crystal was removed from my arm, and my awareness slammed back into the light. Gasping, I slumped back on the chair and felt the lack of Marthil's strong hold on me.

My lungs burned as I sucked in a breath. My mind throbbed along with my body.

"Thank you, my dear. It would seem we have a journey ahead of us," Gordex said. "Take the boy to his room, clean him up. Leave the girl with me and return for her after."

The constraints around my wrists slackened, freeing me. But still my head spun in circles. With a light mind, I looked down to the lingering whispers of agony that crawled up my arm, yet there was nothing to see. My skin was perfect, untouched, yet the pain still sang. It's memory strong within my arm.

Marthil yanked me from my seat and pulled me from the throne room. She had to hold me up, for my legs still would not listen to my commands. All I could manage was a single glance over my shoulder as we left the remains of the doorway.

Nyah was still sprawled across the floor, chest heaving. Gordex now sat in his throne above her. His following words to her chased after me.

"You will be rewarded for your cooperation, my dear girl. I promise you that." He smiled down at her, like a cat above a bowl of fresh cream.

And I have a promise for you, I thought, smiling to myself as I imagined the pain I would cause Gordex in return for his actions.

CHAPTER
SIX

THE *FAMILIAR* ARRIVED a long while after Marthil dropped me on the floor of my room. Whereas my mind whirled with anger, my body was numb. I couldn't stop feeling the pain Gordex caused Nyah. How he used her greatest weakness to get the answers he desired most.

Marthil left promptly. She refused to speak to me, even as I threw insult after curse her way. The bolt on the door scrapped shut, locking me in, keeping me away from Nyah. If I had had the energy, I would have smashed the door down, but I couldn't move from the floor. I stayed on it, face pressed to the cold slabs, waiting for the pain to leave my body.

Soon enough, I no longer felt the agony. It almost didn't seem real in the first place, not when I was left unmarked. It was the pain that took place in my heart that didn't fade.

I pulled myself from the floor, stumbling over to my

bed, which I proceeded to lie on for more silent moments. Then a strange sound, followed by a high-pitched series of clicks and screeches, caused me to look out of the window. Looking up to the open balcony, I could see that the sky had faded to a navy blue, highlighting the heavy snow clouds that pulsed above the remains of the city. But it was the dark outline of the creature perched on the windowsill that conjured a gasp.

My sudden movement must have frightened it. The creature screeched and hopped on the spot. I expected the noise to draw in the shadowbeing guards who stood watch beyond my door. With a hand on my mouth, I listened to hear if they would come in. But to my luck, they didn't.

A knowing sensation flooded me, a feeling of familiarity that made me brave enough to raise my arm for the creature. It soared across the room to me, no longer more than a shadowed outline, and I could see the entirety of the bird.

An owl.

Talons exposed, the owl reached for my arm and rested upon it. Where I expected the sharp cut of its expenditures, nothing happened. Its touch was gentle.

I raised a hand and ran it down the speckled feathered wing, admiring the black and white circles that looked like mystic eyes. Even the owls face gave it a sense of mystery. Sharp and wise, large amber eyes with long white lashes only enhanced its unique appearance.

How this beast had made it to my room was beyond me. Yet here it was.

The owl hooted and twisted its head. It was only a small movement but enough for me to notice the roll of parchment wrapped around its scrawny leg.

"For me?" I said, pulling it free with a gentle tug and unraveling it in my hands.

Scribbled on the parchment was a short note. The handwriting was both beautiful and rushed. And my name stood atop it.

Over and over I read it in my mind, the words melting into one string of relief.

"The flame burns strong. Bide us time."

I read it aloud, being careful to keep my voice no more than a whisper.

That was it. Seven words that calmed the raging storm within me. Answered the one question that had kept me awake, alive and hoping. I sagged in relief, closing my fist around the small note until the crunch of paper became music to my ears.

It didn't last long, not while I knew Nyah was still with Gordex in the pits of the palace. Was he hurting her? No, he needed her. I'd missed what she had told him about Emaline's location, but perhaps he would still need her alive to reach it.

I glanced up at the owl, expecting it to spew more

secrets regarding my Hadrian. The flame. No longer did the owls eyes hold the golden amber of color. Now they were pitch white. This was no ordinary creature, not that I had thought that. But the milky gaze that peered at me solidified the fact that this owl was a familiar. But whose?

Looking into the pearl orbs, it reminded me of Jasrov's familiar. How Bell's eyes would change to white when she shared through her bond with him. Only an elemental could have such a power.

Was one looking at me now?

With one great force of its wings, the owl hopped from my arm and flew for the window. I almost cried out for it to stay. Looking around the room, I searched for anything I could relay a message back to the sender. But by the time I looked towards the window the familiar was long gone.

"What do I do?" I put my head in my hands.

Rustling behind my room's door sent shivers of panic up my arms. I had to get rid of the note. If Gordex found it, he would know I had contact with someone. There was no fire to burn it, and ripping the note would not stop Gordex piecing it together. I only had one option.

I never expected paper to taste nice, but it didn't matter. I popped the now scrunched ball into my mouth and chewed until it was a moist paste. Then I swallowed, feeling every part of it trailed down my throat as I removed it from existence. Taking the vial of Forbian I gave myself two drops as a chaser. The smooth liquid of the herb helped me take down the parchment but also relieved the aches of the bruising Marthil had gifted me.

"Thirsty?" Marthil said from the door. I bolted upright, surprised that I'd not heard her entrance.

"Have you been demoted to staff?" I replied, trying to keep my voice straight despite the anger that burned through my veins the moment she walked into my room unannounced. I couldn't show any sign that her sudden arrival had spooked me.

Marthil had changed since I last saw her. Gone where her dusted clothes; now she was dressed in a gown of deep brown with a clean-cut bodice of beads and threads. She seemed as uncomfortable as she looked in the dress. She didn't look the part of royalty. It was all an act after all.

"Drink it," she said again, voice deeper and riddled with command. She extended the cup for me, water sloshing over its side and spilling on the carpet. I took it, hoping she'd leave if I listened to her.

"What do you want?" I asked, regarding Marthil with wary eyes.

The sky was obsidian. Midnight must have greeted the city beyond. So why was Marthil dressed for a ball?

She paced around the end of my bed, pulling a small brown satchel from her waist. I had not noticed it before, as it blended seamlessly into her dress.

"Come to check on your wound." Marthil began emptying contents onto the bed. I knew she referred to the stabbing mark, but sine I'd last checked, the Forbian had healed it completely.

"You're a marvel," I said. "One moment you wish me pain, the next you want to help heal me."

"Trust me, Zacriah, this is not something I've chosen to do. But it seems that a certain shifter boy is refusing to come up here alone." Marthil raised one corner of her lip. "Scared of someone's reaction he said."

Petrer.

"Then at least one person in this place understands that I'm a threat," I replied.

Marthil laughed, ignoring my comments. "Gordex needs you back to full health. Take your top off and let me see if my concoction has worked."

If I refused, she would stay until she got her way. And with the lack of food, heavy head and tired body, I obeyed. I stripped the shirt off and showed her my skin.

Marthil studied it, talking to herself. "I'm impressed. The Forbian worked quicker than I expected. The dosage must be potent."

This side to Marthil unnerved me more than any other. Her voice was sickly sweat, almost maternal. To anyone else it would be hard to imagine she had the possibility to hurt anyone.

"See? I am fine. You can leave now."

She ignored my jab at her. "I see your bruising has already faded from earlier. You're not taking too much Forbian, are you? We wouldn't want your body to begin relying on it."

From her smile, I didn't trust her worry for me.

Marthil prodded and poked at my head, moving the silver strands of hair out of the way to see the marks she'd left me.

I didn't move or push her away.

"Are you planning on patching up all of my injuries?" I asked as she tipped a vial of water onto a clean cloth and dabbed it across my hairline. "Even the ones you leave me?"

"Quiet, Zacriah," she said, pressing slightly harder than she had before. "Your voice grates on *all* of my nerves."

"Can't say I am not glad." I smiled.

We didn't speak until Marthil was done. Her hands, harsh yet gentle, ran across my arms and neck, coating the bruising with the cool water. It was a pointless act. What was she trying to prove? She knew as well as I that in a matter of time, the Forbian would have cleared all my marks up. This water she doused over me would do nothing.

Just when I thought Marthil was ready to up and leave me, she came out with more unexpected news.

"Gordex has asked me to fetch you for a feast," Marthil said. "And since you have nothing suitable to wear, he has provided you with a new uniform." Turning for the door, Marthil clapped her hands. The door was kicked open by a shadowbeing who walked inside. His face was lifeless and gaunt. A painting of death. As he walked in I spotted a large trunk of sorts being carried between the shadowbeing and the next one who followed in after.

"I don't want his gifts," I spat.

"I'm sure you don't. But this isn't a game of what you want or not. You'll get changed into it. It's only polite to become presentable for the guest of honor."

The shadowbeings drop the trunk and leave, the bang makes me jump.

"Nyah?" I asked, hands clenched on the sheets around me.

"The one and only. Pretty girl, beautiful hair. Shame about the voice. Still, I have a feeling this feast is going to be the best yet, for Gordex is readying for an announcement."

"Wait," I shouted, reaching for Marthil who bent over to pack her satchel. "Is she... is she badly hurt?"

"Get changed." Marthil kicked the trunk on the way out. "And come and see for yourself."

I'd never moved so quickly. The moment Marthil closed the door, I was up, unbuckling the trunk and throwing the lid open. Inside, laid out on plush red silk, were folded black garments. Lifting the first up I recognized it as a uniform a soldier would wear. A black jacket of metal and leather layered in stiff plates of armor. This was not a custom for a feast, this was a statement of war. Within was a pair of black trousers and boots, all of which blended into one another as I tried them on.

The need to know if Nyah was okay was overwhelming, so I threw the uniform on. Not once had she tried to connect with me after I'd left, which unsettled my nerves. Not that I would've answered, but her persistence was at least a sign she was conscious, alive.

In my rush, I left for the door. Marthil surprised me, leaning up against the wall adjacent to my room, eyes dull and bored. She looked up from her nails and regarded me from boot to shoulders.

"Handsome," she said. "No wonder you have a prince falling at your feet."

And there the real Marthil had returned with a malice infested expression and voice thick with disdain. She reached past me and pulled my door closed. "Ready?"

"For what?" I replied as Marthil looked me up and down.

"Our guests?"

Guests?

Marthil nodded, leaning in close to me but screwing her nose in displeasure.

"You stink like muck," she said. "Gordex would have both our throats if you arrive smelling like that."

I raised an arm, inhaling what Marthil had. No wonder she was so offended.

"And in your new uniform!" Marthil scolded. "I will go ahead and tell them of your tardiness. Someone will come and collect you shortly, but you better wash straight away."

I didn't have a chance to question her on the meal, nor did I want to. Marthil turned and left, picking the long skirt of her dress up as she moved through the corridor. I was left with the shadowbeings who guarded my room. Not wanting to be under there gaze a moment later, I ran for the bathrooms. It'd been days since I'd last cleaned myself.

Questions about the feast and guests rattled through my mind, but only one thing was clear to me. If Nyah was going to be there, I might have a chance to communicate with her. My want to tell her about the message I had received urged me on. The sooner I got to her, the better.

CHAPTER
SEVEN

THE STREAM OF water was freezing. It chilled me to my bones, sharpening my senses as it washed days of dirt from my body. I needed to be ready for anything, clear minded and prepared to fight, just like Nyah had been. Already so much has been lost, and I was not prepared for anything else to be taken from my control. My magick was no longer my own, Gordex made sure of that. But my will was mine and mine alone. He could not have that.

I picked the uniform from the damp floor and got changed before the large, gilded mirror in the washroom. Standing before the mirror I fixed my hair, quickly pulling it back into the tight bun and gathering any lose stands into a messy style. This was me, the me from home. I might not have felt the same as I used to, for so much had changed for the boy who looked back in the reflection I hardly recognized.

"Here, let me help," a voice called out behind me.

My gaze snapped to the boy in the reflection, stood feet behind me.

"I thought my threat resonated with you?" I replied, fixing the last strands into place before turning for Petrer. "Or do you need a reminder as to why I have asked you to leave me alone?"

"Pardon my intrusion, Zac." Petrer bowed his head, ignoring my threat. "But I was asked to collect you by the Druid himself, since you've kept us all waiting longer than we care to wait," Petrer droned, eyes trailing me from head to toe. "Now I have seen you, I am glad I came up. Truly. It gives me a moment to admire you. You look delectable."

I wanted to slice his tongue from his mouth as he ran it across his lips until they glistened with spit. His hungry gaze fueled my desire to hurt him.

"Leave me, Petrer, turn around and go." I kept my tone still and tempered. "I can find my own way to the Druid."

"This desire to turn me away only urges me on more. You are wasting energy." He smiled. "Energy you could rid with other means."

Petrer took two strides forward, hands on hips and trouble in his gaze.

I took equal steps back until the mirror's cold kiss touched my back.

"I also have ideas, but I can honestly say they would be different from what you imagine."

"Please, entertain me. Tell me more." Petrer pushed on.

"Why tell you when I can show you?" I replied, licking my own lips and narrowing my gaze on him.

Petrer released a labored breath. "You do things to me. I worry words would fail me if I tried to explain."

He was close now, walking straight into my trap.

I smiled a devilish grin as the darkness bubbled deep in me. It could sense its will to escape.

"Is that right?" I said, voice tipped with innocence. Petrer was so close, his breath tickled my lips. His gaze flickered between my own, my mouth, my body. I could see what he wanted, and I used it against him.

"Finally," he breathed. "It was only a matter of time till you wanted this again. I gave you the distance you asked for, and now you are mine. You remember that I'm good for you."

"Hmm," I said, trying not to scratch my nails up the glass mirror behind me. "Would you like me to reveal what occupies my thoughts?"

Petrer giggled, looking up through his dark lashes. "Do I really need to answer that? You know my answer."

His hungry gaze was enough proof that he wanted me to spill my secrets. His mouth was parted as he breathed excitedly.

"First," I said, raising a hand and calling forth my magick. The darkness shot across every inch of my body, taking a hold of my muscles, blood and mind. "I'm going take every morsel of breath from your body until you turn blue. Until your body burns with starvation and your consciousness titters over the edge of pain."

Petrer's expression melted from hunger to confusion.

"Then, just as your mind begins to protect you from the pain that I cause, I will flood every inch of that vile body until it cannot hold the air I supply you. I'll not stop until your lungs crack under pressure. That is exactly how I want to expend my energy."

It took a moment for my words to register on Petrer's face, then his snarl was a warning of his next action. Lightning fast he reached for my face, spit linking his open mouth as he roared in anger. His extended hands called out for me, reaching straight for my exposed neck. But I didn't stop him, not until the last possible moment. I wanted him to think he was winning, to believe he was always in the control over me. Then I would watch the realization that it was over sink into his wide, dark eyes.

I pushed out my hands, already swirling with the air that longed for my control. As the tips of his revolting fingers grazed my skin, I forced every ounce of strength

I owned behind my magick. The strength of power sent Petrer flying across the room in a blur of panicked limbs. He cracked into the wall, sliding down to the floor. Crumpled in on himself, Petrer choked out.

I couldn't help but smile as the pain creased across Petrer's once desirable face. A face I now only ever wanted to see with this new expression.

"Listen, Petrer, and do it carefully," I said, pushing more magick into my air and holding him in place like a bug beneath pins. "You'll never again step foot near me, look at me, think of me. Because this will seem like pleasure compared to what it is I do to you next. That is a promise. Cause me *any* discomfort from this moment forward, and I will be sure to make you feel it tenfold in return."

He tried to call out, but I rendered him silent by the hurricane that roared around him. My winds ripped across my room, tangling my sheets and slamming the furniture into one another. I could see the silver stings of magick. Heart Magick. This was my mark, and it was gorgeous.

"Do you understand me?" My voice rained across the room, lifted by my air.

Even if he wanted to nod, reply, agree, I wouldn't let him. It was a game to me now. I was in control; I was the master.

I almost laughed when a single tear leaked from his right eye and rolled down his flushed cheek. The feeling was strange and alien to me.

There was something calling to me in the pits of my stomach, a light that tried to cut through the dark that powered my magick. But I ignored it. It was no longer welcome.

Stop, it sang.

This is not you, stop.

Petrer tried to open his mouth, whether to plead or speak, I couldn't tell. His face was changing color, his eyes rolling toward his hairline.

I laxed on my power and willed for my air to retreat, letting his helpless body slump to the ground.

"Petrer," I called from above him, faltering over my own words from the sudden depletion of energy. "I think it is time for us to go, isn't it? As you have said, I've kept them waiting long enough."

He didn't say anything. He only looked at me with fearful eyes and a disheveled appearance.

"Come now," I said, moving for the door and stepping over the clothes that my wind had scattered across the floor. "Lead the way."

CHAPTER
EIGHT

PETRER WALKED STEPS ahead of me the entire way to the banquet.

Every now and then he would peer over his shoulder, face pale and eyes unblinking, as if he expected me to lash out again. In truth, I didn't know what I was going to do. Each step I took I was becoming more myself, realizing my actions were not in my control. Even thinking about what I'd done seemed hazy, as if a darkness was acting for me and burying me deep as a spectator.

But I didn't want to dwell on it. Regardless if I was in control or not, my message was true. I wanted Petrer to stay away, to cease his hungry stares and fleeting touches. From the fear that rolled off of him, I was certain my message had been received.

I missed Hadrian. The feeling had become overwhelming as my mind returned from the dark control. Only did I want him close to me like that. I longed for his touch. *Hungered* for it. How long did I have to go through this punishment to finally return to him?

We paced around the dark palace, past the crumbled walls and dirtied, covered pavements. Shadowbeings filtered past us with jaws open and arms hanging by their sides. I flinched from them, uncomfortable when one got too close.

It was common to see them patrolling the palace. Just their presence was enough to make my skin crawl.

Looking around, I didn't recognize where we'd walked to. I'd not been to this part of the palace before, but from the painted portraits of the queen and her family, I guessed I had made it to her personal dwellings.

The corridors were not exposed to the outside as the majority of the palace but kept enclosed by the towering walls lined with red silk curtains and the plush matching carpets that muffled our footfall.

Muffled voices pricked my awareness.

We were getting close.

Petrer straightened his back and held his chin high as we rounded a corner. We walked towards the set of closed doors and stopped. Petrer would never let anyone see him in this state I'd just witnessed.

His pride was stronger than his ability to fear.

"I do hate waiting, truly. I have done it enough over the past moons."

Gordex's words leaked through the crack in the partially opened door as Petrer reached out and pushed them open.

"My apologies, Druid," Petrer replied, bowing his head and stepping aside for me to enter. "It is my own fault we are late."

Petrer's comment surprised me. I walked past him, eyeing him cautiously but he didn't once look up.

Gordex laid his dark gaze upon me and stood from his chair. He opened his arms wide in a strange welcome. "My how marvelous you look, Zacriah. I see my gift reached you. Thank you for wearing it, my solider. And for you, Petrer, next time do not keep me waiting. I understand your infatuation with Zacriah is overwhelming but keep it for moments when I am not forced to wait."

"Sorry, my Lord," Petrer whispered, closing the doors and walking towards Gordex.

Gordex sick joke was wasted upon me. He didn't know what had happened between us, or did he? A strange glint passed behind his eyes, giving a knowing air to his smile.

"Come sit, my boy." Gordex signaled to the two free chairs on the long table beside him. I barely looked his way when I spotted our guests. Nyah and Queen Kathine sat on either side of Gordex, golden chains wrapped round their throats.

I flinched away from the throbbing of the gold. It was subtle, pulling on the anger once again. It didn't invoke pain as it once had. Perhaps now my Heart Magick was free I no longer reacted as I once had.

Queen Kathine's gazed was pinned my way, whereas Nyah hardly looked up. Her eyes were heavy and lost to the empty plate before her. She looked drained, empty, lost. Bruises covered her exposed arms and crept beneath the collar she wore. The dress she had been put in glittered with green and red jewels. Her hair had been pulled back from her face and secured in a bun, but her expression was anything but put-together.

To her right sat the shell of the boy she had been beginning to love. Jasrov, filled with black shadow and a thoughtless mind. A re-animated body controlled by Gordex's warped power.

Inside I wanted to scream out when I saw him, but I had to keep calm. I couldn't act out, for that is what Gordex would want.

I took my seat, biting down hard on the insides of my lips. The harsh taste of copper laced my tongue and reminded me of what I craved for. Just that thought stirred the darkness within me once again. Its presence was larger than ever now.

"Since we are all present, I trust we can enjoy our final meal within this city," Gordex announced, taking his seat again. He picked up the ivory cloth from the table and folded it in half, placing it into his collar before picking up his silver cutlery from the sides of his empty plate.

Final meal?

As if reading my internal confusion, he looked up and smiled my way, flashing teeth and gum. "Oh yes, my boy, final meal within *my* city. Since your friend here decided to give up the location I need, we have a short journey ahead of us to claim my final prize. So, eat up. I am going to need you at full strength."

My face must have melted from one shocked expression to another.

Nyah looked at me, sorrow plastered across her gaunt face. Her lips, cracked and pale, mouthed a simple word my way. *Sorry.*

I was saved from the awkward silence as the doors opened again, and living servants walked in with trays of food. Given a few moments of relief, I worked to calm my shock and regulate my breathing. News that we were to leave when the note I had received told me to hold off worried me. If Nyah had given up the location, this fight would be over soon. And they needed me to bide time. I had to try.

Once the servants had placed the roasted lump of meat, bowls of boiled potatoes and countless dried vegetables and bread, I was ready to tackle this situation.

"When do we leave?" I asked, calmly.

Gordex paused as he stabbed his fork into a potato and raised it above him. "We leave tomorrow at first light. It is not a short journey to our destination, but the ship I found will make it simpler. It took some blade work to secure the ship, but I have it now."

Queen Kathine croaked, trying to clear her throat. It was subtle but enough for Gordex to notice. His head snapped to her, his hand following until her cheek stung red. "Quiet!"

Despite the blooming of ruby across her face, she did not stop smiling. Hearing of her people's rebellion was enough information to fuel her own rebellion with that smile.

"You said it will take a while. Where is it we are going?" I asked, cutting my own meat whilst everyone else around the table did not touch the food. I looked up at Gordex as I placed the forkful in my mouth, my eyes urging an answer. I chewed the lump in my dry mouth. The thought of swallowing turned my stomach.

He regarded me silently before answering, "Since when have you taken up an interest in my doings, boy?"

"Since I had no other choice."

A prideful smile flashed my way, but it didn't stop the hint of distrust that filled his stare. I needed to know everything in hopes to find a loop hole to create a distraction.

"Where is our adventure taking us next?" My sarcasm cut across the tension between us as I asked again.

"The shores of Morgatis," Gordex replied.

"Home," Marthil added from the doorway where she silently lurked. I'd not heard her come in and had no idea for how long she had been listening.

"I believed you had changed your mind about joining us this evening," Gordex said to Marthil. "Come sit before the food goes cold."

"Not hungry, but I don't want to feel like I am missing out, do I?" She sauntered over, walking right behind me and taking a seat at the far end of the table.

Whilst Gordex and Marthil shot comments at each other like hateful siblings, I had a moment to let the news sink in. If Nyah had told the truth and our team was hiding in barren lands of Morgatis, then I was lost to what to do. Images of the destruction Cristilia told me about flooded my mind as they were the only insight I had into that land. Dust and sand, ruins and stone.

A place destroyed by Heart Magick by the Dragori lost to the past.

I needed to know what to expect. And there was only three people within this city who had the knowledge on Morgatis. Knowledge I needed.

I decided to cease my questioning.

Marthil would never speak of the place she hated most. But Cristilia, there was a chance she would speak up. Regardless of what she did to us, she acted out of the hope to save her sister. If I could convince her I was on her side, then maybe she would tell me of Morgatis and the mysteries of the land. There must be something to use against Gordex in his effort to find Emaline.

Something Marthil said registered through my busy mind.

"They'll expect our arrival."

Gordex replied with a mouthful, "I count on it."

"With enough time, they'll see the ship and destroy it before it reaches land." Marthil voice was unbothered, as if she hoped that would happen.

"Oh, I do hope so." Gordex's response shocked me and Marthil, whose head cocked back dramatically. "The ship, although grand, is merely a distraction. It will not be my means of travel. And it would be wasted breath asking more on the matter. You shall all see soon enough."

No one uttered a word whilst Gordex tucked into the slice of meat slavered across his plate. Methodically he sliced it into pieces, red juices leaking from the cuts and oozing onto his plate.

"Marthil, why the face?" Gordex said without looking up. His comment had me looking her way and noticing the intense red tones that blotched her cheeks and neck. "I thought you would be happy to have a chance to return home, to show them just how much you care for the people who turned you away?"

"You promised me that I'd never need to return back

there, yet you conspire these plans without involving me?" Marthil's tone was pointed and sharp. I knew little about Marthil and why she had left, only pieces of story I had pieced together from Cristilia's comments. Marthil had been exiled all because of the fear rotted in the Morthi's people minds and hearts from the destruction of the previous Dragori. Even now, the story Cristilia told me lingered in the back of my mind.

"Retrieving the final Dragori is greater than any promise I have made you, Marthil," Gordex replied simply. "I expected you not to have a problem with this. Not when the promise of you having revenge can be fulfilled sooner than later."

Marthil frowned, contemplating his words. Her gaze was hard like frost. "Leave me here. I can look over the city and keep her rabble in check." Marthil pointed her empty fork at Queen Kathine.

"What do you fear, dear girl?"

Marthil winced. "I want to stay here."

"You will join us." Gordex slammed his palms on the table despite the sweet nature of his tone.

The air in the room thickened, and the flames from the many candles flickered out of existence. I dropped my cutlery and gripped onto the arms of my chair.

Gordex raised his gaze to Marthil, his eyes had turned charcoal and runes leaked with black shadow.

"You disrespected me, Marthil, on more occasions

than one." His voice boomed across the room, followed by torrents of wind, my wind. I felt him pulling on my magick, twisting it for his own control. "Do not make me regret my choice to treat you with great kindness. I promised you the heads of those who shunned you, and that is what you shall get. Yet why you *still* defy me, I do not know."

Queen Kathine showed her first signs of distress as Gordex unleashed his power across the table straight for Marthil. Nyah cowered, curtains of curly red hair falling out of her bun and across her eyes, as if she was trying to hide. Jasrov's undead body sat still, unbothered, hands moving for his empty plate as the shadows inside of him kept him animated on an emotionless loop.

But Marthil did not cower or hide.

In silent protest, she kept her gaze on Gordex as he used our magicks against her. Flexing his control, he showed his use of air, fire and earth as he made the room quake once again.

"Don't make me go back," Marthil said, voice barely audible over the roaring winds. But the catch in her voice and the wet glaze over her eyes was not a result of the magick. It was the result of fear. Like a frightened child she began to crack. "Please…"

Gordex brows creased in their center as he too noticed the fear in Marthil's eyes. Fear not created by him, but by the prospect of returning back to Morgatis.

"You are scared," he said, tilting his head inquisitively. "I sense it on you."

Marthil lowered her head as the room returned to normal. She didn't admit her fear, nor did she need to. It was as clear as summer skies.

"There is nothing to fear, Marthil, not any longer. But I cannot say the same for those who exiled you. They will feel fear, and you will be the one to place that fear in their hearts."

Marthil looked up slowly, her eyes dry and lips pinched white. "How?"

Gordex took his seat, shoulders back and chin held high.

"Something you will soon learn. Control is the only cure to the virus that is fear. And it is control that I—we will have."

CHAPTER

NINE

ONCE GORDEX HAD finished eating, he stood and left. Without another word Nyah, Marthil, Queen Kathine and I sat watching one another to break the silence. Nyah's hand was on the table in front of her, inches from Jasrov's pale, dead fingers. So close that a single movement of one would make them touch.

My heart ached watching her desire to feel him.

Marthil's chair practically fell over as she kicked back out of it and stormed out. I watched her slip past the shadowbeing guards who burst into the room. Two grabbed me by the underarms and pulled me from my place. I tried to call for Nyah, but she was being dragged out as well.

I shrugged off the dead hands from my body and stayed steps ahead the remainder of the walk. My skin crawled whenever they touched me.

The palace was shrouded in an ominous cloud in the dark of night. The lack of flame only added to the frozen air and brisk winds that intruded from beyond the palace. Although it had been days since a fresh layering of snow, it would only be a matter of time until the next blizzard ate its way across Lilioira.

Once I reached my room, I slammed the door after me. The familiar shuffle of shadowbeings feet responded beyond the door but soon disappeared. Strange. I waited for a sign that they had followed but heard nothing. Opening the door once again, all I could see was the dark, empty corridor beyond.

This was my chance.

It was the first time I'd left my room after dark, and I moved through the palace unseen. I'd grown used to the four shadowbeings stationed beyond my door, the way they moved and the slight hum of the magick that leaked from their mouths.

I didn't wait around to question why they had not arrived, nor did it matter. I only needed time to get answers, and there was only one person here that might be willing to give them. Cristilia.

The route we had taken when our group was imprisoned before the escape was clear in my mind.

My new, black uniform Gordex provided helped me slip in and out of the shadows as I made my way towards the catacombs beneath the palace.

Unlike my own imprisonment, Cristilia had no guards to keep watch. Once I made it down the curling stairs into the pits of the dark place, I felt no presence of anyone else but the woman curled on the floor in the cell before me.

"I thought visitors were not a luxury I would receive," Cristilia whispered, sensing my arrival before I had announced it. "Nor did I think it would be you who would come down to see me. In fact, you were the last person I ever thought would visit."

"No shadowbeings to keep you company?" I shot my comment across the dark space between us. Standing beyond the thick bars, I could see how wild Cristilia looked now. Her hair was matted and glistening with grease. Her body was hollow and bent. As she rolled over and looked up at me, her eyes no longer held the shine to them that once hypnotized with their fake kindness.

"I am no threat, Zacriah, not to the Druid or anyone up there. Not anymore." Her eyes trailed my entire body. "Has he taken you and distorted your mind like he has with my dear sister?"

I ran my hands down the uniform, self-conscious beneath her stare. "No. This—this means nothing. I am on the side of what is right unlike you. You did all of this. Your actions allowed Gordex to take control. May the state of this city and the world beyond it be heavy on your conscious."

"You do not need to remind me," she muttered. "I am no threat, not anymore."

"Because you have been stripped of your abilities?

That is a mere fraction of what you deserve."

"And pray tell, what do I deserve? Death? For wanting nothing more than to be returned with my own blood? My Marthil. Do not pretend you would not do the same if faced with my dilemma. I may not have known you for long, but even you know just what rules you would break, did break to be with your prince."

"Do not compare my story with yours Cristilia, for they are none alike. I have not killed for Hadrian—"

"Not yet," Cristilia interrupted. "But this chapter of the story has only just started. Many more events will take place, many more lives will be taken."

Cristilia pushed herself up from the floor, wincing as she did so. "Why are you here, Zacriah? What are *you* willing to do to save those you love?"

Cristilia, after everything she'd done for her sister, had ultimately failed. I wouldn't admit it aloud, but in truth we were no different, two people seeking to save those they love and do anything to complete that task.

"Tell me everything you know about Morgatis."

From the expression that contorted her face, that was not what she expected me to ask.

"And can I ask why it is you seek knowledge on my home land?"

"Tell me everything," I repeated.

"He is taking her back there, isn't he?" Cristilia swallowed. "She will refuse him. She will never return home."

"Well, it pains me to say it, but we are all going. Although I am unsure about you, I have a feeling you will be left in here to rot."

"It is my just punishment," she muttered, eyes darting around the floor as if she searched for sympathy.

"The story you told me of the Dragori who unleashed destruction across Morgatis… is that the only thing you can tell me about the land and its people?" I sliced Cristilia with a stare as she raised her empty eyes back to me.

"Listen closely. Morgatis and the Morthi people are different than you may believe. Do not be fooled by their distaste for magick, for what they fear is what they also desire. My people will protect you as long as you are not a threat. The moment you remind them why they hate the Dragori is the moment you seal your own fate. They will know the Druid will be arriving, no matter what wool he tries to pull over their eyes. My people will know, for tricks are wasted on them."

If what Cristilia said was true, the Morthi will know either way. I couldn't hide the smirk that pulled the corners of my lips. "And their magick? I know little of it, only what you've shown me."

"You are hoping that they have enough power to tip the scales of this fight in your favor?" Cristilia questioned, catching me off guard.

I shouldn't trust her, not after what she did to us. But something told me I could regardless.

"I simply need to know if they have enough strength to hold Gordex at bay. Enough to cause a distraction."

"You have a loose tongue. You tell your secrets to easily."

"What are you going to do, reveal them to the walls?"

"I could use what you tell me to gain grace with the Druid, have my power restored to me."

"Yet you will not."

Cristilia grinned, flashing her stained teeth. "Are you certain?"

"More than certain," I replied, testing the waters. "Because you know that is not how your sister will be saved from him."

"Keep going."

"We are the only chance of saving Marthil now, and from the reaction she gave Gordex this evening, I think we are not far from doing that. You know this is true, and you'll not risk interfering again."

Cristilia held my gaze, some shine had returned to her eyes. She tipped her head in a nod and provided me with the final insight I would need.

"My people once lived in the sun, providing them with the power to will it for their own desires. Now, since your ancestors drove them underground, they have will over the dark. Two conflicting magicks, power that no one else in this world has. Remember that. My homeland is a divided nation between old and new views. But their memory of what the Dragori did to my peoples ancestors is still as fresh as you could imagine. That is all I have to say."

"Thank you," I said, putting my hand in my pocket and pulling out the vial of Forbian Marthil had given me. "You should take this. It will help with your ailments."

I extended my hand through the bars, but Cristilia did not reach for it. "No, that is for you."

Screams sent bolts of terror coursing through my blood, waking me from my slumber in fits of gasping breaths. I threw myself from bed and ran to the balcony. There I'd have a greater vantage point of the city to see what caused such a noise.

The cold morning air kissed my exposed arms. Dense snow clouds hovered high above, eradicating all source of blue that would normally grace the skies. They hummed with ice, yet not a single flake fell from the heights.

Peering across the city, I could make out the dark shapes of elves filling the streets. They shouted and screamed, attention directed towards something I could not see from this place.

Leaving the shouts of Alorian people, I ran back into the room. Stripping the black uniform from my body, I chose to put on mismatched clothes. I didn't want to wear the uniform that Gordex had provided any longer. The thought made my skin itch with discomfort.

The need to visit the city was the only thing that flooded my mind.

I had no weapons, nothing I could use if needed. Only my magick that still dwelled within me, laced with the darkness that urged me to cause pain.

Reaching for the door, I yanked hard on the handle after unlocking the bolt, but it didn't open. Confused, I placed an ear to the wood and listened. My guards were not waiting beyond it. I could not hear there shuffling and raspy croaks.

I slammed my hands on the door to get someone's attention. It was a wasted effort, but my need to leave was growing by the second. With each bang, my palms came back red and no one listened.

I opted for another idea. Closing my eyes, I extended my awareness into the air around me. Pulling on such power gave me a sweet rush that almost made me laugh. I pushed my concentration until I was air. Then I reached far beyond the door for a sign that someone was close. But the palace was still. I felt no shift of shadowbeings, no use of breath in the corridors beyond. I was alone. Whatever was happening in the city had pulled all the shadowbeings around me into it.

If there was no one to let me out, I would have to

leave through other means.

I turned on my heel and faced the balcony. It was not the first time I had jumped from a height and landed without a scratch. This time I had wings as backup. I let my body ripple as I took wide steps towards the open air, allowing the beast to come free. The closer I got the faster I ran. Only a few more strides until I was airborne.

My wings sprang free and my fists clenched with tension. I grappled for the wind's embrace when a shuffle sounded behind me.

"Wait," two voices chorused.

My hands gripped the frame of the balcony, talons cutting into brick, as I regarded to the two hooded men that stood in the shadows of my room. They were not shadowbeings, nor men in the grasp of Gordex.

"Who are you?" I growled.

"Claws away, kitty," one said.

"I think you'll wanna stay and hear us out," the other added.

They both raised their heads, and I caught intense green as their eyes shone through the shadows of their hoods. The color of emerald I'd looked into so many times before.

CHAPTER
TEN

BOTH MEN WERE dressed in black. Their jackets reflected the dull morning light, catching the many clasps and buckles that held the leather straps in place. The hood they both wore covered half of their face, and the half I needed to see the most. I could see their sharp chins and gaunt cheeks, but that was it.

Although they were both similar in height and equally broad, the only difference was the weapons they held. One had a broad sword held in his hand, the tip touching the stone slabs of my floor. The other held two shorter swords, half the length of his bulking forearms. It was he who stood forward and spoke for them both.

"We don't have long with you," he said, his accent reminding me of home. It was rough like mine, crafted from years around the farms and intense labor of Thessolina's countryside.

The presence of sharp steel was what put me on edge.

"Is there a need for those?" I said, pointing a talon

towards the swords. It was my own way of flashing my weapon as they were doing with theirs.

"Cautionary, yes."

"Who are you?"

The first man with the two short swords turned to the other and nodded. Then they sheathed their steels and removed the hoods, giving me my first view of faces I was certain I'd seen before.

"Negan, and this is my brother Neivel. Apologies for the sudden appearance, but if it makes you feel any better, we've been around a while now. It's only thanks to the distraction out there that we have time to chat with you," Negan said, closing the space between us. He didn't even flinch at my wings, horns or the many scales that clustered across my skin.

"Is that supposed to make me feel better?" I questioned.

"We don't have time for this, Negan, get to the point," the other brother, Neivel, said. His face was expressionless and bored.

His face was so familiar.

The brothers both had hair of fire, deep red with hits of a lighter auburn. Negan had more freckles dusting his face than his less welcoming brother. Twins, they must've been. Their appearance mirrored one another, the only difference being that Negan's chin was rounded then his brother, Neivel's.

We all turned to the balcony when a chorus of shouts raised into the air. Lightning panic raced down my arms.

"Hurry," Neivel hissed.

"Yes, do hurry," I said, urging for answers to who they were.

"We are here to help. The noise from the city is our peoples doing, one we have been planning for days."

"What plan? Whose plan?" I asked Negan, gesturing to the open air behind me.

"That is the many who are sacrificing themselves to give us the time to have this conversation with you," Neivel said, voice deep and tempered.

"You are risking lives for a measly conversation?" I said. "Why?"

"These lives are not lost entirely but misplaced until this all ends. It was inevitable, only a matter of time before the Druid claimed them for his army. But this way they will be overcome with his dark power, but not through death. It was the best option we had during such dire times."

"How do you know all of this?" I asked, mind racing to make sense of what Negan told me. Neivel stood a few feet behind his brother which gave me the best view of him when he turned towards the door. His ear, it was pointed like mine. Then I noticed the glint of red that hummed beneath their pale skin. They were in fact from

Thessolina. "And what are two Niraen born elves doing this far from home?"

The right side of Negan's lip turned up. "You've keen eyes. We do share the same shores as you, but left years ago. We've been working for the Alorian Queen Kathine since we both enrolled in her legions, preparing for war that we never believed would arrive."

"You're twins, aren't you?"

Negan nodded. "We are."

Neivel pushed past his brother, face matching his red hair. "We don't have time for idle chatter. Not when our sister is suffering. If we are going to get her out, we need to leave, Negan. We need to go now."

Sister? My mouth gawked open in shock.

"Nyah." I swallowed.

Both brother's expressions changed, as if her name caused them a strange pain.

"You are her brothers?" My knees almost gave way beneath the heavy weight of realization.

Negan tapped in the air. "Older brothers, yes."

"She told me about you. How you'd enrolled in the Eldnol armies. But we never spoke about it again."

"You must listen, for we don't have long. Since the fall of the city we, as well as the soldiers left trapped beyond, are plotting an uprising. We have shared word with those that surround Lilioira beyond the fallen gate. Regiments are coming together from across Eldnol, and soon there will be numbers far greater than anything the Druid has. Even with his new recruits he is collecting as we speak, our numbers will outgrow his ten to one. It is only a matter of time till we make our move."

I almost sagged on the spot with relief. Before now I had only hoped in moments of wishful thinking of the efforts beyond the closed city that would help us. Maybe this was it? With the Alorian numbers they could overthrow Gordex and end it all.

"When are they moving in on the city?" I asked, my enthusiasm clear from the cracking in my voice.

"Soon," Neivel muttered. "When the time is right. That is why we are here to see you. Queen Kathine has been in contact—"

"She has?" This entire time she seemed broken.

"Kathine is *queen,* she has her ways. Regardless of what they are, she seems to believe you are the best person to question regarding Gordex's timelines. Whatever you know you must tell us. It will help determine when we move."

This new information spoke volumes to me. Regardless of Queen Kathine's weakness she was still able to communicate with those beyond the city. As if on cue, a bird sped past the open balcony. I caught the blur of its blue underwing and recognized it as the birds which Queen Kathine used to spread news across her city. It perched on the balcony and watched the three of us, knowingly.

I moved from the balcony into the room where the brothers stood. This could be the distraction I needed to create more time for whoever sent the familiar. Then it hit me, they could be working with the efforts beyond the city.

"I will share what I know, but you must answer this for me. Are you in contact with Prince Hadrian? Emaline the Dragori?" I said, hopefully.

Negan's expression was enough to break down my hope and smash it into a million pieces. "No, there has been no contact with Prince Hadrian or this Dragori you speak of. The only thing I know is they have left Eldnol's shores for another. I am sorry I've no more answers for you."

I took a silent moment to compose myself. At least they were far from the fight, where ever they were. "Fine, this is what I know. Gordex plans to leave for Morgatis this morning, or so that was what he said. He has prepared a ship—"

From the noise in the city, I couldn't help but feel that his plans were being pushed back.

"The ship we are aware about," Neivel interrupted.

"Then you know there is a limited time to strike. I know little of his plans regarding our travel, for he has called the ship a distraction. We could be leaving before it or after. That is all I know," I said.

"What did I say to you?" Neivel said, angered. "He knows little, and we have wasted precious time. We could have our sister far from this place by now."

Negan didn't flinch at his brother's anger but kept his jade gaze pinned to mine. Even his eyes mimicked his sister's perfectly. "Change of plans, brother, we are not going for Nyah today."

"What?" Neivel's eyes bulged, the whites laced with protuberant veins.

"No, you must!" I added my own shock at Negan's comment.

"Now is not the time. We must wait. If what *he* has said comes to pass, there will be a better time to save our sister. Or, as our sister is famous for doing, she will save herself. This is Nyah we are talking about," Negan said, turning for his brother and placing a calm hand on his shoulder. "Come."

Both moved for the large mirror that was propped against my wall.

"Wait…" I called for them, panicked by their sudden departure.

"In sight we may not be here, but we will be around in the shadows," Negan said, pulling the hood back over his head.

"How? What if I find out more details and need to tell you?" I asked.

"Then talk to the walls. They'll be listening."

I reached out for Negan's arm. "Please, go for Nyah. I fear the longer she is here the more Gordex can hurt her to get to me. I cannot, will not let that happen. You need to take her far away from here."

For the first time, Neivel nodded, agreeing with me.

Negan brushed a gentle hand down my arm. I shivered under the contact of kindness, something I hadn't experienced for a while. There was a selfish part of me that wanted them to stay here. Their presence calmed me.

"It will only be a matter of time till we move in," Negan said. He let go of me and walked back to his brother who waited close to the mirror. "Like I said, speak with the walls if you need. They'll be listening."

I raised a brow and watched both boys walk behind the mirror. Once out of view, I raced over to see where they had gone, but the space behind it was empty, the brick wall untouched without sign that they had ever been here. As if they had ghosted through the stone itself, I was alone again.

For a long while I sat on the end of my bed piecing together the puzzle that was beginning to form.

What I knew so far was that the city was surrounded by waiting armies of light. They would attack when the time was right, whatever that was supposed to mean. Hadrian was not with them, which meant he truly was in Morgatis if that was where Gordex believes the final

Dragori to be. And if the armies failed to stop him before we left, then what else would prevent him from getting what he wanted?

Emaline, was the final piece of his own puzzle. A puzzle that when completed would bring about a time of druids again, using our magick and the Staff with the collected souls of his ancestors to unlock a new reign of terror across our lands.

I only hoped we could stop it before time was no longer our ally.

CHAPTER
ELEVEN

I HALF EXPECTED Nyah's brothers to return, but even when the screams and shouts of anguish ceased from the city, they never did. Not for the rest of the day, nor in the evening when my stomach spasmed with hunger, and my throat cut with the need for drink.

All day I'd been left in my room. I'd given up trying to break the door down and decided that flying from the room would only bring more attention to me. I didn't need Gordex's watching eyes on me anymore than they already were.

I complied. It was all I could do. My shadowbeing guards arrived when the sky turned opal and the clouds were no longer visible. Their shuffles soon become a constant, blending in with the quiet as they always ended up doing. All I could do to pass the time was lie on my bed, facing the high ceiling. I counted the arches over and over, trying to calm my thoughts. For I had so many of them.

What else could I do to give Emaline time? The note

had not long reached me, and change was coming. It hung in the air as thick as the smoke that spilled from the city since the cries stopped. Whatever happened within it today was a mystery, one I was sure Gordex would boast about over breakfast tomorrow.

Just as his name slipped across my mind, my door opened. Gordex entered alone.

His cloak trailed on the floor like water. It skittered across the slabbed floor, muffling his footsteps. He stood tall, runes dull across his skin. His obsidian eyes seemed darker than usual, ringed with shadows of tiredness beneath.

My entire body went stiff. I tried to keep my face expressionless, but his appearance made me feel like every secret I held from him was to be spilled across the floor. All sense of hunger that only seconds before clung to my stomach had left me. Even at the sight and smell of the food in Gordex's hands were not enough to reclaim my desire to eat.

"What a day," Gordex said, sighing with relief. The way he said it would be normal if it was from a father to his son, complaining about the work on the fields. "If I am hungry, you must be famished."

He thrust the bowl of unknown liquid towards me. I turned my nose at it and gripped a hold of the sheets around me.

"What have you done?" I kept my voice steady and

sharp. Gordex pulled a face of confusion, as if my accusation shocked him.

"What needed to be done." Gordex thrust the bowl at me, but when I turned away from it again he placed it down on the cabinet beside the bed. "I do hope you have found ways to occupy yourself today. I am afraid I have been too busy to stop by and check on you."

My cold stare was enough of a reply.

"Are you not going to ask me how my day has been?" Gordex asked, walking towards the balcony, his stare lost to me for a moment. In the faded light of evening he looked old and worn, as if the day had taken a toll on him.

"I know the game you play Gordex," I spat. "From the shouts I've heard all day, I can only guess what you've been doing within Queen Kathine's City. So, why are you here?"

"Why else do you think I am here on a visit but to share my spoils of success," Gordex said. For a man who could cause such destruction, he had an air of calm about him. A stillness that I usually looked over. "Those who dwelled in that city were nothing but a thorn within skin. And I need an army, willingly or not. For the days to come, I must tip the scales of war towards me, and for that, sacrifices need to be made."

"Genocide," I shouted, the darkness bubbling within me. "That is what you have done. Killed for your sick gain. The Goddess will not look down upon you with a loving heart."

"It is not the Goddess whose opinion I care for. Volcras will be grinning, I am sure of it. For I have gifted him with many this day."

The Goddess reigned over light whereas Volcras was the God of darkness. And a God is what Gordex longed to be.

I pinched my nails into my palm, trying to still my urge to fight. When I blinked, I saw streets drenched in blood. I only hoped what the twins had told me about lives not being wasted was true.

Anger twisted deep within me. It was the dark energy in me, Gordex's remaining touch, that willed me to act out. But I couldn't, wouldn't.

"Your hands are stained gold, red and black."

"Oh, hush child. Not all lives have been lost today. There have been a few with gifts I'd very much like to utilize. The rest have joined the shadowbeings as companions."

Just as Negan and Neivel had said.

"You expect them all to journey across the sea to Morgatis?" I replied.

Gordex cracked a tooth filled grin, lips tipping to the skies in pleasure. "In a manner of speaking, yes."

"You will lose." I ground my teeth, hissing through my clenched jaw.

"Will I? Everything I do has a purpose. Whether you believe it or not. For this is my game, board and players. I will succeed."

Gordex placed his fingers to his lips to still himself. "That is enough for today. Enjoy your supper. Who knows if tomorrow brings more."

"Wait," I shouted, unsure why I called for him to stay, but the urgency in my voice was so thick I could practically taste it.

Gordex stopped before the door, black robes shifting around his feet from the sudden stop in momentum.

"Yes?" he drawled.

"Nyah, please. I'd like to see her," I asked, forcing the most fake voice I could muster.

"Of course." Gordex looked over his shoulder to me. The dark rune marks on his skin stretching.

His quick agreement snatched the breath out of me.

"You seem surprised, yet not once have you simply asked."

"When?" I barked. Not once did I ever think he would allow this to happen. "When can I see her?"

Gordex ignored my question, moved for the door, and said his final words just as the door was about to close. "Sleep well, Zacriah. I need you in high spirits for tomorrow. You have a busy day ahead."

My dreams were filled with sand. Orange and reds rolled like waves across barren deserts, straight for me.

Billowing vortexes of dancing sands, burning through cities until they were leveled and buried. I watched through blurry eyes as families ran and cowered together, turning at the last moment to watch my sandy wrath engulf them. It felt so real. Even in this warped dreamscape, I could taste the warm desert, feel the grains scratching across my skin as my winds willed them around me. I could even hear the pleading cries of those my magic finished. Their lives snuffed like the blowing out of a candle.

Suddenly the dream changed, desert stripped back leaving a stone hall I recognized. The throne room from Vulmar Place in Olderim.

It was like looking through a mirror of water. All around the vision moved, waved and changed. But ahead, the boy that stood before me stayed untouched. Hadrian. He was dressed in white. His hair had grown back to his shoulders, and his skin was flushed with warm color and life.

"Petal." His voice carried over the space between us, echoing over and over. "You found me."

I blinked, and he was inches before me.

"You look so handsome," Hadrian sang. "There is not a moment that passes where I do not recognize how lucky I truly am."

I tried to reply but no words came out of my mouth. Instead I grabbed a hold of him, running my hands down his arms and chest. He felt real. Solid and full. Being so close to him, away from the shifting room, I could see every detail of him properly. The long ivory cloak that was pinned to his broad shoulders. The silver clasps winking in the faded light of the room. My fingers brushed across the bead work of his waist coat, twirling shapes that sculpted his taut stomach.

"Are you ready?" he whispered.

The sound of clapping surprised me, causing me to turn back to face the room. Elves stood all around, jumping from their seats as they clapped and shouted for us. I felt Hadrian raise my hand, causing the watching audience to react even louder.

For a moment I was filled with the light of happiness. Until the pain in my hand dropped me to my knees.

The shouts did not stop. Not when Hadrian turned my arm backwards, pinning me with my cheek to the cold floor. I couldn't turn to him, couldn't see why he hurt me.

"Watch as I show them what happens when petals are removed from the flower." Hadrian's voice was no longer his. It had deepened, tainted by a darkness that only belonged to one person. "Let us show them just how each one wilts."

I woke up, gasping for breath, the dream lingering in my mind, body and soul. Daylight streamed on my face, causing me to squint. Even without my vision I still felt the strange throbbing in my arm, as if the dream left its mark on me.

Holding onto my arm, I cried. My ache to see Hadrian was only stronger than before, as well as my need to cause Gordex the pain he showed me in dream and reality.

Curling on my side, I let my tears roll over the bridge of my nose and onto the pillow. I wept until the sun raised high above the city, only stopping when I had no more tears left to shed.

CHAPTER
TWELVE

LILIOIRA WAS BARREN of life, at least from what my eyes could see. Streets were empty, only covered with overturned stalls, broken windows and scorched walls. With the number of people Gordex had turned yesterday, it surprised me that I saw none but the two shadowbeing guards that flanked me as I walked the city. I reminded myself of the armies who waited beyond Lilioira. I looked towards the towering mountain face and imagined the sea of soldiers clad in armor.

We rounded a familiar corner, following a trail of smashed stone that littered the ground. Up ahead, I spotted the fountain that Tiv talked about all that time ago. The very one that Queen Kathine had used as a stage the night Hadrian lost his control and his soul to Gordex. My chest pranged at the thought.

I didn't know why I was being taken here. The shadowbeings only grunted and pulled me from my room once I had changed. Their inability to speak was both a blessing and a curse. This morning I opted to wear Gordex's gifted uniform. I needed to be in his good graces to pass under his nose.

The lack of food from the day before left me weak, too weak to refuse the shadowbeings who pulled me through the city.

We stopped beside the fountain, which was dry and ruined. Splatters of red graced the worn stone base. The place where Hadrian cried blood during his performance. I took a seat beside the stain and placed my hand upon it, wanting to feel close to him as I waited for Goddess knows what.

"You look tired."

I looked up to the light voice as Nyah walked towards me, flanked by two of her own shadowbeing guards.

I bolted up and ran towards her. I didn't care about our guards as I threw my arms around her and held on.

"Goddess, Goddess," I repeated in her ear, squeezing her. "Are you hurt?"

"Zac," she whispered, tapping my back. "Zac, I can't breathe."

"Sorry," I said, flustered as I held her at arm's length. Faded bruises covered her neck and arms like jewelry, the greens complimenting her eyes in a twisted way.

"He let you come. I asked to see you, and he actually made it happen," I said it aloud, although my words were meant for me. Gordex had listened to my question and followed through with his answer. But why?

"Please," she breathed, "can we not talk about him. I would rather not have this moment ruined."

"I like the sound of that," I replied, looking towards her guards and mine before I guided her to the fountain to sit with me. "Dare I ask how you are?"

"Been better." She winched, rubbing her forearms. "But haven't we all? All day yesterday I listened to nothing but the screams from the city. That was more painful than any mark Gordex has given me."

I looked to the empty buildings around us. "It was impossible not to hear the screams."

The burning want to tell her about my visitors buzzed in my mind. But with the guards so close, I did not say a word.

"Well, I felt it as well. A bundle of agony and fright. And I know that is only the beginning of it." Nyah's gaze was lost on the buildings around us as well. "I can't help but feel like we are watching the end rush towards us."

There was silence between us for a moment. An awkward pause that only highlighted the strange distance between us. My next question only added to it.

"Why did you come back?"

Nyah looked at me, eyes glassy. "For you."

"You should have stayed away. Stayed with Emaline," I said.

"Well I didn't, Zac." Nyah was blunt and cold. "I

didn't because whilst we were somewhat safe, I couldn't stop thinking about you all alone with him. I couldn't sleep at night. It was never a question; I should not have left you in the first place."

Nyah sagged, shoulders slumping and back hunching from emotional exhaustion. I extended my arm around her shoulder and pulled her close, this time keeping my touch gentle.

Half of me wanted to scold my friend for returning, but a selfish part of me was glad I had her close. She was my strength after all. I opted to change the subject, for there was many things I had to tell her. But with our listening shadows, I had to be sly with my words.

"When was the last time you saw Neivel and Negan?" I asked, keeping my face straight.

Nyah gulped, taken back by my question. She knew as well as I that she'd never told me their names before. Yet here I was, spilling them out before us.

Her wide, unblinking eyes screamed *how*.

The corners of my lips turned up in response.

"Moons ago, many moons," she replied, shock still a mask across her face. "Why'd you ask?"

I couldn't help but smile. Not matter how hard I tried to hide it, my expression went against me. I felt a rush of mischief run through my blood. My own act of rebellion against Gordex. "I just wondered. That is all."

Nyah gripped a hold of my hand and squeezed. "I

do hope they are okay. I think about them both a lot."

I squeezed back. "I bet that they think the same for you."

Nyah sat up straight, blinking back sudden tears as she read my emotion, something that Gordex would not feel, for she did it without communicating between our link. She sensed what I was feeling, piecing the puzzle together until she knew what I hinted at. But I had shared enough. I couldn't risk sharing my feelings anymore. And Nyah nodded and changed the conversation.

"I can't believe how quickly I can go from loving a place to hating it."

"What do you mean?" I pushed on.

Nyah clicked her tongue and began running her hand across her bruised arms. "Gordex has ruined this city, and I am not just referring to its aesthetic. I don't see how we can ever come back from this."

I reached out and rested my hand on hers. She stopped rubbing at my touch. "We must look towards the light. Keep positive."

"What if I can no longer find the light?" Nyah asked, eyes welling with tears. "What if the darkness has finally snuffed it out?"

"Then we find a new flame to relight it."

"The *Druid* has three out of the four Heart Magicks. And it is only a matter of time until he gets the final. We both know what comes next. If he succeeds in raising the lost druids, then this city is not the only one to end in rubble and death. He won't stop until this world is his, and only his."

Nyah pulled her hand from mine, creating more invisible distance between us. I stayed silent for a moment, unsure on what to say. Seeing the lack of fight in her only made me want to bury myself deep in the ground. Nyah had been my rock from the moment I met her, yet now she was beginning to crumble. What hope did I have if the strongest person I knew had given up?

"He sent me to see you for a reason." Nyah didn't look at me when she spoke. "We are leaving tonight. I don't know where, but my guess is to Emaline since I so easily gave up her location. Gordex wanted me to be the one to tell you."

I looked slowly towards the palace. Even from this low level in the city, I could see the spires and curved roofing which jutted out into the pale sky. Gordex's presence poisoned it, turning its light into a shadowed cloak that lay atop it. I could almost imagine him standing on one of the many balconies as he watched us speak. But I knew better. He most likely had been listening in through his shadowbeings this entire time.

"I did wonder why he let me see you so easily. Doesn't seem like his usual style," I added, shooting the shadowbeing guards a look of distaste. I did hope he was watching through their lifeless eyes.

Nyah stood abruptly and turned away from me. My heart pranged as she almost walked off without saying anything else.

"Wait," I said, the panic crystal clear in my voice. "Just wait a moment."

Nyah peered over her shoulder, her red curls lifeless and limp. "Zac."

"Remember when you came after me on the island? Just before we were ambushed and separated by Gordex in his disguise?"

Nyah nodded silently.

"You told me to stop acting with such negativity. *You* told me that." I pointed at her, trying not to shout. It was not out of anger, but out of the dire hope that she heard the message within my words. "I'm asking you to only follow your own advice. The scales might not be tipped in our favor, but we have hope."

Nyah cracked a smile, lifting her pale lips in the corners. Even her eyes seemed to glow for a moment. Her shoulders pulled back and she stood almost a foot taller. "I—"

"You have a way with words," a voice spilled from the shadowbeing that stood closest to Nyah. "Hope is what drove me all these years. The hope I would see my people again. The hope I would finally get my revenge. Hope. A funny thing."

The shadowbeing who voiced Gordex's words pulled Nyah by the shoulders and left me alone by the fountain.

Hope was a funny thing. But regardless, I had it. And it burned strong within me.

CHAPTER
THIRTEEN

THE OWL FAMILIAR returned hours after I was brought back to my room.

I clapped a hand over my mouth to still my shout of surprise, then waited a moment to hear if the shadowbeings that guarded my room would come in and see what the noise was.

Satisfied that I didn't shout too loud, I studied the familiar. It had only been a few days since I had seen it last, and again it came with a message in its beak like it had before.

"For me?" I questioned, plucking the sun-stained parchment from its mouth. The owl twisted its head around as if to say *yes*.

My fingers fumbled awkwardly with the note, a mixture of excitement and apprehension coursing through me. I read over the sentence numerous times, letting what the note had to reveal sink in. It was a request from whoever sent it. Emaline? Tiv? Gallion?

Retrieve the orb he keeps close. Relight the flame.

The orb Gordex kept close. The same one he flaunted at the druid keep. The one that held Hadrian's soul prisoner. *Relight the flame.* That must have been another reference to Hadrian.

I screwed the note up, taking pleasure at the sounds. But the wave of anxiety came on quickly enough. How would I be able to retrieve the orb when Gordex kept it on him? And how would I get it back to Hadrian? So many questions laced with uncertainty burned through me.

My answer came sooner than I could have imagined.

The entire palace shook. Dust rained down from the ceiling, like fresh snow, settling across the bed, floor and the owl, who seemed unfazed. I held onto my sheets, waiting for another to follow.

Commotion sounded beyond my door, startling the owl into flying back out the window. The door flew open, and Marthil stood red faced beyond it.

"We're under attack," Marthil said, breathless. Her eyes darted around my room, as if the attacker hid within it. "Get up. Gordex requests our presence."

I almost laughed. The note, the attack, Neivel and Negan's promise of armies beyond the city. It all made sense. The attack was planned in time for a distraction I would need to get the orb.

I leapt from the bed and ran for Marthil.

"What is happening?" I questioned, trying to keep my face clear of knowing.

"We are leaving," she said, taking my upper arm in a vice grip and pulling me into a jog down the corridor.

I didn't resist. Not when I knew where we were going.

We passed through the pathway towards the throne room. If the armies beyond the city had really chosen now to start their attack, I wouldn't have put it past them to have early arrivals. I looked towards the walls, wondering if Negan and Neivel followed. Had they gone straight for Nyah? I hoped they had. As long as she was taken away from here, I'd be happy, no matter the outcome.

"Both of you, here, now!" Gordex shouted as we ran towards on the open doors of the throne room. He paced up and down, hands ringing before him. Marthil let go of me and the shadowbeing guards closed the doors, shutting us in.

"How long do we have?" Marthil asked, fists clenched and ready for a fight. "Send me out with our defense. Let me help secure the city."

"No," Gordex said, calmly. "As much as I would love to unleash you to our *visitors* I also know that we will take this time to leave for the next part of our journey."

"You want us to run?" Marthil said, voicing my own

thoughts.

"From one fight to another, yes. Protecting this failed city is not my priority. Finding the final Dragori is. And we can do that whilst those beyond the city are occupied fighting ghosts," Gordex said, looking through the gaping hole in the wall that Marthil had made when they first took over the city. "The ship is ready. You leave for Morgatis now."

Staff in hand, Gordex moved towards us, the long black robes giving him the impression that he floated. I couldn't let us leave. If this was my chance, I had to take it.

"What of Queen Kathine? What happens with her?" I almost shouted my question. Anything to make him stop.

"Still you worry over her?" Gordex asked simply. "Kathine is no longer a worry."

My heart faltered. Surely this couldn't mean…

"WAIT!" I shouted.

Gordex turned back on me like a storm. "Enough! I do not want to hear from you again. I can see what you are trying to do. Marthil, take him."

Marthil looked confused but followed her master's command. She reached out for me, her fingers barley grazing my arm before I acted out.

In that moment I didn't know if it was annoyance at my constant failings, or the panic that my chance to get the orb was dwindling, but I grabbed onto the hot anger that was embedded deep with me. A gift Gordex had given me by unlocking my Heart Magick.

A rush of power cut through every bone in my body until my world was tinted red.

I raised a hand, pushing a cyclone of air towards Marthil, who flew across the throne room. Pinning her to the wall, I locked her beneath my power. It was too easy. The magick that I owned was stronger than any I'd felt before.

Beneath my air, I could feel every part of Marthil. I knew, as clear as day, how much pressure I needed to break her, snap her in two. I was aware of everything.

Gordex made no noise as he lashed out towards me, throwing a black snake of shadow. His attempts to stop my air by using my own magick against me failed. Now he attacked. I caught his advance in the corner of my eye, but even if I wasn't looking, I would have sensed it. The air would have told me.

Perhaps it was the Heart Magick that Gordex could not control. Before he had so easily stopped my attacks. Now was different. And so was the power I willed and controlled. It was stronger, wilder. A different beast entirely. I could sense Gordex trying to grasp on with his own control, but he couldn't become his powers owner.

Raising my spare hand, I knocked the shadow off its course, sending it towards the ceiling where it exploded in a silent puff.

Before he could act again I moved through instinct.

I breathed in, sucking in air from the room until it ceased all noise. More and more my body stored the air, building in a whirling storm within me. I knew when I had enough for my body acted out, pushing all the air back out.

I blew, sending the concentrated stream of wind towards Gordex. It collided with him. Smashing straight into his stomach. His feet screeched across the floor for a moment before he was lifted clean off it. I couldn't count how many times he spun in midair before landing on the floor beyond the room. With the exhale of the explosive breath, the sound of the room returned to me.

Marthil struggled in my web of air, so I pushed more power into it.

"Give me Hadrian's soul," I shouted at Gordex, eyes smoldering.

He laughed, slow and demented. "That is what you are trying to gain from this."

"Give it to me," I said, readying myself for another burst of power.

I allowed him to stand, giving him room to steady himself. Gifting him a false sense of control in that moment.

"Hate suits you," Gordex said, mockingly. "Truly, it is a beautiful thing to watch."

I willed a ball of wind to twist within my open palm. Silvers, purples and plush tones swirled around, visible between my palms. "What do you know about beauty when all you want to do is destroy and ruin?"

I caught Gordex's eye shift towards the floor where the Staff of Light had fallen during our fight. I had to keep him away from it.

"The orb," I repeated, creating my own orb of cursed wind to grow in my hand.

Gordex shook his head, eyes flashing black and runes glowing with dark power.

"So be it," I said, cocking my head to the side. I threw my power towards him, straight for his smug face. With speed I had not seen him use before, he reached up and stopped my ball of wind. In his hands he held it, marveled over it as his short hair tossed from its force.

Defying what I first believed, he grasped onto some minor thread of control.

He pushed his hands together, destroying the ball of air until his hands where pressed palm to palm.

"You forget your place, Zacriah," Gordex smiled, opening his hands to reveal a spear of dark shadow. I raised both hands, dropping Marthil as a result, and readied myself to block it. Gordex flexed his arm and threw the spear towards me. I threw shield of solid air, which did nothing but slow the spear down. I dropped to the ground, my only chance of dodging it.

I blinked, face close to the floor and watched Gordex kick out. A burst of air shot across the floor for me.

The room spun as I flew across it. I collided with a wall, bones screaming under the force. Despite the splitting pain, I scrambled to steady myself, but the room was spinning from the contact with my head against the wall. By the time I looked up, Gordex had the Staff in his hands and Marthil by his side.

"Do you yield?" Gordex said, eyes steaming with shadow.

"You will not win," I said, wincing. The urge to reach for the back of my head was overwhelming.

"This anger is not yours to control," Gordex said, raising the Staff between us until the onyx crystal throbbed with dark light. "It is mine."

As he said it, I felt the anger intensify, and my consciousness being forced into a dark cage within me. I was a puppet, fighting for control as Gordex took over my body. I concentrated, trying to pull on it, anything to stop it. But I failed.

As quickly as I could muster I threw myself into a crouch, pushing my hands towards the ground. My air followed suit, colliding with the stone ground and crashing out in all directions. The force was strong enough to push both Gordex and Marthil backwards, but not strong enough to take them off my feet. I moved again, slicing both hands in front of me. The air reacted, cutting towards them both like silver knifes. Marthil moved, kicking the ground. It raised in response, creating a wall between us and stopping my wind effortlessly.

"Stop him," Gordex said behind the wall that then flew forward me. I had only a second. I used it by raising my hands to cushion the impact. Eyes closed, the stone wall slammed into my layer of protection. The force was so strong that the ground dropped from my feet, and I spun blindly through the room. My skull screamed as I finally came to a stop.

Sapped of my anger, I had no energy to fight, let alone open my eyes. When I finally did, Marthil was standing above me.

"Please," she whispered, "stop this."

Both my mind and body craved Forbian. I felt the vial in my pocket. A single swig and my energy would be fulfilled once more.

Gordex was behind Marthil, pushing her out of the way. "Your behavior will not go unpunished, boy. We do not have time for this. Get up, now!"

Black shadow creeped from Gordex's open palm. It pulsed underneath me until I felt my body lift off the ground and settle me on my feet. His power was strong, slick and cold.

"Bind him up," Gordex commanded. Marthil rushed behind me, brushing a hand on my shoulder before yanking my hands. Rough stone locked around my wrists just as shouts echoed from beyond the throne room.

I laughed, teeth coated with blood. It was too late. "Looks like you are out of time, Druid."

Confidence came flooding back through me at the sound of the pounding feet getting closer.

"You are indeed out of time," a voice said from beyond the throne room door.

My world seemed to slow as Gallion stepped around the doors, flanked by two soldiers dressed in purples and silver. Niraen soldiers.

"Now, Druid, I believe it is time we are introduced properly," Gallion sneered, bent his aged knees, and pounced.

CHAPTER
FOURTEEN

I PULLED ON my constraints until the muscles in my arms burned in protest. Had it been days, weeks since I last saw Gallion? I could not remember. But no longer did he look weak, thin and frail. Vitality glowed off him.

Locked in his dance with Gordex, it left the two Niraen soldiers to occupy Marthil.

Stumbling backwards until I reached the wall, I began smashing my wrists against it, trying anything to break my stone bindings. A shout from one of the soldiers distracted me. I watched him fall to his knees, a pike of stone pierced through his chest. Red blood pooled beneath him. Marthil retracted the spike. The entire city could have heard it rip out the soldier's insides before he fell to the ground.

Chaos ruled this room. And I was helpless, unable to fight. Left to be the audience for this show.

Gallion fought without steel. Instead he whirled two wooden sticks in both of his hands. He threw one after the other towards Gordex, who ducked, spun and missed each attempt by inches.

I wanted to shout for Gallion, but I worried it would distract him. Why was he here? Did it mean Hadrian was close by? Just the thought urged me to smack my bound wrists against the wall again. This time harder.

Black shadow burst in the corner of my eye. It was not Gordex this time, but the Niraen solider. I tasted the shift, as I had months ago. The soldier's sword clattered to the ground right by the paws of a wolf. It was jet black, eyes of ruby blood. Thrice the size of a mundane wolf, the shifter was almost as tall as Marthil.

Marthil took steps back, hands trembling beside her, the floor shaking as it echoed her nerves. I pitched over, face cracking with the ground, as I couldn't soften my fall.

Straining my eyes to look up, I also saw Gallion and Gordex tilting as Marthil caused the ground to move. Her fear of the wolf was evident in her paled face and murmuring lips.

Gordex must have seen or sensed Marthil's fear, for he spared a hand, which extended out for the shifter. In moments, it was locked in a cage of slithering shadows.

"You bring my own creation in hopes to win?" Gordex's voice filled the room. As he said it, the shadowy cage vibrated, and the shifter began to falter.

Steams of black shadow seeped off the shifter, melding into the surrounding cage. Yelping, the wolf fell to its hind legs, tongue hanging free as it shook its head. The shadow was pulled from the shifter, melting from his body until his elven form was left, just as Gordex had done to Nyah.

Gordex simply fisted his hand, and the cage of shadow disappeared. All eyes were on the shifter, who stayed on the ground. That left Gallion against Gordex and Marthil, who side stepped the shifter with caution before bracing for the fight.

"Two on one?" Gallion said, tilting his head to the side as he studied his opponents. "Now how is that fair?"

"War has never been fair," Gordex replied, "old man."

Gallion smiled, a knowing expression. "Rules are for those too petrified of failure."

Gallion's eyes flashed red, the same red that circled Nyah's hands when she used her empathic abilities. Then the stone melted from my wrists, allowing me to be free. Gallion didn't do this. Only Marthil had the power for that. As if she read my mind she looked over her shoulder at me, and my heart picked up in speed. Her eyes, like Gallion's had been, were red. Burning, blood red. She snapped her head towards Gordex and threw her hands up. Gordex was not prepared when the stone floor lifted like free water around his legs.

It imprisoned him in place.

Marthil was no longer Gordex's puppet. She now belonged to Gallion's power.

"Zacriah, the orb," Gallion called to me.

Gordex snarled, finally realizing what Gallion had done, controlling Marthil's mind to do his bidding.

I didn't want to get close to Gordex as I reached out with my own awareness and let the air show me the location of the orb. Wind rushed around the trapped Druid until it brushed across the curves of the orb within the folds of his robes. With a tug of my wrist the orb came free, floating beyond the Druid's body and into my hands.

It was too easy.

"Destroy it," Gallion shouted, his voice strained. "Quickly boy!"

"But Hadrian—"

"If you want him back you need to break the orb. Do it. I am losing my hold," Gallion shouted, his voice building in urgency. His neck strained, and teeth bared as he tried to hold onto Marthil's mind.

Looking into the twisting shadows within the crystal orb, I imagined Hadrian's warm embrace. I held his soul in my hands as he held my love in his. A loud groaning brought me back into reality as I watched the stone around Gordex shiver. He was fighting against Marthil's Heart Magick, but just as he couldn't with me, Gordex failed to fully regain control.

"NOW!" someone screamed.

Was it Gallion? Gordex? Marthil?

Taking a deep breath, I raised the orb above my head and brought it down. It slipped from my fingers and flew for the floor. All sound in the room disappeared as the orb came into contact. I believed it would break instantly, but it didn't. It bounced across the ground three times, each one giving a light noise, beautiful and deadly. On the last touch, it burst into a million pieces.

All across the room, shadow and glass filled the air. I raised my hands, covering my face. I bit my lip as glass cut into my hand.

Gordex's low shout thundered, "No!"

The room shook. His bindings snapped like they were no more than weak twigs in the wind.

I lowered my hands as the room stilled in time to watch Gordex break free from the earthy prison. Marthil sagged, finally free of Gallion's controlling magic. Her knees hit the ground and mouth gaped open.

Gallion stood, arms by his side and smile on his mouth. "You did it, my son," he said, looking right at me. "You saved the flame."

I opened my mouth to scream but was too late.

Before my first note came out of my mouth Gordex raised the Staff of Light and thrust it towards Gallion. In the moments after, I would wonder if Gallion knew what was to happen. He didn't even try to stop it.

Not once did Gallion stop smiling. Not when the pointed crystal embedded into his stomach. Not when Gordex lifted him from the ground until he hung suspended in the air atop the Staff.

He just smiled, eyes locked on mine, pride glowing from his face.

Even when his smile turned red and thick blood dribbled from the sides of his mouth, staining his purple armor, he did not stop. Nor when his skin turned lost its color and his eyes stained bloodshot. The smile stayed in its place.

Enraged, Gordex brought the Staff back down, knocking Gallion's lifeless body from the end and turning back to me. I didn't care what he did now. Gallion was gone.

"Get up, girl," Gordex snapped. His voice was muffled as grief took control of my body, like I was listening beneath a sea of water. "Get up and help me take him."

Soon careless hands grabbed a hold of me and yanked me from the room. I managed to keep my eyes open until Gallion's body was no longer in view.

I closed my eyes, giving into the rough waves that stormed within me. I let it drag me down, deeper into its hold.

You did it, Gallion's voice said again. *You saved him. You have given us a chance. Once again there is balance in this fight.*

I wanted to respond, but I was sinking further into the darkness. The rough hands of despair locked around my ankles, pulling me deep into the dark belly of grief.

CHAPTER
FIFTEEN

I BOLTED UP, pushing my hands into my stomach in hopes of calming the violent cramping. Gagging, I tried everything to retrain my breath.

Just in time, I rolled onto my side and let the liquids spew across the rugged floor beside the bed. My vision was doubled, making it hard to see what was happening. All I could focus on was the sickness. Breathing was difficult as the pain took a hold of my lungs. By the time I retched nothing but air, my head throbbed.

I studied the small wooden room through squinted eyes. My eyes clapped onto a bowl which slid across a counter, then back again. Everything seemed to be moving, tilting ever so slightly, enough to tease my stomach into retching again.

Then the smell hit. Salt. Heavy, overwhelming salt. It was so strong I could taste it in the back of my throat, melding with the thick sick that lingered there. The sounds followed next. Singing of birds, the lapping of water against wood.

I scrambled to the end of the bed, a cold breeze from the circular window tickled across my damp skin. I peered through the window and saw ocean. Deep azure for as far as my eyes could make out.

No city, no palace, no Gallion.

Blinking I saw Gallion. As I knelt on the scratchy sheets of the cot, the memory lingered within me. Gallion's smiled haunted every corner of my mind. The closest I had to a father figure since I left home. Murdered. Dead. Never to return.

I leaned over the cot again and retched. Nothing came out, only air and a hoarse scream.

The last thing I remembered was leaving his body in the throne room. After that my memory failed me. Or did it protect me?

Linking the missing events, whatever happened between then and now, I had been taken to this ship. I couldn't gage for how long I had slept.

I stood, steadying myself against the wall as the ship groaned. My bare torso tingled with fresh winds that slipped through the paneled wall. Even the loose cream undershorts shifted slightly. I didn't want to dwell on who had undressed me, that could wait. I spotted the pile of brown clothes on the dresser. Beside them was the black uniform.

Running my thumb against the tough material, it came back covered in the dust of stone. Proof that the fight with Gordex and Marthil had happened.

Pushing the thought back down, I pulled the brown clothing on, not wanting to wear the uniform again.

There was no mirror to inspect my state. From the throbbing that settled in the back of my head, I knew I had a lump. Running my tongue along the side of my lip, I left the raised mark from where my teeth had cut.

I was numb of emotion.

I opened the door with caution and walked the empty, narrow corridor beyond. Using both hands, I pressed them against the walls to still the incessant rocking.

Up ahead, I spotted a set of stairs. The doors above were open, enough for me to see the sky and the white gulls that danced through the blue expanse above. I didn't reach for my magick to see how many waited for me up top. I didn't dwell on what would happen, how I would react when I saw Gallion's murderer. I would rely on instinct for dealing with Gordex. He had to be punished for this.

There was a cold touch in my consciousness, but I ignored it.

Reaching the top step, I was welcomed by harsh winds. And Marthil. She stood at the helm, hair whipping around her face as she studied the horizon. I looked around, eyes streaming from the bright sun, and saw no one else.

"He's awake," Marthil called, not bothering to look over her shoulder. "Finally."

"You," I shouted back, unable to take another step towards her. She may not be the one who ended Gallion's life, but she didn't stop it either. Not that I expected her too.

"You have been sleeping for an entire day. I was close to coming down and forcing you to get up."

I couldn't take my eyes of her. My hands clenched to fists beside me. "YOU."

Winds gathered around my fists. Marthil snapped her head to me and raised a single finger.

"Unless you want to bury us in the middle of the Coralitic ocean, I suggest calming yourself down."

I looked behind her again at the never-ending sea. It took me a moment to see the difference between where the sea ended, and the sky began. Without the clouds I'd gotten used to seeing in Lilioira, it looked like an entire universe of cobalt.

"Give me a good reason not to. It would rid *you* from the world."

"We're on route to Morgatis. Do that and you wouldn't reach sand to see your friends again."

I burned holes through Marthil with my stare. Her face was a shade of green. Eyes framed by shadows, the whites black with veins.

"Where is he?" I spat.

"Gordex?"

My silence was enough of an answer.

She shrugged her shoulders, gripping the wooden paneling next to her as if it kept her up. "It's almost been two days since he put us on this ship. If he was going to join us, it would have happened already."

She is lying, she must be. I reached out with my magick, searching the ship for his presence. I didn't sense his wretched body. Beside Marthil, I sensed countless bodies in the bottom of the ship. Each moved with great rhythm matching the movement of the ship. Living bodies.

"Why?" I shouted over the winds. "Why leave us alone?"

Marthil didn't respond this time. Instead she peered back out towards the ocean.

She had mentioned it had been two days. Two days since the attempt to save us from Lilioira. Two days since Gallion's life was stolen from me. The mere thought turned my stomach. I swallowed a lump in my throat. I'd not show Marthil any weakness.

"How long till we reach Morgatis?" I asked, keeping my distance from her.

"Days, weeks, your guess would be as good as mine." Marthil peered back at me, the whites of her eyes red. She didn't look well at all.

"Why leave us alone?"

"We are not alone. You sense the soldiers below, keeping us on route. We do not need him with us for him to ensure we arrive as he plans." She stumbled slightly, exhausted from the simple sentence she had forced out.

"They're alive." I reached out again, sensing the honest breathing of the living who keep this ship moving. "Why not send his shadowbeings for the job?"

"Because…" Marthil stopped talking and threw her head over the side of the ship. It was followed by the sound of something splashing into the sea.

"Sea sick?" I sneered, unable to hide my smile. I crossed my arms and watched as she fumbled to cover up her weakness.

"Don't worry about me," she said, walking straight past me towards the steps that led to the lower decks. "You're going to need the energy when we reach the shores of Morgatis. Because when we do, I can promise my strength will return tenfold."

There was an undeniable bite in her reply, clear as crystals. But so was her breathlessness and slight hobble when she walked.

I let her leave me. She knocked passed, shoulder hitting into mine, but it lacked strength. It was Marthil who stumbled backward and turned from green to red. She rushed down the stairs and disappeared into the belly of the ship.

Part of me was glad that she left. I had another

means of conversation to have. If Gordex truly was far from here, he would not sense mine and Nyah's link. Unless she didn't get out.

The thought panicked me.

It took me a moment to regain my use of the link between Nyah and myself. Closing my eyes, I willed the image of the door to glow in my mind's eye. Once it was clear I reached a hand and knocked. Three raps on the solid frame and it creaked open. A rush of warm and light filled every vein in my body.

Zacriah, at last. Nyah's voice was full of relief as it echoed across my mind. *I have been worried sick.*

I can't tell you how hearing your voice is making me feel, I replied, leaning against the wooden paneling behind me.

Likewise.

I've been trying to get through for almost two days. I thought… Listen, just don't leave me hanging again.

I'm sorry. I couldn't respond. Turns out I have been out of it for a while.

There was a moment of paused silence. Foreshadowing of the conversation to come. Nyah sensed it as much as me. I could feel that between our link.

I felt Gallion pass, she said, voice wobbling. Even in my mind I could image the twisting pinch of her face as grief took over. *It was so strange. Like the snuffing of a candle. My brothers found me and got be through the city, and just as we*

✖   155   ✖

left I felt him die. They wouldn't let me go back for him. I needed to go back for him, but they stopped me. Told me it was too late. It hurts, Zac. It really hurts.

I know. The two words were all I could conjure. Even with the ocean between us her sadness was palpable.

What happened to him?

He—he ambushed Gordex. Tried to stop me, to give me time to save Hadrian. But Gordex, he... I couldn't finish what I had to say.

Zac, are you safe?

I am not sure. I am headed to Morgatis with Marthil. I don't know what is happening. I don't know where I am. I could fly, leave the ship. Marthil would not have the energy to follow me. But we have been traveling for two days and land could be far.

A calming warmth raced up the link between us and wrapped around me. *You don't need to go anywhere,* Nyah said. *We have means to intercept your journey.*

I looked out to sea, filled with a sudden burst of hope.

You do?

We would have gotten to you sooner, but since this is the first time you have opened our link, I can start to track you from now. I will relay what I know to Queen Kathine, who will contact the necessary people.

Queen Kathine is with you?

Yes, she got out before Neivel and Negan found me. She is not in the best state, but she is healing fast. Yesterday she was taken to an undisclosed location within the mountains of Eldnol. No one but her closest knows where she is.

I couldn't believe what Nyah was telling me. The ambush on the city was a success, in ways and a failure in others.

Before I could ask any more Nyah spoke up.

I need to leave you now, Nyah said gently. *Give me time and watch the seas. I promise we will get to you soon.*

You always are good at fulfilling promises, I thought. *I have a final question.*

You want to know about Princey?

I broke the orb that imprisoned his soul. Gallion instructed me to do so, but I can't imag—

Zacriah, do not worry. Hadrian will see you soon, and if you let me go, he will see you even sooner.

In that moment my heart could have stopped. I had no words, even breathing was hard. Hadrian was fine. *Hadrian is fine*, I told myself over and over. Hadrian was coming.

I imagined his face, his smell. The way his right cheek dimpled when he smiled.

The memories were as bright as the sun that had begun setting in the distance and blushing the sky with a pale pink glow.

Will you watch out for me?

Until the end of time, I replied.

CHAPTER
SIXTEEN

STORM CLOUDS FLOATED on the horizon, dark portentous beasts that moved in our direction and we in theirs. It started as a rustle in the winds. It woke me up before the sun had lifted into the sky. The rhythm of the boat changed enough to disturb me. Peering over the railing, knuckles white with worry, I watched the storm crawl closer.

Latching onto the winds I sensed its anger. It was like nothing I had felt through my magick before. It was raw, natural, and fierce. It caused the waves to rush over one another, crashing in bursts of white foam. The mast screamed, and the wood frame of the ship groaned with each slamming of wind.

I scanned the ships surface and saw no one else. Those in the pit of the ship guided us blindly into the storm. Or did they know? Was this their act of rebellion, to destroy us so we never reached Morgatis?

But where was Marthil? I couldn't place why the storm worried me, but something didn't seem right. It was hungry. Ready to devour.

"Marthil!" I shouted, running down the staircase and into the sleeping quarters. I found her room quickly. It was the only door closed in the entire corridor. Not a spec of worry surrounded me with fetching her. Not when the storm above was far greater of a threat. "You need to get up."

Her door was locked firm in place. I tried everything to push it open, but it wouldn't budge. Something heavy creaked above me, silencing me for a moment. Then I heard the gentle patter of rain. It was closing in, and fast.

"Marthil." I slammed my hands against the door, then my forearms. "If you don't open this door, I'll take it down."

Even saying it stirred my power. The Dragori within me needed a release. It had the strength and more to take this door down. I gave Marthil a moment to answer, but she said nothing.

Taking a deep breath, I willed my shift. Wings flexed in the narrowed corridor as I readied myself. I stood back, giving me enough space for a run up to the door.

"Keep away from the door," I shouted a final time, hoping she would hear me.

I ran. Shoulder first I crashed into the door, breaking through it without much effort. I was a mess of broken wood and leathered wings for a moment until everything settled, and I stood in the middle of Marthil's room.

She was in the bed, nothing more than a lump

beneath the sheets. Marthil didn't stir in response to my brash arrival.

"We are moments away from being battered by a storm!" I shouted, kicking a piece of wood that rested on the carpeted flooring. "Trust me, I wouldn't be doing this. But we are going into… Marthil?"

I reached for the sheet, pulling it back to reveal the girl. Marthil was ashen, lips pale and eyes rimmed in black. Then I noticed the smell. Sick coated the side of the bedding next to her, some stuck in her hair and the rest dribbled off the cot onto the flooring.

In any other scenario I would have reveled in her dimes, but with a storm brewing I needed all the help.

"What is going on?" I asked, shying away from the puddle of sick.

She groaned, eyes fluttering shut as she fought sleep off.

"You need to get up, I am being serio—"

Thunder rumbled outside, interrupting my panicked plea. It was so loud it shook the ship. Like the roar of a wild bear it crashed on, slowly teetering off to silence again. I hoped that got Marthil's attention, but as I looked back to her she was already fading off into unconsciousness.

I tried shaking her, but she didn't even have the energy to push me off. I had heard of sickness on the seas before from Fa's many stories and could only guess this was what it was. But there was a niggling in the back of my mind that suggested otherwise.

"I'm going to regret this," I said to myself, turning for the door and running as fast as my legs could take me. My Dragori form, although powerful, was heavy and slowed me down. Mid-stride I shifted back and picked up my pace.

I got to my room before the second bout of thunder crashed in the skies around me. Ignoring it, I moved for the black uniform. Picking the jacket, I put my hand into the inner pockets until my fingers grazed glass. The vial of Forbian.

Vial in hand, I ran back to Marthil's room, my lungs burning by the time I reached her.

"Here," I said, breathlessly. "If it helps heal a stab wound, I am sure it will work on sea sickness."

Marthil didn't show any signs of response, so I did what I had to do. Lifting her head from the dampened pillow, I felt just how hot her skin was. To the touch, it could have burned me. Her raven hair was slicked down to her forehead, clumped in thick stands of sweat and sick.

"You're going to hate me for this." I put two fingers on her lips and pulled her jaw open. Keeping them there I uncorked the vial with my teeth and tipped the entire contents into her waiting mouth. Once I was certain not a drop was wasted, I discarded the vial on the floor and closed her mouth. "Swallow up. I'm going to need you"

More thunder growled, agreeing with me.

Marthil scrunched her nose, her eyes still closed, and shook her head ever so slightly. If she spat this out I would have no other means of helping her. I wasn't even certain this would help. But it was worth a go.

With my spare hand, I pinched her nose together then, to my relief, she gulped the liquid Forbian. Instantly her face relaxed and she sagged back onto the bed.

From the thunder and rough rocking of the ship I could tell we were gaining on the storm. And a loud gush of water echoed from somewhere up the hallway.

Just after the sixth crash of thunder, Marthil stirred to life. The usual lush tones of her skin returned and with it her anger.

"What's going on?" Marthil growled, grimacing as she tried to sit up. Instinctively I jolted forward to help her, but she raised a hand to stop me. "Get off me!"

She pressed both hands to her head and screwed her eyes.

"That is not your head," I said, sparing a worried glance to the hallway. "That is the storm that we are moments away from entering."

Marthil looked at me, head tilted and eyes squinting in disbelief. Then a loud crack exploded somewhere above us. I screamed, dropping to a crouch which melded with Marthil's scream of shock.

With my ears still ringing, I jumped up and beckoned for Marthil to follow. The Forbian was clearly working, but we had no more time to spare.

"Faster," Marthil shouted behind me as we left the room.

Such a high dosage had provided her with the strength she needed. She didn't look back to her normal self, but it would do.

I kept ahead, turning the sharp corners of the hallway towards the staircase to the main deck. As I turned the final corner, the ship jolted. Pain coursed up my side as I slammed into the wall. My stomach turned with the ship's sudden movement. As my head stopped spinning I noticed my cold feet. The entire hallway was flooded with water. It cascaded down the staircase like an angry waterfall. Cold sprays hit my face as I waded through the inches of water towards the staircase. Marthil was right behind me, hand on my back as she pushed me on. But we both stopped when we caught our look of the world beyond.

Winds raged on, dense clouds made the sky look like night. Water was everywhere. Rushing around the ships deck, splashing in towering waves that knocked against the ship.

"Get up there," Marthil screamed over the storm, which laughed mockingly above us. She overtook me on the stairs, grabbing a hold of the slick railing and half pulling herself onto the deck. I followed suit, shielding my eyes from the lashing of rain.

As soon as I made it onto the top deck, I was drenched to the bone. My clothes clung to me, wet and cold.

Marthil was wading through the lashings of rain, but it was too dark to see where she was headed. I tried to follow but careened sideways as another wave slammed into the ships side. Slipping, my knees vibrated with agony as I hit the deck.

"Take my hand," Marthil screamed above me. I looked up, hair covering my face in clumped strands, and saw her waiting hand. She'd come back for me. "Zacriah, we don't have time. Take my hand and help me."

Our wet hands clapped together. With a tug, she pulled me up and pointed towards the main mast. "I'm going to lower the mast. You batten down the hatches and stop the water from going into the lower decks."

I nodded, turning from her towards the staircase again. I closed the large shutters over the open staircase as quickly as I could muster. The heavy wooden hatches covered it entirely and stopped the flow of water instantly. There wasn't a bolt that I left untouched.

Marthil moved around the main mast, flapping her arms in panic. I joined her, ready to help when she passed me a large rope that disappeared far above.

"Pull," she said. "I'm too weak."

Even in the darkness I could see her tiredness marked across her face. Most of her color had returned, but the Forbian was not working as I hoped it would.

I wrapped the rope around my forearm and pulled as hard as I could. It pinched at my skin, but I tried to ignore it.

A flash of lightning blessed the dark, illuminating everything in stark light. It halted my attempts. Then another. Thunder sounded straight after, signaling the storms final arrival. It was here, right above us.

Frustration and fear bubbled through me. Marthil was suddenly by my side, taking more of the slack rope and pulling with me. It budged, but still the mast flapped wildly in the skies, dancing amongst the storm that controlled it.

As my anger peaked, another flash of light burst before me, followed by a loud cracking. Sparks rained down around us, a shower of fire. The lightning had struck the main mast post. I dropped the rope, falling backwards just as the post groaned and snapped. The storm taunted us, flashing more lightning across the skies so we could watch as the post teetered to the side and fell right towards us.

I closed my eyes, allowing the anger and power to explode across my body. Marthil screamed from somewhere beside me as she watched our end fall closer. Then, with a single breath, I lost control.

CHAPTER
SEVENTEEN

SILVER LIGHT EXPLODED from my very skin. It formed a dome shield and enveloped us just as the wooden post was seconds from crushing both Marthil and me. Palms raised to the winds, we watched the post break from the force of my protection and fall either side of it. No rain reached us inside of my shield, no wind, no noise.

Marthil looked at me, face white with horror. "Think you're strong enough to take on a storm?"

I smiled, the Heart Magick now fully in control. It was euphoria, a strength I could get used to having. "There is only one way to find out."

"Then save us because if I die, I swear to haunt you in this life and the next." Marthil faced the storm that ravaged around us. "Hurry before it rips this ship to shreds and leaves us for the creatures of the ocean."

I got off the floor, controlling the shield with no more than a thought. Clicking my neck and hands, I closed my eyes and breathed. Without using my vision, I could see the silver light thread through my body into the air around me. My threads. Power I could take, use and give back. This storm was made from air, and so was I.

I pushed out, forcing my shield to explode into the skies. My silver light smashed into the angry clouds and lit them from the outside in. The winds screamed in defiance, and I screamed back.

My threads of power filtered into the sky, wrapping around the natural winds that billowed throughout the storm. I didn't stop until I leashed the storm, making it my own monster to command. The storm blended into my own blood, filling me with its emotion. I relaxed in control for a moment from the shock of this new strength. It filled me with elation. I felt like I could devour anything. I could turn this storm in any direction, urge it on more or end it with no more than a breath.

My blood was lightning.

My body was the billowing winds.

My mind was the hurricane.

Hands splayed to the skies I conjured the winds and turned them back on themselves. Clouds parted, and the thunder cowered. The lashing rains dwindled to no more than a light splatter, and the lightning hid from me in dread, cowering in the dark corners of the dissipating clouds.

My heart thundered in my throat; my blood pounded in my ears. More I pushed until not a sliver of cloud was left.

When the warm sun beat down on my face, I finally relaxed. I dropped my hands to my sides and raised my chin to the sky in relief. All at once my silver light scurried back into my body, sending a shockwave through me.

Light headed I faltered, legs betraying me. The entire boat shifted, and I fell. So much energy I'd expended, energy that surprised me. Every time I latched onto the Heart Magick I felt more in control. As if the limits of my magick were only expanding with each use.

Such a powerful creature, a voice said from the darkness in my mind. *I sense your new power and how much you adore it. Remember, I gave it to you, and I can take it away just as easily.*

"You stopped a storm. I'm impressed. And I am certain Gordex would be."

"I don't care for Gordex and his pride," I said, throat hoarse.

Marthil winced. "Regardless, one day you will. I was willing to take a risk on you."

The warmth of the Forbian flooded me. Its familiar kiss tugged on strength and banished the tiredness. My body fulfilled its craving. Marthil had given me another dosage as I sat on the edge of my cot.

"Get up, we have a mess to clean."

"A thank you for saving your life would suffice, and if I'm strong enough to end the storm, why can't you clean the mess yourself? Is your sea sickness that much of a demon?"

"You think I am weak because of sea sickness?" Marthil raised a brow in jest. "You really still do not know much about our kind, do you?"

"I don't know," I replied. "Like you said, I stopped a wild storm. I think I have a pretty good grasp on the Dragori now."

"Then you know your power comes from your element. I'm not near mine."

Marthil gave away her weakness without more than a thought. Did she really believe I was no match for her?

"This entire ship is made from a product of earth. Surely you can take power from the wood?" I pushed on.

"You truly are stupid. Pray tell how I can take power from earth when my only supply is the product of a dead tree?"

"Well you are still up and about now," I said.

"That is because you tipped an entire vial of Forbian down my throat. Once it wears off, I will be back in bed till we reach shore."

"Which you have no idea when that will be because Gordex sent us on this boat with no direction or clue as to when we will arrive, let alone where in Morgatis this ship will land?"

Marthil opened her mouth but did not respond. She squinted at me, eyes laced with annoyance. She stood from her perch at the side of my bed and moved for the door.

"I have changed my mind," she said with her back to me. "Don't bother following to help me. I fear if I hear you speak again today I might be forced to throw you into the sea myself."

"I can't say I am not disappointed that the life-threatening experience we just shared together has not brought us closer," I replied to her. "I'm starting to regret ever stopping the storm."

"Maybe you shouldn't have." Marthil shrugged her shoulders. "But you are too good. That is your weakness. That storm would have ended Gordex's mission entirely, and you single handedly made sure that his plans were not ruined. Like I said, he would be so very proud of you."

I remembered the voice that greeted me in the darkness after the storm. It had been Gordex. I recognized his gruff tones even without seeing him.

"Do not worry yourself on my behalf, Marthil. I've a certain feeling that Gordex's mission could still falter yet. I suppose time will tell."

She didn't know of my communication with Nyah, and Gordex had clearly not sensed it either. Maybe being far from both Nyah and me meant Gordex lost his ability to sense when I spoke with Nyah.

"Better go up and get cleaning. From the look of you, I think you will be back in bed in a matter of hours," I shouted after Marthil. When she was out of view I looked towards the door and raised a hand. A burst of wind pushed it closed, leaving me in my room alone.

I rolled over in my bunk, the feathered pillow folded around me like a cloud. Sleep was still needed.

Marthil had admitted it herself. I was strong, strong enough to absorb a storm. And she was weak. As long as she kept away from land, she was useless.

I banked on that knowledge for I was certain it would come in handy soon.

CHAPTER
EIGHTEEN

MARTHIL, AS I thought, retried to bed before sunset. I could hear her sluggish movement in the hallway beyond my own room. I didn't get out of bed until her own door closed, and I waited a hundred breaths after that.

No longer did the lingering memory of the storm buzz throughout my blood. I felt awake, alert and in no need for more sleep. The Forbian Marthil had given me really worked in replenishing my energy.

This night would be a long one.

I forced myself to walk the ship and check the damage the storm had left us. The floors and bottoms of the interior walls were damp, stained from the water that leaked inside before I closed the hatches. All along the bottom of the walls dark patches of moisture had been left, causing the paint to peel and flake off onto the ruined floor.

Besides that, a few pieces of furniture had been knocked over and carpets reduced to soggy bundles. The top deck was another story.

The main mast post that broke in two laid across the main deck in splintered pieces. The mast material was ruined. It was spread out, overlapping both the post and damp panels of the ships flooring. Even in the husk of evening I could see the many puddles around me. They winked with the reflection of stars. I peered over the railing and could see that the ship was moving, but slowly. Not at the pace it would have when the mast billowed proudly.

Are you awake? I sent my awareness through the door in my mind and into Nyah's. I could hear my own heart beat clearly as I waited for her response. *Come on, Nyah, I need to talk to you.*

She didn't answer.

I only hoped she was silent because she was in the fringes of sleep. So many other possibilities started to flash behind my eyes, but I buried them deep.

I hadn't spoken to Nyah in a couple of days, and so much could have happened since then. The unknown caused great anxiety to thunder through me.

⌒

There was nothing to do but roam the ship and watch the night sky pass by overhead. A few times I thought I saw the wink of light across the seas horizon but passed it off as nothing but the moons reflection and my strange delusion. I was hungry. Very hungry.

Moving for the galley, I hoped the storm's damage had not reached inside it. I'd no idea how long of this journey was left, and perishing from hunger and thirst was not my ideal way out of this world. To my relief, I found that the water damage was minimal, kept mainly to the door and small parts of the flooring. I found dried meats, bread and the casket of red wine that tickled my nose with its fruitful scents.

I ate until my stomach couldn't take anymore. Leaning back in my seat, I reveled in the feeling. Third glass of wine in my hand, I gulped it back. It masked my mind, numbing the possibilities of the coming days. The drink brought on a welcome moment of a relaxed mind. I gurgled a bubble of a laugh, burping and coughing straight after. It amused me, this wine. It was perfect.

I poured myself another glass and took it to my room. With a full belly and spinning mind, I no longer felt like I could stay awake all night. I was ready to climb into bed and allow the drink to warp my dreams.

As soon as the door closed, I knew something was different. The warning tickled in the back of my mind. Turning, I scanned my room and searched the dark. Wary of every shadow and sat on the bed.

This wine must be good, I thought, almost laughing at my own silly worrying.

I lay back, head swallowed by my pillow when I heard a noise from outside. I was certain it was the hoot or shrill of a bird. Waiting for it to happen again, I felt uneasy.

I sat up, breathing rapidly, and watched the door. It was open.

The shadow of someone stood within it, arms on hips and eyes burning the color of hungry fire. Their outline was tall, broad. Glints of light caught across the silver pin that held a cloak in place.

Everything in the world seemed to slow, my breathing, my mind. The shadow walked forward, a slip of moonlight from the porthole blurring across the visitor's face. It highlighted the high, sharp cheek bones and freshly shaven jaw, thick, dark brows and a plush smile.

"Finally," the shadow breathed.

"Please be real," I pleaded, a croak blocking my throat. I rubbed at my eyes. Surely this was a dream, some sort of illusion brought on by too much wine.

"As real as you need me to be."

"No. No. No," I cried, hitting my palm on my head over and over. "This is not fair. Don't do this to me," I scolded myself.

"Shh," he said, kneeling beside my bed. His warm hands took my own and stopped me from hitting myself. "Shh, my petal, shh. I am here now, and I promise, I will never be taken from you again."

I peered up, worrying if I looked to quickly he would disappear. But he didn't. "You won't disappear?"

He guided my hands in his own and placed them on his face. My palm brushed over his warm, soft skin. I let the tips of my fingers trail his bone structure, from the lids of his eyes to the moist texture of his lips.

"I am not a fleeting shadow," Hadrian said, no more than a whisper. His cool breath tickled my face, minty and fresh.

I had no words, only actions. I sprang forward out of my cot and into Hadrian's arms. He rocked backwards, falling beneath me but clamping his strong arms around my waist to soften the fall.

I buried my head in his shoulder, breathing him in, allowing my tears to dry in the material of his top. He really was here.

"Goddess knows how much I have missed you," Hadrian said, brushing his hand down the back of my head. "Even when I was lost, I dreamt of you. You were with me every day, I am just sorry I was not with you."

"Just hold me," I told him, eyes closed as his voice warmed my entire body. "Please don't let me go ever again."

"I vow it, Petal, I'll never leave your side."

I didn't care for anything as Hadrian held me. Not Marthil in her weak slumber or Gallion where ever he was. Hadrian was here. I was safe once more.

Weeks could have passed in those moments, and I would not have moved. I kept my hands clasped behind Hadrian as he hushed gently in my ear. We rocked on the floor of my room together, breathing in time, our heart beats synchronized.

Out of all the times I had thought about this moment, I could never have imagined just how sweet this would've been.

"I hope my presence didn't frighten you," he cooed, voice a whisper that tickled my earlobe and raised the hairs on the back of my neck to stand. "Since you saved me I have been wondering what I would say to you first, but I could not seem to find my words. When I laid eyes upon you, I forgot about everything else."

"It does not matter." Even as his shrouded figure stood above me, part of me knew the presence was not one to be feared.

"How did you find me? I waited, but Nyah gave me no warning of your arrival."

Hadrian guided me off him and stood tall beside me. "We have a lot to discuss, but for now, I want to climb in that bed with you and hold you."

"I want nothing more. But what of Marthil? The elves in the lower—"

Hadrian placed a gentle finger on my mouth. "Do not fret, dear Petal. I informed Nyah to keep our arrival from you as I worried it would alert those on board. I arrived with a few shifters from Rank Falmia with the night as our cover. My greatest worry was the Druid would catch wind of our arrival and ruin it. And trust me when I say I would never have let that happen."

I released a heavy sigh, one riddled with relief. "I can't believe you are here."

Hadrian smiled, but it didn't reach his eyes. They stayed dull and filled with regret. "Well, I am."

"And Marthil?"

"She has been detained and taken to my ship along with the elven prisoners who have been worked to the bone keeping this ship going. They will be cared for now."

Hadrian placed hand on top of mine. "Marthil did not put up much of a fight when we arrived. Her greeting was lackluster to what I expected."

"We truly do have a lot to discuss," I said. "Marthil is weak when kept from her element. It would seem being lost at sea is one way to prevent her strength from returning."

Hadrian sat himself down on the edge of my cot. He tapped his hand on his lap and beckoned me forward. "Come to me."

I took his reaching hand and Hadrian guided me onto his lap.

"Hmm," he mumbled, amber eyes intense as he

regarded me up and down. "May I ask you something?"

"Anything," I replied, pursing my lips.

He leaned into me, his face inches from mine. His lips dusted across my own but didn't move into me anymore.

"Can I kiss you, Petal?"

"I thought you'd never ask."

I felt him grin, lips pulling against mine. "Fadine has been kind and allowed me a quiet moment with you here."

"Fadine? The guard from Olderim?" I remembered her sharp stare and the elk horned helmet she wore. She'd been Hadrian's friend, the same one who had painted the image of his mother that I had left in my dwellings in Lilioira.

"The one and only," he said. "But forgive me, we have already addressed the need for a deep conversation about the events I have missed. Yet, selfish or not, I would very much like to kiss you. And for that, Petal, there will be no need for talking."

I laughed, a light and freeing laugh that was both pure and honest. It surprised me, a feeling I had not felt in such a long time.

"Hadrian, my prince, I could think of nothing better." I kissed his cheek.

"Oh, Zac…" One of his dark brows raised, corner of his lip following suit. "There is so much I want to say and even more I want to do."

I wrapped both hands around his neck and leaned in. "Is that so?"

"It is. But for now, just having a moment to look into those eyes would suffice." I could see him teetering on the edge of playfulness. Every crease of amusement in his face suggested it. And I wanted it.

"Then look into them because they are not going anywhere. No matter what happens in the lurking future, I am staying by your side and you by mine," I told him.

He wet his lips, running his pink tongue across it as he studied my eyes, then my mouth. I could sense the tension in the air between us, no matter how little the space was. Hadrian rolled his head, clicking his neck but never taking his hungry eyes off me.

"Tell me, Petal, what is it you want from me?" Hadrian's question sent my blood racing.

"Everything," I replied plainly. "I want everything from you."

CHAPTER
NINETEEN

AND EVERYTHING I got.

Night flowed into dawn with the sound of perfect harmonies. It was perfect. All of it. Like a dance, I explored every side of Hadrian as he explored me. His hands left no inch of me untouched. He was the Prince of Thessolina to everyone, but to me, he was a King.

I felt like a King in my own right, for Hadrian treated me like one. He worshiped me with his gaze, his touch, his mouth. I had never experienced anything like it.

When we finished, we began again. This time I took over. Showering him with compliments until his stomach moved with deep laughter. He was beautiful, regal, strong. Muscles rippled under my touch, his head cocked back with his eyes closed in pure ecstasy. His heavy breathing urged me on, keeping up pace until it reached a climax of pleasured groans.

Then we stopped, breathless and tired.

We spent the next moments in silence, both lying on our sides and staring deep into each other's eyes. Hadrian didn't stop touching me, running the tips of his fingers up and down my arms and exposed back.

"You are a miracle," he said, forehead gleaming with sweat. "I am blessed, truly."

My cheeks flooded with warmth. I didn't need to look to know they had pinched red.

I leaned in and placed a gentle kiss on his lips. "That was the most magical moment of my life so far."

Hadrian smiled from ear to ear. He pressed his finger to my lips and whispered. "Another word from you, and I think Fadine will be coming to look for us. We are already late."

"Oh, well, let them wait," I replied, pulling him back as he tried to climb out of bed. "If we have grown used to waiting, why can't everyone else?"

"Believe me, Petal, I want nothing more than to climb back in there with you." He kissed my head. "But we have plenty of time for it. And I have plenty to tell you still."

"You win," I laughed, rolling myself out of bed and picking up my discarded clothes. My body and mind were in the fringes of euphoria. Too much so to dwell on what had happened.

"I am unsure if they have brought a ship to collect us or if we must reach them in other means, but I think it is best we get going."

"And where is it we are going too?" I asked.

"Morgatis, same destination this ship was headed for. The Morthi people know of our arrival, for Emaline has prepared them. But before we dock, we still have much to discuss with the New Council."

I moved through the room to Hadrian and brushed his hands away from his shirt. I began buttoning it up for him, gently threading the silver buttons through the roped holes. I kept my attention on the gentle work whilst Hadrian looked down upon me doing it. His stare was almost warm on the top of my head.

"Just tell me what it is you need for me to do," I told him.

"I am sure we will begin with a debrief of the events you have been through, and the time you have had close to the Druid. Oh, and where this came from would be a good start."

His fingers grazed the side of my stomach.

I looked down and saw the faded sliver of a scar. The Forbian Marthil had provided me had worked wonders in the past days. Besides the memory it left it had almost disappeared entirely.

"Ah, that," I said. "We really do have a lot to go over. Shall we?" I pointed to the door.

"I've a feeling this day will be long and filled with many headaches."

Hadrian's chuckled beneath his breath. "Come then, my petal. Let us cease the pause in our fight and return to the front lines."

He took my hand and guided me from the room. I didn't look back. I allowed the memories to linger in the room as it did in my mind. But in the dark corners was the truth of what happened before Hadrian had found me. I wasn't ready to shed light on that yet.

"Fadine and a few shifters you said." I turned from the view to Hadrian whose hair tussled in the winds.

"You are looking upon our people's greatest asset of war." Hadrian raised a hand and blocked the sun from shining in his eyes. Had we really been lost to each other for this long? It was night not long ago yet the sun now crowns the sky. Even with the lack of rest, I felt reinvigorated.

The moment we stepped on the top deck, all I could see beyond was a fleet of ships. Countless vessels hugged the ocean around us, a swarm of wooden beasts. Flags billowed in the winds, decorated with the Niraen elves symbol of the grand tree and overlapping roots.

"Shall we?" Hadrian asked, squeezing my hand.

I turned and looked behind me a final time. "What about this ship?"

"That is your choice. We leave it here until the Druid realizes what has happened. Or we send it to the bottom of the ocean."

The answer was an easy one. "I want to see it burn."

Hadrian admitted hungrily, biting his lip, "You *are* my

soul mate."

"And you are mine."

I shook myself until my wings burst from shadow at my back and spread wide around us. Hadrian shifted, his dark wings danced behind him, brushing against mine. I let him go first. With a large push of his powerful wings, he was airborne.

I smiled up at him and jfootumped into the air. It took a few pumps of my own leathery limbs to get me to his height. From up high I could see the closest, and by far the biggest, ship out of the fleet had people out on the top deck watching. As we floated over the ocean Hadrian leaned in close and placed his lips on my own. It was a stolen moment with the crowd of Niraen soldiers watching us from below.

"Are you sure you want me to burn it?" he asked again, sun burning behind him and outlining his body in golden light.

"I've spent enough time trapped within Gordex's constraints. Let this one perish to the depths of the sea." My eyes were trapped to the bobbing vessel below us.

Hadrian's wings missed a beat.

"If I can rid one horror for you, it would be a start," Hadrian said.

The next moment blue flame burst beyond Hadrian's fist. It shot down towards the ship, air rippling around it, and landed amongst the rubble from the storm.

An explosion rocked the world. Water rippled beneath the ship as wood disappeared in flame. We watched in silence as the fire devoured every inch of the ship. It happened so quickly. One blink it was untouched, the next the intense dark smoke of the destruction floated up into the sky with us.

I took Hadrian's hand. Looking up to him, I saw Hadrian's amber eyes reflected blue as he watched and willed the flames to devour the ship.

This wasn't how I expected it to feel. Not an ounce of victory rushed through me. Only a part of me wished Gordex could see this. A symbol of our first act against him.

We flew off, Hadrian leading the way, towards the largest ship.

I landed amongst a group of waiting elves, all their eyes were trained to the fire.

No one welcomed us. Not whilst they had such a display of power to witness. Hadrian took my hand and rested it on the railing of his ship. We joined everyone in watching as the ocean finally opened for the ships remains to sink.

Left were a handful of burnt planks floating across its navy surface.

CHAPTER
TWENTY

"I THOUGHT YOU would appreciate this." Hadrian walked back into the room he'd left me in. I turned to greet him, still not over seeing his sharp, handsome face. He carried a tray of food in his hand, balanced perfectly as the other closed the door behind him.

The room was as beautiful as it was grand.

Hadrian had introduced it as the great cabin. Nestled on a top floor of his ship, from one window it overlooked the vast ocean, and the adjacent window allowed us to watch the many Niraen soldiers and sailors mingling across the main deck. There was one door in and out, one desk and a large oaken table that had enough seats for six others to join. The walls were plain, besides a few half-empty bookshelves and the cot in which we sat on.

There was an unmarked carpet beneath the table and flowerless vases. All signs that this ship was new and unused.

"It all looks delicious," I said, mouth watering as I

looked over the assortment of fruits and meats. I'd only just stripped the clothes I'd worn on the ship and changed it for a mundane set of slacks and shirt Hadrian had given me from his trunk. As I thought, the shirt hung loose on my frame, unbuttoned slightly to let the cool winds kiss my skin.

"I could list something more delectable to the eye."

Warmth spread up my cheeks as I thanked him and patted the side of the bed. "Will you sit and have it with me?"

"Hunger escapes me. I will eat later, after the New Council meeting which, I am afraid to say, begins shortly. There is something about the way worrying can affect my hunger. I must tell you, it has been a while since I have had a proper meal. Knowing you were out there, alone. It was all I could think about."

I got up onto my knees and leaned over the tray. Wrapping my arms around his shoulders I placed my forehead against his. "I am here now. Please, eat."

Hadrian hand stalled on my neck where it tickled my skin. "With the weight of events that we have still yet to speak on I fear that I cannot eat. Not until it is cleared."

"Then I will wait until the meeting is over, I can eat with you. It would be lovely to share a meal after this long." My finger lifted Hadrian's chin, so he looked dead into my eyes.

"I insist you eat." It was all Hadrian said.

"And why the sudden command?" I dropped my hands from him and sat back.

"Well, I do not know what you have been fed over the time you have been away. I have spent far too long imagining you starving and weak. Even seeing you and knowing it is not the case, I cannot shake the visions."

Being within Lilioira, I had lost some muscle tone, but not much. I made sure I ate when I could, I knew how important it would be to keep up my energy source.

"And I need you to gather some energy for this eve. The nights are long on ships, and I think we have a new way of passing the time."

Hadrian's fingers lingered gently on my thigh.

"Oh, I see." I chuckled, picking the reddest apple from the bowl of fruit.

"This 'New Council'," I said through a mouthful, "is there anything I need to know before they arrive?"

Hadrian picked up a white napkin and dabbed the corners of my mouth. "You can ask them everything you wonder soon enough. I fear my descriptions will not do justice as it has only been a few days since I met them myself."

Both our attentions snapped towards the door as a shuffling beyond it demanded our attention.

"Here they are." Hadrian sighed. "Never late."

I could hear the light footsteps of those walking up the wooden staircase towards the great cabin. Shadows fussed beyond the door, voices no more than a whisper. Then I heard one above all.

"For goodness sake, I'll go first."

Someone pushed through the crowd and pushed the door open. Fadine. She stood, long dark hair like sheets of midnight resting over each shoulder. She smiled, alluring eyes glowing as she regarded us both.

As I remembered, her features were sharp. Pointed, manicured brows and long lashes. But her beauty was a disguise for the soldier I knew her to be. One look at her unkept hands would give away just how skilled of a fighter she was. Her knuckles were marked with white scarring, and her nails were bitten short.

"Well if it isn't Hadrian and his little play thing." She strolled right up to me, hand extended out. "I jest. It is good to see you, and finally grand that Prince Hadrian will stop his moping about. Between me and you, it was easier when he was out cold for so long. The second he woke up he has been in a thunderous mood."

"He has?" Her grip was tough.

I looked over my shoulder at the boy in question, who watched us, arms crossed and knuckles in his mouth. "That's it, Fadine, spill all my embarrassing secrets."

Fadine laughed, shaking my hand then dropping it. She turned back to the crowd who hovered by the now open door. "Would you just come in? Hadrian, you have picked a council who can't even decide who is to open a bloody door first."

"Those decisions are not what they specialize in," Hadrian replied, putting his hand to the side of his mouth and whispered. "And that is why you are my second in command."

Hadrian guided me to my seat at the oaken table. He found his seat beside me, Fadine next to him than the other three walked in and took their places at the table.

I scanned their faces, noticing their age. Each was as young as me, not marked by aged lines or grays in their hairs.

Looking at their clothing, I felt underdressed, but mostly under decorated. Each of them had countless weapons strapped to them, belts, across shoulders, at their ankles. For a council, they looked more like a war band, nothing like Queen Kathine's council in Kandilin.

"Thank you, New Council, for attending our first meeting with such punctuality," Hadrian announced. "And for your patience whilst we waited for our final member to be retrieved."

"First meeting?" I leaned into him and asked.

"Yes, the first of its kind. I could not host without one of its most important members missing. And now Zacriah is with us, we may begin."

His announcement shocked me. I was one of the New Council, yet he had not mentioned it before this. I supposed we had been too busy, but it would've been nice. Now, I felt even *more* unprepared.

"Perhaps we should go around the table, starting with me, and introduce ourselves so Zacriah has a better grasp on who you all are. Understood?"

"Aye," the table agreed in unison.

"Prince Hadrian of Vulmar, son of the late King and Queen. Head of the New Council."

I didn't hear what he said next. I'd been too lost in Hadrian's arrival and swept in the tidal wave that followed that news of his father's survival had slipped past me.

In truth, I'd not thought of him since I was taken from the city. I needed to tell him. There was a small worry that me doing so it would be part of Gordex's plan, using the sleeping king as bait for Hadrian to return.

I directed my attention to Fadine next, gifting her a false smile as my mind whirled with images of the King in his slumber.

"Fadine, second in command. Is there much else I need to say? I represent the Niraen people."

The elfin girl next to Fadine spoke up next. She had short honey hair, cut close to her scalp. Her eyes were a mixture of azure and gray, and her skin was as pale as fresh cream. She wore a dress, the corset piece beaded and pulled tight. A band was wrapped around her wrist.

It was a snake, made from some metal. The mouth of the snake bit into its tail, completing the piece of jewelry.

"Vianne Mill, cousin to Queen Sallie of Eldnol, wife of the loved Queen Kathine. I represent the voices of Alorian elves. Those who are still on our land during such tumorous times."

It was Hadrian's turn to lean into my ear and whisper, "Without Vianne, we'd never have made it out of Lilioira. I cannot remember much of the escape, but I know that Gallion took me to her. She has a unique skill set. One that would impress you."

Vianne must have heard, as her pale cheeks blushed with gold from her Alorian blood. She fluttered her eyes and peered down at her crossed hands on the table.

Next was an elfin boy who I thought I recognized from Olderim. By the time he'd sat down and finally raised his face, there was something about his rough exterior that rang clear in my memories.

"Samian, shifter of faction known previously as Rank Mamlin," Samian said, rubbing his square jaw. Everything about him was wide. His chin was square with a single dimple in its middle. He had broad shoulders, mirroring his equally broad stomach. I couldn't take my eyes of his arms. They were as thick as his neck, which also protruded with veins and lines. His hair was both blond and auburn depending on the light. Simain had it slicked back over his head but occasionally it would fall over his hazel colored eyes. "I talk on behalf of the shifters in Thessolina."

"Do I know you?" I asked. All eyes turned to Samian besides Hadrian, who had a knowing look about him.

"We shared the same dwellings in Vulmar Palace. Even arrived in the city on the same cart," Samian explained.

Brushing the cobwebs in my mind, I vaguely remember seeing someone like him on the cart once I left Horith. Did we pick him up from a neighboring town? I made a mental note to ask him as we moved onto the third and final visitor.

The final girl was by far the quietest out of the council.

Her sky colored eyes stood out in contrast against her dark skin. Her gaze flickered from her clasped hands to the rest of her peers. Her hair was jet-black and cut sharply at her shoulders. Every time she moved her head to follow the conversation I noticed the shimmers of light that reflected off it. She was short in build, even sitting down I could tell that. Her frame was small, but there was no denying the power her tunic and trousers hid. Muscles practically bulged, stretching the seams every time she flexed.

"My name," she said, voice louder than I expected, "is Kell. I am the daughter of Morgatis itself, and I act as a mouthpiece for the Morthi people on this council."

She bowed her head slightly and said no more. It was impossible to deny the authority in her voice. It sparked my interest in her immediately.

Hadrian cleared his throat. "Zacriah, the floor is yours. Please introduce yourself."

I opened my mouth to introduce myself as every other had before me, but it was as if my own control faltered, and the urge to speak on the King's behalf took over. It'd been too much keeping it from him as I let those on the New Council introduce themselves.

"Hadrian, I've something of importance that I must tell you before we go on any further."

His face melted, sensing something wrong.

"What is it?" he asked, resting a hand on my own. "Tell me."

I looked through my lashes at him. "I have news about King Dalior. I am sorry I didn't say anything before. With everything that has happened, it simply escaped me."

"Zac." The use of my name chilled me. "Say what troubles you."

"King Dalior is not dead. He is very much alive, lost in a similar state that you, Hadrian, had been in. But alive."

In the next moments I could have heard a pin drop in the room. Even the gentle crash of waves against the ships wooden skin sounded terribly loud.

Fadine had her arm around Hadrian as she whispered into his ear. She'd reached him in only a few short movements. His eyes were unmoving from the spot on the table as he listened to her.

"This changes everything," Hadrian mumbled over Fadine, eyes static and wide, his face white. "My father is alive. The Goddess had shown me this, but only now do I finally believe it."

"It changes nothing!" Fadine said back, clapping her hand on Hadrian's shoulder. "Nothing. Until he returns, you are acting King."

"And our mission?" Hadrian questioned, voice quiet like a child, Fadine his acting mother.

"Is the same, unwavering and firm. I know what you are thinking Hadrian, but we can't go. There is too much at stake," Fadine replied.

Hadrian snapped his head around at her. "And my father, your King's life, is not priority over reuniting the Dragori?"

"No, it is not." Her answer clearly shocked Hadrian into silence. "My priority is protecting you, and that means I will not allow you to walk straight back into the hands of the Druid."

"That is my decision." Hadrian gripped the edge of the table, the air around him warming. We all could smell the faint burning, which only stopped when I reached out for him. He raised his hands and revealed the burn marks on the edge of the table.

"Again, you are wrong. It is no longer your decision alone. You created this New Council, you made us all sign the dotted line making it clear that decisions that affect Thessolina must be put past us all until a mutual solution is found. Zacriah has yet to sign, but I am certain he will not want you returning to get your father." She looked across the table at me, urging me to agree.

I nodded. "That was the last place I saw him, and if Gordex wanted to harm him, kill him even, he would have done that by now. I am certain that the King is safe for the time being at least. And I wouldn't want you returning to get him. Who knows if he has been moved in the days past?"

"I accepted that he had died. Now you tell me he still lives. Do you understand the pressure my mind is putting me under? I know it is not wise to return, but he is my father. My last blood relation and the King to Thessolina. His safety is as important to me as yours."

"And I understand that," I said, threading my fingers into his. "But even you know what we need to do first. Rid the world of Gordex, prevent him from raising his fellow druids all before he kills anymore."

"My suggestion, as second in command, is we discuss exactly that," Fadine said. "But if it makes you feel any better, Hadrian, let us pass your request to return for your father. New Council, raise your hand if you are in agreement with Hadrian and believe our priority should be retrieving the King?"

No one raised a hand. It didn't stop Hadrian sweeping his eyes across the table with hope burning within them. He dropped his chin, sighed and took a labored breath. Then, shaking himself off, he looked back to his council and nodded.

I gripped his hand and squeezed.

"For now, we will focus on our mission at hand. But the moment it is done, I want to know of my father and his position. Perhaps we can pass message onto Queen Kathine now that she is out. She may be able to act on our behalf and fetch him."

"Nyah, can you reach her?" Hadrian asked me. "Do you think she can pass on this to Queen Kathine?"

"I can try, but when I last spoke with Nyah, she told me that the Queen has been taken into hiding whilst she heals. I'm unsure how much reach she has during this time."

"It is worth a try," Vianne added. "My aunt has many creatures willing to do her bidding. As she uses birds for messages, I am certain she can scout out your father and see his state."

"Then I will speak with Nyah as soon as I can," I agreed.

Still the room was tense with the truth I had spilled. I could see from Hadrian's expression that he tried to stay present within the meeting but something about his stare was lost to us.

"Vianne, I will need you to help me if I tell it incorrectly." Hadrian looked at her.

She nodded.

Hadrian cleared his throat. "Vianne was able to get us far from danger, but we had to separate. Gallion said it was best for us to return to Thessolina and rile up support, even in my unconscious state. And Nyah was sent to the soldiers around Eldnol to rally them up in hopes to get you out. Which, we know now, did not go to plan. Gallion sent Emaline and Illera to Morgatis for protection. It is a place still untouched by the Druid, so it was the best option in keeping Emaline away from Gordex."

"But the Morthi people despise the Dragori," I added. "Cristilia told me as much."

"Yes, but they hate the druids more. It would seem they are willing to put their discomfort to one side to some extent."

"That is where I come in," Kell said, her voice gruff and deep. "I was sent here to join the New Council and guide you all back to my home. If we were to protect your own people, we wanted security that if the time came you would do the same for us. My task is to ensure that end of our agreement is held up."

"A task I hold seriously," Hadrian said, shooting Kell

a stare that spiked my interest. There was an unspoken tension between them both. A clash of authority. But he must trust her to place her on his New Council, regardless if it is just a political safety net.

The conversation flowed from one topic to another. It ended with me recapping my own events during my strange imprisonment with the Druid in Lilioira.

"The owl familiar, who does it belong too?" I asked, finally close to getting an answer. I had not thought of the owl yet, but it did intrigue me to whose it was.

"The small elfin boy," Fadine said.

"Fadine, his name is Tiv. Quite an interesting boy, full of magick and potential. He refused to go anywhere but our side. Something about being the best solider…" Hadrian said.

I hadn't seen or heard of Tiv being here. I had hoped he was left with Queen Sallie and her children.

"I would like to see him," I said briefly before moving onto my next pressing question. "And what of Marthil now?"

"She is being kept on another ship. If what you suggest is right, she will not be coming off it. I would happily offer myself to keep watch of her whilst you reach shore," Samian said, clicking his large knuckles. "That demon murdered my friend alongside Gallion. I will be sure to make it known what I think of her."

Samian's anger was powerful. The hate in his eyes

would burn hotter than any of Hadrian's fire.

"We need her," I told the group. "If we ever have a chance against Gordex we are going to need as much power as we can gather. Power that Marthil has an abundance of."

"Forgive me, but I do not see how she will ever join us," Hadrian said. Throughout my entire retell he had gripped the cushioned sides of his seat until his knuckles dusted white.

"Regardless, she is a Dragori, and if we ever are going to stop Gordex, we are going to need her power on our side," I said, brushing the tips of my fingers across Hadrian's clenched hand until he relaxed.

"Let me speak with her."

"She doesn't deserve hospitality and idle chatter with us. She should be punished, not kept alive," Samian announced, his face a thunderous storm of expressions.

"Well whatever conversation you are going to have with her will have to be through me," Fadine said. "As Hadrian requested, she is being kept in a sufficient means of prison, and it would be foolish for you to go and also be affected."

"What do you mean?" I asked.

"When Gordex ruled as my father, he'd commissioned more than just one golden cage. When we returned to Olderim, it was Gallion who found them. I thought it best we bring it for back up. A decision I am now glad I made," Hadrian answered.

A memory of Hadrian trapped within a cage of gold on a ship very much like this one flashed behind my eyes. I remember the pain he was in, how it broke him down physically and mentally to unlock his Heart Magick.

"She should be weak enough being away from land," I said, surprised by the deep anger I felt towards her suggested mistreatment. "The cage will not be needed."

"I find it hard to believe you are seriously standing up for her after everything she has done." Hadrian's tone dropped. Simian agreed out loud.

"We are supposed to be better than Gordex and the evil he conjures, yet here we are putting people in cages when they are already on their knees. If that is how you want to rule, it is not something I will condone," I replied, holding his gaze. This was the first disagreement I'd had with Hadrian, and despite the discomfort and arguing, that dark look in his eyes made me want to pounce from my seat and wipe it from his face with my lips.

Hadrian looked to the floor. "Then this will be yet another decision we will vote on. If you truly feel strong about this Zacriah, put it forward to your New Council peers, and we shall vote."

I relaxed my shoulders, pushing my chair back so I could stand.

"New Council," I started. "I would like us to vote on

the treatment of Marthil. I believe we can all agree that she will be kept on the ship when we dock in Morgatis, but her treatment on the ship is what I ask we change. Please, raise a hand if you would prefer the cage to be discarded."

Kell, Vianne and Fadine raised their hands in the air. Leaving Hadrian and Simian sat with them on their laps.

"I appreciate your need to be civil, and I respect that we have been out voted," Simian said, "but remember she is a killer. And those with the capability of murder should be treated with a lack of kindness that you are so willingly able to show her."

"Yet sometimes we are forced to do certain things that go against our true beliefs," I replied, talking to Simian but making it clear to the entire group. "Marthil is no more than a puppet pulled by strings of shadow. We simply must find the puppet master and sever those strings and give her a chance to act on her own. She is easily manipulated by him because all she remembers is hate and fear from her very own, so let us try a different approach."

"Perfectly put, Zacriah," Hadrian stood, his hand grazed my side. "It is voted upon. Fadine, I trust you will oversee the removal of Marthil from the cage. For good measure keep it close."

"I can't believe this," Simian muttered, standing from his seat and marching past us.

"If you have something to say Simian, do." Hadrian waved for the council who watched as Simian walked for the door.

"If any more blood is spilled by her hand, Zacriah, be it on your conscious. Your hands will be the one stained with the blood."

CHAPTER
TWENTY-ONE

I CAME UP for breath after being lost in Hadrian's kiss. Placing my hands on his chest I pushed him away, interrupting the moment we'd shared together.

"He hates me," I said, breathless and flushed. Each time I closed my eyes I couldn't shake the vision of Simian's gaze as he left the New Council meeting. It was our first one, and it had not gone as smoothly as I'd hoped for.

"You saw how he looked at me. And who can blame him? He shares the same view on Marthil as any sane person would. I just cannot bring myself to vote on causing her pain. If that makes him despise me, then so be it."

Hadrian scooped his hands around me and in one smooth move, rolled me onto my back. Pinned beneath him, his damp chest pressed to mine as his finger gentle brushed a lose strand of silver hair from my eye. "Only a fool could despise you, Petal."

"A fool he must be. Simian is a member of your

chosen council, yet I stroll in and create upset in such a short time. I think I'm the only fool here."

Hadrian pulled a face, pressed a kiss on the tip of my nose and sat up, gathering the sheets around himself to cover his modesty. "You forget, the decision that was made happened with a fair vote. The blame cannot and will not be pin pointed all on you. This will not be the first or last time a decision is made that not all members will be pleased with an outcome. It was not an answer I was hoping we would reach in all honesty. But saying that, Simian must come to terms with it, just as I have. Otherwise, he will prove that he is not the right commodity on my council."

"I shouldn't have said anything. I've completely ruined the mood," I said, embarrassment rushing through every limb of mine. "And the last thing I would want is Simian to be removed from the council because of my complaint. They will start seeing our relationship as a means of favoritism amongst the council. More than just Simian will dislike me."

"Petal, do not think like that. We are having a conversation, something that can happen whenever you so desire. It is my pleasure to listen to you." He leaned forward and cupped my face in his hands, lifting it up so I had to look at him. "I will always be here to take on your woes and help you carry your burdens. In regard to Simian, if it truly bothers you, I can speak to him."

I shook my head. "There is no need. By pulling him aside it will not help our cause."

Since we were left alone, we'd been completely and utterly lost within each other. It was Hadrian who instigated, to my pleasure.

In some ways I couldn't help but think this was his way to keep his mind occupied. After learning about his father, I was certain it would be an overwhelming thought. I'd do anything to keep him entertained, it was no bother to me.

"Can I ask you something else, a question you do not need to answer if you don't want."

Hadrian nodded. "Go ahead."

"How did you choose him? I understand Kell and Vianne's positions and of course Fadine, but why Simian?"

"Between us, there were not many shifters left in Olderim when I arrived. It would seem most left with Gordex. And I needed to have someone to be a voice for them, so I picked the one who held the most hate for the Druid. Simian seemed like a perfect choice. Yet his hate for him is clouding neutral judgement."

The coarse hairs on my jawline scratched at my fingers as I rubbed away at it. "And you believe he will comply with other passing votes he might not agree with? Or do we expect him to walk out of every meeting when he doesn't get his own way?"

"That,"—Hadrian placed a hand on my knee and squeezed—"is a worry we both share. But for now, let us not dwell on such topics."

I brought his hands to my lips and kissed them. "I don't blame Simian. He lost a friend that day when Gallion tried to help me. Of course, he would hate Marthil for that. My only hope is he begins to see the issues we are all faced with from a different side or view point. I don't like Marthil but treating her like a caged animal is not a means of building trust."

We stopped talking for a moment. The silence was blissful.

"How we are going to stop him?" I broke it after a sigh.

"A solid plan. Gordex seems to have had one and has succeed thus far," Hadrian replied. "And we have the numbers. We are going to Morgatis not only safety, but to give us time to create exactly that, a plan. It is not too late."

"Our numbers seem to be lacking in my mind."

"Gallion," Hadrian said, almost choking. "Forgive me, Petal, but I have not wanted to bring the topic up yet. Not with everything that has been unearthed today. Would you like to talk about it?"

I'd not mentioned Gallion since arriving. With everything else that had come up, my thoughts had been preoccupied.

"Yes." I swallowed. "But not in here. Could we go for a walk? I think I need some fresh air for this."

Hadrian looked to the door and the flash of night that could be seen through the frosted glass panel. "Petal, a walk sounds like an excellent suggestion."

CHAPTER
TWENTY-TWO

NIGHT HAD SPREAD its blanket of black across the sky, taking its color and replacing it with a chill that sliced through the ever-increasing humid air.

The winds were wild tonight, billowing around the fleet of ships that bobbed on the ocean's surface. In the dark, they looked like nothing more than floating lights. Glows of orange, yellows and reds from spotlights that reflected off the ocean's glassy surface. I was most thankful for the way the nightly winds snatched the tears from my eyes, stopping Hadrian from seeing the product of my pain. It was the first time I'd fully allowed myself to think of Gallion since I woke up on the ship with Marthil. Bad memories banged around my consciousness like an ominous veil.

"Part of me knew that death waited for him, and I truly believe Gallion saw it following him as well. He said goodbye before he left for you, which is a word he had never used with me before," Hadrian explained, looking out over the railing of the ship. "Then, like a pain in my chest, I was sure I felt him pass."

I'd not known Gallion for as long as Hadrian, but I couldn't deny the relationship I had built with him. He was a guardian to me. He'd looked out for me, risking his own life to save mine. Without Gallion helping my father bury my Dragori abilities, I'd never have known who he was. Now, years later, I had only the fleeting memories of him during life to cling onto.

The bond we'd created was one I would never forget. But for Hadrian, Gallion was more than he was to me.

My heart broke all over again for him.

"He is with his sister now," I told Hadrian, squeezing his hand which he had not let go of since we left his sleeping quarters. "And he succeeded in saving you as well as me. Without Gallion I would never had retrieved the orb that imprisoned your soul. It is all thanks to him."

"And I know that." Hadrian cleared his throat which made me look at him. A single tear leaked down his cheek. "I have not allowed myself to think about it out of fear our peers would see me cry. I am supposed to be their leader, yet I cannot even hold myself together for enough time to make clear decisions."

"Hadrian," I stopped him. Taking his other hand, I urged him to face me. I looked up at him, my own eyes glazing with moisture. "That is what is going to make you a successful King. A leader who is guided by their heart and emotion. Two assets with aid for the best decisions. Do not be ashamed to share your true feelings, never. Crying does not make you weak, it makes you self-assured and honest."

We stood there, looking into each other's souls as the moon hung high in the night sky between us. I was unsure about many things, but the love I held for him was a certainty I could cling to. As if reading my mind Hadrian spoke, his eyes clearing of sadness.

"I never dreamed I would experience such feelings for someone. But with you, I feel like I can achieve anything."

I smiled at him, reaching on my tiptoes for his mouth. I was mere inches away when I whispered my reply. "I love you, Hadrian. There are no other words I could use to truly tell you how I feel about you. I just love you."

"And I love you, Petal."

I barely remembered Hadrian leaving our room. In my fleeting memories, someone had called him out of the room. But I'd not found the energy to wake up alongside him and see why he was called so early.

I looked up to the ceiling, going over the events of

yesterday, and more importantly last night.

Once Hadrian had got me back to the room we'd wasted the night entwined together. No wonder I'd slept so soundly.

He drove me to the point of pure exhaustion. It plastered a gleaming smile on my face and relaxed my body until it was impossible to wake from my sleep. There was so much I'd not known about Hadrian before. Small, yet important details, such as the way his bottom lip turned white when he concentrated. Or the scar beside his belly button. The perfect shapes his mouth made as he explored my body. I'd made a mental list, never wanting to forget it all.

He treated me with respect, worshiped me for as long as I could take. I'd never experienced anything like it. With Hadrian, each time was better than the one before it.

Maybe I should have scolded myself for allowing enjoyment into my life when so much had gone wrong. But I couldn't help but look forward to the moments I would have with Hadrian where nothing seemed to matter.

A gentle rap at the door snatched my attention.

"Can I come inside?" a small voice called out. I could feel my heart skip a beat as it registered in my mind.

"Give me a moment," I called back, quickly changing

into something more suitable than my bare skin. Once I was ready I threw the door open and watched the blur of silver run into my arms.

"Tiv has been so very worried," Tiv said, voice smothered in my clothes. I dropped to my knees to hold him better. "I have been hoping and praying that you would come back. Every morning and every night."

His vulnerability pulled on the strings in my heart. "I am back now, and we are all together, all thanks to you." I held him at arm's length, smile bright on my face with pride. "Do you know what you are Tiv? For keeping my friends safe?"

He shook his head, silver locks bouncing and twisting.

"A solider, Tiv, you are a solider. And who knew you have your own special gift? I can speak on all our behalves, we are so incredibly thankful for you."

His smile took up almost half of his elfin face.

A hoot sounded from beyond the room, and we both turned to see Tiv's familiar. The owl bobbed its neck, as if it too was appreciative of my compliment to its owner. I'd not seen it since Lilioira. I almost cried in that moment.

"It is good to see you too," I called to it, which made Tiv laugh. "Tiv the Elementalist. Queen Kathine's best kept secret. And you have a familiar, I'd never have known. Do you have a name for it?"

Tiv nodded vigorously. "Spots."

"Spots." I clapped my hands together. "A perfect name for your companion. I'm sure there is a story about when you found Spots. I would love to hear it. Queen Kathine—"

"Queen Kathine?" Tiv's small voice spoke over mine, smile faltering suddenly. "She will not be proud because Tiv was not able to save her."

"Hush now. Queen Kathine will hold more than pride for you in her heart. And if you don't believe me, you can ask her yourself when we return to her."

"Do you promise?" Tiv said, large eyes full of a clash of emotion. "Tiv has heard lots of people talking. They say that she is not important anymore."

Confusion crossed my face. "Who has been talking, Tiv? Tell me and I will personally remind them *who* is important in this fight."

Tiv just shrugged. "Tiv doesn't want to get into trouble."

"And you won't! I promise that." I welcomed him back into my embrace. Not once had he brought up his own parents' safety, something I could not answer or give him promises about. "Tiv, I have an idea. Why don't you whisper and tell me who it is? Then, no one will know it was you who told me?"

"Really?" he whispered.

"Really," I replied.

Tiv leaned in close to my ear and told me who said it. I expected one name but was wrong. "Everyone. People are confused, saying that we are letting the evil man win. That the King is running away and not fighting back."

I didn't look Tiv in the eyes for longer than a moment because the doubters where right. We had no clear plan on what to do, expect keep away from the Druid. Decisions had not been made, not even I knew what came next once we reached Morgatis. Of course, the soldiers would see this as retreating, running and hiding. But that couldn't happen. Not after the many he had killed and the many more he could.

My silence must have been noted by Tiv because he pulled on my arm, "Have I made you sad?"

"No, Tiv, not at all. I just have much to think about, and I believe another meeting with the New Council is in order. I need you to do me a favor, do you think you are up to helping me?"

Tiv bounced up and down. "Yes, I want to help!"

"Good, now listen carefully."

I brought my own voice back to a whisper, in hopes the secretive nature helped Tiv see the importance in his task. He didn't speak until I had finished. He agreed and practically ran from the door to start his own mission.

I only hoped news spread across the fleet as fast the wind allowed it.

TWENTY-THREE

"NO ONE LEAVES this room until a plan has been thought up." I stood, hands placed on the table, frustration boiling through me. It was a pain to get the New Council together. Fadine had helped me round everyone up, but no one could find Hadrian. He had walked in last, face red but head down. He took his seat, sparing a mischievous look up at me then back to the table.

Once what Tiv had told me sank in, I couldn't help but feel others' annoyance. Was this what Nyah's power was like?

"News has reached me that most, if not all of the soldiers on this ship and others don't believe we are going to reap punishment for the Druid. They believe we are running. A thought that would dampen moral for when the time comes when we expect them to actually fight. Everyone on this table can agree that being kept in the dark is not productive, so that is why I have called everyone together, to finally shed some light on what is going to happen once we reach Morgatis and beyond."

Hadrian spoke up next. "If not to give our own minds clarity, but to make conversation with the Morthi easier we need to know what we have to ask of them. Is it protection, more soldiers?"

"I think both is a priority," Fadine said. "I can't say I haven't heard the whispers amongst my peers, and nor do I think they're not called for. But I think we can all agree that keeping the final Dragori from the Druid's control is one, if not the most important of tasks."

"Agreed. If Emaline is taken by Gordex, then he will be able to raise whatever it is that is kept within that staff," I reiterated.

Simian had his head propped up by his hands. I didn't have enough fingers on my hands to count the number of times he huffed and puffed as I spoke. Kell pulled a face of irritation before turning her full attention back to me.

"Keeping Emaline way from him is part of the plan, but Gordex will never stop trying to reach her. We could hide her in the darkest of places, but he will find his way to her, for Gordex is the one who controls the darkness. We need to stop him before he can complete his ultimate task."

"If you have a suggestion please do share," Vianne asked politely. Every now and then she fiddled with the serpent bracelet on her wrist, turning it around and around.

My own ideas brewed within my mind as fast as a strike of lightning. "Without the Staff of Light, Gordex would have no means to raise the trapped souls of druids."

We all knew it was the main factor to his plans. He'd risked a lot retrieving it. He moved Hadrian, Emaline and me like pieces of a game just so he could re-enter the Druid keep in the mountains to retrieve it. Ever since then the Staff had been by his side.

"Then we break it," Simian said, anger lacing each syllable. "Snap the twig in half and call it a day."

"That is an option. We return, somehow get the Staff from Gordex and destroy it. Then we are left with stopping him." Although I didn't truly believe we should return, I said it only to please Simian, to make him *feel* that I was actively listening and agreeing to his points.

Kell spoke up next. "We end him like he has ended so many. With steel."

"Gordex is smart. He wouldn't let anyone he deems a threat close enough to end him." I rubbed my side on top of the scar he'd left me. "I would know."

"How hard is it to kill him?" Simian practically shouted. "Why can't you just say it? You are dancing around the fact that we will have to kill him. Spill blood, murder. Speak it aloud with conviction. He is no more than a man. How hard can it be to stick him like he has my friends. *Our* friends."

"Simian, lower your voice," Hadrian said, voice deep and threatening. "This is no place to shout. Everyone has their turn to speak."

"Hadrian, it's fine," I said, beckoning for him to stop. "We *will* have to kill Gordex. I just want to make sure that he has no room to return once we do."

Simian looked pleased with my answer.

"I regret to bring this up," Kell said, her gaze piercing straight through me. "But what of Marthil, and you both? The Druid has control over your powers, right?"

I looked at Hadrian, lost, who was already gazing up at me. Kell made a good point. But the answer was hard to explain.

"To a point we are linked with the Druid through the Heart Magick we three possess. That is why we are keeping Emaline away. But he does not control me, nor Marthil, nor Hadrian. He is able to call upon our magicks, use them, bending them to his own will. I am sorry I can't be clearer but, in truth, I do not know what it means entirely."

Did I mention the anger I felt when using my Heart Magick? How it could take over, tainted with Gordex's touch?

"Then we must count that as a risk," Kell said, closing her eyes. "I believe you all have your best intentions, but it is highly important we understand the extent of his power if we ever have a chance of going against him. I do not want to tell my people to fight alongside you if you could turn on them at any given moment."

Fadine coughed, waving both hands in dismissal. "Hold on, that's not a fair judgement to make so flippantly. I know Hadrian so can only speak on his behalf, but he has given me no reason to believe the Druid is lurking within him."

"Then, Goddess forbid, until something happens that suggests otherwise, we keep the worry to the back of our minds," Kell replied. "I did not mean to cause offence."

"You have not," I added quickly. "You are only looking out for the good. I understand."

In that moment I should have told them of the anger I felt when I linked with my Heart Magick, or the phantom voice of the Druid that always followed. But without speaking to Hadrian on the matter first, I would never admit it. It could have all just been in my own mind.

"And what of those left behind in Lilioira? I speak on behalf of King Dalior and the many more civilians in the city. When do we fight for them?" Vianne said. "The few Alorian soldiers I have brought with us are days away from being up in arms about leaving their own. They worry about the families they left behind within the city and of what state they are in now."

"My suggestion is when we arrive in Morgatis, we negotiate a deal of protection for Emaline. Kell, I hope you can help us with this next request, but we need more soldiers. Our numbers are staggering, but we have an army of dead waiting for us in Gordex's shadow. Then we take the fight to him. Destroy the Staff first, then destroy him."

"Then, as we end each meeting, a vote. Raise your hand if you agree with Zacriah's plan?" Hadrian commanded.

To my surprise, everyone but Vianne raised their hands high into the room. I released a sigh of relief and thanked them all, unable to hold Vianne's eye contact for a single moment.

"I understand this plan is still fresh and many problems could arise. But I appreciate your cooperation."

"What next?" Simian said. "We deal with Marthil?"

I ignored the mention of Marthil. "Next, we tell our soldiers. Everyone. I want to be as transparent to them as we are to each other. It will mean they keep trust for us if they feel that their voices are being heard and considered."

Simian tipped his head.

"Then this council meeting is ov—"

"Wait," I interrupted Hadrian from closing the

meeting. "Vianne, something is wrong. Please, tell us what it is that bothers you."

I could tell she was not one to cause a fuss from her ability to keep silent when she disagreed. A skill that Simian lacked. But she looked up, smiled weakly and spoke with a clear tone. "Forgive me, I do believe your plan is desirable in your eyes. But I still have a worry. It is a risk, taking armies across seas for a fight. It is a long journey, one that could drive them to feel weak, tired and unprepared. We have already spent days on sea, and even I can see their attitudes faltering. They will need time when we arrive in Morgatis to rest. We are also at a disadvantage. What if the Druid ambushes us beyond land? We have limited space to fight and could lose many. Besides that, I worry that taking an army back to the city of Lilioira threatens the lives of those stuck within. Their homes have been turned upside down, forcefully made into a battle field. We do not need to bring any more suffering to their doors."

Everything Vianne said registered in my mind.

"I do have a suggestion, you might not agree with it, but I want you to think on what I have to say as I have with what you have spoken about."

"We are here to listen," I said, mimicking what Hadrian had told me the night before.

"What the Druid wants more than anything is Emaline, hence why he sent Zacriah and Marthil to

Morgatis in hopes they would retrieve her. However hasty of a plan that was." Putting Marthil and me on a ship with no clear direction was strange. Almost, rushed.

"At least that is what I can understand from that strange decision of his. Since that plan failed, I am certain he would do anything to get her," Vianne said. "What if we lure him to Morgatis? Bait him. We intervene before he can get Emaline by laying our own trap of sorts. That way the fight is kept away from Lilioira. It would be his army that has to travel, and our soldiers will be rested, ready and strong enough to fight."

There was a paused silence after Vianne finished talking. I didn't want to admit it aloud, but risking Emaline as bait for a trap did worry me. It could go wrong. Something Gordex has said to me rang around my mind like a bell of warning. *Everything I do has a purpose. Whether you believe it or not. For this is my game, board and players. I will succeed.*

"Then we shall vote on it," Hadrian said. "Just as we had with Zacriah's suggestion. Raise your hands if you agree with Vianne."

Kell raised her hand and said, "It is a smart decision. There is much land on Morgatis, untouched by life. Plenty of space for a battle."

Simian and Fadine also raised their hands together.

"Lilioira and the cities people have suffered enough," Fadine added.

Even without my and Hadrian's hands raised, it had already been voted. I surprised when Hadrian raised his own.

Staying in Morgatis prolonged our attempt to retrieve his father.

I didn't have a chance to question it when shouting from the deck reached our room. A single word rang out above the rest.

"Land!"

In unison we turned to the grand window at the head of the room. Beyond it, an orange sliver waited upon the horizon. I had to squint to check it if was land or just an apparition caused by days of travel.

Morgatis. We had arrived.

CHAPTER
TWENTY-FOUR

KELL WENT IN the small wooden boat first. Everyone else stood aboard the ship, surrounded by our fleet who'd taken command and lowered their anchors. Hands raised to block the intense sun, we watched Kell arrive on shore as she was greeted by a huddle of figures.

All I could see of Morgatis thus far was sand. Deep orange and blood red dunes that raised around the group that waited on the beach for us. Beyond that, the bright sun made it hard to see anything else.

I had stripped my jacket off and pulled the sleeves of my shirt up to my elbows. The heat of the penetrating sun had made the little material I had left stick to my skin.

Hadrian did not seem bothered by the heat. Not a gleam of sweat was seen on his forehead, nor did he remove his clothes to cope. Even the entire crew of soldiers and sailors had followed my suit, some even bare chested. Many peered into the sea. I could read the intentions behind their longing stares. I too wanted to jump into the cool embrace of the ocean to wash off the sticky humidity.

Kell told us that she must return to land first and converse with the welcome party who waited for us.

We had to wait, then take it in turns to filter into the many small vessels that carried no more than twenty bodies at a push. Hadrian had passed the command that when the time came, anyone who could shift into an animal with wings would fly alongside the Dragori, excluding Marthil. She was being kept in the ship farthest from land with her own personal guards that would keep watch on rotation. They'd be changed at random, so those on the ship had time to rest on land with us. That was my suggestion.

I caught Tiv out of the corner of my eye cowering within the limited shade the mast post made across the ship. His eyes were squinted tight against the sun, and his familiar was nowhere in sight. His expression screamed with discomfort, yet no one was around to comfort him.

Picking my jacket up, I wadded through the busy deck to him.

"Why are you over here alone, Tiv? You're missing the fun," I whispered to him.

"It is too bright. I don't like it," he said, pointing to the sun with his eyes closed. His top pulled back from his wrist slightly, and I noticed the red marks that circled his pale skin. When he brought it back to him he began itching at it.

"Let me see," I whispered, taking his hand and lifting up to get a better look. I was careful to keep my touch gentle and away from anything that could cause him pain. His skin looked on the verge of blistering. It was red, sun marked and burned. To the touch, he was hot. "You're very warm. When did this start?"

"This morning. It was so warm and sunny, so I stayed down in the galleys with Spots. He doesn't like the sun either," Tiv explained.

I had noticed the sudden change in weather yesterday. Within miles, it had gone from bearable to scolding. With not a single cloud in the sky, it was impossible to get shade. Even the air seemed still and burned out. Breathing was difficult.

"Put this over you," I said, wrapping the jacket around his shoulders. It would keep the sun away from him, even when we had to leave for shore.

Tiv squirmed instantly. "It's too warm." His tears pooled with tears and his voice choked. A few soldiers turned to see what the fuss was, but no one intervened. This young boy would have been left alone if I had not seen him. My heart could have shattered at the thought.

"It's okay. Stay still, I'm going to try something to help you." I brought my palms together and closed my eyes. Concentrating was key for my idea. I didn't want to use too much power all at once for fear of hurting Tiv, but I had to try something to cool him down. I would have called for the air around me, but that was warm from the sun's kiss, so I called for the winds that lived inside, deep in the pits of my body. I controlled their temperatures, breathing out only the coldest of breaths to bless Tiv.

All at once my lungs were full. Making my mouth into a small oval shape I blew out, letting the steams of silver tinted wind escape from my lungs and envelope Tiv.

His face relaxed almost instantly. Wrinkles around his eyes smoothed out and his brows flattened. I watched as the silver strands danced around him, lifting his white curls and blessing his skin with its cool touch. A chuckle escaped him, making my heart leap. I had never had experience with children, nor did I think I ever wanted to. But there was something about Tiv that made it easy to care for him.

"How is that?" I asked as the silver strands faded into nothingness.

"Cold," was his reply.

I leaned in. "What about your magicks? The ice you conjured when you saved us. Can you call on it in this heat?"

"I cannot find it," Tiv said, raising his hands beside him as if he had lost something. "It is too hot for me. It doesn't want to come out."

Far away from Lilioira, which had an abundance of snow to pull from, Morgatis was no place for ice. This sun blessed place was a kingdom of heat and fire. Hadrian was literally near his element.

Hadrian's familiar shadow covered both Tiv and me. "I was wondering where you had gone. Kell has given signal for us to start our travels to shore, and I was not ready to go without you."

Soldiers began filtering towards the port side towards the rest of the small row boats.

"Tiv is struggling with this heat, Hadrian," I said, trying to say more with my gaze. I didn't want to admit in front of Tiv that I was worried about him. "Go ahead without me, and I will get a boat over with him. I don't want to leave him alone."

Tiv hugged onto me from the side, resting his cheek on my shoulder. "You are not going to leave Tiv?" he asked, voice muffled as he pressed himself onto me.

"Not at all," I said, stroking a hand over his head. It was not as hot as before, but the warmth was returning.

"Then we will go together," Hadrian said, extending a hand for Tiv, who took it eagerly. "You stay by Zac's side for the time being whilst I go and get us a boat. How does that sound?"

Tiv nodded, sticking in Hadrian's shadow.

Then Hadrian looked over to me and pressed a kiss on my cheek, whispering in my ear. "You have a way with children. I did not expect that from you."

"Nor did I," I replied.

Tiv's gaze darted to both of us, smile plastered on his face.

Hadrian found us a boat quickly. There was grumbling of some soldiers who were not pleased they had to wait even longer for the next boat to return for them, but none would have said it too loud. Hadrian was their acting King, but it was clear the days at sea had washed away most of their previous values. I made a mental note to talk to Hadrian about it. Now the New Council had a plan, it was only fair the entire crew heard about it.

The short journey to shore was filled of Hadrian rowing, his back to me and Tiv, who peered over the side of the boat. I held my jacket above him, my arms aching as I kept them high.

Every now and then Tiv would shout out and point. I would follow his finger and see fish with colors so bright and beautiful, flow through the glass-like water. The ocean was bright sapphire and incredibly clear, so I could make out every grain of sand below. The only one missing being was Spots, who we left in the dark of the ship. Tiv was certain when night fell, Spots would come looking for him. I only hoped he was right.

A collection of Niraen soldiers had lined up on the lush beaches, more filtering in with each new vessel.

When we breached land and climbed out of the small row boat, we walked straight towards the New Council, who stood waiting alongside Kell and the Morthi welcome party. I jumped into the shallow waters, causing my boots and lower slacks to dampen. The cooling relief was welcome.

I kept Tiv close. Nestled under my shoulder, I held my jacket over his head and shoulders, keeping him firmly in my shadow. It was the least I could do to keep him comfortable until we reached whatever destination waited ahead of us.

"Welcome," the two Morthi woman said. They both wore deep earth-toned robes, hoods covering their heads. Their skin was pale and eyes piercing blue, glowing through the shadows of their hoods like burning orbs. "We have awaited your arrival and look forward to showing you great hospitality."

Kell stood to their side. She had her face raised to the skies, smiling with pleasure as she took in the warmth.

As they spoke in unison I couldn't help but notice their voices sounded emotionless and scripted. Kell showed no sign that she noticed, but Hadrian's eyes told me all I needed to know.

"Thank you for your greeting," Hadrian tipped his head in respect. "We appreciate your help in this dire situation. As you can see, our soldiers have spent days upon the sea to get here, and I would appreciate if we can offer them some time to rest under protection."

The two women looked towards the sea of soldiers that stood behind us, so many that even I couldn't gage a number. Then they looked to Kell, who nodded subtly.

"I regret to inform you all that they are not welcome to follow you into our city. This is for our own peoples' comfort."

That was not what I expected to hear.

"But, to accommodate, we will ask for food and supplies to be brought over as soon as we can pass the message on. Our people will help set up an adequate camp and ensure they are well rested. I do hope you understand; our own peoples' comfort is most important at a time like this. The threat of war is already thick in the air, seeing your army will only set them on edge."

Hadrian paused for a moment, looking to Kell they shared an unspoken word.

"I accept your rules and thank you for help. I will have my second spread the news of this arrangement."

Fadine scoffed beneath her breath and walked towards her soldiers, dark hair swaying behind her. I followed her with my eyes until a sound distracted me. Looking around, I couldn't place what it was. No one else seemed to notice the stir in the air. It followed by the slight vibration that ran up my feet from the sandy bed and into my body.

Something big approached us.

"Sister Shadows, thank you, your welcome is most kind," Kell said, turning to face the New Council. "The city is close, and we will head there together."

"He will have to be left out here," the sister shadows said in chorus, pointing to little Tiv.

"That is not going to happen. Tiv stays with me," I said, sternly. "I'm sure we do not need to vote amongst us when it comes to leaving a child alone out here with in such unfamiliar territories."

Kell looked to her fellow council members then to the Sister Shadows, who seemed amused by my minor outburst.

"The child may come," Kell told the sisters, who bowed, eyes diverting to the floor.

They didn't say another word, as if Kell's was final.

"Then it is decided," Hadrian added before anyone could change their minds. I was thankful for his quick thinking and assertive nature. "How long is the journey?"

Again, a heavy sound vibrated across the ground. This time, I was sure I was not alone in hearing it. Vianne looked to her sides, and Hadrian's brave expression melted.

"By foot it is far, by serpent it is near," the Sister Shadows said, as the ground rumbled once more.

Clouds of sand burst from behind them, exploding up into the still air and raining back down around. I raised a hand to stop it falling into my eyes. Simian shouted out in shock. As everything settled, I got a look at what had caused the explosion of sand.

Snakes. Three of them.

My entire body chilled as the towering serpents raised their pointed faces to look over us. I heard the gasps of our soldiers but couldn't move around to see, for the fear kept me frozen stiff. My muscles seized and blood raced.

They were the size of towers, bodies three times as wide as a bear. Scales reflected the sunlight, showing just how large they were, at least the size of my open palm. Forked tongues licked out at the air around them, eyes gray and misted over.

One opened its mouth, flashing its pointed, needle-like fangs at the watching crowd, which conjured more screams of terror, but they did not attack.

Kell walked over to them and raised a hand in greeting.

The Sister Shadows followed, always steps behind Kell.

The largest of the three serpents lowered its pointed mouth and slithered towards them. I caught a glimpse of the saddles across the serpents back.

"Not a chance am I getting on that." Simion crossed his arms, his hairs standing on end. "I would rather swim back to Olderim."

"The ocean is filled with deadlier beasts." Kell laughed. "At least these will not harm you. That is until they are commanded to do so."

"Is that supposed to make me feel better?" He flashed the whites of his eyes as they rolled dramatically at Kell.

"It was worth a try," she replied, checks flushing briefly before she swiveled on her heal. Both sister shadows tutted at what Simian said.

Kell gestured for them. "It is all in jest sisters, nothing serious."

Whoever Kell was to these two women was important. It would explain their protective nature when Simian spoke to her.

Hadrian flashed me an awkward smile and walked to Simian, putting a hand on his shoulder and pushing him forward. It was Tiv who urged me to move. He took my hand, not a single mark of fear on his face, and guided me towards our mounts.

"What would I do without you?" I managed to choke out, fear closing my throat and making my palms moist.

Tiv looked up, a single white brow raised. "Don't worry, Tiv will look after you."

CHAPTER
TWENTY-FIVE

TIV SAT BETWEEN me and one half of the Sister Shadows. Hadrian opted to go behind me, his strong arms a welcoming comfort as we waited for the serpents to move. I didn't want my fear to show, unsure whether these creatures could sense fear as clear as elves could hear. I swallowed the fear deep.

Hadrian leaned in, muscles in his arms tensed slightly and whispered into my ear, "Think of all the many terrors we face, and these majestic beings will not be as frightening."

His suggestion worked, to an extent. With a simple clicking sounds from the Sister Shadows the two serpents began their move. We were sat high, close to the back of its head, allowing its monstrous body to sliver across the ginger sands before us. I turned to look over my shoulder to see our extensive army watching us leave with hands over their eyes to block out the burning sun. I only hoped the Sister Shadow's promise of cover and supplies would come soon. They deserved a rest, one that gifted them with full bellies and deep, long sleep. Fadine would have passed on the message and would also return to stay with them. I could only see the side of her face as the serpent she rode was beside us, and it was pinched with discomfort at leaving her elven women and men.

The warm winds wiped at my hair. Sands buffered around in torrents and bursts. All around the desert was alive with dancing tones of yellow and orange, with the occasional green shrubbery speckled amongst the skyline.

Morgatis, unlike Thessolina and Eldnol, was mostly flat. Besides the wave of dunes, I could see for as far as my eyes allowed. No mountains, no cities, towns or dwellings. Just sand. Orange and reds.

Out the corner of my eye, I caught movement across the barren desert. Smaller creatures, some scaled and some shelled, scurried across the sands unto unseen holes and homes. This land was thriving with life I'd never seen before.

Tiv was still nestled under my jacket, which meant my exposed neck was burning. I could feel the sun work away at my own skin, constant needle pricks of discomfort. Soon enough the beauty of the view was wasted on me. I longed for shade and could see none in the everlasting desert. No signs of shelter or the promised city we were supposed to be close too.

The serpents moved with great speed, keeping their slick, cold bodies to the sand bed and gliding across it. Occasionally I'd have to close my eyes to prevent the desert from invading them. Sand got into my hair, mouth, nose, only making my longing for a cold drink more intense.

When the creatures finally stopped, my stomach felt sore and empty. I doubled over, hands on my knees, and focused on my breathing. Any moment I felt the urge to expel my insides out onto the dry ground before me.

"We have arrived," one of the Sister Shadow's announced, slipping down the side of the serpent and landing effortlessly with bended knees. "Welcome to the Vcaros, capital of Morgatis."

"Not much to see," Simian said through the corner of his mouth. He panted, lips parted and hands on hips. His hair was slicked down onto his forehead, his shirt unbuttoned almost entirely.

Kell strolled past Simian, unbothered by the sun. "Please follow me. A dwelling above the city has been provided for you. I'll take you there and leave you for the remainder of the day whilst I deal with some issues. Someone will collect you for an organized supper in the evening."

The Sister Shadows began moving on foot towards a

tall wall of rock that protruded into the skyline. It was the only thing for miles that seemed different compared to the flat horizon. No city, nor dwellings could be seen by the eye.

The rocks were crimson and sharp. Both angled towards each other as the reaching sharps of red rock created an arch for us to pass beneath.

Numerous possibilities sprang to mind. Maybe the rock acted as a barrier of sorts, blocking the city from an untrained eye. Maybe similar magick as Cristilia possessed allowed the occupants of Vcaros to stay hidden.

"Are we there yet?" Tiv drawled, whiny and tired. I had to bite my tongue as we slogged through the sands that attempted to swallow my feet. Each step was harder than the one before it.

"I wish I had the answer," I replied. It wasn't his fault for my bad mood, nor could I place what was. Possibly the journey by snake, my least favorite of all creatures or the long, hot walk which my body begged for water. But annoyance brewed within me like a lurking storm.

I skipped ahead, tugging on Hadrian's sleeve as we neared the rock. "Is anyone going to ask exactly where we are going?"

Hadrian turned on me, sweat glistening across his

top lip like the sun across clear water. "A little walk never harmed anyone. Kell does not seem worried about our journey. I have been studying her face, I can assure you. The moment I see a twinge of confusion I will speak up."

"Well, wherever this city is, I hope it has plenty of water. My body is burning for it."

Hadrian's wrapped his arm around mine. "You forget, Emaline is waiting for us. Wherever she is, I am sure she can conjure as much water as you so desire."

"I do hope so," I said, short. Something about his comment pushed me the wrong way. Studying Kell's face? A twinge of jealously pulled through me. A feeling I'd never felt before, one that didn't belong to me, I was sure of it.

Unsure whether to snap or scurry, I quickly faded back to walk with Tiv who took my hand in his. This didn't feel right, this misplaced anger. It reeked of someone. Gordex.

"We have arrived," the Sister Shadows announced in tandem, distracting me from my inner worries. "Please, follow us in a singular file and stay close to the wall."

Confused as to what they meant, I filtered into line with Tiv in front of me and waited my turn to pass around the rock. When I got closer, I saw our destination. Carved into its side was a hole, big enough for Hadrian to walk through on tiptoes.

The entry was dark and narrow, but the air was instantly cooler, so I hurried inside.

Footsteps echoed as we walked down the steps in a circular motion. Down and down we went until the world above seemed far away.

Tiv cooed and huffed at every sound around us. His fear of the dark evident without his need to say it aloud. I trailed my hands down the smooth walls, eyes closed, and felt out for a change in the air. Connecting to my magick, I could instantly sense a large opening we were getting close to. A bubble of space, filled with fresh, cool air that made my mouth water.

"We are close," I whispered to Tiv, answering his question from earlier, when my voice echoed all around us, distorting with each bounce across the stone space. He found it funny, suddenly distracted from his fear of the dark. He began shouting words and listening to them come back to him in different pitches.

I didn't know what to expect when we rounded the last steps and looked upon Vcaros. But what was before me was far from what I imagined.

The space before us was large, hollow and barren of life. Much like the burrows of rabbits, this rounded space within the ground had other tunnels shadowed in darkness that must link to other parts of the underground cavern. This was no larger than the throne room in Lilioira, and definitely *not* a city.

"Where is everyone," I said from the back of the group.

"Far below," Kell explained. "You will be staying on the outskirts of the city for the time being. Thank you, Sister Shadows, for your guidance, I can take it from here."

"We will wait at the entrance if you wish to return to your people," they spoke to Hadrian directly. "Call upon us at the surface."

The Sister Shadow's bowed to Kell and left for the doorway again. Their footsteps were silent as if they were never here.

"And why is it we are not visiting the city?" Hadrian asked. "This is news to me, Kell. Something I would except a member of my own council to explain before we arrived."

"Even after this long, no matter their willingness to help, they do not want the Dragori within the city," Kell explained, moving for the wooden chair that was propped beside the large table in the middle of the room. "My people are hostile to you, even now. It will take time for them to trust being close to the Dragori."

"But Emaline has been here. If she has not been allowed near the city, what have they been doing?" I asked.

"Staying safe," Kell explained. "What my people promised you."

"And I appreciate that, but explain this to me. How do I speak to your King if we are not allowed near the city? We do not have time to wait around here and leave my own soldiers at the shore with no understanding of what is happening."

Kell stood abruptly, face flushed from all Hadrian's questions. "If it pleases you, Prince Hadrian, I will speak with my King now. I will return when I have news. But remember, you are not permitted to wander close to the city of Vcaros. Any sign of your unannounced presence will be looked upon as a threat and dealt with accordingly. You are welcome to return to the surface world but that is it."

"Right now, I want nothing more than to find a steady bed and sleep," Vianne spoke up as Kell left. "We are not going anywhere for a while since we are not welcome, so we might as well use this spare time to rejuvenate our energies."

"I think Kell made it clear that it is the Dragori of the group who are not welcome," Hadrian said. "You, Vianne, are free to go as you please I am sure."

"I do not understand that," Vianne said. "The Dragori are known, or were known, to be protectors.

Beings that helped end the Druid's previous reign. But here you are treated like open threats."

Hadrian looked to me. "Do you want to explain?"

I shrugged, unsure where to start. "There is a reason as to why the Morthi people live in burrow like dwellings beneath the surface. During the time when the previous Dragori lived, something happened upon Morgatis land that caused them to fear us. It was the Air Dragori that leveled towns, killed many and destroyed miles of Morgatis with his power. Now we have arrived, they cannot help remember the great destruction our predecessors left in their wake."

Everyone listened to the story Cristilia had told me.

"Something I've yet to mention is regarding Marthil's reluctance to return here. They banished her as a child, leaving her to the wild with her untamed power. Even to their own, they will turn them away at the sign of magick that left such a scar on their land. She made it clear for her distaste for Morgatis when Gordex suggested we were to return here."

"It sounds to me like they are doing their best to help," Vianne said after a paused breath. "They understand the threat of the Druid is a threat that all continents should take seriously. To allow what they fear most to enter their home is a sign they are willing to help."

"By putting us carefully in a box and hiding us away is not my idea of helping," Hadrian added, pausing from his nail which he chewed with nerves.

"Would you share bread with what you fear most?" Vianne asked, bright eyes full of wonder.

Hadrian didn't answer, hardly looking up from his fingers which he studied.

"We must show the Morthi gratitude. Kell will make sure we have an audience with their King, and then we can barter more soldiers for this fight. For now, we should find Emaline and Illera. How big can this place be?" I said, looking around at the three dark tunnels that snaked off from the main atrium of the burrows.

Fadine cleared her throat, getting all our attention. "Don't mean to be brash, but I would rather return to our soldiers and stay with them. This place is suffocating. If I'm with them I can make sure those 'Sister Shadows' promise of shelter and supplies actually are fulfilled."

Fadine would return to the camp and keep an eye over her soldiers. She'd also pass on word of our plan, keeping them in the loop with the New Council's decisions.

Again, watching Hadrian say goodbye to his long-term friend caused the lurking entity to return. Jealously. Was my tiredness resulting in a lack of control over my own emotions? I turned, battling it down. The feeling was strange, wrong. Like a bad taste that stayed at the back of my throat. Never had I felt this way before. Almost, territorial.

A black shadow of distrust that I had not experienced before. Gordex. It had to be his power lurking amongst mine since he unlocked the Heart Magick. The same anger Marthil had, and Hadrian experienced. But why now?

I forced a smile when Hadrian came and wrapped an arm around my shoulder. I couldn't tell him now, not with Simian and Vianne close by. Only when we had time alone would I bring it up.

"We should find Emaline and Illera," I said quickly, thinking that action would help me control this dark emotion. "Then I need to speak to Nyah. She should be arriving a day or so after us, and I have not heard from her in a long while."

"There is no need for us all to search," Hadrian said, squeezing my shoulder. "Simian, Vianne and I will each take one of the three tunnels. Whoever finds them first must bring them back here. Petal, you stay here and try to contact Nyah. It would be good for us all to hear of her journey and when to expect her."

I didn't want to be left alone, but I didn't admit it aloud. Time alone scared me. I couldn't explain it in words to him, but I worried for this growing shadow within. The pressure was building, a sensation that put me on edge.

He took the back of my head and left me with a lingering kiss. As if it was the medicine I needed I felt the shadow recoil.

"Better?" Hadrian whispered. Did he sense it without my need to admit my worry?

I nodded "Much."

Hadrian smiled, turned on his heel and beckoned for the two to take different tunnels. As they left, swallowed by the shadow of the tunnel-ways a voice peppered in the back of my mind.

See how powerful I have made you? Your power cannot contain itself.

CHAPTER
TWENTY-SIX

I LOOKED FRANTICALLY around the room for a sign of Gordex. His voice was crystal in my head, so loud he sounded as if he was stood behind me. But he was nowhere to be seen.

Not wanting to wait a moment later, I relaxed back in the chair and closed my eyes. It was easier to connect to Nyah when I was most tranquil and still. I searched through my mind for the door, following the fading tether of light that linked me to her. I saw it up ahead, glowing slightly from the light on the other side.

Nyah? I sent my awareness through the door into hers.

I waited with bated breath for her response which came suddenly, laced with exhaustion.

I'm here. Tired, but here.

Long journey taking a toll on you?

I could almost feel Nyah take a deep breath as she prepared to rant. *Try manning a ship alongside your brothers who are nothing but a thorn in my back side. Add on rough seas and bad weather into the already unfortunate mix. That is why I am tired.*

She was clearly annoyed, but hearing her voice always calmed my own storms. *Surely you're arriving soon? We got to Morgatis today and the welcome has not been as warm as I thought it would be.*

You sound hopeful, whereas I am unsure. The seas have not been kind and from what our navigation suggests we are slightly off course. But I have seen birds today, an entire flock of them with long necks and ugly faces. Negan thinks that is a sign that land is close. But if that is what is waiting for us I am not sure I am excited to dock.

Will you let me know when you arrive or at least see land? I remembered what Kell had said about the Morthi being cautious to our arrival. I worried that if Nyah turned up unannounced her welcome would be ice cold compared to our lukewarm reception.

You can be sure I will. How is Princey holding up?

He is much better. Back to his usual self. I didn't want to talk on his survival after losing Gallion. Not when Nyah had been so close to him.

Is that it? That is the only thing you can tell me.

Images of what Hadrian and I had experienced passed through my mind beyond my control. I felt Nyah instantly recoil with a mindful chuckle.

Never mind, she thought. *Perhaps that conversation should be kept for a time when I can't see as well as feel what you are thinking. That and a glass of strong ale.*

Cheers to that, I thought. Nyah always had a way of distracting me.

Hadrian has gone looking for Emaline and Illera, and I really should go and help them. Turns out we are not allowed near the city and are being kept in the levels above it.

Levels above it? Nyah's questioning rang clear in my mind.

You will see. It is amazing, but we are confined to this oversized rabbit hole for the time being. If this is what the city of Vcaros is like I can only imagine how impressive it might be down there.

Then go and help. I need to make sure Negan and Neivel know what they are doing. Can you believe they have had much training over the years, but still at their age they argue like spoiled children?

Sounds like your journey has been an eventful one.

Nyah giggled, awareness fading away from mine. *You have no idea.*

"We have looked over every inch of this place, and take my word for it, it is not as big as you think. And Illera and Emaline are not here," Hadrian said, announcing his fast return with Simian and Vianne following in his shadow.

"The three corridors all connect at their ends and, besides the few rooms that link off from them, there is no sign that Illera or Emaline have even stayed here." Simian crossed his arms and blew the strand of close dark curls from his right eye. "I have a strong feeling that Kell knew that as well."

"That *is* a bold accusation." I stood from my chair, head light from the sudden severing of connection from Nyah.

"She is keeping something from us, I am certain of it," Simian said. "How do you know she is truly on our side?"

Hadrian interrupted, standing in between the four of us. "Are you suggesting I picked blindly for this New Council?"

Something about Hadrian's tone thrilled me.

Simian shrugged boldly. "If that is what you take from it, then that is on you. All I am saying is I don't trust her."

"We do not need tensions between us, not at a time like this. I believe Kell is as in the dark as us. Who knows, Illera and Emaline could just be out and will return soon," I added, feeling the tension between Hadrian and Simian pulling tight like an overstretched string.

"Zacriah is right," Vianne said, her gaze full of anxiety at the agreement before her. "We should not hold distrust for each other. It is not a productive use of energy."

"She speaks." Simian laughed, waving a dismissive hand at Vianne. It was a horrible laugh, one that belonged far away from this New Council.

My mouth dropped, surprised by his rudeness to Vianne. My mouth creaked open to respond but the sound of a heavy clap beat me to it.

"Look down on me again, Simian, and it will not end well for you." Vianne hand was still raised as Simian's cheek grew redder by the second.

Simian's eyes flashed red, black shadow seeping from his skin. I tasted the shift as it began. Vianne did as well, readying herself in a powerful stance. As black fur rippled in place of skin and the snout grew forward, I couldn't imagine how this would end. No matter how shy Vianne was, she was not going to back down.

"Enough!" Hadrian shouted, heat waved over us all. "Simian, enough."

The growl that built in Simian's throat halted as Hadrian's flames creeped close to him. They exploded to life across his open hand, inches from Simian's half-shifted face. All at once, the shadow receded on itself and the mundane Simian returned.

"By the Goddess's name, what are you playing at?" Hadrian slammed his palm into Simian's shoulder, knocking him back two steps. All this fury was turned on the shifter. "How dare you swing for Vianne. I thought you were better than that."

"She hit me first," Simian said, eyes burning with anger and frustration. He sounded childish. His chest heaved with each labored breath. I couldn't stop myself from rolling my eyes. His response was as immature as his frantic behavior.

"Behavior of a youngling, that is all this is. I did not ask you to join my New Council only to cause such tension between it. Then to shift, an open threat to Vianne who has only stood up for herself. I am shocked Simian, utterly disappointed and shocked."

"Hadrian, you do not need to speak for me," Vianne sneered, twisting the strange bracelet around her thin wrist.

"Simian, you need to leave. This is an order from your Prince. Return to Fadine, for you will be staying with the soldiers until further notice."

Simian stood still, soaking in Hadrian's command. His entire body seemed to shake with tension. His fists were clenched at his sides, even his face was pinched as if he wanted to say something. But he didn't. Instead, he bowed, arms waving dramatically before him. "If that is your wish, your *highness*."

Hadrian kept his fiery gaze on the top of Simian's head. I could almost taste his want to strike out at him. The strange twisting of darkness within me longed for Hadrian to do it.

"Hadrian will suffice." Hadrian turned his back on Simian to face Vianne and me.

There was a prolonged moment of pause filled with heavy breathing and the click of bones in hands and necks. Then Simian, in an aggressive stride, burst past us all and left the burrow for the staircase. With his departure came the receding of my own dark desires. Even Hadrian slumped.

"He should not have threatened you like that," Hadrian said to Vianne. "I apologize for my reaction, as I fear it has pushed him further away from us, but I could not let that stand."

Vianne tipped her head. "Before I say thank you, I want to remind you I could have handled it myself. But not all are like me. Simian should have controlled himself and maybe I should not have hit him in the first place. But I think it is clear he was never going to work in this New Council. Not with such aggressive views."

Like the ringing of a bell, something fell into place in my mind. A comment I had to mention. Flashes of Gordex using his power to strip the shifter of his power during the final tussle before my escape. And his mention of using his own creations against him.

"Gordex, he created the shifters," I blurted out.

Both Hadrian and Vianne looked at me with creased brows and pulled mouths.

"Are you sure?" Vianne winched.

"Explain," Hadrian said.

"He said it himself. I watched him take the shift from one of the soldiers who came in with Gallion to save me. It is the shadows, it is just like his power. And the magick that fuels his shadowbeings."

"And you tell us now?" Vianne asked.

"Between everything else that has happened, I am sure you can forgive me for letting this slip through the fingers in my mind," I bit back at her. "I do not understand it. But maybe Marthil knows more? She is the only link we have with Gordex."

"One thing at a time," Hadrian said, placing his fingers to his temple. "We need to find Emaline and Illera. Then once we discuss what has happened in the lost days, we can move forward with this idea that the druids created the shifters."

My mind swam with everything that had been unearthed in the past days. I only hoped we had more days of them in the future to work out exactly what was going on. I couldn't help but feel the threatening vibe that Gordex had woven his web decades ago, which would have placed him leagues ahead of us all. If he had created the shifters, he was more than merely steps ahead of us in this game. He was decades ahead.

Time always favored those on the side of victory.

CHAPTER
TWENTY-SEVEN

IT SURPRISED ME just how narrow the steps down into Vcaros were. If a city was truly below us, surely there must have been a better way in and out? Unless those in control did not want people to leave, and there was no way an army could come charging in unannounced. Not with such little room to move.

Hadrian was first to decline my suggestion to visit the city. But I couldn't imagine where else Emaline and Illera would be, and we had no time to waste waiting for them. With the intense heat of the sun above ground, I was certain both girls would not be passing the time amongst the desert of dunes. My only answer was they were already in the city. Kell had made it clear that we could not go there unannounced, but it was a risk we were willing to take. What could they possibly do?

We were the Dragori, the ones who would put an end to Gordex. They needed us.

The answer came sooner than I expected.

"Halt." The shout reached us before we even

stepped around the final steps onto the open floor. It vibrated across the tall stone walls, disorientating us as we look around for the source.

Hadrian gripped my hand, sensing the violence in the single word that was shouted our way.

The voice that greeted us was male, deep and threatening. It belonged to the Morthi guard who stood in the middle of what looked like a bridge way of stone. His hands were folded over the hilt of a large sword that easily came up to his chest. He was dressed in black layers of leather and metal, if there were natural sources of light it would have danced of the different materials beautifully. The crimson hue the glowing crystals gave off from the cave's walls was enough light to make out all the necessary details around us.

Reaching the bottom of the stairs, I scanned the ominous space we'd entered. It was vast. The ceiling so far up that it was shrouded in black. It was no more than an open cave, gilded with crystals. Stalactite's dripped from the shadows above, browns tinted with gold. Sharp enough to cut but to far up to reach.

The bridge way was the only piece of land connecting the ledge we stood on to the one beyond the guard. The space was no bigger than the one Hadrian and I stood on. Mostly because the brass gate took up most of the wall. Vcaros must be beyond it.

Hadrian stepped past Vianne and me, raising his

hands to show we were not threat. "We are here to see Kell. She is our correspondent and member of my New Council and we believe she is currently waiting for us within the city you so bravely guard."

Vianne shot me a look, showing me that she too noticed the hint of sarcasm that Hadrian threw at the guard.

"Leave."

Even from this distance, I could see his grip on the long sword tighten.

Hadrian peered over his shoulder at me and whispered through the corner of his mouth. "A little help here."

"Could you then point us in the direction of our friends. Emaline and Illera, we are looking for them. We have been told they are staying in the apartment burrow on the higher grounds. But we are led to believe they are currently gallivanting amongst Vcaros. Do you know of them?"

"The *demoness* is and will never be within this city." The way he said it made my heart skip a beat. He spat his words, clear of his distaste for Emaline. For us. "Now leave, before you are made to."

"Understood," Hadrian replied, voice monotone and bored. He turned for the stairs again, already giving up on finding them.

"Wait," I grabbed his upper arm and pulled him

back. I then turned my attention to the guard, willing some sort of command in my request. Shouting didn't feel right so I took cautious steps forward towards him, leaving Hadrian and Vianne behind. "If you could get a message within the city for us it would be helpful. I understand that you—"

My body suddenly faltered. I only managed four steps over when the guard shifted his stance, as if my walking was a threat. He raised the long sword in both of his hulking hands and flashed the tip at me.

"Not another step," he shouted.

"Lower your weapon!" I heard Hadrian behind me, but my mind was swimming with the sudden weakness. I tripped over my own feet, landing on one knee, then looked up at the end of the guard's weapon. Gold. The entire sword was gold. It was not a weapon to be used in a fight but means to keep certain beings away. The Dragori.

I then caught the other handle of a sheathed sword attached to the thick belt of the guard. The one he held was no more of a caution, one that affected me greatly.

The dull light from the glowing crystals danced across the swords surface, highlighting the warm tones that ran through it like rivers of power and strength.

"Stay back," I mumbled to Hadrian who ran forward. But I was too late. He got close to my side and fell beside me. The presence of pure gold taking its toll on us both.

His back shook as he took deep, labored breaths. Hands splayed on the gritty ground his fingers, clenching as he fights against the drowning weakness.

"You were told to leave, yet you ignore." The guard slammed the sword three times on the bridge, sending a heavy thudding vibrating across the cave. Vianne was shouting something at him, but I was too focused on the opening doors behind the guard to notice what she said.

Guards streamed out of the half-opened gates, some dressed in whites, some in blacks like the guard that hovered above us. The only sound that followed was the beat of their booted feet as they swarmed the bridge and circled us.

Then the pain intensified.

With each guard from Vcaros who pointed yet another gold-infused weapon our way, I felt the heavy weight of weakness bare down on me. As if the cave around me seemed to get smaller, pushing down on my body and crushing me, the gold pinned me to the ground. Tears leaked from the corners of me eyes, cheek pressed to the cold cave ground. My body refused me of my senses. Each one disappeared after the other. First my sense of smell deceived me, then my hearing. My vision was the final to leave. Everything I saw was in double until the outlines of figures blurred and obsidian were all I could make out.

I couldn't move. No matter how hard I tried, I couldn't lift my face from the floor. The vision of Hadrian squirming beneath the gold's presence was all I could see within my mind's eye. Over and over it replayed as the world beyond the darkness carried on.

The dark presence turned inside of me, waking from its slumber once again. At first, I thought it was no more than a trick of the overwhelming shadows. But soon I knew I was wrong. The presence, it was all too familiar. Seeing Hadrian in such much pain tugged on the deep buried anger and urged it to wake.

Yes. The voice filled every vein of blood in my body, igniting it with renewed energy.

Gordex's voice meddled with the darkness, growing like the smoke from a freshly extinguished fire. The more it grew, the more I could hear Gordex.

This is how they treat you. They cause you pain. They cause your love pain. Will you let them do this?

I squinted my eyes closed, trying everything to push the dark anger back. But it was strong. It knocked aside my futile efforts to control it and began spreading itself across every limb.

Everyone has a weakness dear boy, but sometimes one's weakness can be the key to ultimate control.

Heart Magick, the darkness was Heart Magick. It fell into place as the shadow filled my body. It was the key for Gordex to control. A darkness I had felt before, but this time stronger.

All at once I was back in the throne room in Olderim, battling Alina with my magick. Anger was the key to my loss of control. Now it was the pathway for Gordex to take over me as he had with Petrer, Marthil and so many more. I belonged to him now. Just like his shadowbeings, I was his puppet.

With the Heart Magick glowing through my body, it protected me from the gold. No longer did it hurt me, no longer did it make me weak.

The wind in the cave was stale. Every sense of mine was overwhelmed with my element, preparing myself to protect Hadrian. All it took was a single breath in to refresh my mind, body and power. Then I readied myself, pulling the cave's air towards my body like a taunt string. I had to protect Hadrian. My Hadrian.

Be unrestricted. Show them that you are to be feared.

Gordex's voice was the siren call which freed me.

The Stalactites vibrated against my force. My wings ripped through the cave, distracting the guards who began reaching for me.

I released the hurricane from my very bones and forced the air to spin in powerful vortexes around us. In a single swipe the many Morthi guards who had only moments before surrounded us, now were sent into the air against my powerful force.

Locked in my control, I pushed everyone away from

Hadrian, sending their golden weapons with them. No longer close to our weakness, I could see Hadrian move from the floor, his own magick burning into life. His eyes glowed with anger and flame. *My* air rippled around his skin which glowed blue, a blue I'd seen whilst he battled his Heart Magick all those weeks ago.

In tandem we moved, both filled with anger. I wondered if Gordex spoke to Hadrian as he did me?

All around me the guards fumbled to stand. I wanted to hurt them. The voice inside of me willed me to create pain, I hungered for it. I scanned the crowd and noticed the lack of them. The force must have knocked a lot over the side of the bridge way. I almost laughed at the thought of their bodies falling to the ground far below.

Stop, I told myself, but the voice was quiet and easily ignored.

A cold brush went against the wall within my mind, but I sent a new force towards it, barricading the door with my own, refreshed power.

White flashed ahead of me. It was so bright it burned at my eyes. Stunned, I raised a hand to block out the light, but as if the very sun had filtered into the cave, it blinded me.

Hadrian called out in discomfort, his heat intensifying. Then the light disappeared. It took a moment for me to come to, but the fist was already aimed for my face.

I swerved my head, dodging it by inches. Eyes wide, I watch the incoming fist open into a splayed hand. It was so close that I could see every line across the pale palm. Then, once again, the light returned. Bright as a star it burst through the Morthi' guard's skin inches from my vision.

I stumbled back, trying to rub the light from my eyes but the damage was done. I fumbled for control, blindly sending my air out in all directions hoping I caught the Morthi.

"Stop, Zacriah, stop!" Vianne screamed, her voice echoing up the large cavern walls. "You need to stop."

Was it Vianne who reached for me, hands frantic and voice panicked? I couldn't use my eyes to see. Roughly, I shrugged the hands off and flew back for my attacker.

More, give them more.

The small part of me that had receded into the dark depths of my mind knew that even if I wanted to stop, I couldn't. I was no longer Zacriah, not when Gordex pulled his strings and made the most out of my anger.

Still blinded by the light, something heavy thudded into my face and knocked me backwards. My spine screamed as I landed on the ground without my arms to soften my fall. Something cold was pressed against my exposed neck, but without my eyes, I couldn't see what it was. The familiar tingle told me it was gold. No pain followed, only more anger.

"Do not move," the voice said, pushing the sword into my throat as my vision began to return. It was the guard who had greeted us. He towered above me, his long sword teetering with my skin. I shifted to spring up at him, but the tip of his sword nicked at my neck and the warmth of blood flowed down onto my chest.

The feeling of release that followed was refreshing. I felt the darkness bleed out of me, allowing my own mind to take control of my body once again. Gordex's presence was receding as the gold nipped into me. His calling voice got quieter as it leaked further and further away.

Hadrian was struggling on the floor, pinned down by guards who flashed light at him from their skin. Their magick was unlike anything I'd seen thus far. Like other Morthi who had control over darkness, these had the power over light.

"Cut him," I whispered, breathless from the loss of my control moments before. The guard was panting above me, face marked with confusion at my request.

"Cut him with the gold," I said again, trying to show I was no longer a threat. The weakness was overwhelming. "Do it, or he will not stop fighting."

Each time I blinked it was getting harder for me to keep my eyes open. And when I could, everything I could see was in double. Two guards, two golden swords, two panicked faces of Vianne.

The guard who kept me down shouted something to those who pinned Hadrian down. Then, moments passed and the heat in the cave reduced. I don't know if it was the sudden relief that Hadrian had been made to bleed like me, or the drained energy from my Heart Magick, but I gave into the darkness. No longer did I need to watch and listen to the guards who shouted slurs at us.

Didn't I tell you I am always here? Gordex whispered, his voice fading fast.

My powerful, powerful beast.

CHAPTER

TWENTY-EIGHT

"YOU COULDN'T JUST sit back and wait for us to return, could you?"

Without looking, I could imagine the speaker, arms crossed over her strong chest and eyes full of mockery.

"Oh no, you *had* to go snooping where you are unwanted. I mean really, Zacriah, I've never known someone so impatient as you. Well, someone more than me, and I never thought that was possible."

Someone chuckled in response.

"My head feels like it is splitting in two. If I knew this was how I would finally come around, I would not have bothered to wake up." Hadrian's voice was rough. I didn't need to open my eyes to know he was beside me. The weight of him in the bed was all I needed as an answer. That and the familiarity of his warmth.

There was an extended pause followed by the clap of hands embracing each other.

"It is good to finally see you."

I opened my eyes against harsh light. My own head thundered with pain as everything seems stronger as I woke up.

"I can't believe I am saying this, but it is a relief, if only slight, to see you as well. Both of you. It has not been the easiest of days sitting back in our burrow waiting for news. I have felt so useless hiding out here. I know Illera feels the same."

I rolled my head and look at Hadrian, then to the girl above him.

Emaline.

I wanted to open my mouth and say something, but my throat was too dry and tongue thick.

"Where is Illera?" Hadrian asked.

"Trying to calm down an entire city after your little trick with Zacriah. I thought they'd have told you when you arrived that the city and those within it do not like our kind," Emaline said. "We've been here for such a long while, and *still* I've not got close to the Vcaros."

"They did warn us," I croaked, sitting up in the small, straw cot. The three of us were placed in the middle of some kind of tent, pitched from bamboo and material. This was not the dwellings we had been taken too when we arrived.

"He wakes!" Emaline clapped, taking a seat on the edge of the cot which made the entire structure quake.

There was already little room for Hadrian and me, but with Emaline, I was surprised the cot didn't snap under our conjoined weight.

Rubbing the sleep from my eyes, I released a yawn that could have moved mountains. "I have a sinking feeling within my stomach that we've messed this entire plan up."

"How long have we been under for?" Hadrian asked.

"Long enough for the guards to escort you from the city and back to your soldiers. You've both lost a day, tops. Do you know just how much your little intrusion has affected the days of time I have spent trying to build a relationship with the Morthi? All that time wasted. I can't say I am not flattered that you came to look for me and Illera, but you should not have gone near the city. That was a grave mistake. You are lucky they did not kill you both."

I watched Hadrian stand, wobbling slightly, then steady himself on the nearest bamboo pole, which was erected in the middle of the tent. "Maybe if they told us they are armed to the teeth in gold we would not have gone near them. That was a pretty important detail Kell has so aptly missed out on telling me."

"You had no idea about that gold?" Emaline asked, peering at the swaying flaps of the tent as if she was waiting for someone to walk in. "Illera noticed it when we first arrived. Everyone within the city carries some form of the metal in some way. Whether it be jewelry or chains, weapons or even false teeth."

"Seems like the Morthi would do anything to keep the Dragori away from them," Hadrian said, pushing his arms through the holes of a shirt and wincing as he did so.

Did his body ache as mine did? Even lying down, I could sense my sore muscles and equally pained mind.

"Like water kills a flame, they want nothing to do with us," Emaline murmured.

I reached for my throat, waiting to feel the mark left by the gold sword when it cut into me. I could feel the dried scab but felt no pain or swelling. "The gold, it—I lost control. What happened was not supposed to happen, I swear it."

"I guessed as much. Sounded very uncharacteristic for you to just let loose for no reason. But I am easy to sway. Kell, is it? She is currently back with her people trying to negotiate the peace between us once again. They think you tried to attack out of your own will. All your little display has done is solidify that we are in fact nothing but danger in their eyes."

"Then we need to speak about what really happened." I tried to keep my voice calm, but I knew what was coming next. I had to tell them about the dark anger. How it latched onto me during the moment of weakness, allowing Gordex to take control.

"Yet another understatement. We need to do more than simply talk. But before we do, you both need something to help your healing. The gold has left its mark when the Morthi guards bled you. It is healing, but slowly."

If only I had Forbian. I craved it.

Emaline fished out a pouch from her pocket and handed it to Hadrian. He pulled a face, tilting his head as he tipped the contents onto his hand.

"Numbing agent, some type of flower that you can find within the Doom. Apparently, when dried, it can help mask pain. It was as best as I could find to give to you both."

"Doom?" Hadrian questioned, handing me on of the dried buds. It was dark brown, shriveled and surrounded me the worst stench. My nose creases as I smell it before I trust it enough to take.

"The desert we are currently situated in," Emaline explained. "Doom is as vast as you could imagine. Illera and I have explored as much as we can, but it is mostly just sand. Exciting."

I sniffed the bottle, nose scrunching in response.

Emaline looked to us both. "Chew it, it tastes better than it smells I promise."

I'd do anything to numb the faint aching. Not even the stench could put me off of trying it.

As I took it down, I thought of Marthil. My body was calling out for Forbian, something she had. But the last dosage, had it burned along with the ship?

"I do have something else that must be brought up."

I looked to Hadrian, who fisted his empty pouch and waited with wide eyes. Somehow, I sensed he knew what I was going to say.

"Bear with me, for I'm trying to make sense of this at the same pace you are. But I believe Gordex, through the Heart Magick, has control over me. Us. To some levels."

Hadrian dipped his gaze to his hands.

"Gold, as we all know well, is the Dragori's weakness and is supposed to subdue our powers. But it was over exposure to gold that was used to unlock our Heart Magick. When we were surrounded, I started to feel this darkness inside. Like the Druid's shadow, I could feel it replacing my weakness with something else. Something warped. Then I lost control. As if I was watching what I was doing but from a locked dark room far in the back of my mind. Only when the sword finally drew blood did I feel the dark presence leave. As if the cut acted as an opening for the irresistible pressure of evil to leave."

Emaline's mouth sagged open, her azure eyes wide

as she listened. I took a deep breath, readying to carry on. She rested her head in her hands, not making a sound as she waited for one of us to carry on.

I expected Hadrian to agree, or to make comment. But he is silent as he too listened on.

"Then I heard him. Gordex. It is not the first time his voice has filled my mind. I have experienced it a handful of times when my anger peaked during my imprisonment within Lilioira. It is as if my anger is the welcoming for him to take over."

"And you?" Emaline turned her attention to Hadrian, asking a question I wanted to know the answer to.

"Zacriah speaks with sense. Even when my body battled the Heart Magick I could feel a dark presence. Then today, it was the first time since Zacriah freed my soul that I felt the anger again. This time I had no ability to squash it, to keep it buried. It was powerful."

"Did you hear his voice? The Druid?"

"I heard something, but it was what I felt that unnerves me. Every inch of my body and mind thirsted for pain. The fire, *my* fire, hungered for it. I felt... lost. Only when I was cut did I finally grapple control again."

"Well this is just great." Emaline stood, hands on hips. "You are telling me that, as well as Gordex using your power, he can control you during your times of intense anger or weakness? That leaves me, the only one free. The only one to make sure this does not happen again. Do you know how much damage you could have caused? Still could cause?"

"If your goal is to keep us calm, throwing your own anger is only going to make me reciprocate that emotion," Hadrian said, chest heaving slightly. "I admit that even now I sense the want to argue. As if the Druid's residue of control has familiarized itself with my body."

"Or is that just your excuse for a good back and forth, Prince?" Emaline said, sarcasm dripping from her tone.

Hadrian just furrowed his brows, stilling her comment in an instant.

"Well then, this changes everything." Emaline paced the room, nails between her teeth. "We need a plan. If the only way of stopping you from losing control is drawing blood with gold we will have to have some on us. But also keep is far away from me and both of you at the same time. Yet another challenge to add to the ever-growing list."

"I like lists," Illera cooed, strolling straight into the tent and pushing the curtain like doors wide. Her sun-kissed hair was gathered into a bun atop of her head. Her face seemed fuller than last time I'd seen her. She glowed with happiness. And the cause of her happiness stood amongst us. I could tell from the tanned sheen of her skin that she'd been out beneath the sun for a long while during her waiting time here.

Illera walked straight up to Emaline, wrapped her arms around her neck and turned Emaline's face to hers. The kiss she gifted her was warm and honest. Both girls lost in each other for a brief moment.

They pulled back from each other, and instantly I watched Emaline relax, a smile cutting across her sharp face. "Is this when I say that you have got the wrong side of the conversation?"

Illera smiled our way. "Zac, Hadrian. Good to see you up and if only you could hear what they are all saying about you around camp."

Hadrian rolled his eyes into the back of his head and released a breath, which pushed the hair from his forehead. "Fabulous. Even more reason for my own soldiers to believe I am a terrible leader."

Illera laughed. "Suck it up. They are singing your praises. Said it is the most exciting thing to happen this entire journey here."

Hadrian rocked back, his spine straightening as Illera's words sunk in. "Well, then they do have sense."

"I have come to get you all. Someone claiming to be part of the New Council, which by the way thank you for asking us to join. They're requesting a meeting. Her face is beet red, so I don't think you should keep her waiting."

"Kell," I said, looking at Hadrian who nibbled on his lip.

"That's the one," Illera said, nestled in the crook of Emaline's arm. "I'll give you a heads up; she is not happy in the slightest."

"Then I guess we should not keep her waiting." Hadrian winked his amber eye and smiled slyly my way.

"Good luck," Illera called at us as we left the tent, her arms still wrapped around Emaline. "From the face on her, you are going to need a lot of it!"

CHAPTER
TWENTY-NINE

KELL WAS FURIOUS even the air around her recoiled in caution.

She stood, hands pressed on the oaken table as she leaned on it. Someone had brought the table to land where it now was now placed in a large tent in the center of the camp. Vianne and Fadine waited, sitting around in silence, only sharing wide-eyed looks. Simian stood by the wall of the tent with a cup in hand and smile across his round face.

"Tell me, boys, just how it took only moments after your arrival to successfully get yourselves banned from Vcaros and anywhere close to it?" Kell didn't look at us as we entered the tent.

I could hear Illera laugh from beyond it as she flittered away after taking us here.

"Perhaps it had everything to do with no one informing us that this place is riddled with gold." Hadrian hardly looked up from his nails as he replied to her. "That seems to be an important piece of information you missed out. Seems intentional to me."

"Is that supposed to be a pointed accusation at me, Prince Hadrian?" Kell said, testing him further.

"Correct, you got it in one. I would have thought the mention of our greatest weakness would be the first comment you would make before we arrived. At least, that is what I would have done to a praised visitor in my palace."

I just stood back as they interacted, unsure of how to add my comments in with such thick tension between them both.

"I'd already warned you not to go near the city. But you ignored that. Do not belittle me and suggest I was not looking out for you all. Everything I have done thus far is to ensure my promise of keeping the fourth Dragori safe is upheld. You are grown. Are you not used to following rules where you are from?"

Fadine cleared her throat, awkwardly interrupting to cool the air. "I do not think that is what Hadrian is doing, is it?" She shot him a look full of warning.

"Oh no, not at all."

Kell and Fadine shared a glance as Hadrian sarcasm washed over them but neither responded to it.

"I have spoken—battled for you to stay on Morgatis. But you are not welcome nor permitted to leave this camp for the remainder of your stay. You both, no matter how true your threat was, attacked the guards of the city. Such violence is exactly why my people do not trust the Dragori after all these years."

Hadrian began to pace, clearly flustered at this news. "What are we to do in the mean time? Wait for the Druid to turn up and finish what he has started?"

"Do not fret," I said, placing a hand on his shoulder to calm his anxiety. "We're your New Council for a reason, we can help plan what comes next. We still have the bones of a plan, it could still work."

"Baiting the Druid here?"

"It is a risk we are going to have to take," Kell said. "My people may not want you close to the city, but they still are willing to help. There is one condition before we can move forward with any decisions."

"Pray tell, what could this be?" Hadrian snapped.

"There is a chance that you both could lose control again, and that makes the city and its people uneasy. We need insurance of a kind, something to make them more at ease to know that you both can be subdued if anything happens again," Kell explained. "It only took one Dragori to send my people below the ground moons ago, and this time around we have all four here. After what happened yesterday I am certain you can understand why I—the King worries."

"We will do what is needed to ensure he can help us in our joint effort to bring the Druid down for once." I stepped forward, nodding with vigor. "Tell us what it is he asks of, and we will do our best to comply."

"He asks for each Dragori present on his land to have a guard of sorts. The guard will be armed with a weapon forged from gold, strong enough to bring you down if you ever lose control again. When I spoke of what happened when the guards bled you both and how it ceased the attack it was the only option to stop it from happening again."

There was a paused silence as our group of four looked to Kell then to each other. It was Hadrian who spoke first.

"If that is what it takes, we will do it."

Kell released a breath which sagged her shoulders and flattened the creases in her forehead.

"I am glad you said that, and so will my people when I tell them you have accepted the clause."

"These guards, will they be provided by your King?" I asked.

Kell paused, lips pulled into a smirk and nodded. "Only if that is what you desire. If not, you are to choose someone you trust with your life. Literally. Someone who will not hesitate to bury gold into your flesh if you ever lose control again."

There was only one person I could think of besides Hadrian to do this for me, and she was on a ship coming to Morgatis. Nyah.

"Do you know someone who you trust enough to do

this?" Kell pushed on.

Hadrian nodded, raising a finger to Fadine. "This is down to you, sister."

I'd never heard him refer to Fadine as his sister before. Fadine's face lost its color for a moment, and I was sure she was going to refuse, but she lowered her gaze.

"If that is what I must do, then so be it," Fadine said, her voice cracked as she agreed.

"What of you, Zacriah?" Kell asked. "Do you need me to retrieve a guard from Vcaros?"

"I am sure they would jump at the chance to take years of disdain out on me, but there is no need. I know someone who will do it without question."

"What of Emaline and Marthil? You will each need someone."

"Give us until this evening to decide who they will have as their guards," Hadrian said. "And Zacriah you must contact Nyah for an update on her arrival. My guess is they will need a guard for us each as soon as night falls."

He looked to Kell and she nodded. "The decisions must be made tonight."

"Being close to gold is both a safety net and a curse. It must be well hidden until it is needed, otherwise we cannot guarantee we will be in control if we are close to the source again," Hadrian added, rubbing his hands together to mask their shaking.

"We have a solution for that already. As long as you stay far from the city you can be certain you will not be put in the way of gold again. Not until it is needed that is," Kell said. "I must return to Vcaros and its people and tell them of your acceptance."

"And what is the chance that I can have a conversation with your King?" Hadrian asked.

"Slim," Kell replied bluntly. "I am afraid it will be me used as his mouth piece and yours."

"Then I trust you will tell him of our plan," Hadrian said. "Word for word."

"Believe me." Kell looked down briefly. "Not a single detail will be left out."

I tapped Hadrian's shoulder. "We must inform Emaline first and tell her before we begin solidifying our moves. It is her we are putting at risk to bait Gordex here, she should know before everyone else."

"Kell, if you just pass on our acceptance and give us until this evening to sort out both Emaline and Marthil a trusted guard. But leave it until sunrise to inform the King of our plans to force Gordex here."

Kell tipped her head, and a subtle smile dusted across her lips. "So be it. I will return shortly."

"We will watch out for you." Hadrian extended a hand for her to shake. "Thank you."

"Do not thank me yet," Kell said, taking his hand

and shaking it twice. "My people are kind, but their minds can be altered as simple as the change in wind."

"Then I better keep the wind calm for a while," I said, pressing my arm against Hadrian's side for comfort.

"Do just that," Kell said before disappearing back off towards the camp.

CHAPTER
Tʜirty

WITH THE ARRIVAL of dusk came a sand storm that washed over the camp and turned everything a shade of burnt orange.

Morthi warriors were sent to warn us of the turn in weather and ensured that our soldiers were secure within the tents. The grand structures were a combination of wood and thick material that let no light out or in. It was promised they would withstand the storm to come, but only time would tell.

Hadrian was the last to be secured in our own, covered in a layer of sand as the harsh, warm winds finally greeted us. He had been out, making sure his own kin were safe.

"This will only prolong the conversation that must be had with Emaline," Hadrian said, shaking his hair until specs of amber sand floated to the rugged ground.

I raised a hand and helped pull his shirt from his damp chest, then carefully discarded it in the corner so the sand would not infiltrate the camp bed that waited for us. The sand storm brought warm winds with it, causing us both to sweat profusely. "It is wasted energy to worry about it now. Until this storm passes there will be no way of speaking with Emaline so don't let it worry you."

"You know she will not be pleased that we have already come up with a plan that potentially puts her at risk." Hadrian's thick, sand-speckled brows creased with worry.

"The entire point of our plan is to make sure she is not in harm's way," I replied. "It is the only hope we have of tipping the scales of victory on our side. Try focusing on the possibility that it will work rather than worrying about the chance it will not."

"Kiss me then," he commanded. "Take my mind away from me."

"If it helps." I smiled as I pressed my mouth onto his. His tongue found his way out and caressed my own, running into perfect circles as they intertwined.

"I want this all to be over with," he whispered, pulling away for a breath. "I want to return home with you by my side. I want to spend time with you knowing that danger is not around every possible turn."

"A time will come when that will happen," I said, honest hope laced amongst my words. "I believe it."

He looked up at me with his large golden eyes, unblinking and exhaled. "If you believe it, then I suppose I should as well."

We kissed again, chest pressed against each other. I could feel the beat of his heart and how perfectly it blended with my own. Even our breathing synchronized as we devoured each other.

"Your father looks like you," I said, pulling away. "I sat with him a lot. Telling him of our stories so far. Sometimes I didn't say anything, but just stayed by his side. It was one of the only comforts I had when I was with Gordex. In a way it felt like I was with you."

"I want nothing more than to see him."

I brushed my fingers down Hadrian's cheek. He leaned into my touch and closed his eyes. "And we will. He is going to be so proud of you, Hadrian, so unbelievably proud."

"That is all I have ever wanted, to make him proud," Hadrian admitted. "After my mother passed, I was certain I'd never see him smile again. It is sad. But what has hurt me most is not recognizing when my real father was replaced with Gordex. I cannot remember the time."

I kissed his cheek just as a single tear escaped from the corner of his eye. The tear made my lips moist. Not once had Gordex mentioned about his time as King Dalior, nor did it pass me to ask him about it.

"Do you want the answers to what it is you seek?" I whispered.

"In ways, I do. But then what difference would it

make? My mind tells me I should find out, whereas my heart disagrees. I see no good coming out of uncovering the truth in it."

What lingered in the past was no more than a memory. Finding out the truth of when Gordex took over as King Dalior would change nothing, only add more anger into Hadrian's heart.

"You look tired." I brushed my finger across the dark circles beneath his closed eyes. "We should get some rest until this storm passes. Even I still feel disconnected after what happened."

"I feel the same." Hadrian yawned, lying back on the bed and pulling me with him.

The sand storm rustled at the material of our tent, battering its sandy presence all around us. But from inside the tent it did not feel as threatening as it would be from the outside. Although the storm caused a slight orange glow as the sands and moonlight melded together it was still dark within the tent. The candles had long blown out, leaving us with only the remnants of natural light beyond to give us vision.

"Any word on Nyah?" Hadrian asked, his eyes closed and voice no more than a murmur. "Surely, she should have arrived by now."

I had already tried when we got back to the tent earlier as Hadrian went out to check on his soldiers before the storm arrived.

"I did try and reach her, but she didn't respond. I am sure she will attempt it as soon as she can. Navigating a ship does not give much free time," I replied, following suit and closing my eyes as we laid about the sheets of our camp bed.

Hadrian mumbled his reply, but it was no more than a mash of incoherent sounds. I cuddled up beside him and listened to his own heart. It beat as silent as an assassin, hardly a sound.

Having time lost within my own thoughts was both a blessing and a curse. Hadrian's question regarding Nyah became its own storm in my mind in the quiet of the tent. I tried reaching out for her, but again, there was no reply.

I awoke to Hadrian's touch. His fingers ran down my arm, tickling me awake. My natural reaction was to roll over and allow his strong arms to pull me onto of his lazy frame. He held me close, every inch pressed onto me in its own way of welcoming me back into the land of reality. Without the need for words we danced with each other. As he laid down I explored his skin with my mouth, moving from his neck to chest to stomach and further below.

He didn't know what to do with his hands.

Sometimes he would lace his fingers with my hair, tugging and moving me like the gentle waves of an ocean. Then they would let go of me, rest behind his head as he allowed me to have my way with him.

Hadrian truly was a beast. In more ways than I'd ever expected. I gave myself moments to worship him with my body, allowing ourselves to have these lost moments together. I wish it could have carried on, but it soon came to a blissful end. I felt it spur before it happened, a warm throbbing in my hands and then release.

We lay beside each other, shoulders touching and clammy hands entwined. No longer did the storm rage on around us. I could see the circular orb of light cut through the burgundy material of the tent.

"I could happily go back to sleep after that," Hadrian whispered, chest rising and falling with his panting breaths.

"No time for that," I replied. "Not with an entire evening of conversation we need to catch up on."

Hadrian almost choked on his deep laugh. "Oh, how simply those words can rid me of tiredness. I suppose you are right, we do have much to accomplish together. But before that…" He rolled over, nose pressed to mine. "We can waste a few moments together before the day goes on."

A blush crept across my face. "As much as I want to just lay here all day we should really go and check on the rest of camp. See just how much damage a Morthi sand storm can do."

Hadrian moaned and sat up, rubbing the heels of his palms into his eyes. "I promise, when this is all over I am going to stay locked within my room for an entire week."

"And how am I supposed to deal with that?" I said. "Not seeing you for an entire week?"

"Oh, you will be locked in there with me." Hadrian laughed, reaching a hand for me.

"Then that sounds like a fabulous idea."

We both changed. I got into a set of silver and purples provided from Hadrian's personal chest. They, like the other clothes I'd been given, were loose. Nothing a tight belt couldn't fix.

Hadrian downed a mug of fresh water from one of the many barrels Vcaros had given to us on arrival. With the back of his hand he wiped his mouth of the dusting of droplets and held the flap to the tent open.

"We must first speak with Emaline," Hadrian said as I walked to join him. "Last night was our deadline to give her a guard so we need to sort that out first. Then I think it would be smart to kill two birds with one stone and tell her of our plan."

"Agreed." We leave the tent, moving through the alleyways of material towards Emaline and Illera's dwellings. "But am I the only one nervous to tackle this conversation?"

Hadrian looked at me through the side of his eye. "A fool would lack nerves."

I squeezed his smooth hand, nodding at the many we passed who stood out in the sun clearing away the storms mess. From where I could see only one tent had fallen, its contents strewn across the sands beyond it. Hadrian briefly stopped to help a couple pick up the main post that held the tent up. I watched him, licking my lips as he displayed his strength. By the time we got to Emaline and Illera, I wanted nothing more than to get Hadrian back into our own privacy where we could play with his strength over and over.

"I will do it," Illera announced, finally pulling her knuckles from between her teeth. She was the only one who didn't sit during the entire conversation. Emaline was perched on the edge of a cabinet, Illera stood in between her legs. Hadrian was sat beside me on a plush, cushioned lounge and Kell beside us in a matching single chair with extravagantly carved clawed legs.

Kell was already with the girls when we had arrived. The moment we walked in their conversation had ended abruptly. Even after we inquired into it, they waved us off.

"Only if you are certain. You must be able to do it without a moment's hesitation if it is ever needed," Kell explained. "Causing someone you love possible pain is a difficult task to ask someone to do."

Love. Neither Illera nor Emaline flinched at the word. They only shared a look and smiled.

"You don't have to do it," Emaline said, her arms hugging onto Illera harder. "It is a lot to ask, and I don't mind having some guard who already despises me put in charge of bleeding me if needed."

"That is exactly why I will do it." Illera would have slammed her foot on the ground if given more room. "No one is allowed to hurt you. My job is to help protect you as you do me. If that means I have to hurt you to save you, then I will do it. As long as no one else comes close to having the chance. And anyway, this only works on the Dragori who have given into the Heart Magick, right? That doesn't concern you, so I don't see how I'll be needed to act on this anyways."

"My lady has spoken." Emaline looked to Kell, a smile on her face. "If Illera wants to be the one in charge of stabbing me *if* I go all crazy like you two did, then so be it."

"And what of Marthil?" Kell asked. "Do you have someone to put in charge of her? I know of many in the city who would happily oblige."

"What of Simian?" Hadrian said. "He is the first person who comes to mind."

"No!" I shouted, surprised at Hadrian's suggestion. "I will not have her life be put in the hands of him.

Simian would kill Marthil the second he got close to her with gold. I don't trust him, and neither should you. Not after how he has acted."

"Petal, I do not trust Simian either. But it was the first thought that came to mind. That leaves Vianne. I trust that she would not act out, so when they both arrive shortly I will tell her of her new task."

"When are they arriving?" Emaline asked. "And why here?"

"We have something else we must discuss this morning." Hadrian's gaze was pinned to Emaline, who began shuffling with discomfort.

"Hadrian," Emaline droned, "what are you hiding from me?"

"Kell, can you go and find Simian and Vianne please and request them to arrive earlier for our New Council meeting? There is no need to wait any longer then we need to."

Kell left without the need to be asked again.

The wait was agonizing. Emaline and Illera whispered to each other but did not speak to either Hadrian or me. They kept shooting tempered looks our way.

To fill the time, I tried to connect with Nyah but was met with silence on her end. I didn't want to admit it aloud, but I was beginning to worry about her prolonged absence.

Kell soon returned with Vianne at her side and Simian a few steps behind, his face streaked with exhaustion and annoyance.

"You do not ask for much, do you?" Simian said, nailed finger pointed at Hadrian. From the state of him, he looked like he had only just woken up. His strawberry colored hair was stuck up in the back and at the corner of his lip was crusted spit.

On the defense, Hadrian stood instantly. "Trust me, shifter, if I did not need you to join our meetings, I would gladly not ask for your presence."

Simian scoffed, mumbled under his breath and took a seat on the two spares that Kell pulled into the middle of the room. Emaline introduced herself to Vianne who wasted no time in doing the same.

"And who is this?" Vianne asked, extending a hand to Illera.

"My partner, Illera," Emaline said. I smiled her way, humored to see the shock on Illera's face that Emaline had admitted it aloud. That shock melted to pride as she took Vianne's hand and shook it back.

"Now we are all acquainted with one another, let us begin," Hadrian announced, standing above us all. "I have called a meeting with my New Council this morning to discuss the plans we have begun to brew regarding the Druid. Our next steps are beginning to become clear, but it is important we keep Emaline part of this discussions, as she plays a crucial part."

"I don't like the sound of this," Emaline said.

Hadrian filled both Emaline and Illera on all the missing events. Emaline's entire body shook as I spoke of her Queen and what she'd been through. Even Vianne bowed her head as if trying to block out the details she already knew.

"We can all agree the Druid needs to be stopped, the sooner the better. It has now been a long while of silence for him, which unnerves me. Besides the mishap that happened two days ago, his presence is still missing," Hadrian said. "I hate to admit this, but it would not surprise me if he is already here. Gordex has the ability to always be steps ahead of us all, so it is smart for us each to not underestimate just what he would do to finally get you, Emaline."

"Forgive me for pointing out the obvious, but why do we not just kill Marthil? Surely, if we sever one of the four Dragori, the Druid cannot complete the ritual to raise the other druids again?" Emaline said.

"At last." Simian almost jumped from his chair out of excitement. "Someone else who thinks with a lick of sense."

I ignored Simian and replied solely to Emaline, "We will not kill Marthil because we are not desperate. Not yet. If we took someone's life, we are no better than Gordex himself."

"That, and we have another idea. One that, if planned carefully could work," Hadrian said, mirroring Illera and Emaline and squeezing my hand.

"Let me guess, this is where I come in." Emaline crossed her arms across her chest.

"This part will involve you, but I promise what I say next is in no way to put you in deliberate harm. So please, let me explain, then you can ask all the questions you have."

Emaline waved a hand for him to continue. Her lips paled with tension and cheek bulging as she bit her tongue to stay quiet.

"We know the souls of the long-forgotten druids are locked within the Staff of Light. We also know that it is important for the ritual after the extents Gordex went to retrieve it. Our options, to ensure it does not happen, is we must destroy the Staff. Cutting off his life line to those souls will mean he has lost. Once we do that, we are four against him. Regardless of the Heart Magick."

"Three of us," Illera added. "Marthil, from the sounds of it, will never help you. Nor should we expect her to. Not after what she's done. To Jasrov, to so many others."

Hearing Jasrov's name caused the hairs on my arms to stand. Not only did it unearth memories of him dying or his lifeless body walking the halls of Queen Kathine's palace as a shadowbeing, it also reminded me of Nyah.

"I agree, Illera." Hadrian flexed his fingers in his lap, enough for me to see just how much his hands were shaking. "We must destroy the Staff of Light, and to do so we must get close to it. We must lure Gordex here, separate him from the Staff so we can destroy it. Then he is all ours to take care of."

"And just how do I come into this?" Emaline asked, confusion furrowed her brows.

"We need something to lure him here. And there is only one thing he needs with such desperation to possess," Hadrian explained, eyes flicking between myself and Emaline. "Because you are the only thing standing in his way of raising his kin. Without your magick, he is shooting in the dark."

Everyone in the room looked to Emaline.

"Emaline, no," Illera plead before anyone had finally admitted aloud what Hadrian meant.

"You want to use me as the bait?" Emaline asked, her voice calmer than I expected. Her hands tapped across the table but didn't show signs of strain.

Hadrian nodded, his eyes focused on the floor. I expected Emaline to shout her disagreement and refuse, but the longer the silence grew the more I felt like that was not going to happen.

Finally, she spoke up, voice crystal clear with a hint of excitement audible.

"Your plan makes sense, and that is why I agree to

help. But under one condition."

"Really?" Hadrian spluttered.

I couldn't stop looking at Illera, whose face was growing rosier by the second.

"One condition," she repeated.

"What is it?"

Emaline took a breath. "Promise me that you will do everything in your power to keep those I love from getting in his way."

I knew whom she spoke of. And so did Illera, who swallowed, wincing at her partner's words.

"I've lost enough, and I'm not willing to lose anymore."

Hadrian's mouth was slack, his words lost. But he nodded again and agreed silently with Emaline.

"I promise with my entire being that I will do as best as I can," Hadrian said.

"Then it is agreed," Kell said. "We lure the Druid to Morgatis, and when he steps foot on my sands—"

"We end him," the room chorused.

CHAPTER
TÐIRTY-ONE

I'D ASKED EMALINE for some company after the council meeting. Hadrian kissed my cheek and waved us off as we left the New Council and began our walk within the quiet of the beach.

Debris amassed along the side of tent walls, slopping like a fresh layering of snow against my home back in Horith. Even the fresh breeze the calm ocean brought was gritty and thick.

I walked beside Emaline on the sea's edge. We had both stripped our dirtied boots off, discarding them before our walk so our hands would be free. Emaline kicked up splashes of water as she waded through the water, its sapphire embrace reaching up to her ankles like a needy child.

Every now and then a splash would lift up unnaturally high. Without even realizing it Emaline was using her abilities. Her hand would clench and relax, willing the water beneath us to follow her command. But her mind was elsewhere.

"Do you really think this plan is going to work?" Emaline said. She'd just finished telling me of the food. Singing the praises of the spices and baked goods that they'd been brought daily.

"I hope so." I didn't want to say yes because it was hard to imagine anything could work. "I can't see anything else the Druid would want enough to travel across the sea to get it."

"That is if he isn't here already." Emaline mirrored a concern I had already voiced. But there was something distant about his voice when it filled my mind. As if he was far away. It was not as clear as it had been during my time with Gordex in Lilioira. "And what about her? She is being awfully quiet out there."

I followed Emaline's finger to the ship that bobbed calmly out of reach of the shore. The sails were down, as well as the anchor that tethered it in place. Even from this distance my eyes could pick up the damage the storm had had on the ship. The hull was dusted in yellows, as well as the piles that covered the portholes on the ship's side.

"She will be subdued whilst kept away from her element." A vision of her in a weak state filled my inner vision. My stomach turned, displeased with the thought. "It may sound odd, and believe me, I have not admitted this to any other, but I want to see her. Not because I care for her. There's something deep down... a part of her damaged beyond repair as a result of her mistreatment. I believe it to be the key to Gordex being able to manipulate her. What if there's a chance we can get her on our side? Show her kindness, enough that she sees there is more than just hate in this world."

Emaline raised a hand to block the morning sun as she looked upon Marthil's prison. "And you truly believe there is a possibility that would work? Someone who has murdered out of cold blood? Do you really believe she could come around from that? Because if I'm honest, I do not see there being a chance."

"Maybe there is no turning back for her, no redemption. But Marthil has shown me windows of kindness, brief moments of normality amongst the storm of anger and violence that seems to follow her."

Emaline turned away from the ship and carried on walking. "And what would that be? Did she give you a nice massage? Did she read you a story during the dark, cold nights you were holed up with them in Lilioira?"

Her sarcasm was palpable, but I didn't laugh. There was not much room for laughter these days. "I was not well. Marthil supplied me with Forbian when I needed it most." I rubbed the faded scar across my side as it ached with the memory. "Without it, I wouldn't have healed as I have now."

"Forbian? I've heard of it before." Emaline rubbed her chin, gaze lost to the ocean. "Doesn't it stay in your system for weeks at a time even when the healing properties last only a day or two at most?"

I shrugged. "I believe so." Jasrov would've known the answer.

"So, why did she need to give you it?" Emaline asked, already suspicious.

Maybe my pause gave it away, but Emaline already released a sigh that screamed "I told you" before I even admitted the reason behind Emaline's kindness.

"Because she stabbed me."

"Ah, you see. When an act of kindness comes as a result of violence, it cancels it out and becomes meaningless," Emaline said. "Do not be fooled, Zacriah, I know by now you are smarter than that."

"What have I done without your insight all this time?" I said, rolling my eyes.

"I was thinking the same thing myself." Emaline knocked into my shoulder and chuckled, the silver acorn necklace bounced out of the slip of her stained, white tunic. She grabbed it instantly, pushing it back beneath the material and out of sight.

Emaline caught me looking at it. "Do you think Nesta would hate me for falling in love with someone new?"

Her question caught me off guard. "From what you told me about her, I do not think she had the capability to hate you."

"I didn't expect it to happen, you know. But Illera, she is so different. Beautiful, open, honest and fiery. She reminds me a lot of Nesta, but on the other hand she is so… new."

"I guess this time together all alone in the far-off lands of Morgatis has really been good for you both?" I said.

"Well, yes, it has. But I fell for her before we arrived here. Perhaps when we first found her all covered in grime and muck in the Thalas Temple. I knew there was something different," Emaline said. "She interests me."

"That explains why you were so territorial." I peered at Emaline who still clutched onto the acorn necklace, her own gaze glued to the horizon ahead. "I can see that you care for her."

"I do." Her reply was simple, short. "She respects me and my choices. Illera listens to me, she understands the way I love and praises it. Being around her is refreshing."

I rested a hand on her shoulder. "Never did I expect Illera, the girl from home, would ever find such a lucky person as you."

"I may not have known her from Horith." Emaline said the name of my town without the need for me to say it. Clearly Illera's and her conversations had not missed a single detail. "But I do know that she is not the person she was when she left it."

"We can both agree on that!" Even now, thinking back to how Illera treated others, her coldness, it seemed like I was imagining a different person. "What have you both being doing here to pass the time? If you can't go near the city, you are limited to what you can do, I guess," I asked, genuine interest in their events as they knew every detail of what happened with me.

"Lots of walking, even more talking. The first few days we were holed up in that cave of a room, but then we ventured to the top level and explored. Watched the Morthi people from a far. Even spent endless moments training, fighting. Sharpening our skills in case of the worst. Nothing as eventful as what you have been through I am sure."

"You say that, but I am certain you know a lot more of this land and its people than anyone back at camp does. Knowledge is an important tool. Care to share it with me? I have some interest in this place as well." So much had happened, and I still knew nothing of what the Morthi guards who we fought could do. Or of the elusive King that was mentioned daily, but never showed up. "What of their powers? The magick I've seen is nothing I knew possible before. Even in passing mention from Cristilia, I still didn't expect it."

"From what I worked out from passing comments and displays is the Morthi have two magicks unique to their people. Like the Niraen elves can shapeshift and that ability is unique to them—"

"Unless it truly was Gordex who is to blame for that," I interrupted. "The shifters."

"Well, for argument sake, let us pretend that each of the three races of elves have different abilities due to the certain blood that keeps them animated. Before the Morthi were driven underground by our Dragori ancestors, or the Air Dragori who single handedly did that, no offence. The Morthi were only supposed to have one power. Blaze Wielder, that is the name given to those who could harness the suns energy. Warriors who could create light and weave it to their own bidding. The power was spread over a minority of the Morthi people. But now, since they live in the dark depths below ground a new power came into existence. They go by the name, Sister Shadows. Only the woman have such abilities."

I remembered the two who'd greeted us when we arrived in Morgatis. Kell had introduced them as Sister Shadows and I'd not known what that meant.

"Like Cristilia, they have abilities to control, conjure and weave darkness. I don't know why they got their powers so late, but my guess is Morgatis is a burning desert of sun and fire. Maybe the people never had the opportunity to unlock this power until they no longer dwelled in the light. The only main difference, from what I can see, is the magick is unique to the women of Morgatis. No man has been recorded to have that magick."

"I want to see this magick again," I admitted aloud, interested in this new display of power.

"I am sure you will soon enough, now we have agreed to the King's requests. He should send warriors to help our cause as promised," Emaline said.

"Their King is another mystery. We cannot see him. I don't know if that is what makes me suspicious or something else entirely."

"Do not let your suspicions get in the way of what is needed to be done. There will be plenty of time to request an audience when the fight is over. I know we all want peace after this, but it will take time to rebuild after such destruction and turmoil."

It didn't matter that the King would not meet us, only that he was supplying us with soldiers willing to help our fight. By the sounds of it, their magick would be welcomed and praised amongst our lines. It was a power that would help us.

"We have walked far enough." Emaline turned, the water swirling with her sudden movement. "Any further and we might venture into unwelcome grounds. Doom desert is large and unforgiving. If those towering serpents are out there, what goes to say that something even bigger isn't?"

"Is that your excuse for actually wanting to return to Illera?" I said, smile on my face.

Emaline shrugged. "You will never know. But, between us, I don't think I want to stray from her too far. I have seen enough distance between those who love each other. I do not think I could cope with us being separated as you and Hadrian have been."

"Well, I suppose," I said, lost to the view for a moment at the mention of Hadrian. "Keep her close. I might stay out here for a little longer and try to communicate with Nyah. Maybe the quiet out here will help me get through to her at once."

That was part of it. There was another reason I needed to stay away from camp for a moment.

Emaline wrapped me in a hug and squeezed tight. She lifted me from the floor then plonked me back down. "It is good to see you again, Zacriah. Here's to hoping we all can stay together again. Don't tell Illera I told you, but even she worried about you."

I pulled the most dramatic face I could make, slapped my hand to my chest and gasped. "Illera, worries for me? Now that is a miracle."

"Exactly." Emaline punched me sharp in the gut and skipped off towards camp. "I hope you can keep secrets."

"You have no idea," I muttered under my breath, turning towards the ship with Marthil was trapped within.

I waited until Emaline was a dot in the distance

before I let the beast free. Wings spread from my back, arching in a giant stretch that shivered down my spine. Talons elongated from the tips of my fingers and the warm rush across my forehead warned the growth of my horns.

Then I sprang into the air and flew for the ship, anxious for what state Marthil would be in when I reached her.

CHAPTER
THIRTY-TWO

NONE OF THE Niraen soldiers stationed on the ship questioned my arrival. My boots touched down first, sand scattering around my feet as my wings cascaded strong pumps of air on the ships deck. The few soldiers whose turn it was to guard the ship gave me the most careless of looks before carrying on with whatever they were doing before I arrived, which seemed to be sleeping on the job.

Some were sprawled out across benches, faces raised to the sun. Others walked past rounds of sand from the storm, not bothering to clean up. There was an air of uncaring about the many stationed here.

I retracted my Dragori form until I was left with rips in my shirt and trousers. For a moment, I longed for the uniform Gordex had created for me. It was made around my ever-changing form. At least I would not need to walk around with such exposure of skin.

There was a strange tugging within the belly of the ship. As if my air recoiled from something it feared.

Marthil. I didn't need to ask where she was being kept. The hum in the air was a trusted answer. Her presence was beneath me, kept in the lower decks were the water was surrounding her from all sides. A prison to keep her powerless. There was no need for the golden cage. Perhaps, with hindsight, it would have given Gordex control to take her over if she was exposed to the gold? At least that was one worry we didn't need to contemplate.

I moved as quickly as I could, feet tapping across the paneled flooring as I ran towards the staircase and lost myself in the lower decks. It would not be long until Hadrian or someone came looking for me. And once Fadine, Vianne and Illera had returned from getting their golden tipped weapons, someone would be forced to become my guard since Nyah had still not arrived. That would prevent me from visiting Marthil alone again.

The prison was easy to find, thanks to the smell that seeped from the half-closed door before me. I gagged, clogging my hand over my nose and mouth in hopes to stifle the stench. Days of heat had intensified the smell, enough to ward off any unwanted visitors. With my foot I kicked the door open, startling the restful guard within.

"I didn't expect my shift to be over with," he said, face red and hands flustered as he flattened his blond curls. He was young, his creaseless face screamed it. I was certain he had seen no more than fourteen moons.

"Stand down," I said, voice muffled by my hand. "I am here to see the prisoner."

The boy squinted, soon realizing I was not a guard but a random visitor in rags for clothes.

"I-I can't let anyone come in. That has been my orders."

"Order's given by myself and Prince Hadrian." I stepped through, into the room, so the light didn't block out my features. I wasn't sure if this would work but as soon as the guard got a properly look at me he dipped his head and scuffled out of my way.

"My apologies, Zacriah, I did not mean to offend." His tone was panicked.

I raised a hand, tapping him on his shoulder to show I was no threat. "No need to apologize, but please, wait beyond the door until I'm finished. Oh, and why don't you inform your fellow peers who are resting and not doing their job that I'm here, and Prince Hadrian will hear about their slack attitude?"

"Of course," he said, not turning away from me as he took steps back from me. "Again, my apologies."

I didn't remind him not to apologize again, as it was clearly driven into him that it was the right thing to do. I only smiled at him and closed the door between us, leaving me in the room with the prisoner.

Weak beams of light cut in through the small slits in the wooden walls, and the occasional portholes made it hard to see a foot in front of me. I tiptoed around the shadows, trying to stay in the thin pools of light that were dotted around the room sporadically.

"Come to gloat?" a voice purred through the darkness. It was rough, harsh and sounded as painful as I was sure it felt to make.

"I've come to see how you fair," I replied, eyes jumping from shadow to shadow, in search for Marthil.

"How convenient."

The rustle of metal made me snap my attention to the left. Raising my hands out before me, I walked cautiously till the kiss of cold iron touched my palms.

"Have you been eating?" I asked, kicking out at a plate of moldy bread beside my feet.

Marthil didn't respond. Her silence was cold, a warning that she didn't want me here. But I couldn't live with myself if she was ignored and mistreated.

"Not hungry," she snarled.

"You really should be eating something Marthil." I made a mental note to ask the young guard to bring some fresh food in as soon as I left.

"Your attempt at kindness makes me sick. It's days too late." More clinks of metal sounded. Even in the darkness of the room, I could almost imagine her turning her back to me.

"If we knew you would not attack us, you wouldn't be kept here. But, no matter what you think, this is the safest place for you right now. So many people want to harm you for what you have done. My choice to keep you here is my own way of making sure you stay alive."

"My savior, how thankful I am." Marthil laughed, making the hairs on my arms stand. "You speak as if you are my owner. That I am no more than a pet you keep locked up in the shadows because you have lost its muzzle."

"Unlike Gordex then," I said. "He lets you roam free with your muzzle on. I do not keep you locked up to control you, to make you do things that are not in your nature, like murdering, hurting."

"You think he makes me do that?" she said, her face suddenly between the bars. There was enough light to see her dirt streaked face and tangled hair. Her frail hands clamped around the metal bars, each nail either broken or riddled with muck. "Gordex doesn't control me. He merely encourages me to do what I want to do."

This was wasted effort. Maybe Emaline was right about Marthil. I turned away, walked towards the door and left her to giggle at her own statement.

"I see your weakness as clear as I see my future," Marthil announced, deranged. "You care too much for others and even more so when others do not care for you. You look for the good, when sometimes there is no good to be found."

I pinched my teeth down on my lip and just kept

walking. I wouldn't let her see that her words got to me.

"It will be your downfall, Zacriah. Just you wait."

Gripping a hold of the wooden door I turned over my shoulder, unable to keep quiet a moment longer. "My heart pains for you Marthil, truly it does. I wish you'd see through your clouded judgement one day. I only hope it isn't too late."

I threw all my weight into slamming the door closed, blocking out her mocking laugh. No matter how many deep breaths, I couldn't calm my anger. It creeped up on me, snaking its darkness through every vein in my body. Maybe this was her plan. Provoke me to lose control, to give Gordex his chance to take over?

The young guard came bounding down the steps, breathless and flushed. "Everything fine?"

I nodded, trying to swallow down the lump that blocked my throat. "It will be."

"Did she speak to you? She has not said a word to anyone else since we arrived," he explained.

"Yes, she did." I walked passed him, readying myself to take the steps up. As I placed my foot on the first, I turned around, unable to stop myself. "Make sure she is fed. Bring her plates of food until her temptation overwhelms her and she eats."

"Everything we give her she leaves to rot in her cell," the young Niraen guard said.

Even with anger threatening my being and her

incessant mocking, I still couldn't leave without commanding that she was fed. My weakness. That was my weakness.

"Try again and again."

"We will." He bowed.

"I want daily updates of Mart—"

I doubled over, hands slapping against the stairs as my mind spun violently. It felt as if the entire floor beneath me shifted, although it was not the ship that moved.

Burning cold cut across my head, Nyah's presence slamming into mine with such force I lost consciousness for a moment. I couldn't open my eyes, not as the slightest bit of light would pain me.

"Zacriah, are you well?" the young guard said, lifting me up from the floor. "Do you need me to call for someone?"

I couldn't response, not with the sweltering panic that now coursed through my body, dousing the anger out instantly.

Nyah.

I pulled myself from the guard and pelted up the stairs, two at a time.

Reaching the top deck, I threw myself over the railing, willing my Dragori form to burst free. It didn't take me long to reach camp, not with the pump of my powerful wings that kept me soaring forward.

Nyah.

I shot down for the sandy beach, landed and ran straight into Hadrian's tent. He jumped, looking at me as I burst through the entrance and interrupted the conversation he had with Fadine.

"What is it?" he said, eyes wide as he saw my own panic.

"Nyah," I said, finding it hard to breath. "Nyah has been captured. Someone has her somewhere in Morgatis."

Fadine ran for help before either of us needed to tell her.

I sagged into Hadrian's arm, unable to keep my legs up. "The pain, I felt her pain. There is so much."

"Shh," he hushed into my hair as he held me tight. "We will find her."

"Hadrian, what have I done?"

CHAPTER

THIRTY-THREE

THE RESIDUE MEMORY of pain was overwhelming. I'd shared images, memories with Nyah, but never a feeling. It seemed that every time I blinked I felt more. I tried to keep my consciousness, but the phantom agony still had hold of me.

"You need to tell us what you know!" Kell was suddenly inches from my face, her own plastered with concern. I could have sworn she was not in the tent before I closed my eyes. How long had I been out for?

Moving my eyes up I saw Hadrian, then I felt him. He'd laid my head in his crossed legs, his hands stroking non-stop across my sticky forehead. "Petal, Kell needs to know. If we have a chance of finding Nyah, then we must start searching straight away."

It could've been Hadrian's urgency, or the mention of Nyah's name that kicked me out of my state. I bolted up, knocking Hadrian's hands away with my quick change in position.

"She didn't speak to me, not like we normally do.

This time was very different. I felt... pain. So much of it. But I saw the sky, sand, sea. And, I think I saw the broken walls of a building. I can't be sure now." Even as I spoke, I tried to contact Nyah again, but there was no presence behind the door into her own mind.

Kell rocked back on her heels, eyes lost to the tents ceiling for a moment. The silence was agonizing. When it finally broke, I could have shed a tear with relief.

"I know where she is," Kell said, eyebrows furrowed above her wide, dark eyes.

"How far? We must leave with haste," Hadrian shouted at Kell as her face melted with clear worry.

"We can, and if my guess is correct, we would reach it in a matter of hours. But there are risks to this."

"Risks?" I said. "You do not know Nyah yet, but I assure you she is worth every risk you could possibly throw at me."

"There seems to be risks with everything at the moment," Hadrian added quietly.

Kell raised her hands and nodded. "I understand your urgency, I do. But you need to understand what we will be getting ourselves into. You have faced hostility from those within Vcaros, you understand the disdain they have for the Dragori. But there are others, Morthi who refused to live beneath ground after the war many moons ago. A small pocket of Morthi overrun with hate for anyone who hid beneath the ground after the Great

Destruction. If that is where your friend Nyah is, I cannot promise she will be living by the time we reach her."

I could've screamed at that moment. I could have teared down the entire camp with a single breath and shown these elves who have Nyah captive just why they should be fearful of us.

"Then we leave right this moment," Hadrian commanded.

"If you go, your guard will need to follow." Kell paced, her nails between her teeth. "And I will come for Zacriah in case the worst happens."

"So be it," Hadrian said, pulling a long sword from the top of the dresser. In a giant heave, he pulled the weapon free from its sheath, allowing the light to dance across its metallic surface. "We must fetch Emaline and Illera. They will join us. I do not want us to be separated again."

"I will return in a matter of moments," Kell said, already moving for the tent's exit. "Be ready."

"Decorate yourself." It was the first thing Hadrian said to me once Kell left us to prepare. His skin blotched with splashes of red as he too had to battle to keep his anger at bay. "Leave no inch of your body untouched by a weapon."

"What if we are too late?" I asked, needing to hear Hadrian's confidence in our task to save her. If I admitted what I really thought, I would've broken down on the spot.

"Petal, let me help you prepare."

Hadrian didn't answer me properly.

We all changed, preparing for the unknown.

Hadrian wore no armor. Nor did he need to. The less he wore the freer he was to shift into his Dragori form. His scaled skin would be all the protection he needed. But that did not stop him from showering his body in weaponry. The long sword was strapped with leather ties down the middle of his back, adjacent to his spine. On either side of his hip, twin daggers hung from a belt. His last weapon was the power that lay dormant beneath his very skin. Looking at him in the streamed light from the burning sun outside I could imagine his entire body combusting and devouring his chosen enemy. It made my knees weak with excitement.

I wore the dark uniform Gordex had gifted me for no other reason than being free to shift without ruining my clothing. Hadrian looked out the side of his eye as I pulled on the pieces. I could see my own reflection in his curious gaze. But not once did he make a comment

"Here," Hadrian said, handing me over a bow. I had not noticed it in the room before now, but as the smooth wood graced my hands I knew of its familiarity. "Do you remember when I gave this to you?"

I nodded, mouth open and wordless.

"Such a beautiful weapon. Fadine retrieved it before she left with our fleet to get us. It was the first item I saw when I finally woke from being soul lost."

I ran my finger over the gemstone that was embedded into its hilt, and the rivers of purple decoration that graced its surface. "I almost forgot this ever existed."

"Then let us hope you have the opportunity to re-familiarize yourself with it when we take down those who have Nyah."

"And her brothers," I said. "The twins. They traveled with her. And what of the Alorian soldiers who helped man the ship? They will be there as well. So many lives we must retrieve, I only hope they are all still intact."

"As do I." Hadrian kissed my forehead, brushing a strand of silver hair out of the way with his thumb.

We left the tent to find Emaline, Illera and Kell each dressed head to toe for battle. Emaline did not have any weapons attached to her belt, but two skins of water that were full and dripping. That was the only weapon she would need. Fadine came rushing over, elk-helmet atop her head which shone with a fresh layer of sweat. I had not seen her wearing it since Olderim, something which filled me with a sense of home.

"I don't know about you all, but I am ready to kick some—"

"Thank you, Fadine," Hadrian interrupted.

"We will be riding the serpents, which already wait for us beyond the camp. I do not believe your soldiers would appreciate the serpent's arriving so abruptly," Kell explained. "Follow me."

It was a short walk to our meeting point. Already my boots began sinking into the sand, and my tunic itched under the heat. Then, as the three serpents caused the entire ground to shake before they burst skyward, they brought with them more discomfort.

Like the first time I saw them, they were both beastly and impressive. The sun reflected off their palm sized scales, causing light to dance all round where they slithered in anticipation. This time each serpent was as black as night, the odd white scale speckled amongst the sea of darkness. Forked tongues licked out at the air as they familiarized themselves with our scent. Then, when they were ready to accept us, they bowed their pointed snouts and pushed their cold bodies against the sandy bed.

"Climb on, two each, make sure your Dragori have your chosen guard with you," Kell said, giving me the eye to follow her to the first serpent.

"Is that necessary if you do not have the weapons for us yet?" Hadrian asked, his discomfort at leaving me was clear.

"Well," Fadine said, hooking her arm with his and walking towards the next serpent. "We do have them."

Even I looked at Fadine as she lifted her untucked tunic and flashed a dark holder at her side. It was not made from leather like the rest of her sheaths, but from a material that mirrored the same serpents scaled body beside her. Dark scales stitched together, enough to hide the small dagger at her side.

"You will not sense the gold until it is pulled free from the Morthi made holder," Kell explained to me as Fadine did the same to Hadrian. From Emaline's unbothered expression, I could tell it was not news to her. Kell then raised her voice to the group, "We will arrive by dusk, if all goes well. Be prepared for anything. Blade and light may be our only greeting when we arrive…"

"Blade and light?" I heard Fadine mumble to Hadrian just as the serpents shot forward. I didn't catch his response as I was too focused on gripping ahold of Kell around the waist to stop myself from falling from the serpent's slick back.

⌒

There was no room for conversation as we rode the serpents into the horizon. We hugged the shore, slipping across the damp ground with such speed that the air whistled past my ears. I quickly learned that pressing my face as close to the creature's body stopped the sand from getting into my mouth, nose and eyes. I followed Kell's actions and let our companions guide us knowingly. I couldn't help but think about how easy this journey would have been with a griffin to ride.

Kell hadn't told us of where we were headed too. Not with the rush we had to get the journey started.

The silence was torture. It left me in the deep pits of my mind, imaging what Nyah was going through to cause her so much pain. Different scenarios filled my mind, flashing from one bloody vision to another. I had to occupy my mind with other thoughts as I risked the anger to grow further. I could not lose control now. Not yet. There was a teasing nature to anger that was both hypnotic and exciting. I knew what would happen when the Heart Magick took over and gave Gordex his welcome to command me. If it meant I could destroy those who had Nyah, I would gladly give up control.

We rode until the sun dipped behind the dunes of Doom desert and the sky morphed into a painting of dark navy. It was a cloudless night, but still humid and dry.

By the time we came to a stop, I was thankful to use my legs. The serpents lowered their bodies, enough for us each to slip down their smooth skin onto the ground. We'd stopped in the middle of a valley of dunes. Billows of sand flew in circles at the peaks of the dunes as the wind beyond our protected pit teased them. We could not see beyond our pit, nor would anyone see into it unless they stood at the top of one of the dunes and looked in.

Beyond its beauty was the reality that our destination was a short walk away and with it was Nyah.

"We must be smart if we are to save Nyah and her companions," Kell said. "Those who dwell in the ruins of the once great city of Merrik have not been seen, nor interacted with in many moons. I can imagine they will not be pleased to see us. With the setting of the sun, those Blaze Wielders will not be as powerful as they would be during the day. But they still have great magick, be prepared."

"Forgive me for stating what could be the obvious, but would it not be ideal to have a plan before we just stroll into the old city?" Fadine asked, dusting sand from her shoulders. The metals of her uniform clinked as she hooked a finger in her collar and pulled it for a moment of relief. For once, wearing this uniform, the temperature didn't bother me.

"There is no time for plans," I snapped, ready to unleash my force on the unexpecting Morthi in Merrik. "Nyah has waited long enough. We go in, find her, and do everything to get her out. She has been through enough trying to save me, it is our time to repay the debt."

"There would be no plan that would help us in this

city," Kell warned.

"Do you know how many there are within Merrik?" Hadrian asked, his fists clenched and knocking against his leg.

"Enough that they will easily cease our efforts in a fight," Kell admitted. "We will not be going into the city ruins looking for a battle. We must be calm, hope that they give us a chance to explain."

"And if they don't?" I said, annoyed at the leash Kell's words had put on me. I would not be able to fight, not straight away.

"Then you better unleash every inch of power you all have and hope all six of us make it back out alive."

Illera and Emaline had their hands clasped together, a united force prepared to face anything together. Hadrian must have spotted it as I had because he soon took my hand and squeezed it.

"For Nyah," Hadrian said, aloud to the group.

"For Nyah," we chorused back to him.

"Come and see what waits amongst the ruins," Kell said, taking lead and walking up the steep slope into the waiting danger beyond it. "Be vigilant."

CHAPTER
TᕼIRTY-ꟻOUR

WE WALKED IN single file, hoods up to protect ourselves for the sudden dip in warmth as dusk faded into night. As my booted feet trudged through the heavy sands, I contemplated on the many possibilities the following moments would bring.

What state would we find Nyah in? Had her brothers, as pesky as they were, found a way to be free before they were captured? How many Alorian soldiers had been on the ship with her and how many were still alive? Time would tell.

I passed beneath an arched wall that must have been the old entrance. Even with the rusted hinges hanging off in tatters to my side, I could imagine clearly the grand door that must've been here before. Once we passed under, it was clear we stood in what must have been the main street of the once grand city. Like an artery, the pathway went on for as far as the eye could see before us. Cobbled stones hardly visible beneath the history of debris and sand. On all sides broken homes and buildings littered the sidewalks. Walls had fallen onto one another, strange weeds wrapped around most surfaces. This place was no more than a graveyard of spirits and destruction.

"Even in its state of ruin, this city is—was huge," Illera said from the back of the line.

From what little of the old city I could see it was clear the pure scale it once was. The first layer was mostly leveled, left only a few buildings half standing. But I could see in the far distance outlines of many yellowed-stoned buildings which cut into the dark sky.

"It will be a challenge to find her. Where do we start?" Emaline added.

"By checking every possible shadow and place of hiding," I answered, my voice as stern as my gaze which hadn't stopped scrutinizing the view ahead of me. "But I have other means to speed up our search."

"Be careful," Hadrian hushed in my ear. "We do not know much about the Morthi. If you use your magick they might sense it which will ruin our sense of surprise."

Hadrian knew I could search for life with my magick. Checking the wind for secrets, asking it to tell me where the life is. A single breath would alter me to their location.

"I will be careful," I said, unblinking. "They will not sense me, not unless I want them too."

"What are you both talking about?" Kell asked.

I explained what I could do. Kell looked as pleased with my idea as I was.

"If they do pick up on it, we must be ready," Kell said, talking to the entire group. Everyone already had a hand on their weapons, in case they needed to pull them free for use. "But this will save us much, precious, time."

"Don't know about you, but I'm ready. It's been a boring time so far, a little tussle wouldn't hurt too much," Emaline said.

"Go ahead, Petal," Hadrian urged me on, although his worried stare clearly stated that he did not want me to go ahead with this idea. "Ask your winds for aid."

For better concentration, I closed my eyes. Raising my hands, open palms, to the sky I envisioned the silver strands of my air. The bright light filled my mind, sending shivers of pleasure across my skin. One moment I was standing in place, the next I was everywhere.

My presence flowed through the city, skittering across stone, sand and sky. I felt the city in ways I would never have thought possible. I felt the birds which flew above us, circling the city in hopes to find prey. I felt small creatures running across the dry ground in hopes to escape their hunter. In my mind, I could see what it once was, before another power came and destroyed it.

As I explored the ruins, Cristilia's voice filled my mind. She told me of the Air Dragori and how he unleashed his dark power, causing chaos. I could see it as clear as if the story played out before me. Walls breaking under the powerful force as it ravaged the city and those who screamed in terror within it.

Stronger than any storm I'd encountered, the power was intoxicating. I toppled the tallest of buildings, sent bodies flying amongst the twisting twisters that devoured anything within its path. In the deep parts of my mind I was scared. My own magick picked up on the traces of memories left, warning me of what could come if I lost control.

As I forgot what I was doing, I sensed movement. *There.* In the heart of the city, a building, newer than the rest, stood waiting. I sensed the shift of air within it, ripples against the wind that filled the many rooms. In and out. I could hear those inside breathing as if it was I who inhaled and exhaled. Snaking through the maze of stone spaces, I brushed across skin, hair and blood. My air recoiled from it.

I retracted my magick as fast as it allowed me to. Coming out of it so quickly caused my head to feel light, enough for me to stumble as I came back into myself.

"Zacriah," Hadrian said, gripping my arms and keep my upright. "Steady now."

At first, I saw double of everyone, but that soon settled.

"Did you find them?" Kell asked, hand tightening on

the handle to her sword.

"I did, and they're close," I answered.

"They?" Fadine asked, one brow raised into her helmet.

"I don't know how many, but as Kell said, the numbers are grander than ours."

Illera shared a worried look with Emaline who gritted her teeth. "But we have three powerful beasts, a shapeshifter, a girl with a horny helmet and... well, Kell. What is it you do?"

Kell shrugged. "You shall see."

"We have the element of power on our side," Hadrian said. "I only hope we do not need to use it."

"Are there any Sister Shadows hiding amongst this city?" Emaline asked Kell.

"No, those who stayed here never lived beneath ground. That power never graced them."

"Ideally, I would prefer we did not go in expecting a bloody brawl. Negotiation, that is our first attempt. When that does not work, then we can unleash everything we have in us to get Nyah out."

Emaline's knuckles clicked so loud that it startled a bird on a nearby building wall. The flap of wings made everyone jump.

"You did not mention animals during your strange search!" Fadine called, biting back a curse.

"I didn't' think—"

"STOP!" Kell's panic made me choke on my reply. "Be still."

Her arms were raised out beside her, willing us all to crouch down.

"What?" Hadrian hissed, his hand ready to call forth flame.

"Those birds, they do not look for food. They look for us. The Morthi who have your friend, they will know we are here when that bird gets to them," Kell explained as we watched the dark shape of the creature fly into the heart of the city.

"Then let's get there before the bird does," Hadrian said, his wings sprouting from his back and spreading wide behind me.

"Someone stop it," Emaline snarled, lowering into a crouch and pouncing into the air. The moment her feet left the ground her wings were free and forced her in the direction of her prey.

We all ran forward. Illera moved with grace. First, she started on her legs, but soon black shadow seeped from her skin. Once it cleared the white lioness sped off into the dark, dust billowing where her large paws ripped at the ground.

Hadrian soon followed into the sky after Emaline, but I did not. I kept on the ground, shift hidden. I didn't want to leave Kell and Fadine, the only ones without their own type of power. Not that they would not be able to look after themselves. It was more so they could keep an eye on my back.

Our feet pounded through the streets of the ruined city in chase after the bird. At this rate, our own noise would alert the Morthi before the bird arrived to divulge what it had seen.

It didn't matter anymore.

I peered into the sky, searching for Emaline or Hadrian, but it was too dark to make them out. Only when brief spouts of flame filled the sky could I make out their location. Each explosion of fire would be followed by a large growl of frustration from Hadrian, which could only mean he had missed.

"Kill the bird, it no longer matters," Kell panted beside me. "The fire and growling will alert them of our arrival."

Kell searched the darkness of the inner streets, her head turning in search for an ambush or threat.

"Hadrian is not one for subtly." Fadine scoffed, eyes rolling.

We kept our pace up, only stopping when Emaline and Hadrian were stood on the street up ahead.

"We lost it," Hadrian said as Illera prowled in her lioness form behind him. "The damned beast was impossible to catch."

"What now!"

"We wait," Kell said, hand on the handle of her

weapon.

On all sides we were open to an attack. We'd stopped at a crossroads of sort, giving anyone who wanted to watch us, the best view. Kell had her ears pointed towards the darkness waiting for a noise to single they were coming. Without mention or command we all moved, backs to each other, and watched the shadows of the ruined city.

"Be ready," she said, reaching for her sword and pulling it free. She bent her knees and held the sword up in both hands.

We followed her command, each of us pulling forth our own form of weapon. Hadrian was beside me, flames licking across his two waiting hands. I could hear the swish of water from behind me were Emaline was stood and the growl of Illera who was ready to pounce beside her. I called for my wind, willing it to wait for my instruction. It hovered around my hands, twisting silver trails which linked in and out of my twitching fingers.

I squinted into the street ahead of me and could see shadows detach from walls and walk forward. I had to look carefully to decipher if it was a trick of the dark, or reality. And it was real.

Countless figures walked in a line, side by side, towards us. Risking a glance towards the two other streets I could see out the corner of my eye I saw the same. More outlines of figures walking towards us.

The entire group tensed, readying ourselves to fight.

"A little *birdie* told us to expect visitors, we have been waiting for your arrival," a voice rained out, but I couldn't pinpoint where it came from. "Lay down your weapons, your magicks, and let us talk. I am sure you do not want to cause a scene, and neither do we."

"We are here for the girl you have taken," I called out, unable to keep myself quiet. The unseen voice did not scare me. I had faced worse. We all had.

"Of course," the voice called back. My mind picked up the familiar voice and recognized it above the rest. It was as if it wanted me to know she was here. Nyah.

"Listen to them, Zac," Nyah called out, stepping forward into the weak beam of light. She looked untouched, not marked by pain at all.

It's safe. Her voice filled my mind.

"What is going on?" Hadrian shouted.

Nyah took another step forward, hands raising to show she is fine. "I'm sorry for the means of getting you here, but let us all talk. It will make sense once you hear these people out."

CHAPTER
TῙIRTY-FIVE

NYAH DIDN'T TURN back to look at me. Not during the entire walk through the ruins of Merrik. Not when we were escorted passed crumbled walls and shells of old homes. Not when she leaned in close to the elven man she followed, her lips moving but not a sound flowing out of them.

Every time I swallowed I was greeted with the strange taste of concern. Something was terribly off here. Different. A different that twists my anxious mind into a knot of overwhelming emotions and thoughts. I tried reaching for Nyah across our connection, but she didn't respond. She showed no sign that she even felt my attempt to speak with her.

This was not what I expected. Far from it.

Hadrian took my clammy hand in his without caring. His fingers linked perfectly with mine, tethering me back to reality as we followed the many Morthi. He held on so tight I could feel his heart beat between our clasping grasp. Or was it mine? It was hard to differentiate as we both shared in the unknowing that was to follow.

The group slowed down as we rounded towards a newer building. It felt the same as the one I'd sensed during my search of the city. Dark outlines of large birds circled the skies above the towering block, some filtering in and out of dark covey holes far at the top of the building.

They were the same as the one that spied on us, long black wings, pointed amber beaks. Beady eyes which seemed to know more than I cared to find out.

Made from a lighter color than the many ruined homes around it, this once stood tall. Fresh bricks layered on top of each other, glassless windows glowed with orange from within. Flapping curtains left half-drawn, barely hiding the watching faces of many who peaked on us from their heights.

This place was no military base. No fortitude of weapon and war.

Clothes, rugs and other materials had been hung out the windows to dry. I spotted the garments thanks to the movement of people watching from within squared windows. They stood back from the windows enough that their features were cloaked, but their outlines were not.

"None of them are armed," Hadrian whispered, following my pinched stare. "They should be, from what we have heard it does not make sense."

Amongst the movement of the windows I didn't spot the glinting of silver and steel. Those who watched were no more than children, beardless and youthful. Not Warriors.

"Nothing is making sense," I replied. "There is something very strange going on with Nyah. This is not like her to ignore us completely. These people, they don't seem as hostile as I thought they would." Or hoped. I didn't want to admit it aloud, but part of me needed a fight. Maybe it was the dark presence that had burrowed itself deep into my very soul that made me feel these ways.

"I count us lucky," Hadrian whispered. "So far. Anything can change."

We entered the courtyard of the base, under another arched wall reminiscent of the one we had walked through to enter the once great city. We followed a pathway in silence, passing numerous pillars which dwarfed us all from either side. Each had a large pedestal on their rounded tops, a place for the many dark birds to perch on and watch us walk beneath them.

Flames burned in brass holders, untouched by the subtle winds. They shone across each slab of stone we passed over. The moon acted as the main source of light.

The doors to the main building were flanked by civilians. Their faces where covered in masks of a kind, only showing a sliver of their eyes which were a mixture of obsidian and stars. Each held a curved blade the length of their arms. The handles were wrapped in a dark leather, mirroring the choice of dark clothing they wore. Tight trousers clung to their long legs and corseted long-sleeved shirts highlighted their taunt, yet slim frames.

The closer I got, the more I expected them to raise their blades in warning. But to my surprise, they did not. Before they opened the doors, they bowed their heads, ever so slightly, in our direction. It was a brief display of respect, enough that Hadrian noticed. Perhaps they knew they were in the company of distant royalty. Perhaps they were just not the monsters Kell had made them out to be.

If I was impressed with the grand features of the exterior, I was amazed beyond belief when we entered the building. Long corridors flanked by doors of smooth wood, each still clinging to the smells of their origins.

Carpets, each woven with detailed images and vibrate colors. I almost felt guilty to walk across them, scared I would ruin the art and skill. Curved glassless windows showed glimpses into the many rooms we walked past. I could see the interested faces of younglings and their elders who hovered above them, each with a different emotion plastered across their faces. But the one thing they each had in common, they all tipped their heads as we passed.

I looked towards our guides to see if they were in

fact the source of this admiration from the elves watching. But they showed no sign that they noticed. Not a single one looked me in the eye long enough for me to decipher what they were thinking.

Kell walked at the back of the group. I looked back to see her, but her eyes were glued to her feet. Illera and Emaline walked behind us, hand in hand and faces a painting of pure intensity. Emaline caught my glare and raised a brow carefully. Then, with a swift brush of her free hand, she flashed the handle hidden beneath the hem of her shirt.

She would be ready at any moment, that is what it meant. Besides the water skins I'd not thought she'd brought any weapon so when ours were all taken away they had missed that one.

My eyes couldn't stop skittering across the details of this place. A taste of nostalgia licked at my mind, reminding me of the first time I had walked through Vulmar Palace back in Olderim all those months ago. How my mind couldn't stop chasing the many beauties of the place. Here was no different.

Nyah and her guards turned at the end of the corridor for another pathway, and we followed. We walked around the stone courtyard that framed a large waterless fountain in its middle, made from a white stone, which looked dry and unused. Sand dusted the ornate surface, proving that it had been a long while since it was last used.

Once we came to the end of the first turning of pathway I almost walked into the back of one of the Morthi guards. I looked ahead to see Nyah knocking on yet another set of doors. These were made from metal.

Her knuckles rapped loudly, each place she hit making another hypnotic sound. She stood back, waited, then doors opened from within. When she turned to beckon us to follow her eyes finally rested upon mine, and she winked. It was so quick. One emerald eye flashed closed and open as if it never happened. But I saw it.

Play along, it said. *Be smart.*

Our group ambled into the room. Guided to stand in a curved line facing the chair which sat center stage, the Morthi guards deposited us and stood lining the walls.

In it sat a man. His skin was dark bronze, weathered and aged. His short hair was pure white, not a spec of any other tones within it. Even his thick brows were tinted cloud grays to match. But his eyes. His eyes were large, wise and bright. Like Hadrian's they burned with fire, yellows and oranges mixed together in a dance of swirling hues. It gave him a sense of youth when all his other features suggested otherwise.

The chair he sat in was no throne, nor did this man where a crown or signifier of any royalty. It was times like this that I knew knowledge gave those with it the power to control a conversation. But I knew nothing of this man or those around him who looked to him with respect.

"I admit, I never believed I would see your kind again," the man spoke. His voice was how I imagined it to be. Deep and tense. "Yet those with great minds do say that in desperate times comes the need of desperate measures. I thank your companion here for calling you to us."

He gestured to Nyah who stood at the side of his chair looking out at us with wonderous intent. Her arms were folded behind her back, shoulders broad and chin held high. *What was she playing at?*

Hadrian moved beside me, taking steps forward to control our side of the conversation. Princely and confident his spine was straight and eyes unblinking. "Forgive us for our entrance, but we were led to believe our companion was in danger."

"This must be Hadrian of Vulmar. Prince of Flames, or is he known as the King of Blaze?" The man ignored Hadrian's comment and turned to Nyah with the side of his plump mouth raised in humor. "I say I have heard much about you."

We all looked to Nyah to witness this bond she had created with the leader of these Morthi elves. She raised a hand and covered her mouth as if to stifle a laugh. Was she using her abilities over emotion to get on his right side? Knowing when to act and how by studying him? Or perhaps she was just being Nyah. Princess to the people, able to put even the greatest threats to ease.

"And yet we stand here knowing little about you." Hadrian bowed his head but didn't drop his eyes from the elven man.

"Oh, you will know all. But you can see that Nyah is not in any danger, not here. I will let her explain in a short moment why we had to call you here, for I am afraid our first encounter was not as positive as it should have been."

Hadrian pinched his gaze and narrowed in on Nyah. "If it is a conversation you are after I must ask your name. It is only polite after all."

"Mother told you not to talk to strangers?" he replied.

My heart almost stopped. I snapped my attention to Hadrian, but the only sign he had heard what the elven man said was the clenching of his fists. Even Nyah cringed were she stood.

"Have I missed something?" the leader questioned, looking between Hadrian and his new friend, Nyah.

"Name?" Hadrian just asked again.

"My name, although slandered by most beyond my city, is Paytric. I am the grandson of those who first stayed within this city after it was laid to destruction by your very ancestors many moons ago. It was my mother who followed her father in taking control of those who stayed here. It is our duty to protect them from any threat, just as our own king should have done before he ran for the shadows in fear moons ago." Kell shuffled her stance as Paytric turned his attention to her. "For years me and those brave enough to create homes, families amongst the ruins of the once great city of Merrik stayed with me. So welcome, for this is your home as well as ours. Especially you all, Hadrian, Zacriah and Emaline."

Paytric stood, bowed but never dropped his stare from us. All his followers copied him, each bowing our way. To us, the monsters who ruined this place. But why?

Once Paytric straightened, he gripped the edges of his seat and sat back down, gesturing for Nyah to take the floor. "Forgive me, but I am tired. Age is not a friend, but in fact a foe. Nyah, please, I will let you take this next part. I am still reeling from shame after our first encounter."

Paytric wasn't. Not with the lick of dry humor that thickened his words.

"Is this the part when I apologize for worrying you all?" Nyah said, shrugging her shoulders and wincing slightly. She spared us each a glance, moving her mouth into a silent apology as she looked to Emaline and Illera.

"That depends," I said, walking forward. "For the reasoning behind it."

I wanted to be angry for her misleading me, but I couldn't muster the necessary emotion. This was the first time I'd spoken with Nyah properly since our encounter in Lilioira. I was greatly relieved to see her on these sands.

"When we last spoke I told you we had experienced some, rough seas, so to say. Saying it put us off course is the biggest understatement. It was Neivel who spotted land. The crew was tired, and the unexpected heat had become close to unbearable. We took the chance and went towards it, unknowing that rest from the ocean was what we all needed. By that point we couldn't cope with staying on the sea a moment longer. When Paytric saw our ship, he did act as anyone would when unexpected guests dock on your land. It is safe to say that they believed we were a threat, and with the current situation we all face, I don't blame him."

I looked towards Paytric, whose jaw tightened, physically embarrassed by what happened so we did not push. That was a conversation for another time.

"All it took was a mention of you three and to prove we were not a true threat for them to lower their anger and welcome us," Nyah explained. "Since the initial meeting they have shown myself and the crew I brought nothing but respect and kindness."

"When you sent me all those feelings of pain, I thought you were in trouble," I said, annoyed at Nyah's actions.

"That would be my fault," Paytric called out. "As I said, we did not welcome her with kindness to begin with."

"I was beyond exhausted which made me act out." Nyah rubbed her wrists without realizing. "All is forgotten. We have common enemies to focus our attention on. That is another reason why I did not tell you that all was well Zac. I needed you to come, and I knew you at least have Hadrian tethered to your side. But bringing Emaline was a bonus."

"Why is that, Nyah?" Hadrian questioned her. "Pray tell, why is our being here important?"

"We are linked in more ways than you know," Paytric interrupted, his voice rough until he cleared it with a forced cough. "It is a new custom for the family of the chosen ruler of this city to sit beside his or her elder. But as you see the space beside me is bare, which was not always the case. I had a son. *Had.* Taken forcefully from me, only his tongue left as a token on the ruined sheets of his bed. I believe you are aware of what it is I refer too?"

I looked to Hadrian who was confused as me. But the coin soon dropped.

"Ah, I see the spark of knowing in your eyes for you recognize of what I speak on, even if it is tainted with the time that has passed since you laid eyes upon my son."

"Paytric refers to the Morthi prisoner Gordex presented to us when we first arrived in Olderim. The bait he used to entrap us in his not-so perfect lies and to help us join the new legion he wanted to create."

As Nyah said it, I could see the trail of black blood coating the flag-stone floors of the throne room in Olderim. I saw the hooded figure being dragged between two Niraen soldiers, then dumped on the ground beneath, who I thought to have been, King Dalior's feet. His tongue missing, his face swollen and peppered with bruises and cuts.

Fadine clapped a hand over her mouth to stifle the cry of shame. She, being a solider, would have interacted with the prisoner, not knowing the truth behind his life.

"My son, he was taken from his own room. One moment he was there, the next he was not. Only until our spies within your capital sent word back about the Druid's return and after they found his body in the dark cells beneath the palace, did I know the truth. This Druid," he spat. "He took my son and used him as a way to create conflict with our people. He pinned the blame on us, used lies to knot the truth into his own bidding. Why he took my son, I do not know. One day, as my power blinds him and sword pierces him I will ask. Was it coincidence or was it planned? Either way, he is our enemy as he was before when he manipulated the chosen

Dragori all those moons ago. When his people used them to level cities and spill blood. Just as I know my son leaving was not his choice, nor was it your ancestors' choice to kill so many here. We all know that." Paytric gestured around the room to this guards. "That is why we stayed. Those fearful elves in Vcaros hide from the truth, finding it easier to blame you all even to this day. They cover themselves in articles of gold as protection. They face every visitor with distrust and hate. Not us. No."

I looked to Kell to see her reaction, but her face was expressionless. It was as if she wasn't listening at all. Eyes unblinking, sweat rolling down her dark skin.

Not once during our entrance here had I felt the presence of gold. And the bowing of heads, the signs of respect. These elves did not fear us, far from it.

"I am glad, Dragori of three, that you have arrived within this city. I believe it is the Goddess's own way of showing you that we are not in fear, we do not hold hate in our hearts for you."

"Your kind words are appreciated," Hadrian said. "And my deepest apologies regarding your son. My heart"—Hadrian placed a hand atop it—"pains for your loss. I understand what it is to have one of your own blood leave for the next life. My deepest sympathies."

Paytric displayed his honest smile. "Nyah has told us of why you visit, and of what drove you here. She has added what may follow. That is why I have great wishes to speak with you. Me and those who entrust their lives in my family's hands, we have a proposition for you. As a united people, we offer you our numbers for the coming fight. It would be our greatest pleasure to stand by the Dragori's side and rewrite history. We have our own quarrels with the Druid, and if you have us, we would delight in sharing the field with you when it comes to the final dance."

This entire meeting had gone down different paths since we arrived, but this. This was never expected.

Hadrian stuttered, losing his sense of confidence for a moment as Paytric's offer settled in. Since arriving in Morgatis and witnessing Vcaros's reluctance to help our fight we had grown used to the resistance. But for these people. These strangers to offer their support without the need for promises was refreshing as it was needed.

"We would appreciate your help in the war to come, for it comes at a much-needed time. But you must forgive me for my brashness, this question would also be asked of me if I willingly offered up soldiers to strangers. What is it you want out of this?"

"I want nothing more than to repay the debts of my son. I wish to show this Druid the agony and torment he bestowed on me since my only heir was stolen. We all do."

Pain cut across Paytric's aged face for a moment. His

eyes glazed over and filled with a sheen of tears. As if his people sensed his sadness the entire room exploded in agreement. There shouts refreshed Paytric's smile once again.

Hadrian bowed, knowing this was not his time to question further. "So be it. We graciously accept your offer."

Paytric slapped his hands on the chairs arms and stood again, wobbling on his old legs. "Then we must feast this night and come sunrise you will return with Nyah to Vcaros's borders. We shall follow behind with our heads raised high. It is the greatest honor to face the uncertainty beside you all."

Hadrian walked towards Paytric who beckoned him over with his frail hands. Each took the others hand and shook, signifying the acceptance of our new allies.

CHAPTER
THIRTY-SIX

WE SAT AROUND on plush cushion, legs crossed, and hands occupied with fresh tankards of water. I rubbed my thumbs across the condensation of the tankard, watching the droplets form against the lines that marked my finger prints. The sunbaked air was not as hard to swallow during the night, but a fresh cold drink did help cool the insides that the night couldn't reach. Nyah was the only one who couldn't sit still. After attempting it she opted to pace the floor as she spoke to us.

"They are here, enjoying the fruits of this place. Negan is not as bothered about staying, but Neivel seems to be enjoying himself just a little too much." Nyah answered my question about her brothers, since they too had been on the ship and absence since we arrived. She's already told us news of the Alorian soldiers who occupied them on their journey. News had already been sent to their sleeping quarters within the building to prepare for our journey tomorrow.

"Nyah, how is it I never knew that you had siblings?" Hadrian asked once he finished chewing his piece of dried meat.

"You never asked. And besides, they are part of the Alorian armies, not the Niraen side. I thought it was too sensitive for me to bring them up since they left Thessolina to join another legion."

Nyah and Hadrian share a glance.

"I can assure you it does not bother me, not now when we all must fight as one," Hadrian answered.

"Have I missed something?" I said, clearing a drip of water from my thigh.

"It is unheard of for those born on a certain soil to join another's army. It happens, but it is not common." Fadine took over explaining the strange tension regarding Nyah's brothers. "My guess is they too are magickly blessed in some way, that is normally an easy route into joining Queen Kathine's many ranks."

Nyah tapped her nose and pointed at Fadine, "That may be the reason. Being of half Alorian blood, my brothers have the option to choose between which army they joined. It is their right."

"I am not disagreeing with you there!" Hadrian raised a hand in surrender. "Will these elusive brothers of yours be joining us tonight?"

"I hope not," Kell yawned. "It has been a long time since we have all been in the same room, but after spending extensive time with you on that ship I would be happy not to see them for another hundred years."

We all chuckled as Nyah pulled a dramatic face and put the back of her hand to her forehead.

"The only person I want to meet is a bed and who ever blesses us with dreams," Illera said.

"Here here!" Emaline raised her tankard. "Some sleep would be welcome."

Kell promptly stood, swaying her sharply cut black bob and walked off towards one of the doors in this room. We all ceased our laughing and turned to her. Not once had she said more than a single word since arriving.

"Kell?" I asked through a mouthful of spice bread.

She looked over her shoulder, "I'm going to get some rest."

"Has something bothered you?" Hadrian asked. "You have been distant since we arrived."

Kell shook her head. "Nothing that concerns you." Raising a splayed hand, she waved any more questions off and bade us goodnight.

"Is she always so talkative?" Nyah asked, taking Kell's now empty place on the floor.

"Something is off with her reaction here. I understand the tension between her people and those here, but the tension is palpable." I sipped my tankard.

"Zac, if she is your guard shouldn't you be staying with her?" Nyah asked, nodding her head in the direction

Kell had taken.

"I am sure one more night of privacy will be fine." I didn't need to look to Hadrian to know he was looking right at me. I could feel the warmth of this stare lingering across my skin like a kiss.

"There are three rooms, and forgive me, Fadine. I do not think I won't to be staying with someone I don't know."

"Nyah is right," I said, brushing Hadrian off with a flirtatious smile. "You stay with Fadine tonight, and I will stay with Nyah. She will be my guard now anyway."

"I still have not agreed to that, Zac," Nyah said, hands on hips. "Do you really think I have the capability of making you bleed? I don't think so."

"What if it was me?" Hadrian asked, opening the floor for yet another sarcastic reply from Nyah.

"You know very well I would have no problem doing it to you." She smiled. "No problem at all."

Hadrian clapped a hand to his broad chest and opened his mouth wide. "Me, your Prince. How could you."

"Listen up, Princey, you know full well that you are under the love-sick protection of Zac here. I would not be getting close to you by any stretch of the imagination."

"Oh, Nyah, it pains me to admit it, but I have missed you." Hadrian laughed, genuine and bright. It was infectious.

"I suppose I too have missed you," Nyah replied as she tried to stifle her laugh which shook her shoulders.

Hadrian stood up, stretched his large arms with a monstrous yawn. He then bent his legs and leaned down for me. With his smooth, yet powerful hands he cupped my face and brought his lips down on mine. Our kiss lingered on, fading the small audience we had into the background.

"Steady on." Fadine scoffed, almost spitting out her apple-stewed cake. "I'd very much like to enjoy this without the need to spit it all back out."

"What she said," Nyah added, raising a hand to block us out as if we were the sun.

We both turned, cheeks pressed together and looked at the two of them. Fadine focused on her tankard with more intent than she should have, and Nyah was peeking through the slits in her fingers.

"Rest well, Petal," Hadrian said, gifting me a final kiss on my forehead. I found it hard not to arch my back up to him and pull him down for another.

"And you," I replied, blushing red from my neck upwards.

"I suppose this is my cue." Fadine stood, stuffing the rest of the cake in her mouth and picking another slab up for the journey. "Night all."

Hadrian slipped off with Fadine following behind,

leaving me and Nyah alone.

We both released a breath at the same time. Each as labored as the other.

"Can you believe, after everything we have been through together, we have made it this far?" I said it, unsure why the sudden sadness made me choke on my words.

With everyone else gone the return of a still silence overwhelmed the room. No one else was here to take our minds off what myself and Nyah had shared within Lilioira.

Nyah released a breath and dropped her chin to her chest. Her red curls had been pulled up into a bun, only a few free stands tickled the sides of her face. "Even with my brothers close by, I have never felt so alone as I had when we were on that ship. Then, when we docked, I was scared. It seems they are the only emotions I have experienced in such a long time."

I reached a hand across the space to her, taking hers in mine. "We are all together again and soon this will be over."

"Do you really believe that? Because I don't. I have a terrible feeling in the pit of my stomach, one that I cannot seem to shake. It makes it hard to breath; my throat feels tight and dry. I believe these are all signs for something to come."

"We have a plan—"

"I know you do, but I don't see how it is going to work out. Playing Emaline as bait, hoping that Gordex just falls into place. I don't see how he will fall for that."

"At this point, it is our only hope. We need to destroy that Staff, then worry about doing the same to Gordex. He is only a man. And we have numbers. If we succeed in bringing him here, how is he going to bring the dead with him? Not only do we have soldiers sent from the King in Vcaros, thanks to you we have allies in Paytric and his people."

"And if this does not work? What if Gordex succeeds in his plans of raising the druids once more?" Nyah winced as she said it, rubbing her wrists again.

"Then we face that struggle, together. Like we do everything else," I said.

A single tear escaped from Nyah's emerald eye. It ran down her check, following the curves of her bone structure. She pushed her plate of food away.

I reached out and cleared the escaped tear with my finger.

"I dream of Jasrov you know." Her comment had me stumped. "When I was in Lilioira, Gordex paraded him around me every chance he got, ever since then I cannot stop seeing him in the dark of my mind. I can't sleep because of it. Every time I get close to shutting eyes I am terrified of what I might see."

It explained the obsidian circles that framed her

yellow-stained eyes. She was tired, even her skin had an ashen tone to it. I had put it down to long travel and a lack of fresh water.

"I am here tonight, and I will make sure you sleep. Nothing can harm you, not with me watching," I said, pure displeasure at seeing my friend like this raced through me. I had never seen her teetering on the edge of so many feelings before. I wondered what I would feel if I shared in her empathic abilities. Would I see her soul in tatters as her mind was?

Nyah slid from her pillow and encased me in a hug. The fresh salts of sea clung to her hair, reminding me of my own time on the ship. We held each other, friends sharing in a moment that was both rare and special.

She meant a lot to me. I made it my own mission to help her through this time as she would with me. I also dusted the list in my mind, the one which kept the many promises I had made to Gordex.

For hurting her, I would hurt him tenfold.

"I need more time to organize my people," Paytric explained for the third time that morning. I didn't know if it was his age that had him repeating himself or the excitement of joining our side. "Will you be fine traveling the way back alone?"

Kell tipped her head. "As fine as we were when we arrived here without help. Do not worry, I will have the camp prepare for your arrival, so you have a place to rest. Do not worry."

Since meeting with Kell this morning her allusive mood from the night before had simply evaporated. We'd found her sharing words with Paytric over breakfast.

"For the first time in moons I hold hope for a new time between *our* peoples." Paytric smiled, eyes closed and skin glowing. It was more than a natural glow. It was as if the burning sun above favored his skin and took home in it, shimmering from the inside.

"Do not make that judgement just yet," Kell replied, shaking Paytric's hand for a final time. "I have much to do. Many minds to change."

"I whole heartedly believe you capable of it." Paytric bowed his head, resting his age-spotted hand over his chest.

Kell had already called for our serpents which waited beyond the city's fallen walls.

It was decided the Alorian elves would march with Paytric's people. Hadrian had suggested as much after talking with them, Emaline in tow. Another day's rest for them would ultimately do them good for the fight to come.

Paytric agreed and promised that he would feed, water and help guide them back to us when the time was ready.

Once we all said our goodbyes, we only had to wait for Nyah to return with her brothers. It would seem that they'd been having a good time, too much to bother leaving when we had called for them. When she finally walked towards us, brothers walking steps behind her, we all were drenched in sweat and more than ready to leave.

"Negan, Neivel meet my friends. Friends, my brothers." Nyah introduced them. In turn, my companions shook her hands and greeted one another. I was last.

"Good to see you both again in better circumstances," I said, taking their hand and shaking in turn.

"And you, Zacriah," Neivel said for the both of them.

"I admit, I didn't think this would be our next meeting place," Negan said through the corner of his mouth. "Not that I am complaining." He waved a hand to a Morthi girl who stood in the arch of a nearby ruined building. Her pale face blushed, red creeping up her neck as she waved back, blowing a hearty kiss for Negan who reached in the air to grab it.

Nyah rolled her eyes and pushed past her lust-sick brother, moving for Kell who secured the reigns on the serpents.

The twins towered above everyone, including

Hadrian who seemed shocked at their height when they got close. They both greeted Hadrian by bowing but that was soon stifled. Hadrian never had enjoyed that type of introduction.

"It is great to meet you both, but truly there is no need for formalities. We are all a far way from home, so let us leave the bowing and titles for when we return."

"What Nyah said was right," Neivel joked to his brother.

Negan smirked, mumbling a response under his breath.

Hadrian's face twisted in confusion as he regarded both boys. "And pray tell, what has she been saying now?"

Both brothers elbowed each other, holding the secret between them.

"Nothing but good things one hopes," Hadrian pushed on, unblinking.

"What did you expect of me? That I would sing your praises? Someone needs to bring you back down to earth," Nyah shouted over at Hadrian from where she stood with the serpents.

"I'd very much like to get moving," Kell added from beside Nyah. "I am ready to get all this traveling over with."

Whilst Nyah and the rest began their preparations for the journey, I took the opportunity to speak with

Emaline and Illera.

"Did you both rest well?"

"As well as you can when it is hot and sticky in that breezeless place," Emaline said as Illera helped tie the belt back around her waist. It had ripped clean off when she shifted yesterday. Her hair was wet, her skin glistening with equal moisture.

Illera too still rung her golden hair in both hands, causing drips of water to fall onto the sands beneath her.

Hadrian had told me that they'd both visited the shore this morning to refill Emaline's water skins. But I could see their tardiness was a result of something different entirely.

"I couldn't agree more," I said. It was awkward speaking with Emaline, knowing that each day was one closer to using her as a lure. I knew it was all in my head, but the thought still made me cringe with discomfort.

"When we get back I think we should all discuss our plan again, finalize the details that we have missed out on."

Emaline thanked Illera who finished. "We talked about that last night. I know we plan on using me but have no idea how you want to do it."

"And I will interject here. I am all for supporting Emaline's decision to go along with this plan of yours, but I will have a say in just how you are going to be using her," Illera said, brows pinched.

"I can assure you nothing will be passed if we all do not agree."

Illera spoke up again, "Another thought. We should all get some training in. Shifting yesterday and the way my body aches today proves that we are not close to fighting yet. It has been a short while since I have had to, and I feel rusty."

"I am sure we can do that," I replied. "I think we could all do with some practice and training. It is a good suggestion."

"Always up for another duel, Zacriah," Illera said, a hint of mischief in her voice.

"Somehow I don't think we will be doing that. Not after how it ended last time."

"Hmm," Illera shrugged. "Maybe you are right. But that Simian seems to be a perfect choice for a partner. I could do with getting some tension out on him."

I hadn't thought about Simian for a while, and even with distance I still didn't like him.

"I am glad I am not the only one who is suffering with his appearance in the camp."

Emaline added, "I don't think many like him. Hadrian must've been desperate to pick him as one of the New Council."

Despite my dislike for Simian, I could see why Hadrian did it. To give everyone a voice.

With our three new companions we had to travel in groups of three. Kell was quick to pass over the concealed golden weapon to Nyah and offer for the twins to travel with her. She said it was for better company, and I could agree to some levels.

Hadrian sat up front, me behind him and Nyah at the back. Her face was pressed into the stiff material of my tunic as we began our journey.

After her broken sleep last night, I was sure she would take this chance to catch up on the journey.

She'd woken me with shouts of terror, eyes sleepy and glazed. Whatever visions troubled her must have been bad. I had never seen or heard someone in such a state from a dream alone.

<hr/>

"Get up." Hadrian jolted, causing my cheek to sting under impact. "Zacriah, now."

The use of my full name rid me of any slumber I was clinging too.

I was ready to argue, shout my discomfort at being awoken, but noticed that all three serpents had come to a stop beyond camp. My eyes were blurry from sleep, only rubbing them a couple of times helped them still the vision before us.

Tents lay strewn across the grounds. Rocks protruding in places that had not been before. Destruction lay out before us, as huddles of our soldiers began shouting for us with arms waving in panic or relief, I could not tell.

But the part that had my heart skipping beats was the ship. The prison in which Marthil had been kept in.

Through its middle a spike of earth caused it to rise from the sea. It hovered, hanging in almost two pieces, with planks of wood and rubble floating in the water around it.

The spear of rock was unnatural and impossible. Impossible unless made from someone with the power to command earth.

Marthil.

"GO!" Hadrian shouted, urging our serpent to speed for the camp as we all expected the worse.

CHAPTER
TDIRTY-SEVEN

THE NIRAEN SOLDIERS who greeted us were each covered in sand and grit. Unarmed and unprepared, they stood in panicked huddles, some faces streaked with tears, others cut with anger. Morthi warriors I didn't recognize muddled around them. They were dressed in dark coal uniforms that were untouched by the same destruction our soldiers were covered in.

Sent from Vcaros I was sure. They were armed, points of their swords and readied palms aimed at the empty, destroyed camp before them.

"What in this world has happened here?" Hadrian shouted, running the final distance to his people. The sea of soldiers and warriors alike parted for Hadrian and closed in around him. Shouts erupted.

"The prisoner, she broke free," a young solider said, her chestnut hair bounced in curls down to her small waist. Her narrow nose and sharp eyes were pinched in stress, face pale from shock and something else.

"Marthil, where is she?" I asked, trying not to shout.

Peering back to the ship, I knew they would not stay there. It was moments from snapping in two and falling to the pits of the ocean.

"No one saw her leave. She came in the fringes of night whilst most of us where either sleeping or enjoying the relaxation the dark brought with it. We didn't expect a fight, nor did we give her one."

Hadrian rubbed his strong jaw, surveying his soldiers and the state they were left in. "Tell me everything from start to finish. Do not miss out on any details, no matter how small they might be to you it could be important."

The soldiers looked around, waiting for someone to take control and speak. It was a broad-shouldered guard who stepped forward and answered Hadrian. He had a leaking cut below his left eye. But it was not his only wound, the other was invisible to the eye. He hobbled over, held up by a companion whose arm strained as he helped him stand.

"I was stationed on the ship when it happened. There was a monstrous crack that was followed by towering spikes, which exploded through the center of the ship. It was as if the earth wanted to swallow us whole. All I remember after was the sea. I'd fallen into it and watched, beneath the waves, as the ground beneath snaked up like water. In the rush it was hard to make out what was happening. I tried to swim to shore, but I'd hurt myself in the fall. By the time I got there, it was too late to warn them."

"How many are hurt?" Kell said, gesturing for one of the Morthi warriors to come over. "We will need more supplies immediately. The wounded must be helped and those displaced need a new place to stay."

"Everyone is accounted for," Vianne stepped through the crowd, face splashed with muck. Her dress no longer looked the pure white it had been when we left her. It was stained, ripped at the hem. "Besides one. Simian."

That single name silenced the entire crowd.

"Why?" Hadrian said, voice tempered and dark. Even I knew Simian was linked to this the moment Vianne did not suggest otherwise.

"There was a conflict between us both after you left. It was about Marthil. He blindsided me and took the gold weapon. I would have stopped him, but I didn't come to until it was far too late." I could see the bruise that was in her hairline and the cut that sliced her right brow in two. "He is the only one who has not been seen since Marthil escaped."

"Did anyone else see Simian before Marthil's escape?"

Soldiers turned to Warriors with raised shoulders, yet no one stepped forward.

"Simian told me what he planned," Vianne murmured.

"From stealing the weapon, I can guess what it is he wanted to do," I said, fists clenched at my side.

"To kill her whilst you were all away. Simian knew that no one would stop him besides me, so he dealt with me. But it would seem that his plan failed him."

"We need to go to the ship." I turned for the view, looking at the vessel. Orange and pinks melted into the sky as the morning sun was reaching its zenith. "There will be answers there. Perhaps Simian is trapped within it."

"For his safety I hope he is not," Hadrian growled.

"I have sent soldiers to scan it, but it is too dangerous. It is hanging on by snapped wood and could give way at any moment. I highly suggest it is left alone," Vianne said, twisting the band around her wrist.

"I need to go and see for myself." I brushed off Vianne warning of danger. If Marthil escaped, I had to know why. "In the meantime, you must all prepare for a fight. She could return at any moment, and we must be ready. All of us."

Emaline grabbed a hold of my upper arm and pulled me. "I will come with you. If that ship does break, I can help if we fall into trouble with the water."

I nodded, glad not to be alone.

"Fadine and I will organize our soldiers and get them ready. Kell, could you speak with your King? We will need his support urgently," Hadrian said, rolling the sleeves of his shirt up to his muscled arms as he prepared to get helping. "Tell your King of Paytric's offer to help us, perhaps it will bruise his ego enough to send his soldiers in full force."

I must not have been the only one to catch Kell wince.

"I'll try, that is all I can promise. Marthil is as much of a threat to the city as she is to you. He will want to make sure his own are secure and safe before he assists you," Kell said.

"If that is the case"—everyone listened in to Hadrian carefully— "then we will do it with what we have."

Kell wasted no time in leaving for the serpent, which soon headed off towards Vcaros.

"We will need scouts," Fadine said. "To make sure that all perimeters of the camp have eyes alert to prevent any more surprise encounters with the demoness."

"You know the soldiers better than me. Fadine, you are the best thing I have to a First Commander. Help me with them. I believe that no one can do this job better than you." Hadrian took her shoulders in his hands.

"No need to panic," she replied then rushed off into the crowd of waiting soldiers.

Emaline and I took that moment to head for the shore. Once our booted feet touched sea, we both looked upon the ship.

"She was held in the lower levels of the ship, that is where we will need to look."

Emaline held a hand over her eyes, blocking out the sun which reflected off the glass-like ocean and into her eyes. "This is not good, Zacriah. If she has escaped, she has few places to hide within the Doom. I really don't see her staying away for long. And now she is reunited with her element…"

"I know," I replied, chewing the skin of my bottom lip. "I'd like to know what gave her the strength to escape in the first place. Being out in the water should've kept her subdued."

"And if Simian is still alive?"

A bubble of deranged laugh slipped out of my lips. "Then I hope you can stop me from finishing what Marthil started."

I was the first in the air. Emaline was a beat of her wings behind me.

The rock formation had been conjured from the bed of the ocean. It was wet, rivulets of sea water dripping down its sharp face onto the broken panels of the ship in which it had penetrated. The force of the rock had lifted the vessel clean out of the water, causing it to hang above from the sea's surface. White gulls danced around the formation, their mocking calls irritating and unwanted.

When I flew close enough, they scattered in the wind, not wanting to get close to me. But soon flew back to the point of the spear of rock as if something that far up caught their attention.

I had to hover above the ship's deck, scared that my weight would be all it needed to fall back into the ocean in two separate pieces. From this distance I could see enough.

There were no bodies strewn across the ship, and the absence of rowing boats suggested those who had to get off had done so in time. Or perhaps they simply jumped overboard like the broad solider had told us. But Simian. He would be here somewhere. He had to be.

I clenched my fists at my side, pointed talons cutting into the palm of my tough, scaled palm.

I looked to Emaline and pointed towards the open doors that would have led down into the prison cells in which Marthil had been kept. There should have been enough room for us to fly within without causing a tip in the scales. Emaline nodded, urging me to go first. I paused through the doors and into the corridors below. My wings at full stretch almost touched either side of the walls.

"I won't fit," Emaline said, hanging in the air above the door. "There is no way we can both go down there. Can you manage it alone?"

"I'll be as quick as I can," I replied.

"If you don't find Simian, do not go looking deeper. One touch on this ship and it looks like it will snap clean in two—"

As Emaline warned me the groan of wood screamed around us. It echoed down the mess of corridor, followed by sharp clicks and screeches.

"Be wary," she warned.

"Good luck."

Emaline turned, wings flexing and buffeted wind atop me. She flew off out of view, which left me to the ruined corridors of the lower deck.

I tried to keep as compact as I could as I traveled into the pits of the ship. Only once did I brush my feet across the flooring, which had my heart skipping a beat. The ceiling at that part had caved in slightly, causing me to duck and be closer to the floor.

Ahead of me was the door to the cells, and it was open and waiting. Whereas before there was only a few beams of light, now an entire part of the room was lit thanks to that monstrous, jagged hole in the wall. It gave a view of sea. Nothing else. Where this portion of the ship was tipped and now facing downwards it sent my stomach spiraling. Water lapped up in greeting, so close that splashes dampened the floor of Marthil's cell.

Now I could see how she escaped. Straight through the wall. No one had let her out, she had found it on her own. But how? Where did her power come from when she should have been kept weak amongst the water?

I flew close to the cell, stopping just before the metal bars which I leaned on. Nothing seemed out of the ordinary except for the plate of rotten food that was resting up against a wall within the cell. I noticed something green beneath it, but it was turned upside down, so I couldn't get a better look.

Reaching for my magick I extended my will and used my air to flip the plate around. It settled back down, giving me a glimpse of what looked like a plant growing from the rotten mound of molded food. I reached out again, forcing the plate to skid across the ground towards me close enough for me to pick it up.

Scrutinizing what was in fact a plant, I tried not to inhale the vile scents the rotten food gave, but there was also something sweet about it. Coming from the three plump, amethyst bulbs which dangled like lanterns from the fresh vine. These bulbs, the plant, I had seen it before. Forbian.

It was all beginning to make sense.

Marthil had told me she'd used the Forbian up, but

perhaps she didn't account for the seeds she would've carried without telling me. She'd grown a new supply from the rotting food that had accumulated during her imprisonment. She'd not eaten on purpose. Biding her time, she had waited for the right moment. Simian's arrival must have just urged her to act sooner.

I lifted a stem with my finger. The jade green vine had been ripped. Marthil must have taken one of the bulbs and devoured it when he arrived. It would have masked her weakness and given her a renewed strength as it had when I fed it to her during the storm.

She'd played us.

"Zacriah! You need to come and see this," I heard Emaline shout from beyond the ship. Even without seeing her I could hear the discomfort in her voice. A panic that was alien to her usual calm attitude.

Urged to rush and leave, I plucked the remaining three bulbs of Forbian from the stem and dropped the plate on the floor. It landed on its side, rolling out through the hole and landing within the sea in a loud splash. Pocketing the bulbs, I turned back for the door and flew beyond it, trying to reach Emaline with as much speed as I could muster still without touching the floor and walls of the corridor.

"Up here," her voice came from above me. I looked up, shielding the suns glare to see her hovering next to the formations tip high above. Pushing as much power into my wings I flew up to meet her, unsure what it could be that sparked her panic.

The gulls had given her space but flew at a distance around her. Their angered cries cut right through my head.

As I got close to her the smell hit.

Simian.

The tip of the rock had burst right through his stomach from his back and all the way through. His arms and legs, lifeless and limp, dangled as he was suspended far above the boat. Dead. He was dead. Red stained the dark rock, dribbling down for as far as I could see. Sea birds hung in the air around us, waiting. It explained why so many had been here when we arrived.

As they flew around us, I spotted their red-stained beaks. This was a feast for them and we had interrupted.

"It would seem his plan truly did backfire on him," I said into my hand, covering my own nose and mouth from the stench of death.

Emaline held a hand over her mouth and nose which muffled her voice. "Do we leave him here or bring him back to camp with us?"

I contemplated leaving him, yet even after everything I knew we had to take him back. Not out of respect, but to show our soldiers what Marthil is capable of. She may have only killed one during her escape, but she would be back and could do it again.

"If we leave him, the Goddess will look down on us. On the other hand, every time we look towards this ship it will be a reminder of what happened here." I couldn't take my eyes off his face. His wide eyes were nothing more than empty sockets, black and crusted. Had the birds already devoured them first.

"In that case, you can do the heavy lifting. I am *not* touching him." Emaline cringed away, waving her hand for me to start.

"I will." I flew closer and stopped at something that was first unseen from the angle he hung at. "Emaline, look."

Sticking out the side of his neck was the hilt of a buried dagger. I had not seen it before because of the angle we viewed him from, but it was clearly there. The dark handle stood out against his ashen skin, in death it had taken on a pearlescent tone. "This is what killed him first. He was already dead by the time the earth pierced him."

This was more of a sign, a mark that she left to say she had been here. For me, I knew its meaning. *My power is back,* it said. *I am the threat now.*

"Let me," I reached forward, wrapping my hand around the handle and pulling. At first, I thought it was just the reflection of the sun that caused the blood-coated metal to gleam gold. But then I felt the instant drain of my power and the violent turning of my mind.

Emaline slammed her palm against my fist, causing me to drop the dagger. We both watched from our height as it tumbled far below, landing on the ships broken deck. I didn't hold it long enough to fully be drained from its presence. Seeing it fall from view stilled the sudden spinning.

My mind was still spinning from the quick interaction I had with the gold. Being so close made me feel weak in such a way that my lungs hurt to breath. Even Emaline looked flustered being close to it.

"We need to get away from here," I said, noticing some of Simian's blood had gone on my fingers from touching the dagger. I tried rubbing it on my trousers, but it only seemed to make it worse. Spreading the red down my fingers and into the belly of my nails.

"That would be wise."

Emaline was already backing off from the body as I followed.

I reminded myself to send someone to retrieve it after we arrived. But my first port of call was telling them all what I had found. My initial thought about taking him back had disappeared the moment I'd pulled the golden dagger from his neck.

Our wings carried us away from the ship. Emaline didn't turn back to look at the body the entire way. But for me, I couldn't help but keep peering over my shoulder.

Once my feet touched down on the shore of the camp I looked back for a final glance. Even from this distance I could see the cloud of birds, each fighting for their turn to take a piece of Simian. Then a single thought passed through my mind, making me sick and ice cold.

Perhaps, when they returned to get Simian's body, there would be nothing left to bring back.

CHAPTER
THIRTY-EIGHT

HADRIAN PULLED OUT the items of dark clothing which had been brought back after being cleaned by the Morthi after I returned from Merrik. One by one he laid them out on the bed. When Gordex had given it to me, it was a way of using me as a representation. A costume. But here it was the best choice I had for protection if a fight were to come. It would allow me to shift freely without worry that I would rip and destroy the material.

The plated leather top was pulled over my head. Hadrian was careful not to catch my skin upon the silver points that the scaled armor presented. My boots went on last, something I could do by myself. The tent lacked a mirror, so I relied on my touch to make sure everything was in order. I ran my hands down the cold material, fingers bumped across the scale-like stitching of my skin fitted trousers.

Only my neck and face were free from protection, every other part of my skin was covered. The gloves which were part of the top part of the uniform only had slight slits at the tips in case my claws needed to grow free.

I flexed my fingers, testing the durability of the uniform for yet another time.

"It may be taboo for me to admit this aloud, but you look beautiful in it," Hadrian purred, standing back and admiring me from a distance. He had his hand on his chin as his head tilted, eyes scanning from boot to head.

Hadrian's hungry eyes had not stopped devouring me. Even with material to cover my body his eyes lingered across me.

"Beautiful? Some reason I don't think that was Gordex's incentive when he gave this to me," I replied.

"Beautiful, deadly, wonderous, beastly." Hadrian listed off words, counting with his fingers as he did it. "So many things I could say about you. All as true as the next."

"Well, Prince Hadrian. Would you like me to list the many things I think about you?" I stepped close to him, running my hand down his Niraen uniform of purples, earth-browns and threads of silver which linked the different parts together.

"I would like nothing more than that," he whispered. "But we must help our soldiers, and I worry that you have so many wonderful things to say about me that it could take us all day."

We had only taken a short while away from camp

and already Hadrian was itching to return. After Emaline and I had returned and informed them all on what happened with Simian we had got straight into cleaning up camp. Was it selfish that I wanted a few more moments with Hadrian to speak only with him?

"She will come back, won't she?"

"Kell has strictly told us that besides Vcaros, the deserts are empty for miles. She has not got many places she could be hiding. Eventually, she will come back. But the difference is, this time we are all here. This time we *will* be ready."

I released a sigh. "And when she does, we take her down?"

Hadrian tapped my nose. "Correct, Petal, we end her reign of destruction together. She has killed one of our own, again. We may not have agreed with Simian, but he is still a life lost. Marthil will be held accountable for that."

"She had it planned all along," I reiterated what the New Council had discussed when me and Emaline arrived back from the ship. "Savoring the rotten foods until she could grow the Forbian and regain her strength. Maybe Simian was right, I should never have trusted her to see the right and wrongs. I feel a fool. He warned me that the next death would be on my hands."

I blinked, and in the dark I saw his red blood staining my palms as it had on the ship when we found his body.

Hadrian cupped my cheeks. "The only fool in this story is the one ready to go up against us. It is your ability to see the best in others that I find so endearing. Do not let this experience taint that part of you."

"It is hard not to."

"Well, let me help you. Once Simian is brought back and we show our soldiers that we care for each one lost in this war, we will restore your own hope in hope."

"Hope in hope, how clever?" I forced a smile and a laugh.

"That is me all over... clever," Hadrian said, handing rubbing my shoulder and trailing down my spine.

I went up on my tiptoes and planted a kiss on his lips. It was a hard, passionate kiss one that helped take my mind off everything.

"Thank you, for staying by me," I said.

"No need to thank me, Petal. It is my honor to be the one here with you. I do it for you because I know, if and when the tables are turned, you would be doing the same for me. Goddess knows you have done it for me. It is I who has been the burden, you have done nothing but try and help me."

"I love you."

"So much," Hadrian replied, his lips pressing into my hair line. "As do I."

The entrance to the tent burst open, followed by the

two soldiers who Fadine had chosen to retrieve Simian's body. They were both shifters, my age, who I recognized from the initiations when we arrived in Olderim. I could not remember what it was they could do, but Fadine had suggested they both would not need to touch the ship to retrieve Simian. My guess was they both were birds of sorts.

I pulled away from Hadrian, waiting for their update.

"Forgive us for the intrusion but it is of utmost importance that we saw you."

"No need for the apologies, please speak up." Hadrian waved for them to continue whilst holding onto my hand and no letting go.

"The shifters body is missing your highness."

The soldiers comment shocked us both. How could he have gone missing when I had seen him hours before? Surely he could not have been devoured so quickly.

"We searched the entire ship, but neither of us could find anything. There was blood on the deck, below the rock in which we were told he would be. It is as if he fell from that great height. But there is nothing more to see."

"And you looked everywhere?" Hadrian's brows creased in worry.

"Every possible place we could reach. The only other option is he fell into the sea once his body dislodged from the rock."

The moment of paused silence caused both soldiers

to hang awkwardly at the entrance of the tent. Behind them the sky was darkening into night, giving birth to the many stars that filled the clear sky.

"Thank you both—"

We all turned when a hearty growl broke the silence beyond the tent. All the hairs on my neck stood on end as the entire camp washed into silence. The silence lasted only a few beats of my heart.

Something was wrong. Only one creature in this camp could make such a sound.

Hadrian and I ran. The soldiers followed. Out feet kicked up sand as we moved through the darkening camp. My boots, plated underneath, made it easier to run across the sands making me get to our destination first when another growl sounded within the tent ahead. Emaline and Illera's tent.

The roar lit up the night, shaking the very world around me. Shadows of three figures moved within the tent, highlighted by the candle light within.

Throwing open the tents entrance I took in the scene before me. Emaline lay sprawled across the carpeted ground, dagger stabbed through her stomach. Illera, in lioness form, tossed her monstrous head from side to side as she shook the lump of flesh she held in her mouth.

By the time she spat it out I had already unleashed my own magick and aimed it at the figure. My air lifted him from the ground, causing the flame of candles to flash over its face.

Simian's face.

Black smoke snaked from his eyeless sockets, matching the slithers of smoke which bled from his wounds instead of red blood. His veins, prominent and black, protruded from his skin. He snarled, full of dark power. His body was still in the grips of death, but that no longer mattered. Not when the Druid now controlled him.

"What a welcome." Gordex's voice seeped out from his puppet. "How grand it is to see you again, my boy. And here I was thinking it would have been sooner. But I did tell you that timing is key."

Pure anger was my reaction. It exploded from me as I screamed towards Simian's body. The tent ripped from the ground, leaving us all exposed to the night and sky. I no longer worried about Hadrian, Emaline or Illera. My focus was on Simian and the deranged power that riddled throughout him.

"How beautiful anger looks on you. It blossoms with such grace. I am proud—"

"Enough," I cried, throwing my arms forward and with it my storm of power. It ripped sand from the ground beneath me and with a simple turn of my palms I directed it to spin in a vortex around us. It blocked out everyone else. I didn't want them to see what I was to do.

"Where are you hiding, Druid?" I spat.

"When you seem so irritated towards me? Why would I divulge that information to you?"

I began to close my fist, which caused my control vortex to close in on us. It wouldn't harm me. But Simian, it would scratch away at his remaining skin until he was nothing but bone and shadow.

"You are close. I know you are." He couldn't control his shadowbeings at a distance. He'd told me that himself back in Lilioira.

"And you are alert, as I have always told you."

I screamed my frustration, bending my knees and thrusting my hands upwards. His compliments urged my anger on.

My mixed emotions caused the air to lift Simian's body from the floor until he dangled inches above it. His emotionless face did not seem bothered because in death he would not feel this. But I knew Gordex was watching through his eyeless sockets. Let me show him exactly what the power he had given me could do.

"I often think about my Alina. She was a kind woman. She'd do anything to please me, anything. Then I think about you and your powers. How you revealed yourself to me that day in the throne room of Vulmar palace. What a dreary place that was. Do you remember how it felt when you killed her? Do you ever dream of the lingering strength that follows when taking a life—"

"Quiet," I sneered, looking through my lashes as my air imprisoned the shadowbeing.

My winds picked up, mirroring my growing anxiety.

"I hungered for that power, and now I share in it with you. As I share in your Prince's and Marthil's. And soon, the final piece will fall into place."

Gordex had always enjoyed sharing in his achievements, but this was sick. Warped and strange.

"You will never get to Emaline, I promise that."

"Will I not? That promise is moments too late my boy," Gordex said, his voice full of amusement as it slipped through Simian's unmoving mouth.

A vision of Emaline on the floor beyond my vortex broke through my mind. The dagger. All at once I wanted to drop this power and check on her. I'd been blinded by Gordex's presence that I pushed her to the back of my mind.

Gordex's laugh brought me back from my mind. "You are a dream, my boy. So easily distracted."

Then Simian's body sagged, the black smoke disappearing all at once. Gordex was gone.

Taking a deep breath, I was able to push my anger down enough to lower my winds. I could see beyond at once at the many soldiers who stood around, weapons drawn and shifters ready.

I could not see Emaline or Illera, but Hadrian stood waiting with golden blood spilled across his hands and a face to match that shock that mine must have shown.

Simian's body thumped to the ground, and out the corner of my eye I watched a handful of soldiers rush it. He would not be a bother now, but I would have his head removed in case of Gordex's return.

"Where is she?" I asked Hadrian, still pushing my winds down. The silver strands that filled the air around me were pesky and unresponsive, revealing in their freedom for the moments they could.

"The dagger, Petal, it was the same one you and Emaline had pulled from Simian's neck."

"No," I breathed, winds picking up with my anger once again. My knees almost gave way, the realization slamming into me.

"I had to remove it, but Emaline is still not responding." It explained the gilded blood that dripped across his hands. Alorian blood. Emaline's blood. "Nyah has been sent with her to keep check on her. I worry when she comes around, it will be too late. The gold would have tainted her."

"Heart Magick," I said, my words no more than a whisper. "Hers will be free."

Hadrian closed his eyes and nodded, sighing in defeat.

"We've failed before it even began."

Hadrian grabbed a hold of me, taking my shoulders in his large hands to calm me down. "Stop it, Zacriah."

His use of my full name shocked me into silence. "This is no one's fault. We were not to know that Gordex could control a body from such a distance. Only with hindsight could we have stopped him."

"You are wrong." Tears of frustration and panic for Emaline slid down my checks. "Gordex is not far. He is here. It Is the only way he could control Simian."

"Are you certain?"

I simply closed my eyes in response. From what I'd seen and heard whilst in Gordex's presence, I knew the limits of his compulsion of the dead. He was here, and now he had Emaline we'd be seeing him in the flesh soon enough. That I was sure of.

CHAPTER
ThIRTY-NINE

EMALINE'S DARK SKIN was coated in a thick layer of sweat. Shadowed circles ringed her closed eyes below the four lines that had creased her forehead as she struggled with her pains.

Her agony was written in every wrinkle, mark and flutter of her lids. Her expression was one of pure horror.

Illera sat at the side of the cot, holding Emaline's hand in both of hers. Occasionally she would release one hand, so she was free to dab the sweat from Emaline's upper lip and forehead with the cool cloth the Morthi healers had provided on their short, brief visit. Even the King's healers were not allowed to stay away from the city for long.

Someone had cut away at the material of her tunic to reveal her stomach which was now covered in layers of swab and material to stunt the flow of gold-tinged blood. We had been waiting for the return of a healer who was going to stitch the wound back together, but with each passing second, I was closer to helping myself.

"I can feel it trying to take over," Emaline mumbled in her state of hysteria. She pulled a hand free which shook as she pointed above her stomach. "It feels cold inside. I am trying to fight it."

I'd seen many civilians from my own home to know what deliria looked like. Emaline was in the rough fringes of it as we all looked down upon her.

"Shh," Illera cooed beside her. Tears leaked from her eyes, dribbled down her cheeks which proceeded to fall to the ground in quick succession. "You need to get some sleep. Rest is going to help you, Emaline."

"I'm scared."

I clapped a hand over my mouth to stifle my cry.

Illera leaned forward and buried her head in Emaline's chest. Her shoulders shook as more torrential sobs took her over. Emaline tried to raise a hand to comfort Illera, but she winced at the movement and released a labored breath of pain.

"Will you stay with me? Will you keep me safe in the darkness?" Emaline whispered, face paling.

I bit down on my finger, trying not to cry myself. Hadrian pressed himself up behind me, wrapping her arms around my waist as we watched the two before us share in this desperate moment.

"What kind of question is that? I will be here to slay the monsters and vanquish the dark. Just make sure you stay with me because I might need saving as well."

The corner of Emaline's lip lifted. "Don't fret. I am not going anywhere for long. I just need to sleep this off."

I admired Emaline's act of bravery. We knew she would pull through, for Gordex would not want her dead.

Perhaps that was why the Morthi healers were not helping as efficiently as they should have been. Maybe the King told them not to, to keep Gordex at bay for as long as possible. But I couldn't just watch this. The bulbs in my breast pocket would help Emaline heal, but it was a double-edged sword. If she pulled through and her Heart Magick was free, then Gordex would come. But to have any luck at winning this fight we needed both Emaline's mind and brawn.

"I am sick of waiting for someone to sweep in from Vcaros and help her." I couldn't hide my annoyance. Seeing someone, someone I cared about, in so much pain stirred me the wrong way. "Marthil left Forbian on the ship. That was how she was able to regain her strength, enough for her to break out. Here." I pulled two bulbs for luck from my pocket and presented it to Illera who looked confused.

"What do you want me to do with that? I haven't a clue how to make that edible."

"Nor do I, but it is best she takes it in raw form than

leave her to drown in her pain. She will heal quicker if she takes it," I said.

"Tell me why you think I am going to let you feed that to her when you or I have no clue just how the herb will affect her in its raw form. You don't know of the side effects, or dosage. No, we will wait for the proper healers to arrive." Illera put her foot down on my idea, but I still had room to persist.

"Illera, listen. I know you are upset right now. I get it. But there is a possibility that this darkness she is mumbling about is Heart Magick. The longer we leave her to fight it, the weaker she will become, and the more likely it will take over. I strongly suggest we give this to her."

I didn't want to admit aloud that it was likely too late for Emaline.

Illera spared Emaline a glance, one full of pity and sadness. It was interesting how quick her iron wall could be replaced when she looked anywhere else, but the moment she looked to Emaline, she melted like fresh butter over a fire.

"Do you trust me, Illera? If I truly believed this would harm Emaline, I would never suggest it."

Illera took a moment to respond. She furrowed her brows above her sad eyes and nodded, more like she gave up then agreed.

"I promise you, Zacriah, if you hurt her…"

Fadine did not need to finish her threat.

I reached out and touched her shoulder. "Trust in me as I trusted in you."

She smiled weakly then stood so fast her stool almost toppled over. "I'm not watching."

Illera walked herself to the corner of the room, where she stood with her arms crossed and knuckles in her mouth. I spared her a sympathetic glance but turned my attention to Emaline and the bulbs in my hand.

"Emaline, I am going to feed you something, and I want you to try your best to swallow it. Do you think you can do that for me?"

I waited for a nod of approval or her to audible agree but the very best I got was her closed eyes squinting as her dream scape held her captive.

"Hadrian, help me lift her head. I don't want her choking."

I focused on my shift, trying to capture it within my hand. My skin replaced with scales and nails elongated into sharp points. The rush of euphoria was heavy with this shift. My secondary form thrilled with being free for this moment.

With the added strength I placed the two juicy bulbs within my fist and clenched it tight. I was sure the entire camp could hear the noises that followed. The squelching of wet against dry. The loud crunches of the flowers petals which had dried slightly since I had picked them.

I could feel the Forbian juices dribbling amongst the lines of my palm, some even escaping and dripping on the floor no matter how hard I held my hand closed.

I lifted my fist slowly above Emaline's mouth which was gray and blue. A splash of the juices fell and landed on her bottom lip in one fat droplet. Soon after her pink tongue lapped it up, her mouth opened slightly, expecting more.

I soon relaxed my fist enough for the juices to fall free into her waiting mouth. The purple juices mostly went in, except for the few drops that ran down the side of her cheeks and stained the white pillows with its intense color.

All that was left with the pulp of the bulbs and I didn't want to give that to her. I had never eaten Forbian, only taken its juices so this would have to do. Even in the few moments that followed, I could see the rich color of her beautiful skin coming back to its once glory. Her cheeks flushed with life, and the dull tones of her lips faded back into the plush pinks they once were.

"That should be enough. We need to let her rest now, and she should start coming around soon enough. Illera, will you call for us when she wakes?" I asked.

Even from her distance I could see Illera roll her eyes. "*If* she wakes..."

"She will, in time," I replied. "Call us if you need

anything. I will come back and check on her soon enough, but I need to make sure we are prepared for anything in the meantime."

Hadrian wrapped his arm around me and guided me towards the tents entrance just as Illera called back for me. "Zac, wait. Before you go I need something of you."

"What is it?"

"If Marthil or Gordex come back, send someone for me. I have something I would like to tell them."

I stared at her, unblinking, "There may be a line waiting for a conversation with them both."

"So be it. I can wait and when it is my turn I will unleash everything I have to say... do to them."

I was certain her skin rippled, teeth flashing sharp for a moment.

That was all she said before turning her attention to Emaline again.

Hadrian muttered in my ear as we walked into the cold nightly air beyond the tent, "Your quick thinking may have helped Emaline before it was too late. I am really proud of you."

"Hold back your pride, it may be premature. We don't know if it is too late."

Hadrian clicked his tongue and looked into the dark sky, admiring the many stars and what would be hiding amongst them. "If Emaline's Heart Magick was free already, then Gordex would be here. I have no doubt in my mind that he would not wait until she got back to full strength—"

"Wait. Say that again."

"Gordex would be here already?"

"No, the part after that," I said.

"He would not wait until Emaline was back to her full strength."

"Why is he waiting? Why does he possibly need the Dragori at their full potential for his sick plans to work? If he just needed our magick for the ritual to work, then he could do it with us dead, sick and weak. But he wants us all alive. He needs us all for something, he needs more than our magick."

One simple comment caused a chain reaction of other ideas to fall into place in my head.

"We need to gather what remains of the New Council before Emaline heals. Because when she does, I have no doubt that Gordex will be here, waiting and ready. And we need to be as well."

CHAPTER
FORTY

THE AIR BETWEEN the New Council twanged with tension. It was so thick even the dullest of blades could've cut through it.

Hadrian had stepped back, allowing me to take control of the urgent topics. Which also gave me a say of who else joined. With Simian gone, the council was unbalanced. Following Hadrian's original intentions, I asked for Nyah to fill the spot as she was as much as shifter as Simian.

"Kell, will you tell us of Vcaros's comments? We have not noticed an increase in numbers within our ranks which leads me to think we are not getting help sent anyway," I said.

"That is what I believed until word of Paytric and his willing offer to help has reached the people. Warriors have been requested for you. They'll be sent to us with haste. We should expect them before dawn."

"That may be too late." Hadrian splayed his hands on the oaken table and straightened his back. I could see just how tired he was. The entire council looked exhausted. How could we fight in such a state?

"Better late than never." Fadine scoffed from her seat, her helmet resting on her armored lap. "What Hadrian means is 'thank you'. Thank you for adding your numbers to ours. My men and woman will be thankful to have others next to them on the battle field."

"Preciously," Vianne said. "And what of Simian's body? After what has happened, I have heard whispers that your soldiers do not want it near them in case the undead beast returns."

"That will not happen. I have seen to it that Simian will no longer be a pawn for Gordex and his dark power. He *has* been taken care of."

I turned to Hadrian whose amber eyes pierced the shadows he sat amongst. No one needed to ask more on Hadrian's comments. There was only one way to prevent the shadowbeings from returning ever again.

"We must all be prepared for a strike at any moment. Gordex's ability to control his shadowbeings is dependent on his distance from the dead. For him to control Simian would suggest that he is close by." Even saying it aloud made the hairs on the back of my neck stand to attention. As if a cold breeze tickled my skin, haunting.

"How do we fight a shadow?" Nyah said, head

bowed in defeat.

"With light."

We all turned to the tent's entrance as Emaline walked in, her arm wrapped around Illera's shoulder who helped her in.

"Emaline, you should be resting." I stood abruptly.

She waved me off as I walked over to help her. Even from the short distance, it was impossible to ignore the life that had returned beneath her skin and the shine within her eyes.

"You feel better then?" Fadine questioned, worry creasing her face.

"If your question is in regard to the Heart Magick, I am afraid that it is too late for me." Emaline frowned, her gaze glassy and defeated.

"How can you be sure?" Kell said, hand resting on the golden dagger concealed at her waist.

"Let me see. I can sense the very water rushing around amongst your bodies right now. I can feel the remnants of it in the ground beneath my feet, and the warm moisture in the air around you. That, and the anger I feel like the seed of an oak tree, growing at a rate too fast for me to keep a lid on it. Oh, and the taunting voice of that bastard who is trying to talk to me as if I even want to have a conversation with him."

"I think you should sit down," Hadrian said, offering

up his chair.

"If it helps, you don't look like death reincarnate anymore." Nyah threw her addition to the conversation at Emaline.

Emaline smiled weakly at her then hobbled over. "Shame, because I feel like death warmed up."

As she bent to sit down we all saw the wince of pain across her face which prompted Illera to rest a hand upon Emaline's shoulder.

"We have failed then," Kell said, Vianne nodded. "If the Druid has all four of the Heart Magick's what is stopping him from raising the druids? We should just offer ourselves up, stop the spilling of more blood when it would be a wasted effort."

"You are wrong," I said, grinding my teeth to still my frustration. "It is not too late. This brings me to yet another reason why I called for you all to gather. Emaline, Illera, I'm glad you have also come to hear this. It is important we all are on the same page before our book is destroyed, and we have no more pages to plan on." I took a deep breath before carrying on. "Kell brings up a good point, one Hadrian not so long ago mentioned. It stemmed for Emaline surviving. Why, when you can take her Heart Magick, not just kill her afterwards? Why leave us so we are here to still try and fight against him? The only plausible answer is he still needs us, the Dragori. He needs us strong, all at our full potential for the ritual to work. Our magick is not the only part of us he requires, and I am certain we will find out exactly what the next part of his puzzle is soon. But until then, we must be ready for anything."

"The next question is, do we let him use us to get close or do we keep him far from your reach?" Hadrian said, his brows furrowed and cheeks flush red.

"We should still do anything to get the Staff from him, to destroy it," Vianne spoke up.

"Agreed," Hadrian said.

Illera cleared her throat. "Do what you need, but I will not sit back and send you off to him when he has the ability to do anything to you. I can't lose you to him again, not when I came so close to that last night."

Emaline looked up at Illera and took her hand to her mouth, planting a kiss on the back of it.

Illera's hand was shaking as Emaline pressed it to her mouth. It only calmed slightly beneath her kiss.

"We need to think about this," Nyah said. "If our aim is to get close enough to Gordex to destroy the staff, then maybe we use the Dragori before he can use you. Get close enough, overwhelm him, destroy the staff, then we can all focus on him without the worry of him completing this ritual he harps on about."

"And how do you suggest we do that? He has

Marthil and our Heart Magick. Our numbers may be too much for him, but his power is far greater." Fadine looked at Nyah then tilted her head in interest. "But that face you are pulling suggests you already have an idea."

The corner of Nyah's lips pulled into a smirk. "I needed something to think about during the long journey here. I can say with my hand on my heart that I made use of the quiet hours and have conjured up many ideas on how to take Gordex down. Most are nothing more than ideas of grandeur and fantasy, but one might suffice."

We all listened in complete silence to Nyah's idea until we all mirrored each other's cunning smiles. If this worked, Gordex should never expect it to happen, or at least surprise him at most which is all we needed for it to work.

Nyah shared her plan in whispers, not wanting word to get out. If this was to work, she needed few to know about it.

Everyone left Hadrian and me to prepare for the possible events to follow. With Emaline healing at an incredible rate, it would not be long until Gordex struck. I could taste the anticipation within my air. Perhaps it warned me with its shift in feeling.

Vcaros's promise of extra soldiers arrived shortly after the New Council meeting concluded. Nyah was nowhere to be seen for the greeting, but I knew she was off preparing her part of her plan.

The heavy footsteps of the arriving soldiers echoed across our busy camp, causing all heads to turn in the direction of the desert. Like a mirage, the rippling outlines of bodies could be seen through the darkness, and soon enough, the bright light of the moon exposed them to be the soldiers we had waited for. Kell went forward to greet them, soon welcoming them all to join our camp and help our soldiers with their final preparations. Every Warrior she passed bowed to her, only raising their heads once she'd fully passed.

The gray uniforms of the Morthi warriors blended in with the silvers and purples of the Niraen soldiers. That was not the only differences between them. The Morthi were shorter than most of the Niraen. Compact and muscular. Their pointed ears were hidden amongst the sharp, pointed helmets that gave their skulls an elongated look. It was Hadrian who pointed out the next visual difference.

"Do you see those warriors." He pointed towards a group of three who helped secure the armor of the Niraen soldiers closest to us. "Their gloves look like they are made from metals."

I squinted, getting a better look. "I'm sure they can pack a punch."

"I do not doubt it, Petal. As long as it is not we who are on the receiving end."

As we greeted the Morthi soldiers, I noticed that not one bowed for Hadrian, nor did he seem to care. He was nothing to them. Nothing but a beast who attacked their front gates. But as Kell passed them, I noticed how their shoulders raised back and their faces where held high.

"I trust that you believe Nyah can succeed in her plan?" he asked out the corner of his mouth.

"That's like asking me if I trust that Illera and Emaline are in love. Of course, I trust her to do this. Even as she told us, her eyes burned with determination. If he doesn't catch on, this might be our best chance—"

Out the corner of my eye, a blur of white caught my attention.

"Hold on," I told Hadrian, already walking towards the ale barrel that concealed the small elfin boy I had seen running behind it.

"Tiv?" I asked, peering around it to see him curled in a ball, face to his chest, trying to hide. "Tiv! What are you doing here? It is not safe for you this far from the city right now."

I couldn't hide the angered tone of my voice. I'd never reprimanded a child before but seeing Tiv in a place that would soon become a field of steel and gore panicked me.

"Tiv's sorry." He screwed his face, peaking at me through one eye. He was covered entirely, only his eyes and nose showing. The sun was still bright and warm, too much for Tiv to cope beneath it. "I just wanted to come and help. You told me I'm a solider like my father. I wanted to join you and make you proud."

I moved quickly, pulling him into a hug. "Oh, Tiv, you can't help. This is not safe for you. Whoever brought you made a mistake—"

"No one took me with them," he said, voice muffled in my stomach. "I snuck out myself and came to find you. You told me you would come and see me in that city, but I waited, and you never came."

I peered to Hadrian, who pulled a face, showing his teeth as he too felt awkward at Tiv's comment. How did I tell him why I couldn't come without sounding like a monster with no control?

"I tried to come, but they wouldn't let us close to the city. We have been preoccupied here. I am so sorry, Tiv, I really am."

"Then you will let Tiv stay with you?"

"We cannot," Hadrian said, walking over and laying a protective hand in Tiv's stark hair. "What Zacriah said is true, it will not be safe for you here. He... we cannot let you stay where you are in danger. You must return to the city immediately. The King and his people will keep you safe."

"King?" Tiv said, pulling a face of confusion.

"*What* is the youngling doing here?" Kell interrupted, strutting across the sands to us.

Tiv looked up into Hadrian's eyes, his own glistening with tears, pleading as he wrapped an arm around his leg.

"He snuck out alongside the warriors," I explained. "We were just telling him that he must return straight away, weren't we Tiv?"

"Please don't leave me again. Not like my family has."

My heart almost shattered into the million fragments as his pained voice registered over us both. I squeezed onto the small boy, Hadrian joining as he sniffed in my ear trying to still his own emotion for Tiv.

"You will see them soon, but to be sure of that, we need you to return to Vcaros. Will you do that for us?" Hadrian said, kneeling on the ground to get to Tiv's height. "And when this is all done, not even the soldiers at Vcaros's gates will stop us from seeing you. Promise."

Tiv nodded.

"And Tiv, the city still needs brave soldiers like you to protect them."

"They do?" He wiped his nose with the sleeve of his

tunic.

"They do, isn't that right, Kell?" I peered up at her.

She nodded. "That is right."

"I do not doubt it for a moment. I cannot think of anyone else as brave as you to make sure they are all safe down there," Hadrian said. "What do you say, do you feel up to it?"

Tiv turned his face, beaming with a smile as his tears dried up on his alabaster checks. "Tiv is ready."

We both watched, hand in hand, as Tiv went under the protective arm of Kell. Every now and then he would turn back to look at us. His hand raised in goodbye.

I had to stop looking for the worry that my heart would just stop working.

CHAPTER
FORTY-ONE

MORNING CAME AND with it the crippling exhaustion from the lack of rest. But even with such terror waiting amongst the skyline I couldn't deny the beauty of the morning. The hot weather had created colorful displays whilst the sun rose across the vast ocean. This morning we were blessed with the warm orange tones which danced throughout golden yellows, unbothered by clouds or birds.

The entire world seemed still. As if it was waiting, watching for the events to come.

I'd spent the morning sitting amongst the warm sands, watching the sun rise above the busy camp. My gloved fingers picked up fistfuls of the grains which proceeded to spill through my open fingers back to its home of origin.

Hadrian had noticed my clumsiness brought on from my tiredness. He told me to take a break which I didn't miss the chance on having. He gave me this moment to rest, but the guilt for taking it was strong. I could see that our soldiers and the Morthi warriors amongst them could not rest. Why should I when the fight was so close? We all knew it was coming.

Before a storm raged its havoc, the air would seem frozen in place. Not a single breeze would taint the wind, even the earth seemed to stop. The air was tranquil. The ocean glass-calm. It was Hadrian who shattered the rest as he trudged over, his own face pale and eyes heavy.

"Let me guess, couldn't sleep?" Hadrian said, walking up behind me.

"Not a single blink," I replied.

His warriors' uniform must've been awkward as he complained when he dropped to sit in the sand beside me. "I brought you something to eat. That might help rejuvenate your energy. And if that does not work, then maybe my company can take your mind off it."

I leaned my head on his shoulder and smiled. "I like the sound of that."

He passed me a piece of crusted bread that had been ripped from its loaf and a slab of hard cheese which had spots of blue on one side. I took it with a thankful smile.

"I have had an earful from Kell. She thinks being stuck with the ocean behind us will do us no favors when Gordex turns up. I get her point; we will be cornered in. But if we are all out in the open it gives Gordex his pick of direction to attack us from. I am holding out hope that Nyah's plan succeeds, that way it will not matter where we are because the struggle will be swift."

I looked towards the glistening water which lazily caught the rays of sun and reflected like crystals. "But I don't see what Gordex has to fight with? His shadowbeings in Lilioira can hardly travel here without being seen. We would have spotted a sea of ships by now."

"Death does not ignore Morgatis, the grounds will be full of those who have passed." Hadrian lost himself to the view. "And he has Marthil, a very angry Marthil."

"Do not underestimate our own anger." He knew as well as I just how powerful our own anger could be. It was undeniable. What was a worry was whether or not we could control it. That was down to Nyah. "And if it is mounds of bone that Gordex wants to call upon, then he can be our guest. I do not see how they still stand up against us," I said.

I began picking at the bread and stuffing its fluffy innards in my mouth. The full ache within my stomach soon ceased.

Hadrian wrapped his warm arm around my waist and pulled me close to him. We both lost ourselves to the view, sharing in the silent pause. I could imagine doing this with him for the rest of my life. Seeing new days arrive and biding old one's goodbye. I wondered how many views of this world we would see together. Would we have the chance to see another sunrise again?

"EntDistract me with your thoughts, Petal, what is it that occupies your mind?" he asked quietly.

"You."

His hand softly squeezed my waist. "Only good things, one hopes."

"Just you. Everything about you."

"At least I am not the only one who cannot get someone else out of my head, no matter the circumstance," Hadrian replied, his voice steady.

"I cannot imagine what my life was like before you were in it. It's as if you have been by my side for all eternity. And what makes it worse is the thought of losing you again. I don't think I could handle that again."

"I am not going anywhere. I promise," Hadrian said, fingers squeezing into my upper arm.

I opened and closed my mouth. That was a hearty promise to make.

"How can you be sure? All bad things come in threes. You can't promise something that is wholly out of our control."

His gloved finger found my chin, and he guided it until I faced him. "I refuse to believe that our lives are beyond our own control. This will not be the first time we face something together, but regardless, these are our lives we are talking about. I rebuke the idea that we will fail. It will not happen again. I will be certain of it."

Looking upon Hadrian kindled the hope that

sparked like embers in the very pit of my soul. His honest belief that we would win this helped my own overcome the doubt, even just a slither.

Hadrian extended his hand, fingers splayed before me. "What do you say, Petal, ready to face this together?"

I placed my hand on his and he held on tight. "If you are by my side, I am ready to face what we have to come."

"Glad you said that." He winked, turned my hand round so my palm faced the sand. Quick as he could he pulled my finger out from his hold and slid something heavy onto it.

"What is this?" I asked, catching the glint of dull silver.

Hadrian raised my hand up for me to get a better look. His lips twitched towards a smile.

"A gift, a promise, a ring. It has many meanings I guess."

"Is this a strange custom you royals' keep up within your tall towers and hearth warmed rooms?" I laughed, tears pooling in my eyes.

"I guess, but it is one I hope to share with you one day."

"Hadrian." I paused.

My entire body felt warm. Comfortable and light.

"I have made many promises to you, but I ask of one in return. When we get through this fight and both make it out on the other side, I will tell you exactly what this ring means."

If it wasn't for the form fitting uniform and armor I would have jumped on top of him, rolled amongst the sands and kissed him for eternity. My answer to the question he had skirted round lay thick on the end of my tongue, ready to be shared.

Hadrian raised my finger to his mouth and placed a kiss upon it. Pulling it back he looked deep into my very soul. "I think we have had enough rest for now. What do you say? Are you ready to face another danger together?"

I was too focused on the reflection of light that bounced off my ring to reply with words. Instead I planted a kiss on his cheek.

Hadrian helped me stand, and we walked back towards camp, not once letting go of each other. With every step towards the camp I felt more prepared than the one before.

Soldiers waved hands towards us, some even bowed. Out the corner of my eye, I noticed one point towards the silver that stood out against the glove on my hand. I wanted to shy away, but another part of me wanted to hold my hand high with pride.

My instant thought was to find Nyah, to tell her of what had happened. I could imagine, in another life one without the coming fight, that we would share this idle gossip over the lips of cups filled with steaming tea.

I searched for her amongst the crowd. Even keeping an eye out for Emaline and Illera. They all were important to me, so I wanted them all to know.

As we rounded past the first tent, my legs simply stopped working and my mind spun violently.

I slipped from Hadrian's grasp as my panicked shout slipped out. Hadrian tried to reach for me, I felt his fumbling hands, but he too joined me on the sandy bed. As well as all the others who stood near us.

At first, I thought it was my own fault, brought on by the tiredness of hunger. But I knew the moment I looked up that I was wrong. Then, as I pushed both palms into the sand to get up I felt the shiver run throughout the ground. A vibration of tension that caused the very grains of gold and yellow to dance up off the floor.

Tents shock, some even fell. Hadrian's unblinking gaze looked into me, laced with worry. Another wave of power caused the ground to shake, taking more soldiers down to their knees and hands.

"Marthil," I breathed.

It was the only explanation to this unnatural quake.

"It is time," Hadrian replied, causing my heart to sink deep into stomach.

CHAPTER
FORTY-TWO

I STOOD AMONGST my friends on the front line, watching the cloud of dust and sand rush closer to us. Sparing a glance behind me I looked over the sea of soldiers and warriors alike, each ready and waiting to greet our guests with steel and magick.

Amongst the ranks, shifters prowled the sands, some circled the skies above. Arches stood behind us, arrows readied and waiting to be unleashed. Fadine's closed fist raised beside her, a waiting signal. The moment that fist opened, the cocked arrows would fly.

Morthi warriors boxed our soldiers in as they rode armored serpents, ready to careen across the ground for our enemy. For as far as I could see, we had elves behind us, all as ready as the next to lay their lives down for the future. Even the sea, which sat peacefully behind us, was still. The only sounds I could hear were the muffled breathing behind helmets and the occasional clink of metal against metal.

Hadrian stood, chin high, to my left, Nyah to my right. Illera padded the sand, walking around Emaline who was already back to full health. Her wound had healed, only the silver mark of a scar was left. Vianne held two short swords to her sides, her long sun-toned hair laying still down her back. Even Kell kept her unblinking gaze on the sand dunes before us. We were as ready as the elf next to us.

The initial quake that alarmed us was not the only one to come. As our camp rushed to congregate, the ground proceeded to shake violently after paused moments. Each more intense than the last. The gap of stillness shorter than the next.

It was when they finally stopped that a scout noticed the rolling cloud of sand that raced across Doom to greet us. It was far enough away that we had time to prepare.

"Zac, you know what to do?" Nyah said, tapping my arm with her hand. "Don't hesitate. You've got this."

"Will you be ready?" I asked, trying not to look at her.

"I'll be fine, but you must not be aware of my doings until the last moment. We can't let Gordex catch on to our one chance."

If I looked at her I worried my wall of strength would crumble. Nyah was putting herself at risk, arguably more than Emaline, Hadrian and me. I wanted to hug her, wrap her in my arms and tell her how much she meant to me. But now was not the time.

"I suppose I should tell you now how clever I think you are, wouldn't want to miss out on my chance."

"I know." Her reply was simple. "No need to tell me."

I had to glance out the corner of my eye at her as she smirked to herself. Her red hair had been tamed and pulled back into a tight bun. Only a single strand had escaped and tickled the side of her face.

"Have you concealed the dagger on you, somewhere he will not see it?" she asked.

I lifted the hem of the black uniform and flashed the handle which rested close to the skin of my hip. "It's ready and waiting. If everything is taken from me, he shouldn't find this one unless he pries."

"By that point it will be buried in his head, no need to worry." Nyah's fingers grazed mine, and I took it and squeezed.

Good luck, I sent the thought to her.

You too, friend.

Black smoke seeped from my side and Nyah was no longer next to me. The archers behind her gaped in shock at her sudden disappearance, but I blocked out their gasps and focused on the sand clouds.

It was hard to ignore the tickle that crawled down the lip of my neck and rested across the bare skin of my chest.

Hadrian didn't let go of my hand.

Not as I took steps ahead of the front line, readying myself. His hand held on, fingers pulling to keep me next to him, but he knew I had to go. If the sand storm reached us, we would be blind to Gordex and Marthil's attacks. I couldn't let that happen. Not when we still didn't know what else waited in the storm. Had he found dead to control? Who else fought by his side, willing or not?

Eyes closed, I willed my shift to take over.

Once the weightless presence of my wings flexed behind me and the strong touch of the curved horns protruded from my head, I opened my magick to the world.

My intrusive silver strands of control lit up the sky around me. I pulled on the tight tethers, pushing my awareness all the way across the Doom for the sand storm. I reached into it, searching for its eye, its origin. I had to understand the storm if I was to stop it.

My wind tickled across two figures, concealed inside the wild sands. They walked, pulling the storm along like a dog on a tether. The power was shared between them. One controlling the air, the other controlling the sand. Then I recognized the faint pulling of my power. A feeling I'd grown used to every time Gordex used my own abilities.

This was no different.

The rushed winds got closer, enough that my hair

began twisting from my head. That was all I would allow this unnatural magick to do.

I raised a hand, blocking rogue grains of sand from infiltrating my vision. Pinning all my attention on the horror before me, I breathed. Then, as the wall of orange and darkness got close enough I unleashed my full potential.

I threw up my own wall of wind, solidifying it into a hard, surface, invisible to the naked eye. My scream fueled my power. It lured the anger out into my body and willed the full potential of my Heart Magick to run free.

The wild clouds of sand slammed into it, barreling with all its might. A single droplet of sweat beaded on my forehead and ran down onto the tip of my nose. My concentration was being pushed to its limits.

As if my shield was a door and I was putting my weight behind it to keep it closed, I felt someone—something else on the other side kicking it open. I fought against the pressure, holding my own.

Like a monstrous wave of water crashing into a stone wall, the clouds of sand splashed up against my own protective layer and hung there with the presence of a hungry beast, ready to devour. My feet dug into the desert ground under the force which I kept at bay.

I could feel the banging of feet from the soldiers and warriors behind me, urging me to keep strong. Their presence and support encouraged more of my power to join my protective wall. But with each force I gave up, I felt one going against me from the other side. Gordex.

He used my own magick, the Heart Magick, to keep his counter force attacking against my efforts. In my mind's eye I could see him, standing within the shadowed eye of the storm, pushing energy into the angry winds, making them stronger and hungrier. I could hear his snigger, see his smirk, feel his enjoyment.

I knew he wouldn't stop. He'd never lapse in his own counteract until I gave up on my own. No matter how much energy I put into my wall, with the ever-growing pressure it would not hold for long.

Marks had been made in the sand where I was being forced backwards. My wings began beating, trying to keep me in one place. Like glass, my shield was cracking. I could feel it in my bones. The sharp snaps building until it would smash and allow Gordex's power to reign free. I had to act fast.

"Hadrian, I need you!" I shouted over my shoulder.

Hadrian was by my side in moments, his own beastly form free.

"Tell me what to do," he said, calmly.

"I need you to throw as much flame as you can into the storm. But not yet! Wait for my signal."

He didn't refuse me. Instead, Hadrian widened his stance and readied his hands. Small flames conjured across his waiting hands, tickling around his fingers and reaching their cobalt kiss across his wrists.

I couldn't get distracted. Blocking Hadrian out for a moment, I focused back on my shield as another enormous crack spread through it. This time it conjured an audible bang to spread through the sky and across us all. A thunderous noise that caused the shifters to roar and squawk.

My brows furrowed. Time for my next move to be played.

"Now!"

I dropped the shield, allowing the built-up pressure behind it to race faster towards me. Hadrian shouted his frustration towards the clouds and threw his arms to greet it. Flames sprouted across the distance and clashed with the clouds. The moment his fiery touch met the storm, I threw my shield up anew, this time knowing how much strength I would need to put within it. My shield sucked the very breath out of me.

I turned my face to the side as the flames came close to touching me. Even Hadrian raised an arm to protect himself. But the storm never reached.

Behind the newly formed shield the flames devoured the storm, fueled by the wild winds it burned, making clouds of magenta fire. All I could see beyond the wall was flame.

It was beautiful, majestic, horrific.

No longer did the pressure from Gordex press up

against my own force, it receded like a scolded creature, running from a beating. He would use the power to protect himself against the wild flames, I knew that.

The fire reflected across the soldier's armor as I turned to see if they were untouched. Some hands were still raised, expecting the fire and wind to reach them at any moment. But many screamed with pride.

It had worked.

We both watched as the inferno dwindled into nothing. No longer did the ravage winds roam free beyond. The sand was back across the ground, charred and black. Some even shone, reflecting the bright sun high above. The clear space gave view to the two beings stood atop the nearest dune, looking down over us all.

Gordex and Marthil stood side by side, hatred glares laid upon us all.

Marthil's wings hung high behind them both, casting a devilish shadow across the desert.

Gordex was dressed in black, much like me, with layered plates of amour, and a sheer obsidian cloak that billowed in the light winds left behind from his use of magick. The Staff of Light was held firm in his hand, the crystal winked as he took a step forward. I was certain that shadow seeped from its crest, hungrily.

The dark rune marks that covered Gordex skin seemed darker than I had noticed before, his skin paler. The hood of his cloak covered the top of his face, blocking his piecing gaze from being seen. But the shadow didn't stop me from feeling it. I could sense his wretched eyes running their way up and down my body, then shifting to Hadrian and Emaline, who was still on the front line behind us. He regarded us all as Marthil snarled, pointed teeth lapping over her thin lips.

They were both monsters in their own right. A right they'd both earned through their terrible actions.

Even from such a distance his voice carried over the space between us, loud enough for the entire regiment.

"Dragori, I give you this chance to prevent the blood shed that could soon follow. Give yourselves up, and I shall spare your kin. Do not, and I will unleash horror across these plains, and I will not stop until you are the last ones standing. The choice is yours."

My mind almost made me step forward, but my heart screamed for me to stop. It was Hadrian who shouted back.

"I speak for us all when I say we are not in a mood for bargaining today." Hadrian's voice equally carried across the barren desert to Gordex.

"Shame." Gordex turned to Marthil slightly and we watched him tilt his head towards her. "Remember when the desert runs with blood that I gave you the chance to stop this. Be it on your heads when death spoils the air."

Marthil licked her lips and opened her fists into threatening claws.

"Ready!" Fadine shouted, commanding the archers.

"Zacriah, you can stop this." I felt Gordex run his gaze over me again.

"Nock!" Fadine screamed, shared with the loud grunt which was followed by the notching of arrows and raising of bows. I recognized the slight sounds which was music to my ears.

I could stop this. If we gave him what he wanted, no more death was needed.

"Mark!"

I looked over my shoulder to see Fadine, face red, shout for her archers

"Draw…"

All Fadine would need to do is open her first and a storm of iron tipped arrows would rain down upon Marthil and Gordex. It would not stop them, but it was enough deterrent to cause Marthil to falter on her move.

"You had the choice," Gordex said a final time, sighing.

"There are two of you," I shouted. "And we are many. Do not make the mistake and go against us."

"Ants work together, small creatures with such great strength. But it only takes a single boot to kill an entire colony. I am that boot."

"LOO—"

Gordex laughed, the ocean listened. His joy did not make sense until our soldiers screamed out in terror. I turned around out of panic to see the shallow waters explode with bodies of dead beings. Shadowbeings rushed out of the sea, rusted weapons raised, and rushed the back lines of our regiment.

By the time I looked back to Gordex, he was no longer standing amongst the dunes. Only Marthil was left, a cunning smile plastered across her face.

She brought her hands together, and the ground split at her feet, creating a crevasse that snaked across the desert straight towards me.

CHAPTER
FORTY-THREE

MY ENTIRE FOCUS was on Marthil. I couldn't worry about the soldiers dealing with the surprise attack. Not when Marthil planned to bury us all before the shadowbeings even struck.

I threw myself into the air, my wings pumping with vigor. Only seconds after my feet left the ground did it open beneath me, the crevasse greeting me as it caused the ground to split in two. Sand fell into the darkness that waited below.

It kept moving, snaking for the front line. I reached a hand to my side and pulled it through the air to my side. It caused a sharp slice of wind to rush straight for Marthil. She had not seen it until it was too close. She dropped her own magick and dived to the side, missing my attack by inches.

This would have been the perfect time for the archers to unleash their arrows, but they were all turned towards the hordes of dead that rushed them. Hadrian was already flying above, sending liquid fire down across the ocean to stop the bodies from crawling out. But without removing their heads, the shadowbeings kept coming. This time covered in hungry flames, which only benefited them. Their dampened bodies didn't hold onto the fire for long.

I searched for Marthil, but she had fallen behind the dune. I was about to fly for it when a boulder the size of a cow came flying through the air towards me.

Spinning out of the way, it missed me. But then another came, and another. One after the other the boulders flew from behind the dune, each one getting closer to hitting me. I tried volleying them with wind, but I was either too weak, or too slow for my efforts to matter.

My wings carried me higher into the air as another boulder came for me. My feet pushed upon it, but the sudden force caused me to lose balance.

I tumbled through the air, spinning wildly.

The ground collided with me. My back screamed, and my lungs burned as the air was knocked out of me. I was certain I heard a rip sound from my left wing, but no pain followed, so I ignored the noise.

I gasped out, trying to regain my breath, but I was deprived as the sharp pain settled. I rolled onto my stomach, looking towards the fight at the shore. The boulders lay amongst the ranks, bodies squashed beneath. Blood in shades of black and red stained the sands. From my position, I could see a single arm reaching out in death from beneath one.

Anger boiled in my stomach in reaction. Death, already, death had graced the soldiers. It did not discriminate who it took. It hungered on any soul that stood in the wrong place.

A shout of frustration, laced with guilt, burst out of my mouth. I pushed myself from the ground and turned back to where Marthil last was, but she was now standing inches behind me. Her arm flashed out for my stomach, but I slammed my own palms down, knocking her attempt from touching me. She moved again, wings reaching for me with their curved claws. Its sharp tip caught my uniform but did not pierce it. The layered material was all the protection I needed for that.

In the rush, I didn't see her open hand reach for my hair until my scalp shrieked in pain. My natural reaction was to pull away, but she had a firm grip on my hair. Under her force, she pushed my head down, bringing her knee straight into my face. Blood burst out of my nose, filling my mouth with the harsh taste of copper. I choked on my own gore.

Marthil's fist rained down heavy on my face, knuckles connecting with bone. Even her punches felt like rocks, so strong and unbreakable. Adrenaline was no longer enough to override the sense of pain. It barreled into me, stirring the anger within me to twist like a snake following the sound of its prey.

She turned me, back facing her where she wrapped her forearm around my neck and squeezed. Her face was close to my ear as she laughed, causing spit to fly from her deranged snarl. Her arms bulged as she held on, squeezing as hard as she could.

"Watch them all," she said as we looked upon the struggle of my regiment going up against the shadowbeings. "See how they fall under his power."

Tears of frustration leaked down my dirt-covered face. From the angle Marthil held me, I could see the bodies of our soldiers falling by force of death. I watched my friends blur between the shadowbeings as they fought for their lives. I longed to help them, but she had me trapped.

Putting all my strength behind my legs, I rocked forward, almost causing her to fall on top of me as I tipped to the ground. As my face got close to the sandy bed, I closed my eyes and blew. With as much might and magick as I could muster, wind exploded from my mouth, giving me enough force to slam the back of my head into her face. Sand sprayed, scratching at my face and closed lids. But from Marthil's scream and the way her hold on my neck loosened, I knew it had gotten in her eyes.

She called out profanity just as I flexed my wings, sending her stumbling to the ground. She scratched blindly at the earth, sending sharp spears of rock out of the ground and towards me. Her moves were clumsy, as she couldn't use her vision to direct her power. I was able to dodge her attempts and finally get close enough to her.

I jumped into the sky, wings pumping. Hands raised, I conjured my winds to batter down from above her.

Her body folded in on itself, collapsing to the ground. The air danced with silver tones as the Heart Magick intensified and pushed down on top of her. It kept her in place, long enough for me to talk.

"Where is he?" I asked, licking a dribble of blood from my lip. My nose was blocked with the congealed gore, which made my tone sound muffled and my head throb.

Marthil laughed, gritty sand stuck in her teeth. "You shall see him when he needs you most."

"Cut the mystery and tell me, or I *will* kill you."

"Will you? You've had so many chances, each one you passed on." Marthil laughed, teeth covered in sand and her own black blood. "Even if you tried, Gordex would never let you kill me, as he will not let me kill you."

Turning darkness was close to taking over as she looked deep into my eyes. Could she sense it? She seemed pleased about something.

"You don't know what I am capable of, Marthil." I focused more pressure into the wind that kept her down. The sand around her pinned frame flew in all directions as she began to sink into its hold.

"Nor do I care to know. I only need one thing from you, Zacriah, and you are close to giving it to me. You are easy to read; it is your downfall."

"Bitch." I tilted my head and squinted at her.

Marthil paused before replying. She laughed, rolling her earth-toned eyes at me. The ground seemed to rubble, mimicking her growing giggle as she peered up at me. What was so funny? I had her trapped. I could pull the very breath from her lungs, snap her bones with my unrelenting force. Yet she laughed in my face as if I was no threat.

Then she spoke. "Are you angry yet?"

"Wha—"

The ground trembled again, this time enough for me to notice it for what it was. The sand around Marthil vibrated and in the blink of an eye she was gone. Absorbed into the earth, only the outline of her frame left beneath me. I relaxed my power, turning in all directions, expecting her to come back up at any moment. But she didn't. All she had left me with was her final words.

Are you angry yet? It's what she wanted. She wanted me to lose control, to give myself to Gordex and become his puppet. It would've worked if Nyah was not helping me. Her own task was to keep my anger at bay. It was necessary for our own plan to work. I placed my hand on my heart and reached out.

Did you get hurt?

Not as bad as you. Will you be able to carry on?

Keep me calm and I will be fine.

I closed off our connection and threw myself into the air. Wings flapped behind me, and I flew straight into the heart of the battle.

Up ahead was a clearing within the fight. I aimed for it, landing I brought the force of wind down with me, reaching for the shadowbeings and sending them in all directions. Being up close, I recognized the damp, water stained uniforms from Eldnol. Alorian soldiers who no longer belonged on the right side of the battle.

I spun my wings around, catching dead flesh beneath my claws and ripping. Heads tumbled free, rolling across the ground.

Up ahead I saw Emaline. She was standing ankle deep in the ocean. Water ravaged around her, reaching for the many shadowbeings that still climbed out of the water. Before they could pass she sent hungry waves reaching for them and pulled them back with great control. She held silvered swords with white handles in both hands, spinning them around with detailed control. No blood touched the swords. Only wisps of black smoke from the severed shadowbeings that floated in the water around her.

Not a single shadowbeing tried to attack Emaline. They tried to get past her for the soldiers, never once sparing her more than a glance.

Illera was close by, pouncing from one shadowbeing to the next. She didn't have the same blessing as Emaline. Multiple shadowbeings tried to attack her.

Her white fur was stained with red and black blood from those who fought beside her. Claws flashed as she swiped at one shadowbeing who was seconds from piercing a Morthi warrior through the gut. The warrior's helmet had been knocked off, showing the pure fear in her eyes. But Illera soon rid the warrior of her issue.

The shadowbeing toppled to the ground, legless but still withering. The Morthi warrior kicked herself into standing and pulled the same rusted weapon that almost killed her and sliced it clean across the shadowbeings neck.

Everything passed in a blur. I stepped over bodies searching the crowds for Hadrian. I had not seen him since Marthil had attacked.

"Skies!" someone cried beside me, pointing to above to the dark clouds that cut across the sun. I squinted, getting a better look, only to see that it was not cloud that caused it. But flocks of dark creatures, led by one I would recognize anywhere.

Petrer flew through the skies in his raven form, the monstrous dark creatures following shortly behind him. His glossy dark feathers were slick as he shot through the skies and aimed for a place in the distance. A place I could not see through the rabble of fighting. The creatures that followed him where the same as the ones that had attacked Hadrian, Gallion, Nyah and me before we had truly found out the truth about Gordex.

Their screeches filled the skies, some fighting themselves as they clumsily flew for their target. In daylight they looked different to what I had imagined in the dark. A strange mixture of birds, insects but with humanoid figures and claw like hands and feet.

I ran through the fight, pulling my Dragori form back into its hold. My wings receded, the gaps in my armor closing in after them. Over bodies I leapt, Niraen and Morthi alike. I didn't stop running until I could see what the creatures and Petrer aimed for. In truth, I knew before I laid eyes upon it.

Hadrian was in the middle of a cleared circle of

charred bodies. He was forced on his knees, small animalistic creatures holding him arms, legs and waist down. Petrer stood in front of him, his back to me. He too was dressed in black, his dark skin blending seamlessly into Gordex's chosen uniform.

Like Emaline, none tried to stab Hadrian, instead they held him in place. But I didn't take the chance that they wouldn't harm him for whatever reason.

I overstepped a bow on the sand, not wanting to give away my presence.

Petrer was bent at the waist. From where I stood it looked as if he was whispering something into Hadrian's ear. Hadrian's face was red. Flames licked up his skin, but the strange creatures were unbothered.

Their skinless arms seemed unaffected by the flames, even their insect-like wings were untouched.

My feet trudged over the sand towards them. Hadrian noticed me first. He lifted his stare from the spot in the sand and looked directly at me. His face was pale, eyes wide. Petrer then turned his head slowly around to look at me.

"Zac, how good it is to see you again. I was just having words here with your Prince. It seems that you missed out some important details during your stay with me. Since you are here, why don't you finish of the story I was telling him. I got to the part of when I visited you in your room."

Anger pulsated from Hadrian. Even from my distance I could see him shaking, trying everything in his will to pull free from the creatures that held him down.

"Nothing happened, Hadrian, don't listen to him."

"Are you certain nothing happened?" Petrer lied. "The way I remember it must be very different. Don't be ashamed, Zac, I understand why you didn't want to tell him. It would've made him very angry wouldn't it."

He was lying, trying to make Hadrian angry so Gordex could take over.

"Hadrian! He is tempting you. He wants you to be angry. Do not give in to your Heart Magick," I screamed, my voice full of tension and anxiety.

Petrer looked away from me and proceeded to lean back into Hadrian's ear. I wished I could hear what he said, but from Hadrian's growl, I knew it was not good.

I could sense Nyah trying to calm me, but once Petrer laid his fingers across Hadrian's jaw and ran the nail the length along it, I thought I was going to explode. Not matter how much I felt Nyah's empathic presence, it wouldn't work.

"What a sweet mouth he has," Petrer said louder than the rest. The creatures holding Hadrian cried out as the flames intensified, turning an azure blue. Heart Magick. It was coming. I had to stop it.

"I'd be lying if I said I have not been craving it ever since."

Before Petrer had the chance to turn to me I dropped to the ground and swiped the bow and arrow up. Its frame was only slightly charred from Hadrian's fire. Thankfully the haired string was still intact.

I lodged the arrow in place and held it up to my eye.

My heart beat pounded heavy and fast in my chest, enough to distract myself from my shot. But no matter what, I didn't lose my focus on Petrer. It was not the first time my arrow had found a mark on Petrer's body. But this time, it would be the last.

I took a breath and released it. The arrow sliced through the air, iron tip spinning.

There was no hesitation this time. Not a wasted moment. Even if Petrer had tried to move, it would have been too late. The arrow skimmed through the air, reaching its target. It buried deep, even the wood of the shaft disappearing into the flesh of Petrer's neck.

It lodged deep, from the back and out through the front.

Petrer faltered where he stood, reaching for Hadrian to still his fall. Then all at once he dropped to the sand.

"The first arrow should have killed you," I shouted, spit shooting out from my mouth. I couldn't tell if Petrer knew what I said. Or what it meant. But as he toppled to the ground I remembered when I first had shot him with my arrow back in Olderim. That one should have killed him, it would have solved so many problems, stopped so many deaths.

Red blossomed beneath Petrer's body, seeping from the fresh wound that I had gifted him. His eyes stayed open and unblinking at the skies above.

Then, as I reached out with my air, I felt his final breath. It escaped into the waiting embrace of the winds. I dropped the arrowless bow back to the ground and swayed on my feet. Hadrian tried again to pull free from the creatures to reach me but failed.

Dead. Petrer was dead.

CHAPTER
FORTY-FOUR

THE SMALL BEASTS holding Hadrian down cried out as an overwhelming fire engulfed them all. Even Hadrian disappeared within the bright, sun-like flames. No longer were they blue, not entirely. Not as Hadrian tried to fight the anger.

I rushed forward for him but was halted by the intense heat, causing me to recoil. Burned, twisted corpses of the creatures littered the ground around Hadrian as the fire dwindled. Then he rushed forward, stepping over Petrer without a glance and took my hands.

I felt Nyah work her magick. It flowed through me, making my head light and airy. Hadrian's forehead calmed, lines ironing back out back until his skin was unmarked by wrinkles and marks. His pupils dilated and no longer looked as if his eyes were overwhelmed with black holes.

"He wants us to lose control," I panted, feeling Nyah lax on her power. "If we do, he will become unstoppable."

"Then we must stay close, have Nyah help us when she can."

The tickling of small legs on my chest told me that Nyah agreed.

We both looked upon the fight. As far as we could see soldiers and warriors alike fell beneath the weight of war. Shadowbeings kept coming from the sea, all in different stages of death. It was hard to see Marthil, but Emaline's beastly outline was hard to miss as the unnatural waves behind her shot forward, dragging hordes of shadowbeings back into her watery grip.

Still none tried to hurt her.

"We will not win this fight. Already we have lost so many," I said, my hope dwindling like Hadrian's flame.

Hadrian took my hand. "Then let us help."

We both shot into the air, flying for the middle of the fight. Landing beside each other, we played our cards. Hadrian pulled the broad sword from his waist in both hands and flashed it around at the shadowbeings. Flames sprouted from the swords handle and laced the entire body of the blade.

As he brought it down upon his enemies, they too exploded in flame.

I moved my own magick, slicing daggers of wind towards bodies until they were sent cascading through the air and out of view.

Something hard pulled at my wings. I spun, to see

two shadowbeings taking another swing at me. They were both weaponless. Their dead hands reached for my leathery limbs once more to try and pull them down.

I pulled my shift in and returned to my elven form, my head rushing with the sudden shift.

The hand of the dead girl passed through the space where my wing had only just been. She lost her balance, enough for her face to connect hard with the ground. Before the next could act I pulled the short dagger at my hip and flashed it towards the seconds neck. It sliced straight through, her skin rotten like old fruit. The Druid's dark smoke seeped out of the wound, acting to try and stitch the skin together, but it was too late. It soon disappeared into the atmosphere, off to find its next body. It was then when I noticed the Niraen and Morthi soldiers reanimated in death. With each solider we lost, Gordex gained another.

The shadowbeing beneath my foot tried to push up. With as much might as I could muster, I threw the dagger down upon it. It blurred down towards it, soon disappearing to the hilt in the back of the shadowbeing's head.

This had to end. The longer the fight went on the more died, only adding to Gordex's numbers.

Gordex wanted for us to watch our ranks thin, to prove that he would even use our own against us. But what were the limits to his power? How could he control so many? I wondered as I ran through the fight if that is why he is staying away. Was he most vulnerable when exuding so much power? If there was even a chance that he was weak we had to take it. We had to end him.

Hadrian unleashed waves of flame. Emaline conjured an inferno of ocean which spun in small vortexes around her. Everyone was being pushed to their limits. I should have unleashed my own magick, but I needed to find Kell. I needed her help.

I picked up a rusted axe as I ran, sweeping it from the place beside a decapitated body.

The deeper I got into the heart of the battle, the more I saw the damage. Niraen soldiers battled their dead companions. Morthi warriors sliced at their own as well. The shadowbeings were scattered across the floor, their jobs complete.

Emaline and the outlines were working their hardest at keeping more shadowbeings from joining, but it didn't matter. Not when Gordex had us fighting ourselves.

My muscles ached as I swung the unbalanced axe at those who stood in my way. I had to block out who it was that my weapon reached. The rusted metal passed through purples and silvers, and my guilt grew.

They are dead, I told myself over and over. *Like Petrer, Gallion, Jasrov, Browlin and many more. They are dead.*

I recognized the crest of nightly hair up ahead.

Kell was covered in blood, her cheeks flushed red

and armor ripped in places. She swung twin blades at those who got close enough to feel her wrath. Her short frame helped as she dodged the many attempts at her life. She slipped in and out like water through sand, air through forests, missing each one and stabbing her own blades which never seemed to miss. She was surrounded by Morthi warriors, each moving with equal grace.

"Kell." I passed through the circle of her guards, pushing my back to hers. "I need your help."

"Talk and fight," she said, dodging an attack and bringing her own blade up through the head of a dead Morthi warrior bursting with black smoke. "The bastard has turned my own people against us. The BASTARD," she shouted, bringing both blades, overlapping them and slicing them like shears at the neck of shadowbeing. It tumbled, headless, to the ground.

"We will not win. Our numbers are getting smaller, and his numbers are getting bigger. We have to stop this."

"Tell me something"—metal screeched as it sliced across my armor—"I don't know! If you have a suggestion, I'd love to—*aargh*—hear it."

One of the living Morthi warriors that protected her flashed his mirror covered hand towards us. Light exploded from his skin, intensified by the mirrors into a concentrated beam. It shot forward, catching a shadowbeing in the middle of his forehead and burning a hole straight through.

I'd not noticed the shadowbeing, severed from his waist down, pulling itself through the sand and reaching up at me until the Morthi unleashed his magick. I tried to thank him, but he turned, spinning his unique magick at those who tried to break into our circle.

"I need to find Gordex alone. If there is a chance he is weaker whilst controlling so many, I need to take it. It might be our only time to strike."

"No," Kell snarled, blade thrusting into the chest of an attacker. "No. If you leave, he has you. Hadrian will follow and Emalinc will be forced to go as well. Do not even think about it."

"Kell…"

"No. If you give up, hand yourself over, this will all be for nothing. All these lives lost for nothing."

"I'm not handing myself over, I am taking a risk and ending Gordex before he can use any more of us."

"Act with haste, Zacriah, and expect an unpredicted ending. I will not stand back and allow you do to this." Kell's face was red, her upper lip glistening with sweat.

Frustration at Kell's dismissal bubbled deep within me but soon was swept away by Nyah. She was working her magick again, trying to keep me from losing control.

Something blocked out the sun. It caused both Kell and me to look up. A serpent danced, body erected into the sky, as it snapped its needle-filled jaws out at those who attacked it. Its pointed nose was covered in gore, even scales were missing across his majestic body.

"MOVE!" Kell screamed, colliding with me. I landed awkwardly across mutilated limbs of the dead. Kell fell heavily on top of me.

In the sudden move, I missed what had caused such alarm. It took shuddering breaths to calm the pain of air being forced out of my lungs from Kell's weight atop of me.

The serpent had fallen. Toppled over, its monstrous body lay dead across the ground. Limbs of unexpected shadowbeings and warriors had been pinned beneath it, legs and arms squirming then settling down into stillness. Kell rolled off me, blocking a dark sword as if tried to strike her from above. She'd lost one sword in the fall and raised the second instead. Her muscles shuddered as she tried to stop the shadowbeing from reaching her.

I threw my palms forward, sending a spout of wind directly at her attacker. The shadowbeing flew off into the busied distance. No longer surrounded by the Morthi warriors, half of whom were either squashed beneath the serpent or occupied in a new fight, it gave room for many to swarm us both. Face's with black eyes and rivers of obsidian running through their veins flashed before my face. Too many to count.

I lost Kell in the overwhelming presence of the shadowbeings.

Blindly I threw out my magick in all directions, trying everything to rid the shadowbeings, but my attempts failed. They threw their vile, deathly bodies atop of me until I couldn't see. The heavy bodies pressed down on my chest making it hard for me to breath. My arms were held down at my sides and my cold hands pressed down on my neck. I couldn't fight back. I was a fly trapped in their web of aggression.

The ground seemed to rumble beneath me. I didn't know if it was my imagination until I suddenly saw sky and no longer felt the pressure of hands at my neck. I looked up, my vision double from the lack of breath to see two faces of one man. His hand was offered up to me, his dark skin glowing bright as if the sun lingered beneath his very skin.

"Sorry we are late," he said, my vision stilling. I blinked a few times, rubbing my eyes to see who it was. The figure moved his head, blocking out the sun and giving me my first look at his face. Paytric. "We met some trouble on the way, but soon took care of it."

I clapped my hand in his and with great strength he pulled me to standing.

"You came!"

"Of course, we did. Never would I turn down the chance to fight alongside the blessed. I have always wanted my name to be in the history books, and this is my chance."

As he pulled me up I saw the wave of his own warriors rushed forward to join our fight. Dressed in worn browns and faded coal grays, they joined out fight.

"Come." Paytric let go of my hand and raised his palms before him. "Let's end this, shall we? I have a debt that needs to be paid, and I will not stop until the Druid's tongue is in my hand."

He raced forward with conviction and vigor, throwing himself into the fight and unleashing his own strength against the unexpecting shadowbeings.

CHAPTER
FORTY-FIVE

THE SCREAMS WERE overwhelming.

If I was not occupied with my wind in one hand and a sword in another, I would have wanted to pull out my own hair. These noises would never leave me. Not the final calls of life from the soldiers, or the unnatural noises the shadowbeings made before their heads were sliced from their necks.

I could feel my own energy disappearing, Sapped up by the constant use of my magick and muscles. How long would this go on for? Until not a single life remained?

Even with Paytric's added forces, who swept into the battle field with conviction, we were still losing. More of the living fell, soon raised once again by Gordex's horrific powers.

Emaline no longer stood within the sea. Nor did I see any water around her as she swiveled through the bustling crowds of dead. Illera was no longer in her shifter form but by Emaline's side, swinging her own sword through lifeless flesh and leaving a trail of bodies behind her.

I had long lost the direction in which Hadrian had gone, and when I heard his roar above the loud noises of others, I knew something was wrong. My blood could have frozen in place as blue flame sprouted into the sky. A tidal wave of azure molten cascaded into the clear sky and fell back down across the battle field. Hadrian's outline hovered in the air far in the distance, but I knew it was too late. His Heart Magick had taken over.

"Contain him," I shouted to Emaline who was already looking at Hadrian. I could see her exhaustion as clear as I felt my own. She shook her head, knocked a shadowbeing over and ran for Hadrian's direction. I was close behind. My gaze shot across the ground as I leaped over bodies and shadowbeings who still reached for me. Their heads still connected meant Gordex could still control them.

But Hadrian. Gordex could control him unless I reached him.

I threw wind beneath my feet that sent me jumping through the air. I landed heavily, the bones in my legs and spine vibrating in discomfort. With each jump, I got closer to Hadrian.

Emaline popped the cork on her water skin and threw her arms wide the moment we burst into the circle of flame Hadrian had created. No shadowbeings dared get close to him. He was no longer a threat, not as he too was the Druid's puppet.

Hadrian was kneeling in the middle of the blue flames. His head was in his hands, his skin glowed as blue as Emaline's eyes. His shoulders heaved with each labored breath. He was fighting it. He was fighting Gordex and the Heart Magick.

"Hadrian," I said, hands forward to reach for him. I just needed contact, skin on skin for Nyah to calm him. I could feel her now, tickling across my chest, readying herself to help Hadrian. "Hadr—"

With my next step, I saw something sprawled out behind him. Fadine was laid out on the sandy ground, her skin white and her lips blue. Her eyes were open, stuck to the smoke filled skies above. Her arms were positioned naturally beside her, and so were her legs. To anyone it would look like she was simply resting. But I knew that was not the case.

Death looked beautiful on her. Her horned helmet had tumbled off away from her, allowing her long, sheen midnight hair to flow around her. A trickle of deep ruby snaked its way out from her armor until it trickled down her chest to her neck. Against her shell-pale skin it stood out, like the sun against blue skies or the moon during the night. I followed the river and saw what caused it. The messy wound which bled her gore across her naval and down her trousers. Stabbed.

The murder weapon was next to her, still connected to the severed hand of the shadowbeing that had done it. Burn marks covered the neck of the shadowbeing who laid armless inches away from Hadrian. Smoke still slithered off its cold skin, the smell as pungent as freshly baked pastries. It was sickly sweet, enough to spill the contents of even the strongest of stomachs.

"I cannot hold it off," Hadrian mumbled to himself, head still in his hands.

I took my eyes off Fadine for a moment, reaching forward to help him. "I can help you. Let me, my love, let me."

"Gordex, he killed her. My sister is dead," Hadrian wailed. Slowly, he lifted his chin, looking straight through me. His gaze reflected fire that devoured the sands around him. His large, bowl-like iris were dark and ominous, no longer the Hadrian I love. He was a shell. An empty body.

"He is weak," Hadrian said, but it was not his voice. "He is mine."

"No, Hadrian, listen to me. You are stronger than this. You don't need to fight it, let me help you."

"He does not need help." His voice was darker now, deeper and hard.

Emaline bent her knees and raised her watery tentacles in preparation. "Hadrian, listen to Zacriah, or we will do what we need to do to subdue you."

Hadrian laughed, but it was not the laugh I had come to love. It was shrill like a bird, yet deep like a beast. "You can try, but my you will fail. Your move."

Gordex challenged me through Hadrian's body.

Lightning fast, Hadrian threw his hands out towards us both. The flames behind him raised into pillars of striking light before shooting back down towards us. I couldn't move, so Emaline did it for us. She willed her own counter act, blocking the flame with a wall of water which tripled in size. Steam exploded as flame and water touched, sending hot air across us. I raised a hand to block it.

The water hummed as Emaline pushed it towards Hadrian. It cascaded over him, layering his skin in liquid to calm his flame. When it settled I expected to see his skin back to normal, but not a single fire was put out. Even the blue flames across the ground still spread hungrily towards us. Emaline reeled backwards as Hadrian moved towards her.

He kicked out a leg, sending a whip of flame towards her and another flash through the air.

She raised her hands, conjuring the water from the sand to return to protect her. But there was no way she could do it in time. Not with Hadrian's added power. Before the flame could reach Emaline, I sent my own force of magick towards it. My wind ripped sand from the ground and doused the blue flames. Emaline tripped over Fadine's body, scrambling on her hands and knees to get away. My move had given her enough time to move. But now Hadrian's entire focus was on me.

"How romantic." Gordex's voice seeped out of Hadrian's mouth. "It would not be a true love story unless one killed the other during a fit of rage. Isn't that what your stories depict? Morbid I thought, but now I can see the beauty in it."

More angered flames careened towards me. I willed a storm to battle it back, but the blue fire was strong and unwavering. Water could not stop it, nor could air.

"Fight it," I shouted at him, spinning a vortex of wind and sand and throwing it in his direction. I didn't want to hurt him, I only wanted to throw him off balance or distract him enough to break past Gordex's control. I could hear the battle raging on behind us, but none of the dead tried to help Hadrian. Gordex must have been controlling them to stay away. "It is me. It's Petal."

I ran forward, dodging a whip of fire which got close enough to warm my skin. I dropped to my knees before Hadrian and sent a palm of wind to the ground towards his feet. It was strong enough for his leg to be thrown out from under him. With the sudden loss of balance, he dropped to the ground.

"Emaline, hold him down!" I commanded, pushing wind towards Hadrian's body to keep him down.

"Zac," she said from behind me which made me look.

Fadine, in death, stood behind Emaline with a dagger of gold pressed to Emaline's throat. Fadine's eyes swirled with dark smoke.

The gold dagger was given to her as a way of stopping Hadrian. But now Emaline had it running across the skin of her neck. Enough for her golden blood to trickle gently. Her eyes began to roll into the back of her head, signaling that the gold was taking its price on her body and magick.

"Enough," Hadrian commanded. "I need them in one piece."

I looked between Hadrian and Emaline, confused on what to do. One simple move, and Fadine would pierce Emaline's waiting flesh. And Hadrian, under my air, did not fight back. He knew what I was to do.

"Give up."

"No," I said, a tear rolling down my cheek. I could feel my muscles shaking with tiredness, but my mind and will were still strong. I couldn't let Gordex win.

"Zacriah, look around you," Gordex said through Hadrian. "Be witness to this moment of truce I show you and what is left of your soldiers."

I raised my chin and looked across the battle ground. The shadowbeings moved away from the fight, all the dead running but stopping in a large circle which encased everyone who remained. With the separation I could see just how small our numbers were. Blood covered soldiers held the wounded up, faces still strong with intent. I could count the number that were left. The rest of their companions either dead on the ground or standing amongst the shadowbeings which they had now become.

We were all trapped in the circle of the dead.

"Give up."

"Don't do it—" Emaline snarled but was cut off as the golden dagger was pressed deeper into her neck. I could see her eyes rolling into the back of her head as the gold drained her of her power and strength. Within a couple of blinks Emaline sagged in Fadine's hold, unconscious. Illera screamed from the group of survivors and was held back by a blood-covered Kell.

"I control two Dragori, the other is not in a state to help you. It is only you who is left to resist. This next decision is for you. Do you give in? If you do, I shall spare those who stand and watch. Or do you want this conflict to proceed? You know as well as I how it will end. The choice is yours to make. Do it wisely."

Even as Gordex's voice spilled from Hadrian's mouth, I could feel my own magick receding. I turned to my friends, the many who had given their lives for this fight. How could I put them through more suffering when we all had lost so much?

"Show yourself!" I shouted into the sky. Maybe the

Goddess would hear me and send help. Or maybe it was a wasted attempt. If she wanted us to win this war for her, she would have sent aid at the beginning. But she stayed silent and watched as we failed on the grounds she created.

I stumbled back from Hadrian and searched the skyline for Gordex. The true Gordex. Not one of his puppets or mouth pieces. I wanted to see him. "Come to me, and I will tell you my answer."

I didn't bother to wipe the tears of defeat from my face. It would've been pointless.

The desert rumbled behind me. I turned fast to see three figures walking over the dune towards the battle ground. I raised a hand to block out the sun and we all watched as they got closer.

"You call for me, and I have returned," Gordex said as he walked forward. "To hear what it is you have to say to me. What shall it be? Will you decide the fate of your friends or will you save them? The choice is yours."

The third figure was hidden behind Gordex before I could see who it was.

"How do I know you will keep to your word?" I asked.

"Here." Gordex pulled the small child into view. Tiv, his white hair a mess and face red with stress. He was pushed forward, stumbling slightly over his small feet and tried to run for me. But Gordex raised a hand as the black smoke which raced out pulled him back. "If you need more motivation to finalize your decision, I would be happy to give it to you."

"Tiv." I almost choked on my own word.

"Go on, little youngling, tell the Dragori here what it is he needs to hear."

Marthil laughed, the ground grumbling alongside her.

"Tiv's scared," Tiv said, crying hysterically in Gordex's dark hold. "I want to go home."

My knees gave way under the weight of Tiv's small, sad voice. I hit the ground, arms sagging and head bowing to my chest.

This feeling, the heavy presence of emptiness in my chest, must have been failure. Heavy, dark, ominous failure.

Hadrian towered above me, his eyes entirely black.

"No more fighting," I whispered. "It's over."

The crowd of remaining soldiers shouted at me, angered voices raising into the sky as I sealed their fate. I tried to block out their shouts with my own cursed thoughts.

The sunset light was choked out by something before me. Gordex had moved so close, kneeling inches away from me, a genuine smile creasing his rune-covered face. His dark eyes flickered across my face, searching and his brows creased.

"Wise choice," Gordex said, looking behind me at something, then patted his hand on my shoulder twice. He treated me like a dog, praising me with his unwanted touch.

I conjure a gob of spit for him, but something hard connected with the back of my skull. My eyes rolled into my head, but not before my mouth filled with sand as I face planted the ground.

CHAPTER

FORTY-SIX

I WOKE TO a sharp pain in my arm. My initial reaction was to reach for the origin of discomfort, but my hands were bound. A feeling I was overly familiar with now.

Once the disillusion cleared, all reality came rushing back, a tidal wave of bad memories. My eyes shot open, but for a moment my vision was unclear and scratchy. Sand, I could see it in my lashes and taste it in my mouth. I longed for a drink, the thirst as agonizing as the slicing cold across my forearm.

My vision settled and cleared so I could see Marthil, who flashed her teeth as she hissed with pride. "Stay still, I don't want to waste any." She looked away from me back to what she was doing. I followed, slowly with a mind of cotton, and watched her drag a dark knife from my wrist and up to the crook of my elbow.

Crimson rivers snaked down my skin, dripping into an iridescent bowl beneath. The bowl was covered in marbled lines of white, until my blood stained them red. I dug my teeth into my bottom lip to still my scream, but it soon burst free. Marthil cringed, dropped my arm and stood with the bowl in hand.

"And we can't kill them now?" Marthil asked over her shoulder.

"After everything they have put me through? No. I want them to watch me succeed. Then their lives are meaningless. I will have no need for any of them."

"Put us through," Marthil corrected him. She wasn't looking at Gordex's expression, but I was. I saw how his eyes creased and his nose turned down, as if he was fighting not to respond to her. All he needed to do was roll his eyes, and it would have been clear just what he thought of Marthil. "Who next?"

"The girl." Gordex pointed to my side.

I tried to catch my bearings, but the dark sky and lack of light made it hard to see beyond my own body. Night had fallen upon Morgatis. No longer could I see the hordes of shadowbeings, but I could still sense them. Standing in the darkness, still in their circle around us all. But I could not hear the survivors. Not a scuffle of feet across the dry sand, or the sniffling of noses. It was pure silence beyond the glow of the fire before me.

Fire burned hungrily in a pit before me, casting a plethora of oranges and reds across the sand, which caused me to notice the two bodies lying in heaps at different points around the fire. I tried to stand, but my legs couldn't find the strength to hold me.

"What are you doing?" I asked, voice husky and weak.

"What I have waited long enough for. And now, there is not a chance you can stop me." Gordex shoulders shook as he laughed. "You tried and failed. So many lives, so much time wasted on your pathetic chance of stopping me."

"There is still time," I said.

"Time, I have certainly had plenty of that wretched thing. But I am afraid to be the barer of bad news, your chances are up. It is too late."

I didn't need to look at my arm to know the bleeding was slowing. It had only been a few days since I had stopped taking Forbian, perhaps it was still in my system? Not wanting to take my eyes of Gordex, I was relieved to hear Emaline shouting at Marthil.

"You," Emaline spat. "Get away from me, you bitch!"

"Stop fussing." The annoyance in Marthil's voice was strong. It was followed by the clap of a hand.

I turned to look and saw Emaline's cheek blossom with red under Marthil's slap.

Emaline was also bound, but her legs and feet were free to kick out against Marthil. She had a few attempts before the ground shivered, and the sand rose above her flailing limbs. It soon solidified, keeping her ankles bound to the ground, yet it didn't stop. Emaline kept fighting, knocking out her head for Marthil, even spitting and turning her torso violently. She put up a good fight until a sharp intake of breath caused us all to look to Gordex.

Illera was held before him, his hands wrapped firmly around her throat. Her eyes were clamped shut as she was tilted towards the flames of the fire, which seemed to reach up for her. The smell of burnt hair instantly filled the still air. Illera cringed as much as she could whilst imprisoned in Gordex's hold.

"I'll stop. I'll STOP! Don't hurt her," Emaline shouted, veins in her neck bulging. Marthil wasted no time in digging the knife into Emaline exposed arm whilst she was forced to watch Illera being held over the flames. I could see the tears in Emaline's eyes, whereas Illera shed no tear and showed no sign of sadness. Her face was as hard as steel, her gaze unwavering as she watched Marthil slice into Emaline's skin.

Golden blood dribbled from the cut straight into the same bowl in which my blood was cooling within. Thick, it caught the light from the fire which gave it a multitoned effect. Morbid beauty.

Marthil had to go in again with her knife as Emaline's wound knitted itself together quickly.

Only when Marthil stood, satisfied with her collection did Gordex throw Illera down. She tumbled, rolling across the fire for a moment and landing in a heap. One flick of Marthil's hand and the sand raised to trap Illera in bindings.

"Our blood," I said, trying to stall. "It's important to you? That is why you needed us alive."

"Oh, very. Without it, I would not succeed in raising my kin again." Gordex reveled in sharing these details. I knew it from the warped pride plastered across his face. He raised his hand and flexed three fingers. "First, I have your Heart Magick. A component to your soul, the key element to this ritual. The main ingredient you could say. But it is not enough, not for what I need to do."

I didn't need to press on for Gordex to spill his truth.

"Blood comes next, but it cannot be stale and old. It must be fresh and pure."

"That is why you kept us alive, allowed us to leave you in Lilioira? Because you knew we would be safe. The shadowbeing could have killed Emaline, but that would have ruined your plan. Everything, from the placement of the wound. It was to keep her alive."

"It was a must, I could not have anyone hurting you. Not until I decided the time was right."

"Petal," Hadrian mumbled, lifting his head from the sand. His skin was coated in a fresh sheen of sweat, causing grains of unwanted sand to caress his skin. I wanted nothing more than to rush to him, dust him off and hold him close. But we were held at opposite ends of the fire, both bound and weak.

"He wakes, finally. My *son*, it has been long since I have laid my eyes upon you. One could almost say I had got used to seeing you during my time in Olderim."

"Sick BASTARD." Hadrian lurched forward awkwardly but was caught by his own bindings.

"Is that such a way to greet your father?" Gordex laughed.

Even from a distance I could see the tightening of Hadrian's jaw.

"Do not speak with such idiocy, you were *never* my father. Even during your guise as King, I knew something was wrong. Never had he been so weak, so frail. You could never be a King."

Gordex scrunched his face and shrugged "And here I thought I played along quite perfectly. Never mind. Marthil, take his blood. I have waited long enough."

There was only a slither of impatience shone through the almost perfect cracks in Gordex's confidence.

"The ritual, how does it work?"

Hadrian squinted at me.

"Zacriah, you can watch and see. There is not a need to question when you have the best view when it all unfolds. Marthil, his blood."

Marthil hurried over to Hadrian who tried to fight back, but she did not make the mistake she had with

Emaline. She called forth her element once more and secured Hadrian down. Then she ran the knife across his arm until his blood joined ours. The droplets of ruby as they cascaded sounded grotesque. It grated on my mind, body and soul. Hadrian winced ever so slightly as his wound wept its gore. Unlike Emaline and me, his did not heal.

Forbian still dwindled amongst our blood, Emaline more so than me. But it was enough to speed up the healing process with such shallow slices.

The flames jumped as Hadrian was bled. But it was as much as he could muster. Even the air within my very body seemed the recoil when I reached out for its help.

"My magick," I called to Gordex who reluctantly looked at me. "It does not listen."

"You do not need it anymore," Gordex dismissed.

"You've taken it from us!" I accused.

"Enough of your idiocy. Linked with your bindings is gold, enough to still your usage of magick." That explained why I struggled to keep my eyes from closing from heavy tiredness. "I cannot risk having an outburst whilst I perform the ritual. Do you really think I would let you intercept again at such a late moment?"

"I have no doubt you have covered all possible issues we could've created for you," I replied.

"That is enough, Marthil, I still want him conscious to watch. Bring me their blood."

Marthil stood and left Hadrian in his exhausted heap, his eyes rolling into the back of his head. She'd not taken as much blood from Hadrian, but it still leaked from his wound out onto the sand.

"If you don't help him, Hadrian will bleed out."

"So be it," Gordex mumbled as he raised the bowl to his nose and took a deep breath. His gaze was wide and hungry, unwavering from the mixture of gore inside of the obsidian he held. "I have his blood now, which brings me onto the next component, if not the most important."

"Don't you want him to watch?" I called out, panic clear from the crack in my voice and how I couldn't tear my eyes away from Hadrian.

"Then I will hurry this up, for him that is. He was my son for a short time. I can spare kindness when he has shown none. That is the type of person I am, the way I will rule during the new world that will rise with my kin."

His answer was not what I or Marthil expected. She cleared her throat.

"You seem to keep forgetting about me?" Marthil stood tall, shoulders pinned back with confidence.

"Ah," he waved a finger and proceeded to take the knife from Marthil's hand. "How could I forget how important of a part you shall play in my New World, Marthil dear. So important indeed. Yet I still need your blood offering, then we can begin."

She nodded, extending her hand after rolling her sleeve up for him.

Gordex lifted the knife carefully and held it above her skin. It hovered there, waving slightly, then he held it still.

"But there is one last component that I will need, and Marthil, it would be ghastly if I did not start with you. Turn and face your fellow Dragori. Let them watch as you take the first step into greeting my new world. Just as I promised you."

Gordex sang his command whilst twisting Marthil to face us. Her lips where turned up into a smile even the dark night could not hide. Her teeth peaked through her lips, her brows raised high with a mixture of pride.

Then another smile was formed.

Gordex extended the knife over her shoulder and pulled it across Marthil's neck. A streak of black spread from her skin and gushed down her chest and into the bowl Gordex held ready. Marthil's face flashed with confusion before she rocked back into Gordex's arms and sagged to the ground. He made no effort to still her fall. Down she went, hitting the sandy bed, which shook violently with her final moment of life.

No one made a sound. Not as Gordex took his black-stained knife and rubbed it across his nightly cloak. Nor when Gordex lifted his leg and stepped over

Marthil's unblinking body and stood with the bowl of blood full to the rim.

"The final ingredient is body. What better way to raise my druid brothers and sisters than to gift them with the bodies of the beasts that destroyed them years ago. Like poetry, isn't it? My ancestors gave your kind life then your Goddess took you away from your rightful owners. But like the never ending circle, fate always ends back at the same place in which it started. With you."

CHAPTER
FORTY-SEVEN

"YOU KILLED HER," I said, watching Marthil's dark blood as it leaked into the sand and stained her skin. Before all of our very eyes, we watched Marthil's life spill into the bowl and onto the sand. Just like that, she was gone.

Gordex's greatest weapon, dead.

"She looked up to you," I mumbled, unable to locate the right words. "How could you do such a thing? Why?"

Marthil's eyes peered at me, unwavering. Her head bent on the sand as it was positioned to look directly at me.

Her stare still left alive, no matter how her skin paled and her lips turned blue.

"Sacrifice is important, Zacriah, you should understand that by now. You will all have to join her soon, but for now, you can watch and see what happens to Marthil here. Then, it shall be your turn."

Gordex flashed a final smile and raised a hand before him. The air around his open hand rippled. The darkness seemed to vibrate and split, opening a slither for him to enter. For a moment, his hand disappeared up to his wrist, then when he pulled it back he held the Staff of Light within his grasp.

"She told me of the promises you made to her."

"And I shall keep those promises, in ways she will still be with me, you all will. But your souls will be lost, replaced by the souls of those trapped within this Staff." He tapped it twice on the sandy bed. "And if you have not noticed by now, Marthil expected too much. She should not have been so... how do I say it... entitled. I will be glad not to listen to her all-knowing voice from now on."

Gordex eyed the Staff hungrily. The light from the fire reflected off the sharp, obsidian stone, giving it a new depth than I remember it before. Its name was wrong, it was no Staff of Light. I knew what it contained. And soon, we would see.

I felt the tickling of legs across my chest, reminding me of our final chance.

Gordex looked around at us all, to Illera who had scrambled close to Emaline, to Hadrian who was hardly conscious from blood loss. Then back to me. "I suppose I should start."

My mouth dried, and throat closed up. This was it.

Gordex raised the Staff of Light in one hand and the bowl of our blood in the other. He faced the flames of the fire and looked up to the clear skies, then he began to sing.

I didn't know what to expect, but the moment the first notes left his mouth, the entire atmosphere shifted and changed. The air got thicker, the earth seemed to move. The flames grew higher with each beat of my heart. Even the sound of the ocean in the dark grew in volume with the crashing of waves and the moving of tides. Every element awoke as Gordex sang to the skies.

The notes and words were foreign to my ears, a mix of sounds of a language long forgotten.

As the song picked up in tempo, aided by the roaring elements, his runes glowed with nightly light.

Highlighting the many curves of the marks, shadows seeped from them, wrapping around his body in a cocoon of darkness. My ears stung as I listened on. The words were not words, the sounds not sounds. Everything was peculiar. If my hands were free I would have clapped them over my ears to block out his words. It made my skin crawl with discomfort.

The flames moved erratically, reaching out even against the strong wind which attempted to manipulate it. Then, so suddenly that if I blinked I was sure I could have missed it, the flames stopped. Like frozen tendrils of ice, the fire stilled into sharp points. From the heart of the flames the color changed. Morphing to a stark cobalt that matched Hadrian's Heart Magick, then to bright whites that were hard to look at.

I shied away, squinting against the harsh light. Illera wrapped her hand around Emaline's face to block the light, and Hadrian didn't seem bothered. Regardless I wished I was next to him, holding him in what was looking to be our final moments.

Gordex ceased his song.

His gaze was pinned to Marthil's body which was sprawled out beside the still flames. It was easier to see her in the new light. Bright white highlighted her ashen skin and blood-stained surroundings. The line on her neck was dark, clean cut. My stomach turned, even seeing her in such a state.

I wanted to shout for Gordex to stop, to plead and beg. But it would be wasted. He was shouting into the skies, calling forth his brothers and sisters to join him once more. As his screams filled the night, he pulled the dark crystal from the crown of the Staff and threw the rest into the flames. Holding the crystal up he shouted about imprisonment and freedom, then he threw it down to the ground and slammed his foot upon it.

It cracked like it was no more than glass.

Beneath his weight it sounded as if he had stood on an egg.

The noise was quiet, but with all the elements now still, it was easy to hear. Gordex's chest heaved, and he smiled. Raising his foot, a snake of dark smoke raised from the broken crystal slowly. His gaze followed it, eyes rimmed with tears. His face was a portrait of glee.

The darkness hummed and throbbed, lifting before him where it proceeded to hang in the air before his face. I couldn't hear what he said next, but Gordex's lips moved as he whispered secrets to the cloud. Then he raised his voice for us all to here.

"Witness them, see the bodies I gift you upon your return."

The smoke seemed to turn our way, forming into a hulking shadow of a figure. Its shadowy arm raised and pointed to Marthil, then to me.

"Yes," Gordex said in reply. "They belong to you now. Your hosts."

There was something childish about Gordex's tone. He even looked upon the shadow through his lashes, like a youngling looking up to a parent. Gordex began to snivel, his eyes completely black now. Not a spec of white left. His humanity fading before us.

A chorus of clicks and snaps sounded from the pit of the shadow. Whatever communication Gordex was having with the shadow made him smile and shake with nervous excitement. He took the bowl from his one hand and held it in both. "The final part." He brought the lip of the bowl to his lips and tipped.

Now. Nyah's awareness shouted into my mind, followed by the shuffle of her small legs across my chest and up to the collar of my uniform. Looking down I saw her small wings relax as she climbed out of her secret protection, and she flew towards Gordex. But not before her shadowy hand reached out of her shift and snatched the hidden dagger we had concealed before the battle began.

Time slowed. Part of me wanted to slam my eyes shut, to not watch, but I couldn't tear my gaze away from Nyah as she got close enough to Gordex and shifted.

His eyes widened as Nyah burst into smoke, shifting back fully into her elven form mid-flight. Her ginger hair flew free as she held the dagger in both hands and brought it down towards Gordex. Her scream was infectious, but I couldn't join her. I could hardly breathe as I observed Nyah close in on him.

Straight through her shadowy figure, which dissipated around her, Nyah thrust the dagger out towards Gordex. I couldn't see what happened once she reached him. Nyah blocked most of Gordex out with her tall, strong build. The world seemed to stop as I watched their still embrace.

I could hear my own heart beating in my chest as the hope for her success took over all rational thoughts.

It was an intense paused moment of waiting. Then they both staggered. Gordex took rocky steps back, the bowl tipping in his hands and spilling part of its contents onto the ground, then Nyah too stumbled back. Her head was bowed, looking at something I couldn't see. Then she turned around, allowing the bright light of the fire to unveil all secrets.

Buried in the center of her abdomen was the dark knife Gordex had used to cut Marthil's throat. I couldn't take my eyes of the blood-stained hilt. Nyah's hands shook as she regarded the knife, looking up at me with confusion at what was going on. Her lips quivered as if she was trying to say something.

The screaming that filled my head hurt my ears until I realized it was not in my mind after all.

My throat ignited with pain as I screamed for Nyah.

She took a step towards me, hands extended, but tripped over her own clumsy feet. She fell down, cheek pressed painfully to the ground. I waited for her to move, to squirm, to cry out in pain.

But she didn't.

My wrists shrieked as skin ripped beneath the stone constraints. I tried everything to break free.

"Silly girl," Gordex cooed from the shadows, standing forward. His gaze was focused on his own wound. Nyah's attempt to stab him had worked, she had reached. Besides the crease of discomfort on Gordex's face as he plucked the dagger from his shoulder, he was still standing. "Such a waste."

I snarled and spat, shouted and cried. All emotions causing a storm to burn through me. I felt the want of my magick to respond, but the presence of gold kept it at bay. It didn't stop me from trying.

The shadow reformed, hovering above Nyah as it looked down on her.

"There is still enough for this to work," Gordex said to no one, looking into the bowl that dripped with the mixture of blood.

Rivers ran down the smooth surface, but even I could hear the slosh of contents that was inside.

"Petal, look at me." Hadrian's voice was a slur as he shouted for my attention. "Do not look anywhere but me."

But I couldn't listen. My eyes searched Nyah's body for movement, for the raise of her chest but even the light would not let me see that. I strained my back, trying to break free.

I caught movement out the corner of my eye then Illera was suddenly by Nyah's side.

"Don't touch her," I screamed, but Illera ignored me. Illera took Nyah under her arms and pulled her away from Gordex and towards Emaline. My neck screamed as I tried to follow Nyah as she was taken away from my line of sight.

"Look at me!" Hadrian shouted again. I pinched my eyes closed and shook my head, opening them with burning hate for Gordex.

"You try to blind side me even after I keep you alive

longer than I needed," Gordex said. "Again, I prove that your attempts are futile and wasted. You cannot stop me. I have your Heart Magick, I have your blood, and I will have your bodies. Do you have any other secrets hidden that you would like to share, or will you force me to kill another to get what I need?"

I hissed with each breath. The sadness and panic for Nyah buried by intense anger. I couldn't reply to him; I had no words that would do justice to the thoughts in my mind.

Nyah. My Nyah. My friend.

I spared a look to Illera who was pushing her hands onto Nyah's stomach and pressing her mouth onto her lips.

Slithers of the shadow figure came together once more, standing beside Gordex. A series of sounds came out of its mouthless face and Gordex nodded.

What I would have given to have understood their language and speak it in return, to tell both the shadow and Gordex what passed through my mind with lightning intensity.

"Apologies," Gordex mumbled, looking up and down at the shadow as if he was too frightened to look for too long.

The shadow replied, causing the hairs on my arm to stand.

Gordex lifted the bowl back to his lips and tipped

the blood into his mouth. The lump in his throat bobbed as he devoured our gore, showing no sign of repulsion.

Once he finished, he lowered the lip of the bowl and flashed his stained mouth, now a smile. His yellowed teeth now looked black. A dribble of blood seeped from the corner of his mouth and down to his chin, yet he did not wipe it away.

"Blood of the hosts," Gordex said, eyes rolling into his head. "It is time."

The shadow figure split into four. No longer did it seem transparent, its outline became clearer and features flexed into existence. Gordex dropped the bowl to the ground, his hands spilling more shadow as his lips whispered a string of words. The shadows he conjured fed into the four figures.

One of the figures moved for Marthil, leaving footprints in the sand. It bent down, regarded the body and slipped into Marthil's slack mouth. As if Marthil took a hulking breath, the shadow disappeared within her.

Then, as if it was a trick of the light, her chest rose.

"One down, only three to go. I am sorry, but this is as far as I can let you watch. It is time to gift your bodies as the hosts for those who need them more." Gordex stepped forward slowly, his eyes looked heavy and empty. He lifted his cloak and pulled a curved blade from a hidden sheath at his waist and pointed it to me. "You...

you will be my next"—Gordex cleared his throat, brows turned down in confusion as he battled something within his mind—"next to die."

Marthil's body began convulsing on the ground, her skin shook and her limbs jerked wildly. The three remaining shadows followed him as he walked for me, blade raised. One step he almost missed, his feet clumsy and legs weak.

I clamped my mouth closed and looked to Hadrian. He was smiling at me, a knowing smile full of sadness and love.

"Be strong, we will see each other soon," Hadrian said, looking right at me.

I broke into messy sobs. "I'm scared. What if you can't find me?"

It didn't matter who watched us, in the moment all I could see was Hadrian.

"I shall always find you, Petal, always."

Gordex clapped his hand on the back of his other. "I want you to watch as I take your... your life. There is something beautiful when seeing life seep from one's eyes. I do not want to miss it this time."

I could see my terrified reflection in the blade's steel body.

I spared Emaline and Illera a smile, seeing Nyah and knowing I would join her. Perhaps she waited on the other side?

"Do it," I said, biting down into my bottom lip.

Gordex didn't respond with words. Instead, he raised the curved blade with both hands and blinked heavily. I noticed the twitch of his face as he fought something off.

His mouth opened, but his eyes closed, face relaxing as the monstrous yawn took over his body.

The shadows seemed to click and scream as if panicked by something, then Gordex lowered the blade slowly and rocked back, eyes wide.

"What... What have you..."

CHAPTER
FORTY-EIGHT

YET ANOTHER YAWN broke Gordex's face. His entire body seemed to sag, then he dropped, his legs no longer working for him.

Straight to the ground he fell in a heap, eyes closed and chest rising slowly.

Marthil's body stopped shaking and the shadow of the druids flickered in and out of existence. They twisted and jolted, horrific screams cutting across me.

I looked around for answers as to what had happened. The sky was full of unnatural noises as the shadows were forced to leave. But why?

Everything happened so quickly. Illera moved with speed and threw herself over Gordex who showed no sign that he knew what was happening as he slept beneath her. His mouth ajar, breathing shallow and heavy.

With all her might Illera cried and thrust the same knife he had used to kill Marthil and Nyah and brought it down into his chest.

Once, twice, three times Illera brought the weapon down. By the fifth time, the shadows disappeared entirely, the frozen white flames returned to their natural orange and reds. The wind sang, the ocean calmed in the distance and the ground was still, unmoving.

Illera was bent over Gordex, his chest no longer moving. She pressed her forehead to his body and sobbed loudly. A warmth filled my body and moved down to my stomach. It spread across my limbs, neck and spun around my mind with such speed that I became dizzy.

My head pounded as the world returned to its normal state. No longer did the shadows watch above. The air was empty of their presence.

In beats of my heart, we were surrounded by Niraen soldiers, faces I recognized from our fight. Some pulled at my arms, slamming hilts of weapons and boots onto my constraints until they cracked as if they were as weak as a shell. No longer fueled by magick. Like the dead vines in the temple in Eldnol. They crumbled to dust.

It seemed that every time I blinked, I missed something. The world was in perfect chaos. Someone lifted me from the ground. My wrists were wrapped in damp, cool cloth to still the dull ache left from the rubbing of rough stone. I turned around in circles, watching all the survivors block out my view. I looked to Nyah who was huddled over by countless others.

I ran for her, trying to push everyone out of my way. Faces blurred before my eyes.

"She is in safe hands," a warm voice said from behind. "Shh, leave her with them."

I spun on Hadrian, turning to face him as he stood feet away from me. He looked weak, tried, but alive. Then he wrapped me in his arms and held me tight.

"What is going on?" I questioned, my mind clogged with fog and confusion. Everything around me was happening so quickly that I couldn't grasp onto anything. Only moments before Gordex was going to sacrifice me. Now I stood free as his dead body was laid on the ground near me.

"It is done," Hadrian. "Gordex is dead. It is over."

Dead. Gordex is dead.

Looking over Hadrian's shoulder, I saw the Druid's body on the ground, chest covered in open wounds. Illera was not near him, but I could see that he was unmoving. I could almost feel his lack of power in the air, in me.

"How?" I breathed.

"I do not know what has happened yet, but it does not matter now. Just hold me and do not let go."

And hold him I did.

I squeezed onto Hadrian, ignoring the pain in my body and mind. I relaxed in his hold, giving into his welcoming presence as the world moved around us. Soldiers and warriors ran around, helping others. Leaving us uninterrupted.

CHAPTER

FORTY-NINE

AS NIGHT LEFT us for early morning, the sky tinted with beautiful pastels I could see the full extent of what happened. Shadowbeings littered the ground around us, a circle of dead no longer in need and full of power. Puppets without a string, for their master was no more.

That is how the soldiers had come to break us free. Once Gordex was killed, they were no longer kept from us with the barrier of dead.

"The blood he drank was tainted," Emaline said, scratching her head. Unlike Hadrian, she was not covered in bandages. The Forbian was so fresh in her blood, all marks of war had healed. Mine had worked to an extent, healing the grazes and cuts on my wrists, but I still needed assistance once Paytric helped set up what he could of a camp for us.

"Forbian has a different effect on non-shifters," Emaline said. "And that devil just drank more than enough of a dosage to knock him clean out."

I found it hard to fully listen to everything I was being told, not with Nyah on my mind.

"Like the first night in Olderim when Gordex as King Dalior polluted the food and drink to weed the shifters out, all the mundane fell asleep. That is the affect the herb has on anyone else," Illera explained.

My mind whirled, shocked by the turn of events. Something I never expected to happen.

"Our blood, Emaline, mine and Marthil. We each had taken a dosage of Forbian recently. The concentration must have been pungent in our system." I could still see Gordex's face twist in confusion as he began slurring over his words and yawning. How his body could not control the sudden, overwhelming tiredness that took over him. "His own plan backfired on him in the end."

"And that is what this is," Hadrian said. "The end. It is done."

Even though I knew Hadrian was right, that Gordex could never come around for the wounds Illera gifted him, I still could not find happiness. Not after everything we had lost. Even the things that still hung in the balance. I kept looking towards the flaps of the tent, expecting them to come and give us news on her. I hadn't seen Nyah since a group of Niraen and Morthi picked her from the ground and rushed her into the first erected tent.

"What comes next?" Emaline asked, dropping into a seat.

"That is a good question," Hadrian replied. "I suppose we return to our lives before, rebuild them, start new ones. Gordex may be dead, but I can speak for myself and say the damage left behind in his wake will take a long time to fix. He has left cities as wastelands, towns in ruins and separated many from their loved ones. That will take time to heal."

"I want nothing more than to return home," Emaline said. "To see my family, if they have survived."

Illera raised a glass of water before her. "Home."

Home. It was a hard word to wrap my mind around. After staring into Gordex's eyes as he raised the blade I truly believed I would never return to Horith. I'd never see my parents let alone hold them again.

But I was fortunate. I could make the choice as to where I went now. Whereas Gordex had stopped so many from ever returning to their families. Instead he left bodies, in which where being prepared for the long or short journeys to their homes outside, would all they would get. Empty vessels of shadowbeings being separated into Niraen, Morthi and Alorian to ensure they are taken to the right soil for families to claim them.

"I'm finding it hard to feel relief," I blurted out to our group.

"Me too," Emaline agreed. "Doesn't seem right, the

way this has all ended. It is hard to believe it."

Kell and Vianne walked through the door, both stripped of their ruined, bloody uniforms for mundane slacks and loose tunics supplied from Vcaros.

"We have both watched Gordex's body burn to nothing but ashes. I truly believe he will not be returning after this. His power was great, but not great enough to survive what he controlled, death." Kell pulled a stool and took a seat. "As requested his ashes will be separated between all three continents."

That last comment was pinned to Hadrian for it was his idea.

"Any word?" I asked, almost shouted. My nails had been chewed down to stumps as we waited.

"I've supplied the very best healers I could muster from my city. Paytric has also offered up help."

I noticed nothing wrong with what Kell said, but Hadrian did.

"Your city?" he questioned. "Would it not belong to your King?"

Vianne spared a knowing look to Kell, who scrunched her nose and replied, "No, my city. I said it correctly."

"You don't have a King, do you?" Hadrian rubbed his hand across his sharp chin.

Kell just shrugged her shoulders. "Surprise?"

"Surprise indeed." Emaline straightened in her seat.

"Care to explain?" Hadrian waved a hand, although his expression suggested he had already worked it out.

"I'm sorry I have not told you before, but I thought it best to keep this knowledge to myself for a time. Vcaros has not had a King for years, in fact he gave rule down to his daughter before he passed. I am surprised Paytric did not tell you, for he attended my father's burial."

It all made sense. Why Kell had so much say over her warriors, how she was protected in a circle of them during the fight.

"And you chose not to tell us because?" Hadrian questioned.

"It would make no difference if you knew or not. Part of protecting the queen is keeping her identity secret from strangers. Think of it as collateral. Enemies would never know who to strike."

"Then who is..." Emaline began to ask, but I answered for her.

"You are Queen," I said. It was a statement, not a question.

Kell raised her hands in defeat. "You've caught me."

I should have known. We all should have. Kell's ability to communicate and control. Her strong delegation and command. It was all signs that she was not only the voice for Vcaros, but its very mouth piece.

"And Paytric knew about this all along?"

Vianne sniggered into her hand.

"And you did?" Hadrian looked to Vianne, eyes wide.

"It was not for me to say," Vianne replied, one brow raised in humor. "A woman's secret is as sacred as the being keeping it."

"Here, here," Emaline said.

We spoke more on Kell and her control over Vcaros. For a moment, I felt my mind being occupied with other thoughts than Nyah and her state.

"I actually have come to say goodbye," Vianne said to everyone. "It has been discussed that I should return home as soon as I can. I worry for Queen Kathine and my aunt. What state has the city of Lilioira has been left in? So many questions rush around my mind which I am anxious to get answers for."

"We understand," Hadrian said. "And my father? Will you send word when you return?"

"It will be one of my first tasks to find him. I can assure you word will be sent to you the moment we know of his condition."

Emaline stood, Illera hand in hers. "Then I will join you on the journey. I am as anxious to return home. And I think it is safe to say that I am no longer needed here."

Knowing Emaline would be leaving pained my heart. Saying goodbye was not something I wanted to do, yet I knew it was impossible to ignore it.

Gordex had only just died, and everyone was ready to pack up and leave. I didn't know what I should have expected after this was all over. In truth, I never thought we would all make it through. But here we were on the other side, preparing to leave for the next chapter of our lives. A chapter not riddled with the Druid and his threat.

Illera was looking everywhere but me. And I knew why.

"You are going with her, aren't you, Illera?"

"I am. If I returned home I am giving myself back to a family who will belittle me, treated me without kindness. I can't stand the thought of leaving all this behind. I hope you understand, but Emaline is my home now. It is my choice to stay with her."

"I understand," I said. "You both deserve to enter this new era of calm with each other."

Emaline and Illera linked hands and smiled my way.

"Shall I tell your parents of your decision?" I asked Illera.

She shook her head. "Unless they come asking for me, they do not need to know. Never have they worried about me thus far, so I do not see why they would start now."

Although I felt a burning desire to share my own word with them. For what they had put Illera through.

"And with my help we may reach Lilioira faster," Emaline said. "Although without the Heart Magick…"

I looked up at her, and so did Hadrian.

I hadn't thought of it. My mind has been such a blur that I had not noticed the return of normality to the pit of my stomach. Reaching for my power, I knew it was true. No longer did the darkness threaten me like a lurking predator every time I reached for my magick. My power was no longer overwhelming by any means.

"The Heart Magick is gone," I said. "I can't say I am sad."

"So it is," Hadrian said. "Now that is something I will not find difficult saying goodbye too. But Emaline is right, with your skills you could help return back to Eldnol sooner and with it means answers would soon follow."

"What of the small child? The Elementalist?" Vianne said. "There will be room to take him with us?"

Hadrian looked to me, but before I could open my mouth to reply, two red-headed twins poked their noses through the tent. Their freckled faces looked tired and gaunt from the dark shadows beneath their eyes and which were rimmed red.

"Zacriah, she is ready to see you."

I jumped from my stall in an instant, causing it to clatter across the ground.

"How is she?" I asked, running for Neivel and Negan.

"Come and see," they replied in unison before

dipping back out of the tent. I followed after them, forgetting the conversation I had just been a part of.

But as my hands went to push the tent I turned back to Emaline, Illera and Vianne. I had a feeling, deep in the pit of my chest, that this was the last time I would see the three of them for a long time.

I paused and offered them each a smile. I hoped they could see just how much I cared for each one of them with my subtle expression. Goodbyes were not something I had practice with, but even I knew I would not been good at them. Instead I raised my hand and placed it on my heart. Emaline and Illera followed suit.

Goodbye friends, I thought. *May our paths cross again.*

CHAPTER
FIFTY

NYAH'S EYES WERE closed as I entered the makeshift medical tent. She must've heard the tent flaps open as she rolled her head to the side and forced a smile in her state of exhaustion. Her pasty skin was coated in a sheen of sweat making her deep-crimson curls stick to her forehead and neck. Dark circles framed her hollow eyes. She was a portrait of weakness, but it didn't matter. She was alive.

"Oh Nyah," I breathed, rushing to the side of the cot. I laid both hands on her arm and rested my head atop them. "I really thought I'd lost you."

"It is going to take more than a knife to finish me off." Nyah's chuckle was scratchy and rough. She winced but didn't stop her little laugh. "And you really think I would ever leave you without saying goodbye?"

I sobbed in response, holding my friend as if it was the last time.

"Zac, really. Stop crying. I have a headache as it is... your emotions are not helping ease it."

"Sorry," I choked out half a laugh and half a cry. Wiping my nose with the back of my hand, I looked my friend deep into her emerald eyes. They were squinted, the whites flecked with small red veins. Her left eye was almost completely bloodshot.

"I have realized something."

"What?" I said.

"It could be the strange healing plants the Morthi have given me to help increase the production of blood, or the fact I lost so much that causes my moments of deliria, but you may be the only person I'd take a knife in the stomach for. I hope that makes you feel special."

I squeezed her arm gently, thanking her with my eyes. "Like the most important person alive."

Nyah sighed. "Alive." Closing her eyes and laying her head back down on the pillow. "Tell me we can go home soon. I need the comfort of my own bed. I do hate to complain, but these cots are the worst."

"You are in all your right to complain about anything you want. In fact, I will never tell you to stop ever again."

"Goddess, you really do like me." Nyah opened one eye and the corners of her mouth tilted up for a slight moment.

"We will be leaving as soon as you are well enough to travel. Rest will help you heal." I spied the bandage that had been strapped down on her exposed abdomen. A small faded red stain could be seen through the white material from the fresh stitching the healers had given her.

"And you don't have any Forbian left that could help speed this up?"

"Would seem that Gordex drank it all up when he took down our blood," I joked. It felt strange, but a relief, making light of what happened.

"That would explain what I've been told. My brothers said he just fell asleep in the middle of his ritual. I didn't believe them at first."

"They speak the truth," I said. "It's hard to fully grasp it but it would seem that the very same drug he used to get us together in the first place has also kept us together."

I shook my head, taking a cool cloth from the basin beside her cot and rubbing it across her head. "Don't worry. We will be home soon enough, then you are free to do whatever it is you want to do."

"Strange concept, isn't it? Knowing that this is all over," Nyah whispered. "It sounds silly, but I feel like I am lost now. Unsure where life is taking me next. I should be happy that the drama has been put to bed, and I am! Yet I cannot deny the small part of me which worries about the next chapter."

"It's not silly." I wrung the cloth out and dabbed her head again. "But think of it like this. Up until this point, we have been living through a story already set. Yet now, we have turned the page, and it is empty. We can finally control what it is that happens in our lives, no longer controlled by a present destiny or conflict. The story is finally ours."

Even I was proud of my explanation, but Nyah laughed. "What ever happened to the boy who grabbed me as he escaped the kitchens in Vulmar Palace? Now he is a poet, you sound more and more like Gallion by the day."

"That boy… I don't know what happened to him."

I didn't. I felt different now.

"I do." Nyah lifted her hand and rested it on mine, stopping me from wiping her forehead. "He became brave."

My heart quivered. "He had to."

"We all did."

Nyah fought a yawn, her lips shaking as they opened dramatically. That was my cue to let her rest, she needed it after what she had been through.

"How about I come back later and see how you are getting on? If you want to get home you really are going to need to sleep and let your body work," I said, stretching my knees to stand.

"Could you"—she stopped me—"stay with me until I sleep? Don't tell anyone else, but I am finding it pretty hard to navigate the darkness at the moment. Wouldn't want anyone thinking I am a pansy."

"Of course, I will stay," I said, sitting back down. "I won't go anywhere till I hear you snore."

"I don't snore!" Nyah laughed.

"We will soon see about that."

Nyah was asleep within a few moments.

I watched as her eyes settled beneath her eyelids and her chest leveled out to her regular breathing. Even after she slept, I didn't want to leave. But the Morthi healers, the King—no, Kell—had sent for had returned and ushered me out.

As they guided me from the tent with words of kindness and trust, I spotted Hadrian who was leaning up against a tent pole.

"How long have you been out here?" I asked.

"Since you went in." He pushed himself off and walked to me with open arms. Taking my hands in his he explored me with his eyes from my toes to my eyes. "Forgive me, Petal, but it may take me a while to get used to you being out of harm's way. For the time being I just want to be close to you."

I smiled, cheeks warming, and it was not thanks to the burning sun. "Would you like to go for a walk?"

"A walk?" His eyes lit up. "I would love to do anything, as long as your hand is within mine."

I would have guided him towards the sea-shore and along it, but still Morthi from Vcaros were cleaning up the remaining shadowbeings. In the distance above camp, a large black plume of smoke stretched into the sky. Instead we walked around the small camp.

"Kell has surprised me," Hadrian said.

"I think she has surprised us all."

"I will miss her when we return to Thessolina. But for once I am confident to say that we have a relationship with Morgatis even if it was created in such dire times."

I peered up to him. "Your first act as King."

Hadrian didn't smile back. "My father is still King. I only hope he returns soon enough. Did the curse the Druid placed upon him break with his death, or is my father still stuck in his eternal sleep? Those are the question that blur in my mind."

"I wish I could give you the answers," I said, pressing the back of his hand to my mouth. "But when Vianne reaches the city, we will be able to put your questions to bed. We must wait and hold out hope that your father is safe." Even saying it I could see the vision of the sleeping king in his glass casket.

"Have they left?" I asked.

"When you were with Nyah? Yes."

"What of Tiv?" I asked. "Did Vianne take him?"

I'd not seen him since the aftermath of the fight. He was huddled between soldiers and kept at a distance even after Gordex had been killed. Seeing such fear in his small, innocent eyes broke me at that moment. The thought of saying goodbye to him was sickening, especially since I knew little of his parents and if they survived the attack on their home.

"He is still here," Hadrian replied. "Until Vianne can assess the city, I believe it is no place for a child."

"I would very much like to see him," I said.

"And we shall, but I have something for you. Emaline gave it to me to pass on to you. She said you would understand."

Hadrian pulled a tangled silver chain from his breast pocket and handed it over to me. The silver was cold to the touch and it tickled my palm as he laid it down. The small silvered acorn being the last thing he dropped.

I released a breath and a single tear. It made my heart ache and flutter with understanding in a single moment. I fisted the chain, pressed it close to my chest and sent a silent pray to the Goddess for my friends. Emaline's final act, giving me this necklace was all I needed to remember her. Just as Emaline had given it to Nesta, and Nesta back to Emaline it had made it all the way to me. I would cherish it till the end of my days.

"It seems that there is a story that comes along with that gift," Hadrian said.

"There is," I replied. "But one for another day."

For this moment I wanted to keep it as my own little secret.

Grief shadowed Hadrian's face for a moment. It was

brief, but there. He tried to rid himself of it by plastering a smile on his face, but I could see through his illusion.

"Do you want to talk about it?" I asked.

Fadine. Her death had not been brought up.

"Not yet," Hadrian said. "But when I am ready, I promise it will be you I speak with."

I squeezed his hand, trying to show my understanding.

Hadrian tugged my arm and pulled me in a different direction. "Let us go and see the youngling. I have a feeling that will make him very happy."

"Tiv?" I said, approaching him as he was sat on the carpeted floor of the tent with his back to me.

His ears tickled as he heard me and ever so slowly he turned around. The moment his eyes laid themselves upon me, he sprang for the floor and ran for me. Jumping, he flew through the air and collided with my waiting arms. We both toppled to the ground.

"You came back for me," he half cried half laughed. "Tiv is so so sorry, I didn't want the bad man to find me, but he did, and then he wouldn't let me go. I tried to fight him, I promise I was brave."

"Shh," I cooed, hugging him tightly. Hadrian knelt beside us and wrapped his arm around us both.

"You were very brave, Tiv, just like a solider," Hadrian said.

"Like you?" Tiv asked.

Hadrian shook his head. "You are even braver than I."

Tiv's white face beamed with pride. His small hands lifted and ran down Hadrian's stubble. "You remind me of my father."

"I do?" Hadrian said.

Tiv nodded and looked to me. "What if the bad man took them from me? I don't want to be alone."

"You will never be alone," I said, peering to Hadrian for an answer but deciding for one alone. "Because you are coming to a castle in a new land until we know it is fine for you to return home. That is if you want to."

"My castle," Hadrian added. "And we will look after you for as long as you need. How does that sound?"

"Is there swords?" Tiv asked, one white brow raised.

"Many."

"And shields?"

"More than you could imagine."

Tiv nodded. "Tiv wants to come."

CHAPTER
FIFTY-ONE

ALL THAT WAS needed were three of the Niraen ships we had arrived on. The rest we offered up to Kell and her city, who took them graciously. It was the first gift of many between Thessolina and Morgatis. A way of thanking the Morthi warriors for their lives during the fight.

Hadrian and I were the last to get on the small row boat to take us on to ship as we had goodbyes to say to Kell.

Hadrian spent his time thanking every Morthi warrior who aided in our fight, even Paytric and his people, who stood amongst the crowd. Once hands were exchanged and thanks was given, it left Kell, Hadrian and me alone to share our final moments.

"You know you are always welcome to return to Vcaros," Kell said. "And I promise next time there will be a considerable lack of gold amongst the city. I think you have helped me prove just how little of a threat the Dragori really are, so thank you."

"That was your plan all along?" Hadrian said.

Kell closed her eyes and smiled. "My father's rule, and his father's before lived in fear of your kind. Without showing, proving to the people of my city that you are no threat, I would never have won their trust to abolish traditions that they had been brought up with. I can assure you, everyone in Vcaros will discard their gold in thanks and memory of you all."

Hadrian took her hand and shook it. "It has been a pleasure."

"One that has been all mine," Kell replied. Once she dropped her hand, she turned to me. Instead of offering hers to me she opened her arms, and I embraced her in a hug.

"Thank you for everything, Kell," I said, breathing in her spicy aroma that clung to her garments.

"It has been a pleasure fighting beside you."

"Oh," I whispered into her ear. "Thank you for saving my life back there. Without you, I'd still be being scraped from the scales of a serpent."

She patted my back. "And thank you for saving the world from potential reign of darkness and despair."

I laughed. "When you say it like that…"

"Sounds important, doesn't it? I am certain the history books will tell stories of you all for years to come. How we all came together after years of being so apart. I feel proud to be a part of that."

"And I am proud that my name will be in ink next to yours."

Kell waved us off the entire way to the main ship. My arms ached by the time we reached the ladder up to the ship from waving at those who watched us leave. Once we climbed to the top deck and looked back, I could see the crowd walking off towards the direction of the city, Paytric included. It was good to see that their long feud was over. Yet another achievement from Kell and her secretiveness.

The ship was a blur of movement and excitement. It had been almost three days since the death of Gordex, and the remaining Niraen soldiers were just as excited to return home as we were. Masts were raised, oars where placed into the ocean, and we began moving. We slipped away from the land of Morgatis into the never-ending expanse of azure. Sky met sea seamlessly, giving it the impression that it went on for eternity.

"I promised Nyah I would sit with her for a while," I told Hadrian, who stood behind me as we overlooked the ship's hull at the horizon. His arms were wrapped around my stomach, his chin rested on my shoulder. His cool, minty breath dusted gently across my check as our breathing became in sync. "But the longer you hold me, the harder it will be to go."

"Then I know what to do to always keep you with me."

My heart skipped a beat. "You do."

The light caught the ring Hadrian had given me. It was still nestled on my finger, perfect and clean. Not a spec of war tarnished its smooth surface. Hadrian picked my hand from the railing and lifted it before us both.

"You never did give me an answer," he said. "And you promised that when this was all over, you would."

"I did, didn't I?"

In one slick move, Hadrian spun my hand, turning me around to face him. My back pressed up against the railing now and face inches from his.

"So?" he asked, amber eyes glowing with intrigue. "What will it be, Petal, do you fancy facing the new world together?"

I tilted me head and grinned. "I could think of nothing better in this entire expanse of the world that I would like more than to be next to you for the rest of my days."

Hadrian's mouth crashed into mine, laying his extreme passion and love upon me. His body pressed against me, and mine into his. I felt the hard groves and shapes of his body as he kissed me deep, uncaring of the many who gawked on behind him. When he pulled back he was breathless and beaming.

"Then I will take that as a yes," Hadrian said, lips swollen and red.

"Yes, Hadrian Vulmar Prince of Olderim and King

of my heart. Yes."

His chest heaved as he released a breath, which tickled all my sense. With a tender hand he brushed the hairs away from my head and the tipped my head back in his hand. He kissed me until the world slipped away and we no longer could sense anyone but each other. With the sun beginning its long descent behind us, we glided on the ship towards home.

It would never matter where that might be. With Hadrian in my arms, I would always find comfort. Home.

EPILOGUE

I LOOKED BEYOND the carriage window at the rickety house, the place in which I was born and raised. It had been months since I had looked upon the rough brick work and white faded window frames with dusted glass.

Buds of roses were almost in bloom across the overwhelming bush which took up most of the side of my home. Deep green leaves glistened with the early morning dew. Small insects would be bathing amongst the small balls of water for refreshment from the warm weather as they always did. I used to watch them from my window every morning. A window that was open, curtains drawn as we looked upon it.

"Such a beautiful place," Hadrian hushed from beside me. "Even now I look upon it and can almost see you growing up here."

"I can't believe I am back," I said. "The last time I saw home was when I was in the back of the cart being taken out of the town to Olderim. So much has changed since then, yet this place seems untouched."

"So much has changed," Hadrian agreed, rubbing his smooth thumb against my ring.

"I must admit I'm feeling terrified right now."

"Frightened of your home? After everything you have faced, Petal, I know you are not scared." The Niraen guard who had taken us here opened the door to the carriage and extended a hand for Hadrian to get out. I noticed the new emblem he had embroidered onto his purple uniform. It was the antlers of an elk. In memory of Fadine.

Instead of taking the guard's hand Hadrian thanked him and climbed out alone. Hadrian walked around to my door, smiled through the window and opened it for me. "Come on, we will do this together. I am here every step of the way."

Without thinking my body moved, took Hadrian's hand and climbed out. My eyes still pinned to the door of my home. I could imagine Fa preparing the morning fire and Mam making fresh breads as she did every morning. What would they think of me when they saw me? Would they recognize the person I had become? Would they be proud?

Hadrian guided me with a smile towards the rickety gate and pushed it open. The familiar squeak settled the nerves in my stomach. Even this far down the line, Fa still had not oiled the rusted hinges.

We walked up the small, slabbed path towards the front door. Every step I took, my heart beat faster. I expected the door to fly open, but I knew better. Neither Mam nor Fa would hear us approach. Not with their morning argument over what meats to cook before the day starts.

I pulled Hadrian back, dropping his hand and rubbing my own down the deep plum jacket that I wore. It was held together but gold painted rope and had multiple buttons and clasps covering it. Even my form fitting trousers screamed riches. Something my family had never had. And now here I was, standing before my home, but not the same as I was when I left it.

"Do I look ridiculous?" I asked him.

"Even with a funny hat and oversized shoes, you could never look ridiculous. Stop worrying my love and let it happen. When they see you, they will not care what you wear, or how you look. It will be the last thing on their mind."

"I hope so," I breathed, trying to calm myself down.

"Ready?" Hadrian smiled down at me.

I nodded, and he took my hand again, walking me all the way to the step before the scratched, dark wood door. Hadrian step aside and silently waved me forward.

My knuckles hovered over the door for a paused moment. My mind raced with possibilities. Then I heard them, Mam shouting to Fa about something mundane and pointless. My heart warmed, and all my anxieties disappeared.

I rapped my fist against the door three times, wondering if I should do a forth. Before I could even contemplate it further, the door swung open to the back of Fa's head.

"Let me deal with this." Fa turned around and laid his eyes upon me. His face morphed through many emotions before settling on pure shock. His eyes filled with tears, something I had never seen before. Then in the next breath, I was in his arms, and he was screaming for Mam.

"What is all the fuss," I heard her say but my head was buried in Fa's strong arms. "Oh Goddess…"

Mam snatched me from Fa and held me close. This time, she was buried in my embrace.

"My son," she cried, tears staining my velvet jacket. "You have come back, my son, my son."

It was a chorus of tears and heavy breathing as the three of us didn't let go. I heard doors of neighboring homes open and hushed whispers about Prince's and caught some even clapping from their doorways.

When they finally pulled back, they caught Hadrian standing in the corner of the pathway. It was Fa that rushed over to him, wrapping him in a hug. Mam soon followed. They accepted him as their own in that very moment. I stood watching from the top step as they all laughed and clapped hands on backs. My heart could have exploded at that second.

Hadrian was guided back to the door with Mam on one side of him and Fa on the other. They ushered us inside, closing the door to the outside world.

"We have been so worried," Mam said, taking strands of my hair in her fingers and twisting like she had done most evenings back when I was here.

"I know," I said. "I am sorry for making you worry. I am sorry I ever had to leave."

"None of that," Fa said, squeezing my shoulder. "You have nothing to apologize for. You are home now, you *both* are."

Hadrian wouldn't stop smiling whereas I couldn't stop crying. Seeing them all together, as ridiculously as it sounded in my mind, was a dream come true.

Mam straightened her apron. "Goddess I have never had a Prince in this house. I suppose I should put some tea on."

"Ale will do fine, dear," Fa said to her as he guided Hadrian and me to sit by the fire. He called for Mam to join us.

We sat before the warm fire, boots off as it warmed out toes. Fa gave us each a tankard of home brewed ale and sat back down with his own.

"We hear you have been on quite the adventure," Fa said. "Why don't you tell us all about it?"

"It is a long story, Fa," I told him.

His smile was honest and true, beaming from one ear to the other. "My son, we have all the time in the world."

Fa was right. Time *was* finally on our side.

With a big breath I readied my mind and told them everything.

We shared our story for the first time, Hadrian's hand in mine as we recited it from beginning to end.

❧ THE END ❧

ACKNOWLEDMENTS

To everyone who trusted me with this series and allowed me to tell my truth. Woven amongst the words are secrets I have never shared, stories I never dared to tell. Until now. You have each given me the strength to write this world and I thank you with all my heart.

I love you.
I adore you.
I thank you.

See you in the next world I create.

About the Author

Ben Alderson is a collaborator in the NYT bestselling anthology, *Because You Love to Hate Me*. He grew up in Berkshire, England. In addition to writing, Ben also runs Oftomes, a successful micro-publishing house. He enjoys reading, traveling, Greek food, music, and anything fantastical.

Visit Ben on the Web:
www.benjaminoftomes.com.
www.oftomes.com

46011668R00326

Made in the USA
Middletown, DE
23 May 2019